shadow of the sun

Book one
Timeless Series

LAURA KREITZER

iUniverse
Bloomington, Indiana

iUniverse books may be ordered through booksellers or by
contacting:

iUniverse
1663 Liberty Drive
Bloomington, IN 47403
www.iuniverse.com
1-800-Authors (1-800-288-4677)

Front cover artwork by Igor Šćekić

ISBN: 978-1-4502-0689-1 (sc)
ISBN: 978-1-4502-0690-7 (ebook)
ISBN: 978-1-4502-1175-8 (dj)

LCCN 2010901559

Printed in the United States of America
iUniverse rev. date: 1/29/2010

This is for you, Mom and Dad.
Thank you for believing in me.

shadow of the sun

LAURA KREITZER

CONTENT

An angel can illume the thought and mind of man by strengthening the power of vision, and by bringing within his reach some truth which the angel himself contemplates

St Thomas Aquinas

prologue

It's too late, a voice echoed in my head. I gasped and knelt beside the angel. There was no puddle of golden blood, no marks—just a lifeless body. It was in that moment that I realized I'd never be able to speak to my beloved angel again.

I stared straight ahead, feeling hollow. The dark wooden casket taunted me, telling me it was entirely my fault. I had thought I knew what pain was before, but I was wrong. So incredibly wrong.

The rain scattered across the ground, soaking the flowers that were lying upon the tomb of the forgotten angel. Someone had told me that when it rained, it was God weeping for the beloved who were lost. Today I believed this more than on any other day, because this was a more grievous death than that of any mere mortal.

All around me, those who had been blessed by this glorious being wept and held on to each other, coming together as one entity for the support they each needed. In the distance, I could see angels beneath the shadows of the encroaching forest. Their golden tears glittered in the small glint of the sun beaming down through a slit in the clouds. No one else seemed to be able to see them, but I could—in all their magnificent glory. They had always possessed a celestial glow, but today it had been taken away. There was a darkness that surrounded them as they mourned the one they had lost. The one I had lost.

I was silent as the tears descended my face, contributing to the heartache around me. A perfectly smooth, warm hand found its way to mine. The thumb compassionately stroking my palm was soothing. I never looked to see whose hand was holding mine, and its owner remained slightly behind me, out of view. That was just fine with me; I needed time to grasp the concept of this monumental death.

It was then that I looked down at the mound of dirt that would soon be covering this benevolent angel. In that moment, it felt like something was breaking away from my heart. It fluttered away, and the hole it left would forever be there. A reminder.

As the service came to a close, the crowd dispersed and the angels seemed to vanish before my eyes, some just completely fading out of existence. I stayed to watch when they began to lower the body into the ground. I stayed to watch as the ground swallowed the coffin whole.

The warm hand never left mine, even when I collapsed to my knees, unsure if I would ever be able to leave this place, and leave this angel who had never left me. Something inside of me sank down with the coffin, as if I was being suffocated by the dirt that was now being thrown over the angel. Still, the support of that warm hand never left mine, as if we were melting together.

"Gabriella," a gentle voice spoke softly in my ear. I hadn't noticed that he crouched beside me. "It's time to leave." His breath was so affectionate, so *healing*, that some new strength grew inside me.

"You?" I cried as I recognized his face.

He pulled me to my feet. I just looked into the eyes of the angel through my own water-filled ones. They were deep pools, so blue you would think that someone had painted them that way. Perhaps someone had.

"What are you doing here?" I asked. It wasn't out of exasperation that I had cried out; it was pure intoxicating relief.

His hand tightened in mine before he released me. He wrapped his graceful arm around my waist to move me toward a black limo. "No time for questions. It's not safe here anymore," he whispered.

I mouthed the words back questioningly as he pushed me towards the car door. Wasn't this death the end of it all? The door flung open on its own accord, and suddenly we were inside and speeding away.

His hand still had not left mine, and he continually gave me the strength I so desperately needed. My head rested upon his shoulder as tears continued to trickle down my face to land on his jacket, staining it with salt water.

"I'm sorry," I said softly as I tried to wipe away the tears on the fabric. He caught my hand to stop me, as if this action displeased him.

"Don't ever be sorry about weeping over an angel. This truly is a heartbreaking day for my kind." He cupped my chin to get a better look at my face. Again, just the warmth of his hand was enough to feel that he was healing me. And perhaps he was.

He kissed the tears on my face and then wrapped his arms around me protectively. "It's just you and me now," he breathed. "I'm your Guardian now."

The road curved some as we headed out of the cemetery. "And where will we go?" I asked, my lips against his collar bone.

He shuddered slightly.

I ignored the meaning of that. "And what about Aiden?" My question was muffled against the lapel of his jacket as I tried to avoid his skin.

"The dark one." He nodded, as if to some thought

4

he had just had, still ignoring my first question. "He is not far." He pressed a button, and the window between the driver and us slithered away.

"Driver," he called out. "How much longer till—" Sudden and violent metal twisting against metal echoed in my ears as the limo seemed to bend sideways. It was as if my reality had just warped into something new. Then I was exposed to the elements. Rain splattered across my face and wind rushed through my hair as I felt my body being pressed tightly against the angel's hard chest. My head felt faint, but with all my might I clung to him, absolutely confused at what was going on.

Something hot and wet seeped from my head and down my neck. My hand automatically went up to a sore spot on my temple, and when my fingers came away they were covered in blood. When I looked into my protector's eyes, I saw they were full of regret and torture. All I could think about was soothing him, even though he was here to protect *me*.

There was no time for that now, though. We were in danger. He hastily deposited me onto the ground next to a tree and sprang forward, shielding me.

"It's him," I whimpered. "Aiden. Just like he promised." This was my fault. If the angel was killed, I would die too. Surely there were no other Guardians left for me. This would be the end.

The ground shook beneath us as a dark shadow loomed overhead. My protector tensed for action as the ground shook again. We were in complete darkness now, only the headlights of the limo illuminated the vicinity. Fire sprang up and ringed around us, and the rain seemed only to intensify the raging flames that licked at the air.

"Only one Guardian?" a vicious voice said mirthfully. "It's so easy to pick you off one by one."

The encompassing fire crackled and flickered into an ominous red as a shape appeared before us. Fire shot from the palm of the dark creature. My Guardian ducked, and the fire-ball hit a branch above us. The branch came clattering down, and then, as a new darkness began consuming me, I knew I was finished.

#

"Ella? Hello?" A hand waved furiously in front of my face. "Ella! Are you in there?" The annoying wasp lowered her voice to barely a whisper. "I always thought you got here by sleeping."

That was just *another* one of Sally's nasty innuendos that she'd mutter under her breath just loud enough that I could hear it. I stared at her, my aggravating redhead assistant, through narrowed eyes. Her hand continued to flap in front of me.

I took a deep breath. "Sally, would you stop that?" My voice was like ice. "I haven't even had my coffee yet. And *don't* call me Ella. It's Gabriella. And really, you should be calling me *Doctor Moretti*."

She glared at me as she pointed to the coffee mug on my wood desk, completely ignoring my name tirade.

"Oh," I answered, feeling completely idiotic.

My eyes immediately shot to the missing coaster and reached over my desk to place one underneath the mug which was misshapen and had a picture of a rainbow painted on it. It was made by my niece, Jules, who loved to draw me pictures and make me pottery. She was only five and very sweet. My sister, Jenna, had brought her over to visit just the other day. I missed them both. We just don't see enough of each other.

I grabbed the mug, blew gently over the surface of the liquid to cool it off and watched as it rippled under my breath, then took a sip. It was room temperature. I gulped it down loudly as my assistant still stared at me in anticipation, a smug look eclipsing her features.

"It's cold," I said irritably. This just wasn't the day for her to pull her usual crap. It wouldn't surprise me if she didn't put it in the fridge before bringing it to me.

"Well," she said, straightening her back importantly, "you've been daydreaming at your desk for over an hour."

I could tell by the look on her face that she still couldn't believe I had my position and was unquestionably envious, but some days I would gladly give my position to someone else. My occupation could be stressful, and the long nights were overwhelmingly exhaustive. Not many people understood my profession, and I didn't expect anything less. Even my assistant was oblivious to the secrets below me—the secrets that were now weighing heavily on my shoulders.

"I wasn't daydreaming," I insisted, looking at her shirt, which was an eye-watering color of green. Absently, I continued speaking, "I was thinking about my new discovery—" I cut myself off, realizing that I had almost told a very top-secret piece of information to someone with much lower security clearance than myself. I desperately needed sleep; my brain just wasn't functioning under all this stress.

"New discovery?" Sally placed her round bottom on my very expensive desk and leaned in eagerly.

Good job, Gabriella. Now she'll never let it go, I thought bitterly. "It's just something I was working on in the lab." I fluttered my hand in a gesture to let her know it was nothing really. But it was. Boy was it something—something amazing and frightening.

She continued to look at me expectantly. The soft white light behind her head made every single tiny red hair stick out and cast the rest of her features into shadow.

"You know? *Top secret* experiments?" I whispered with a quizzical half smile, just to goad her a bit. I knew it was wrong, but it was so easy to get her riled up.

She grimaced. As always, Sally hated it when I brought up the fact that she wasn't allowed in the lab. Sometimes I saw her staring longingly at the "Restricted Access" sign on the door to the underground labs. But she wasn't hired to do scientific work; she was hired to assist me in other ways. Some days she just couldn't grasp that concept and I had to remind her—like today, for example.

"Will you take this to the post office?" I pushed a blue and white custody-sealed cooler her direction. The nearest post office was a fifteen minute drive and wouldn't be open for a while. I knew this errand would keep her occupied for a bit while I took time to absorb the night's events. "This needs to be in New York City by tomorrow morning." There it was—the reminder of what her job was.

Sally dropped down from her perch on my desk with narrowed eyes and seized the cooler furiously. Without another word, she turned on her black high heels, and spun so fast I almost thought she would turn all the way around.

I decided to press her a little. It was only fair; she did it to me every day with dirty comments whispered under her breath. "And could you pick up my dry cleaning? Same place."

She froze mid-stride and turned around more slowly this time. "Again?" she grumbled through gritted teeth. "Can't *you* pick up your own dry cleaning?"

Here comes the explosion . . .

I plastered a huge grin on my face, ready to put her in her place. I'm not a mean person, honestly. I had just lost all of my patience because I had been up all night dealing with things that I couldn't fathom telling someone as small-minded as Sally.

Keeping the mocking smirk in place I said, "Sally, you were hired as my assistant. If I need you to flush my toilet, you will flush it. But since I am not a horrible monster, I am not going to give you the crap jobs." I laughed at my own wordage. *Oh, the hilarity.* I really required sleep; I was slowly turning into a giddy school girl who laughs at *potty* words like "crap." "If you can't handle running *one* simple errand, then I will need to hire someone else." I added. "Is that clear?"

She nodded, her eyes reduced to slits now. "That won't be necessary, *Doctor* Moretti." Her voice sardonic. "I'll pick up your dry cleaning."

Some people never learn, but you take what you can get, right? "Thank you," I said sweetly and then waved her away. She shut the door firmly behind her.

Good riddance.

I sighed, folded my arms on top of the desk, and lay my head down to relax.

I knew that at the young age of twenty-four, I was lucky to have such a lavish office. This was also the same reason that Sally seemed to take offense to me. The walls were a pleasantly rich crimson and decorated with black-and-white framed photos of some of my favorite destinations. My eyes caught sight of a beautiful snow-capped mountain that I captured on my last ski trip. I was an excellent skier and would have loved to be on the slopes right now.

The light-blue tint of a new day came through the window behind my desk. The light was bright enough that the reflection off the glass from a framed photo of my sister and me hit my eyes and burned. I closed my eyes and put my head down against the desk while yawning loudly—just another reminder that I desperately needed sleep. I was getting thoroughly sick of these all-nighters at the lab. Last night was different, though, because I discovered something so incredibly ground breaking that I was sure the government would try to cover it up.

I am a supernatural specialist. Whenever I discover something, it is *never* ordinary, and the government is *always* interested. I perform experiments and conduct research on things no one believes are real, like aliens and ghosts. And mostly, they're not. But, last night was my biggest revelation to date, and I wouldn't be surprised if at any moment men in military uniforms converged upon me.

Zelko Corporation, where I currently work, has many different laboratories for diverse kinds of scientific work. The lab I work in—also nicknamed "the fishbowl"—has been involved with research on supernatural beings for several years now. There are many private investors that keep the lab running, but the largest investor of them all was the U.S. government. They always want to be the first to know about anything new we uncover, mainly so they can cover any evidence right back up, especially if they think it would scare the American public.

This definitely would. It almost scared the pee right out of me, and I am not one to frighten easily.

I've made several small discoveries before, but nothing of great interest really. So far, the only *major* finding we have established is a few corpses—or skeletons—with large fangs. Of course, the FBI came in, snagged up all the scientific documents on that case, and had them shipped to who knows where. Whether vampires exist or not is still a mystery to me, but I think not. Some people just have extra-long teeth that appear to look like fangs. Plus, aren't vampires supposed to be immortal and vaporize in the sun? But I was the skeptic here—never the one to truly believe until there was undeniable evidence to back up the claims.

I always thought that the kinds of experiments our investors wanted us to perform were ludicrous. I've investigated everything from a man covered in mostly scales to a "werewolf," who was actually just a really—and I mean *really*—hairy man. Everything seemed silly, honestly . . . until last night.

Three corpses found in the mountains of Italy were shipped to us at Zelko Corp, and there seemed to be absolutely nothing unusual about the delivery until I opened the boxes and realized that the bodies hadn't decomposed—*at all*! Their skin was still flushed with blood, though none had a pulse and there were obvious signs of aging on their disintegrating clothes. I checked the paper work and realized there was a colossal problem, and then called my colleague in Italy, hoping for answers.

"Hello?" Adriana answered in her thick Italian accent.

"Hello, Adriana! It's Doctor Gabriella Moretti."

"Gabriella, it's so good to hear from you. What can I do for you?"

"Um, yes . . . you shipped three bodies with paper work?"

"Yes. Did everything arrive there okay?"

"Well, I'm not sure," I said hesitantly, trying to think of how to word our predicament. Well, *my* predicament now. "According to your paper work, your laboratory dated the bodies back to 100 B.C., but these bodies are so fresh you would think that they died only minutes ago."

My eyes glanced over to the first opened box. The skin on the body seemed to be glowing.

There was a long calculating silence on the other end. I waited, very impatiently.

"Stefan?" Adriana finally yelled to someone on the other end. The rest of their conversation was muffled Italian. "Gabriella? Are you still there?" she asked after a minute.

"I am. Is something wrong?" I started to panic. Three fresh corpses, yet no sign of death, and most definitely no sign that they had been dead for over two thousand years. Was I losing my mind?

"Are you near a computer?" Her voice quavered a little and that only made my nervousness rocket.

"Yes," I answered wearily.

Again, a long silence. "I am sending you pictures of the bodies we sent you. These were taken only four days ago."

A few clicks with the mouse later, I opened up the attached file to see the pictures of three bodies that were decayed, leathery, and absolutely, undoubtedly *dead*. Since I was only ten feet from the bodies, I gasped in complete shock. I could feel the blood draining from my face. The phone dropped from my hand as I stepped back, tripped, grabbed the nearby table and knocked some instruments over that met me on the

15

floor with a resounding crash.

The light on the phone was still on. I seized it quickly, and then scooted across the floor as fast as I could. I couldn't get away from the bodies quick enough.

I could hear Adriana shouting on the other end. "Gabriella? Are you all right? Gabriella? Hello? What is going on?"

"Adriana." The shaky whisper left my lips in fear that the bodies might hear me. I know, it was stupid, they were dead after all. "I'm going to have to call you back." I hung up the phone, not waiting for a response.

After I gained some of my composure back, I grabbed the edge of the table beside me to lift myself to my feet. I moved so quietly and slowly that I probably could have popped over the edge of one of the boxes and scared the corpse back to life. I peered over the top of the first box to see that the body hadn't changed at all since I had made my phone call. Surprisingly, I was somewhat relieved; I had thought by now that they would certainly be alive. That gave me pause. What if they *did* come back to life? My heart jumped wildly in my chest at the image.

After a few more seconds to take deep, steadying breaths, I pulled my latex gloves on and then turned to take a sample from the first body. I cut a small piece of his skin and placed it in a tiny vial. Carefully, I put it in a rack for later testing. I turned around to take another sample and screamed in bewilderment.

Instantly, the door to my left flew open and three lab technicians from another lab burst in, trying their best to look knightly. It was difficult not to laugh at this show of chivalry. But considering the reason I had screamed, it was probably best that I didn't start chuckling or people would think that I had lost my mind. After what I thought I had just seen, maybe I had.

"Are you okay?" all three men asked in unison.

"I don't know . . ." I whispered, stepping towards the box that held the corpse.

I approached the body with the three men shadowing me. Then I looked over to the vial on the counter. It was still there.

"He . . ." I paused to look back and forth between the body and the vial again. "He grew his skin back," I breathed.

The three men looked at me like I had just grown a second head.

"Oh, just hand me a vial," I barked irritably.

Three vials all appeared in front of my eyes. "Thanks," I replied, grabbing one without looking to see who I took it from.

As I bent over the body to take another sample,

the three men followed my movements, all of them watching what I was doing with nothing but questions in their eyes.

"Watch carefully," I whispered. I was afraid I'd wake the dead man, especially after what I had seen.

Using my scalpel precisely, I cut a small piece of flesh from the body and placed it in the vial. Then, we waited. After only a few seconds, one of the men beside me yelped, and the other two visibly gulped.

The skin on the man's arm had begun to heal. It grew until we couldn't tell I'd ever cut the flesh away. Any second now I expected the fingers to twitch or for the corpse to become animated and sit up. All four of us took an involuntary step backwards. The only noise in the room was the heater turning on. The three mens' expressions were lined with horror. I bet they regretted the knight role now.

"Seal the fishbowl until the director comes in," I ordered, keen to vacate the scene. "Now!"

The three men stumbled over each other, trying to reach the exit. Backing away, I left through another door, and within seconds the room was sealed from the outside world. There was only glass between me and the bodies now, but it made me feel safe instantly.

Yes, last night had been very . . . remarkable.

My eyes opened, the memory still fresh. Dawn had broke over the sky, the colors mixing together pleasantly—pearly pink and misty gold through my window. Sighing at the memory, a dreadful blast of realization hit: I'd have to go back into that lab. The thought actually sent a wave of terrified excitement through me.

#

ven though my coffee was cold, I continued to drink that same cup of coffee Sally had left for me while staring into oblivion. The events of last night were still swimming in my head, and I was nervous about going back down to the lab. Would those dead bodies still be dead? Or would there be three humans—supernatural beings?—standing in there waiting for me?

The door to my office flew open and slammed against the wall, which caused one of my photos to rotate sideways, as Sally backed in with my dry cleaning and a large box in her hands. As she struggled to bring it all to my desk, I sprang forward to relieve her of her burden. I wasn't always a complete jerk. She hung my clothes in the closet as I set the box on my desk.

"Thank you," I said in a way that she would know she was being dismissed.

"Yeah, no problem," Sally answered bitterly, smacking her lips in an irritating fashion.

"*Doctor Moretti*," I corrected for her benefit. What could I say? I was in a vindictive mood and she was begging me to play this game with her. Unfortunately for her, I always win.

"No problem, *Doctor Moretti*," she growled and then she slammed the door behind her. She must have fumed the whole way to the post office. I smiled at the thought.

Forgetting the box, I locked my office door and went straight for the clean clothes. I grabbed the first business suit I saw and headed toward my bathroom. Because of the many nights that I ended up staying here to perform research, the director was kind enough to have a shower unit installed at the office. It was either that, or they moved the lab to my house, which was not an option as far as I was concerned. And luckily for me, there just aren't many other people willing to do this job; and of those that are willing, few have the credentials or the patience to study both cellular and molecular physiology and biomedical sciences. Ergo, a bathroom. I earned it, simple as that.

The hot water ran down my back, which helped to calm my hyperactive nerves. It was difficult to be completely terrified about what was downstairs in the lab at this present moment. The only motivation behind applying for this post was the prospect of discovering

21

something not of this world, or even better, something so ancient and mystifying that my life would find some definitive significance. My sister had thought I was absolutely nuts.

"This isn't about your parents, is it?" Jenna had asked me.

"Of course not!"

"Well, I would understand more if it were. The mysterious circumstances of your appearance were strange enough."

I sighed and ignored her talk of my parents who had abandoned me and never came back to claim me. "My parents are the same as yours," I told her flatly.

"I know. Our relationship goes beyond some blood bond." She hugged me, and I hated the fact that she felt the need to reassure me. Her past wasn't any better. "I was just happy to have a sister when they adopted you," she said.

I knew she loved me, and I loved her too. She was right: our relationship went far beyond any type of blood link.

I was five when my adoptive parents first came across me. My memory was gone, and they never really told me the circumstances or what had happened. They said it was probably best that I didn't remember. It could have been something so tragic that my subconscious refused to remember it. "Retrograde amnesia" is what they called it. I had made peace with my diagnosis, but it didn't mean I didn't want an explanation of why I was abandoned.

"That place doesn't hold the answers," Jenna said to me one day after she caught me trying to find out about my past through Zelko Corp's wealth of knowledge. "You are just going to drive yourself mad."

We had agreed to disagree, but now I was beginning to wonder if I really was slowly losing my mind. I didn't believe in things that went bump in the night . . . *but I wanted to*. That was why I had taken the job at Zelko Corp. It offered me something that other companies couldn't. There have been some weird and unexplained things I have come across, but nothing yet that really changed my world. Nonetheless, I never, ever, thought I would come across something as paranormal as this.

My whole body felt extremely shaky as I grabbed the soap off the dish and lathered up. I became aware of a strange feeling, as if there were a vine wrapping itself around me and sending something peculiar through my throbbing veins, making the hairs on the back of my neck stand straight up. It made me want to unseal the room below—to visit the undying creatures . . . which was a strange sensation, considering how absolutely frightened I had been only hours before.

It was paramount that I try to forget these deviant desires that were gradually leaking into my brain. Were the creatures really undying though, or was there some scientific explanation for the whole incident?

Rotating the hot water tap off seemed to simply intensify the escalating compulsion to descend to the lower levels—to the fishbowl—to open the doors and see what secrets those wooden boxes were concealing. What was wrong with me? My body craved to unearth the treasure concealed below. That was what this discovery amounted to: a pile of knowledge so rich it made my head swim with imaginings of the possible scientific findings.

Again, it felt like there was some force pushing me to descend into the depths. I just needed to breathe. Calm down. *Resist the urge.*

What would Jenna say now?

Wiping some of the fog away from the mirror, I looked at the wet tangled mess on my head. Though my friends praised me for my locks, I never understood their love for my loose, brown, natural curls that I thought were nothing but a pain. Couldn't my hair just decide to be straight or curly? Honestly, this should have been the least of my worries considering the magnitude of what lay only a few levels below my feet in the fishbowl.

There was a soft, rhythmic noise in my office, like paper being printed from my computer. In the mirror, my sea-green eyes dilated in alarm. Why did the sound seem so sinister? I didn't know.

My heart made a plunge-dive through my chest as an odd creeping sensation found its way to the pit of my stomach. Panic shot through me. In my head, I was replaying the scene where I had purposefully locked my office door. Maybe it had all been in my imagination? Why did I feel like I was in some awful horror movie?

Hastily, I dressed and dashed across the black and white tiled floor. To the best of my ability, I made my way to the door without any noise, and then I put my ear against it like it was some large telephone receiver. Nothing: complete and utter silence.

I held my breath and tried to slow my speeding heart as I gently pulled the door open, turning the handle at a measured pace so it wouldn't make a single sound. Anxiously, I glanced through the minuscule gap that I made. The office was vacant. I breathed a deep sigh of relief before I pushed the door fully open.

I inspected my desk and noticed that nothing had been displaced or tampered with, and nothing was on the printer tray. Even though things appeared to be orderly, my gut was screaming for me to leave and advance down the stairs to the figures in the three wooden boxes. I was really starting to get annoyed at this excessive longing, but no matter what else I thought about, every second that elapsed compelled me to find my way down below again.

I first ascertained that the door was still locked, just to be sure. My tense posture deflated some at this discovery. *So I had been alone.* When had I become so paranoid? My imagination was playing some exceptionally barbaric tricks on me. I had to remind myself why I chose to work here.

My body had just relaxed drastically—and then I circled around and saw the box on my desk. It had been shredded at the top.

I stopped dead. My breath caught in my throat as I inched silently over to it, eyes darting wildly around the office. Maybe it just hadn't been securely fastened in the first place?

Who are you trying to convince? A voice in my head said.

It didn't look as though someone had cut the tape; it was as if someone had punched a hole through it, or something had exploded from the inside. I grabbed the box cutter off my desk, to use either as a tool to open the box further or as a weapon in case of an intruder . . . or possibly something else. The paranoia was becoming familiar—unusual, for a supernatural specialist; but this seemed to be an excellent day for lines to blur between reality and fantasy. Everything I had ever known was being thrown into doubt and uncertainty. *Isn't this what I wanted? Divine intervention?* As the goose bumps rose on my skin, my body had to disagree with my thoughts.

My trembling hand reached out to sever the rest of the tape. A strange feeling of foreboding hit suddenly, as if a wave of piercing cold had broken over me. After flipping the cardboard flaps away, my eyes dove deep into the depths of the hefty box. There was a small, ancient looking chest inside. The lid was askew and fractured, torn off its hinges. I speculated briefly. *Was this how it was received, or did something happen to it while I was in the shower?* I couldn't tell.

The room seemed to grow perceptibly darker. Before I had the opportunity to look up at the lights, I found myself falling to the ground. My head hit hard against the floor and the box cutter slid several feet away. Then it was dark.

Now I didn't feel so dumb for being paranoid.

Staring through the haze of pain from my head, I could see that the lamplight in my office was barely penetrating through a black force that surrounded me; the only color in my view seemed to be a deep-red mixture of blood. Whatever it was, the blackness—like a shadowy mist—began gradually wrapping snugly around my body, warping and evolving as if it were a ghost. I tried to scream, but the shadow smothered my voice. My heart beat out a jagged rhythm as the blood pumped through my veins, burning like liquid fire.

A tall inky-colored creature emerged from the blackness, appearing momentarily unfocused before he set his eyes upon me. Everything was abruptly in startling clarity. His eyes were ablaze with fire and staring right into mine. I couldn't look away, as if I were hypnotized. *I'd take the bodies downstairs any day*, I thought stupidly, realizing the situation was not going to have any sort of a happy ending.

"Don't wake them," the burning-eyed thing hissed, hostile and issuing a clear warning. I tried to recoil at the steely note in his tone, but he only held me tighter in the blackness.

My lips parted to speak, but no noise would surface. The creature bore down into my eyes with his. He made a movement with his hand, as if he were granting me my wish to speak.

Suddenly, I could address the black creature before me. "Who?" I asked, choked. As I lay on the ground,

my heart continued to pound so profoundly I was surprised it didn't explode from my chest. *Please let this
be a nightmare*, I chanted to myself.

"The angels," he said matter-of-factly, like I should
have known this all along. His eyes flashed with a fiery
heat as he leaned over me. His whole body looked
chiseled from a large piece of charcoal. His hair was
shaggy and black, though the only feature I seemed
able to look at were his blazing eyes—like firestorms
trying to escape his body.

"Angels?" I squeaked. My head was spinning,
and suddenly it felt like the darkness was suffocating
me. I choked on the air. The creature tightened his grip
around me, though his hands had never left his side—
he was controlling the dark cloud.

"Bury them in the earth, where they belong." His
voice was smooth and calculating.

"The . . . angels?" I repeated like an idiot. Maybe
this was just a very ghastly dream. *Wake up*! I shouted
in my head. *Wake up now*!

No luck.

"Yes," he spoke coldly, though the air in the room
only seemed to blaze with his heat.

There was an explosion of sound, and suddenly I
was swept up in a windstorm in my office. Papers flew
off my desk, spinning wildly around my head; the com-

puter crashed to the ground, sparking; and chairs were flipped over. My favorite black-and-white photographs crashed to the ground and the glass shattered. The box that held the ancient artifact flew across the office and landed with a thud against the wall. Everything was spinning wildly around me, inducing vertigo.

Then, as if I were being shaken from a dream—which I so desperately hoped was the case—I heard the door handle jiggle. The darkness disappeared as quickly as it had come, leaving behind a trail of destruction. I fervently thanked all the gods known and unknown for that small door-handle jiggle.

My mind began oscillating between each of the events that had just unfolded before my eyes. To my great relief and surprise, I was alive—and instantly I was trying to analyze every word the creature had said. *Don't wake them . . . the angels.* I lay my head against the front of my desk, exhausted. *Of course you wouldn't be resigned from an unsolvable mystery*, I told myself angrily. *Seize the day or the revelation. You know—just grab it by the horns. How many hours does one person have to be awake before they go crazy? I've completely lost my mind,* I decided.

"Gabriella?" The voice gave me a start of surprise. "Are you all right?" It was the director, Darren. Concern was obvious in his voice. "I received your urgent message. Will you unlock the door?"

My mind was still whirling with the events.

Darren knocked on the door again. "Gabriella?" His voice heightened a little, his anxiety peaking.

I realized I hadn't answered him yet. "Yes, I'm fine," I said evasively as I pulled myself to my feet and walked over to unlock the door.

Darren was about six feet tall and roughly forty years old. We had worked together at Zelko Corp. for the last five years, and never once had I sent him an urgent message of any kind. His dark, apprehensive eyes looked over me, noticing my distress. He pulled his hand through his thick dark hair as his eyes roamed over my shoulder and into my office. Curiosity flashed across his face and then I realized I was an idiot, which seemed to be a constant theme for the day. The room was torn apart, and now here was Darren to see the disaster. How was I going to explain this one?

Um, yes . . . this creature came out of the box . . . Nope, that definitely wouldn't go over well—unless I wanted to be hospitalized.

My heart had barely slowed, but now it began pounding like a drum through my chest again. But when I looked back over my shoulder, ready to explain, my office was just how I had left it before taking a shower. Darren's eyes were focused upon the sealed box on my desk. Everything else was orderly. My papers were in their usual neat piles and folders, the photos on the wall were straight, the filing cabinets upright, and the computer screensaver that said *Zelko Corporation* was still bouncing from one side of the monitor to the other, as if the mouse had never been moved. Only moments before, I had seen that computer crash to the ground and short circuit.

My jaw hit the floor. *I really was losing my mind.*

celestial being

We descended to the lower level in the small elevator. When we stepped off, fluorescent lights flared to life in the room outside the fishbowl; the incandescence made me blink to reorient myself. My heart still pounded profusely as Darren advanced into the room. He seemed somewhat oblivious to my overwhelming anxiety at the strange events in my office.

There were rows of computers lined around the glass walls of the fishbowl. There were a few monitors that would mirror back whatever was happening in the lab during major autopsies or experiments.

I lingered outside the elevator door, now undoubtedly terrified at what was behind the glass. The lab was cast in shadows. The ominous darkness was still calling out to me. The push to go towards the lab was even more powerful now that I was only feet away from it, like a physical force was thrusting me in that direction. I fought it.

Darren noticed that I hadn't followed behind him and turned and gave me an incredulous look. He held out his hand, a gesture I didn't expect. I stared down at it.

"What's gotten into you?" he asked and moved towards me, smiling, his hand still out stretched.

My mind was still reeling. It was bizarre to actually find something this . . . *mystifying.* Yet here I was, completely blown away by this extraordinary finding. Of all the people to come across something so incredibly ground breaking, I supposed it would be a supernatural specialist. But right now I felt as if I had just won the lottery without ever playing it in the first place—although it was still up for debate whether this win was a good thing or a bad thing. My instincts begged me to go towards the bodies in that darkened lab. My brain, however, was screaming "*no!*"

Darren took my hand when he realized I wasn't going to move and pulled me into the overly bright room before letting go. Staring through the glass surrounding the sealed off lab, I was praying that what had happened upstairs had just been my wild imagination. Something deep inside me continued to repeat the dark creature's words. *Don't wake them . . . the angels.* Weren't angels good? God's creations and everything? What was so bad about that? But I knew from personal experience that not all of God's creations *were* good. Still, from everything I'd learned about angels and about the Bible—which was very little—weren't angels some sort of celestial being?

No matter how prophetic the dark creature's suggestion—or demand—had been, being near the angels seemed to make all my worries about the fire-blazing creature subside, and I suddenly felt safe from it. I imagined the angels battling against the dark creature two thousand years ago, and I wondered what had happened, and what they might have been fighting over.

Our reflections were crystal clear as we approached the glass. My mind must have been in another dimension because, during my contemplations, I hadn't noticed that Darren was speaking to me.

". . . the bodies from Italy?"

He reached for my hand and squeezed it when he realized that I was somewhere else in my head. Somewhere far from here, more like 100 B.C., the time period the angel bodies were supposed to be from. He shot me a questioning smile, but my brain was still on another wave length. *It's remarkable they were in as good a shape as they were in the pictures*, I contemplated, *but now they are practically living*.

Even in the shadows of the lab, I could see that their skin was still flushed. This made me even more anxious about unsealing the doors. Again, my body felt the pull towards the lab. It was stronger than ever—a stupid, excessive longing.

"Gabriella, are you all right?" Darren asked, concerned now.

Surely my face was showing just how nervous this whole situation had made me. There was no hiding my feelings, at least not at this juncture.

I turned to him, nodding. "Yes . . . There's something . . ." I didn't know how to tell him about the bodies lying in the dark on the other side of the glass. Usually a visual demonstration would be the preferred way to explain a case, but this time I didn't think we should enter the room—even though everything in my body was screaming for me to slide my key card for access.

Darren eyed me eagerly, awaiting my continuance. An urgent message from me was the equivalent of a radio signal from an alien planet, telling him that the earth's people had three days to vacate or be destroyed. So of course he was still expectant to hear about my findings.

He finally gave up on any response when I moved towards the lab door. I wasn't entering; I just flipped on the light switch next to the entrance. I decided the best avenue of attack would be to show him what was lying behind the reflective glass. The glow of lights bore down on the angels (a much better way to think of them than "the bodies") like spot lights.

Darren reached out with his plastic key card to unlock the door. "Don't!" I screamed out. All the air vanished from my lungs as I launched myself towards him, practically diving through the air to stop him. My old baseball coach would have been proud of that save. He retracted his hand immediately, looking extremely startled as my back slammed against the door, my body now between Darren and the angels—protecting them.

Protecting them? What was I thinking?

My hand gripped the door handle with all my might. As soon as I touched the cold metal of the door, electricity shot through me, a low current that was pleasant in every way. I almost collapsed at the rush of emotion that spread through me. My breath caught in my throat as my body slid slowly down the metal door. ". . . Wait," I whispered.

What the hell just happened?

Darren bent down to me, an unreadable look on his face. "Doctor Moretti," he said formally. "First I receive an urgent message in the middle of the night. Then I show up and you are locked in your office, looking absolutely frantic. And now you won't let me in the lab. What. Is. Going. On?" he said testily, distinctly pronouncing each word.

With a great effort, I rose to my feet, noticing that this time Darren didn't offer his hand. Was I just overacting about everything I had seen last night? Was it all in my imagination? I peeked through the glass to see the angels in their wooden boxes. They looked alive still. I blinked twice, trying to clear my eyes in case of some paranormal disturbance. Nothing had changed. I was starting to think like one of *those* people. You know, the ones who are convinced they are being haunted because the central heater is making a noise.

"Do you see those bodies?" My voice was high-pitched and somewhat hysterical. I pointed towards the glass, hoping I didn't look like the lunatic I felt like.

He nodded impatiently; the fishbowl was always full of the deceased. His eyebrows came so close together they formed one severe line. "I see them, Gabriella. Now explain. What about them?"

I turned to look through the glass, almost expecting one of them to rise from their holding boxes. *Don't wake them* echoed in my head. "Well . . ." I said cautiously, my finger outlining them against the glass. "These bodies . . ." I trailed off, my mind wandering elsewhere as the pull towards them grew exponentially. I craved to be near them. *Stupid, stupid, stupid!* I chanted to myself.

Darren sighed heavily at my back. "I'm growing impatient, Gabriella."

In the reflection, I could see him close his eyes as

if praying for more patience. Any second he was going to tire of our conversation and just unlock the damned door himself.

When I still didn't answer, he grabbed my shoulders with his big hands and spun me around so I was looking right at him. His eyes searched me, almost apologetically. Instead of staring back at him, I began looking over his shoulder at the line of computers which were set up for those working alongside me in the fishbowl. Sometimes I made lab technicians stay on the other side of the glass when I was working with sensitive materials. Better safe than sorry.

"Let me show you something." I pointed towards the computers and gestured for him to follow me. He did, raising his eyebrows and looking exceedingly reluctant. *Maybe he does need more patience,* I thought, though that was sort of like the pot calling the kettle black.

I opened my email and clicked on the attachment from Adriana. Pointing to the screen, I said, "This is what these bodies looked like four days ago." I wanted to say, *Now do you understand my hesitation?* But I thought that would be rude. Instead I gave him a significant look.

He stared in disbelief at the photos and then at the boxes in the lab. All the blood drained from his face.

He whispered under his breath, but the only words discernable were *supernatural, not possible,* and *unorthodox.*

Tell me about it . . .

"And," I continued, breaking into his muttering, "I took a sample from one of the bodies—a skin sample, to be exact. And when I turned around to put the vial in the rack, the skin had grown back. There wasn't even a scar or mark of any kind."

For a second he looked as though he was struggling to comprehend what I was saying. He was standing so still you'd think a group of industrious lab technicians had carved a statue in the middle of the lab, though I could tell by his frozen expression that his brain was working frantically. If I thought his face couldn't turn paler or more skeptical, I was wrong. His jaw dropped so quickly I thought he might have dislocated it. He visibly gulped before fiddling in his jacket pocket. His cell phone flashed to his ear. I knew what that meant: the FBI would be here soon. I wanted to kick myself for bringing this to his attention before I had researched everything more thoroughly. It seemed like a brilliant idea two minutes ago.

The conversation on the phone was quick. I roughly translated from the one-sided conversation that we were flying to D.C. with the FBI in tow. They were also going to ship the supernatural beings—the angels?—along with us. I'd only been there once before as a little girl and wondered what exactly they expected us to do there. Actually, I was surprised that we were coming along in the first place.

I opened my mouth to speak but Darren had already begun dialing another number and within seconds he was speaking again, eyeing me with mild apprehension. "Yes, this is Darren Halistor," he said with a determined calm. He walked across the room to give himself privacy. I didn't know who he was talking to.

After the brief conversation, Darren closed the space between us again. "I'm going to request that the lab techs stay out of the fishbowl until the FBI arrive."

"That's all right. This is their lab, too," I insisted.

He nodded slightly and then turned around to walk back toward the elevator. "Gabriella?" he said over his shoulder. "Keep the fishbowl sealed until the FBI arrive."

"Okay," I whispered.

For twenty-six minutes I stared at the angels through the glass walls like they were fish in an aquarium. That was how the lab became known as the fishbowl. And for those twenty-six minutes, all I could think about was how they ended up here—in *my* lab.

Was it all a part of a conspiracy or was this just by chance?

As I sat at one of the lab tables, the place began swarming with laboratory workers and FBI agents. It was like a sea of white coats and black jackets had taken over.

The outsiders marched in, preparing to escort everything we had received from Italy to another laboratory in Washington, D.C., and now several of their scientists were groping all over *my* equipment. *They better watch their hands once inside the fishbowl.*

I was very displeased, and I was sure it was obvious on my face. Of course, it was only natural that the U.S. government would be *very* interested in this kind of discovery. This had happened a few times before, but for some reason this time they had sent double the number of agents.

My poor associates crowded together in a corner, eyeing the newcomers suspiciously. One thing everyone had in common was the fact that they were all waiting for me to open the lab and enter first. Even Darren seemed afraid to pass through the doors first after what I had told him.

I stretched my hand out towards the door handle, the key card in my other hand. Both of my hands were trembling nervously, but as soon as my fingers touched the metal on the door, my whole body relaxed. All I could think about was moving towards the angels inside. What had possessed me? This time I slid the key eagerly through the lock. When the door opened, air came rushing into the lab, and the movement made me take several steps into the lab involuntarily. My heart calmed, my nerves died down, and suddenly I felt like I was being welcomed by the angels lying in front of me.

People anxiously flooded into the lab behind me.

"Doctor Moretti." A taller, older man approached me. He was definitely an FBI agent. His muscles filled the black, wrinkle free suit perfectly and his full head of hair was sprinkled with salt and pepper. There was the ear piece I always saw in the movies, curled and wrapped around his right ear. To top the look off, he was even wearing dark sunglasses indoors. "I've been informed this is your field, and you're the best. To think that you graduated with your doctorate at nineteen—amazing."

I nodded, not sure how to respond. I guess my brain had always functioned at a higher level. Also, my specialty was unique in every aspect. How many people were paid to prove the paranormal—or to try to disprove legends and myths?

A terrible thought came bobbing to the surface.

What if this was the last time I'd ever see these angels?

The agent continued, not noticing my mind working a million miles an hour. "I'd like to request you join us at our P.I. Laboratory, to continue your research on this project."

That was a surprise. It was like he read my mind. "P.I. Lab?"

"Paranormal Investigations," he answered with a slight twitch of his lips. He obviously thought something was funny about this. Maybe he didn't believe in the supernatural.

Over his shoulder, Darren nodded approvingly; so I also nodded. I was still in a daze. Someone could have asked me if I liked ketchup over my ice cream and I would have agreed.

The agent stared at me for a moment, trying to read my face, maybe. I wasn't sure.

"Excuse me—" I groped for his name, realizing he hadn't given me one. It wasn't like the FBI had name badges that said "Hi my name is . . ."

"I'm sorry. I forgot to introduce myself. I'm Special Agent—" He put his finger to his ear piece and frowned angrily. "You can just call me Jeff." He smiled at me, the gesture seemed fake. Something familiar in his eyes blazed from beneath his sunglasses. Gooseflesh ran up my arms and down my spine.

"Well . . . Jeff, I'm Doctor Moretti," I said, using my formal name.

Before he had time to respond, he looked up over my shoulder. Someone must have said something over his ear piece, because he pressed his finger to the small device again and then said, "Excuse me," and walked away. I was relieved and felt a rush of gratitude to whoever had contacted him. My mind just wasn't coherent enough to respond and I could feel my concentration sliding away. I felt a fervent desire for the day to end, but it had only just begun.

As the busy workers packed up the other artifacts that had been shipped from Italy, I stared at one of the boxes that held the human remains—if they were human. There were two males and one female. What I was seeing, though, was the opposite of remains.

My fingers curled around the box that held one of the males. All my previous fear seemed to evaporate being this close. His long black hair was shiny; it looked freshly washed, and his cheeks and chest were full. His skin color was superbly browned, as if he had been working in the sun for hours. However, his clothes were old and torn to pieces, consistent with being buried in dirt for hundreds of years, although the necklace around his neck appeared completely untarnished by time. This man just couldn't be the same dehydrated corpse in those pictures. But what bothered me even more than his strange appearance or the fact that he looked alive, was that I thought he was beautiful.

4

necklace

An alluring, statuesque woman with long, brown hair positioned herself on the other side of the box that encompassed the marvelous male angel. She was perfectly fitted in a black suit that showed her every curve, but I could tell she had no clue she was in the presence of an angel. Unless it had all just been in my imagination—the angels and the dark creature—all things I had just invented. Maybe I had eaten some hallucinogenic mushrooms. Maybe I wasn't even really at work . . .

"Hi. I'm Agent Austin. You can call me Karen," the woman said with a companionable inflection. "I'm with the FBI." She held out her hand for me to shake. She had a charisma about her that I was sure made every woman envious of her. Even I felt a pang of jealousy at her outstanding perfection and breathtaking beauty.

"I'm Doctor Moretti." I shook her hand. "You can call me Gabriella, though." I tried to smile at her convincingly. There was something compassionate and fascinating about this woman, and I immediately liked

47

her, jealousy be damned.

"Gabriella," she tested my name on her tongue. "That's a striking name." She returned my smile. Even her teeth were white and straight. Maybe she was an angel too. Why not? If I really was on some trip, she could be whoever I wanted her to be.

"Thank you." I continued to stare down at the angel before me. I was afraid if I ripped my eyes away from him now, he would vanish. I wondered why I had been so anxious to get away earlier when I felt so peaceful in their presence now. Each second I spent next to this box, the more I wanted to touch the man inside.

"Are you the one who specializes in supernatural beings?" Karen questioned, clearly intrigued by my profession. I didn't hold it against her; many people were curious, though most just looked at me like I had lost all my marbles.

"I guess you could put it that way," I said, pursing my lips. "Really, though, this is the most mysterious thing to happen here. One time there was an uproar about vampire bones, but you know, it was just in everyone's head."

Normally I wouldn't talk this much to anyone about what I do, I was practically babbling. Keeping so many secrets could be difficult sometimes, but I didn't have to here.

Karen looked at me, eager and delighted. "So that myth is squashed?" She sighed, as if she wished the stories were all true. Maybe she was one of those people who dreamed of a vampire to come and bite her neck. Something in her ear piece caught her attention and she looked up from the angel, pressing her finger to her ear. I followed her gaze. Her eyes met with none other than Jeff's, who was standing at the far side of the fishbowl.

When Jeff realized I was looking in his direction, his eyes burned into mine. Again, behind the sunglasses there was that familiar blaze within them. Sinister, somehow.

"Crap," Karen muttered. "I'll be right back." She spun around gracefully, like a swan in water, toward Jeff.

My eyes turned back to the angel inside the box. He looked peaceful, blind to all the fuss going on around him. A lab worker came waltzing up and stared at me expectantly, without saying a word.

"Yes?" I finally asked after several long, silent seconds.

"Director Halistor wishes for me to prepare these boxes for shipping to Washington," the boy said timidly. He continued to look at me, and finally raised his eyebrows. His eyes roamed down my arm to where my fingers were curled around the box.

"Right," I said, my mind somewhere far, far away. "Darren is the boss."

"Huh?"

"Sorry. Director Halistor," I corrected.

Darren absolutely hated his last name. There was nothing wrong with it, he just preferred his first. Only his lower subordinates called him Director Halistor. Sometimes it even took me a second or two to register who my employees were talking about when they called him that. Secretly, I knew they also called him *hook foot*. It had something to do with fishing. Something I never cared to hear.

Backing away from the angel, my heart ached slightly. It was hard to move away now that I had gotten so close. I scrutinized the room now that the box was being nailed shut.

Karen and *Special Agent, you can call me Jeff* were still talking rapidly to each other. Their whispered discussion was intense, and several times Jeff shot a look my direction—targeting my forehead, as if he were shooting laser beams through my skull. I had to resist the urge to recoil from the glower. We were on "friendly" terms only moments before, right?

Weird, I thought, trying to shrug off the odd feeling.

My eyes kept darting in their direction, stealing glances, unable to suppress paranoia. Karen incessantly rubbed her mouth and neck in noticeable exasperation; she even looked a little indignant. I wondered briefly what they were talking about, and then decided it wasn't worth the additional thought. My mind was too busy dealing with the situation at hand: the angels.

Now that I knew they could be revived, I wanted to do it. But I didn't know how. *It would be a travesty if they never awoke*, I thought out of nowhere.

The lab employee was now carting the first box away on a steel table with wheels. The other two boxes were still open. This time I loomed over the box that held the woman.

If I thought Karen was stunning, this angel blew her out of the water. She had hair down to her chest, and it was a dark auburn color that I thought only women who dyed their hair could achieve. Her skin was dark and covered in tattoos—symbols I'd probably never understand. I gazed down at the angel in heavy concentration, as if it would mend her. She also wore a necklace. It was small and simple; a circle with a shield in the middle of it, resting just above her disintegrated clothes. It was small, delicate and for its age, it appeared shiny and new. It was identical to the one the male angel wore. I wondered what their meaning was, and whether I would ever get the chance to find out.

I was transfixed. Without conscious thought, I went to reach for the necklace; something was compelling me to remove it from her. I felt determined to seize it. It was as if my muscles were writhing with the urgency—the desire—the necessity of it. My heart began racing.

There was a funny prickling on the back of my neck. I ignored it. My fingers were only inches away when a flash of steely fingers reached out and stopped me. The force of the grip was painful and I let out a howl of distress. I looked up to see Jeff glaring down at me, his face disapproving. Through his dark glasses, I could see a gleaming red. A vivid image flashed across my mind—the dark creature and his blazing eyes.

His fingers tightened around my wrist when I tried to recoil, and he yanked my hand back to my side forcefully. Karen was behind him, a look of utter disgust on her face. It wasn't aimed towards me, though. It was addressed right at Jeff, as if she were bursting with unpleasant retorts.

What had their conversation been about?

The tension rolled off both of them.

"Let go of me," I said in stunned disbelief, each word punctuated.

I may only be twenty-four, and I may be thin, but

I had made sure to take plenty of self-defense classes when I was going to school. On the weekends, I used to box with my cousin Nicole. Our furious wrestling matches were actually pretty entertaining, or so we'd been told.

"You were going to take that necklace," Jeff accused, nostrils flaring. The malice in his voice was unmistakable. He was more enraged than one should be about the whole incident. It immediately made me suspicious of his anger.

He redoubled his grip, his fingers like an iron band tightening around my bone. Was he generating waves of hate that everyone else could feel too?

"I was not!" I shouted back, feeling provoked.

The noise in the lab died down as everyone took notice of what was happening.

"If touching it is considered stealing, then yes, I was about to do that!" I said tartly. "Now let go!"

His fingers only tightened on my wrist until it was so excruciating that moisture was building in my eyes. *Stupid tears*, I thought bitterly. My heart was thundering, unheard.

"Let her go!" a booming voice echoed from behind me. The tone was astute and domineering, and I felt a little relieved, though I hated being rescued by a man.

Instead of waiting for assistance, I decided to fix

this situation myself. With my left hand free, I pulled it back and let it snap around, hitting Jeff with all my might—right into his kidney at his back. The pressure disappeared from around my wrist.

There was a roar of displeasure. Jeff looked taken aback that I had punched him and was now bent over. He straightened, and his face only showed irritation before he cleared his expression, as if someone had just wiped it away.

The blood rushed back into my fingers so quickly it was like tiny needles were poking every inch of the skin there. Karen had a fleeting expression of satisfaction before Darren came running up, a look of deepest loathing in his eyes.

"How dare you accuse her of stealing?" he shouted, waving a threatening finger at Jeff. "If she wanted—" he stared at me for a second, not sure what Jeff thought I was stealing.

"That necklace," I pointed to it and then shot Jeff an insolent stare.

"—the necklace, she could have stolen it at any time. Why would she wait until the place is teeming with people?" I'd never seen Darren this upset before. His teeth were mashed together tightly. "*FBI*," he muttered angrily.

Jeff, realizing the battle was lost, backed away.

One of the FBI appeared out of nowhere and put his hand on Jeff's shoulder. "I told you to treat Doctor Moretti with nothing but respect. She is not a thief." The man's voice was deep and authoritative. He looked at me and then said, "I'm very sorry, Doctor Moretti, Agent Vittorio will not bother you again, I can promise you that."

They both walked away, the one FBI agent pushing him out the door roughly.

Karen stared after them, a look that only spelled out *good riddance*. I wanted to scream *amen*.

Darren leaned down to look at my wrist. "Oh, my. I'm so very sorry, Ella. I should have gotten here quicker." It surprised me when he used my nickname, one only few—*very* few—have called me, and usually only those close to me . . . *intimately* close. His fingers lightly traced the horrible red marks left on my wrist. They would be bruises by tomorrow, there was no doubting that.

Karen was speechless for several painful seconds before she spoke up. "I'm very sorry, Gabriella. He's got a temper," she said sweetly. That was the understatement of the year.

Darren looked up from my wrist at Karen, only a few feet away. It was funny what happened next. They both froze, staring directly into each other's eyes, as if they had been searching for each other their whole lives and had finally found the other. If it weren't for the fact that he had called me Ella, I would have shown a nauseating expression. Instead, I smirked—secretly pleased he was interested in her. I'd prefer never to hear him call me Ella again. *Ever*.

Darren cleared his throat loudly.

"Oh! Sorry. Darren, this is Karen. Karen, Darren."

They both smiled and shook hands. They appeared as if they were in a daze-like trance. Out of everything that had just happened, it was wonderful to see these two happy, just from seeing the other for the first time. *Match-making: accomplished. Rhyming: accomplished.* I giggled under my breath at my thoughts. *When had I become so delirious?*

I walked away, ignoring the sting in my wrist, and the strange looks, and went to the next open box. My eyes fell immediately upon the angel. My curiosity was like an ache, a need, like one would thirst for water.

The boy who had marched off with the male angel was still gone, so I had a little bit of time before the other two angels would be taken away. It seemed that I was the only one who wanted to be near them. Was I the only one who felt the forceful push in their direction—the innate power, begging me to protect them?

This second male was obviously tall. He had long

blonde hair and his skin was very light, the opposite of the first specimen. There was a peculiar feeling while I was near these angels, as if they were suffused with some indescribable sense of power. He also had the same circle and shield necklace. And just like before, I wanted to take it off of him. I wanted to remove it so badly that it ached deep within me. The clasp was close to the pendant, so it was doubly tempting to remove it.

Karen, without making a single sound, appeared and held out a box of latex gloves. One of her lips twitched up slightly; she appeared curious to see what I would do.

"No one will think you're stealing if you're wearing these," she whispered conspiratorially. Her face was set in lines of amused skepticism.

Darren must have run off to do something. It was funny, but I already immediately thought of them as a couple, though they had only said a few words to each other.

"True," I laughed nervously. There was something about Karen that made me think we were best friends in another life.

I grabbed the violet gloves out of the box and slipped them on, delicately avoiding my sore right wrist. Slowly, I reached out to unclasp the necklace. My heart began to race and my blood was speeding through my veins, all while I was being robbed temporarily of breath. I was excited, I realized.

I held the necklace up in the air to get a better look at it and my heart beat even faster. Warmth suddenly spread from the tips of my fingers down to tips of my toes. The golden glow the necklace had seemed to have had when it was on the angel's chest faded immediately; it was losing its luster. A heavy weight disappeared from my shoulders, even though I never realized it was there in the first place. I felt free, and a strong desire to laugh bubbled to the surface. It was as if the life had drained from the gold and into my body, though I knew that wasn't the case. It was something else; I just couldn't put my finger on it. Thoughts and questions exploded in my head like tiny nuclear bombs.

Karen held out a plastic bag for the necklace, and then handed me a label so I could tag the bag for shipping. I couldn't quite read the look on her face. Her eyes were wide—with astonishment? Amazement?

"Thanks," I whispered, eyeing her carefully.

"It's the least I could do after Jeff—Agent Vittorio." She looked anxiously over her shoulder.

What was with this Jeff Vittorio? And what was his problem? "He's not there. I guarantee that Darren went to help escort him out of here by now," I said. We both got a good chuckle at the image. Slowly, we were building a sort of camaraderie.

Karen's eyes were oddly bright. "Do you want to take the necklace off the woman, too?"

I nodded; but when we looked up from the male angel, the boy who had carted off the first angel was back, already nailing the lid shut. She looked highly disappointed.

I shrugged. "I'll do it in D.C."

Karen looked around the room. "Well, is there anything else we need to pack up to take with us?" she asked in an offhand sort of way.

I suddenly remembered the box on my desk upstairs. Surely it had something to do with the shipment from Italy. I shuddered at the thought of the dark creature, but now that I was down here, away from the horrid chest, I was beginning to think the whole incident was just a dream. Deep down I knew that was wrong—I had not been dreaming. Those bodies *were* angels. I had no doubts in my mind, even though I wished I did. Being assured seemed worse than uncertainty.

Was this just some cruel joke the universe was playing on me? Or was I really barking mad?

"Maybe," I said thoughtfully.

She only raised an eyebrow, and I beckoned her to follow me back up to my office.

guardian

the elevator was quiet; no music here. The ride was painstakingly slow, but Karen and I finally made it to my floor.

Sally was absent, and I wondered where she was. I checked my watch to see if it was time for lunch. It was still reasonably early in the morning. Maybe she had quit? Nah, I couldn't be so lucky.

We approached her desk. It was cluttered, and dotted with Post-it notes and randomly splayed files. I felt embarrassed that someone from outside our office was seeing this, but Karen walked on by as if it were no big deal.

My gaze turned from her disaster of a desk to the door of my office, which I suddenly noticed was ajar. My heart gave a horrible jolt and shivers ran up my spine. The images of the dark creature flickered again in my already exhausted brain.

Had I not secured my door? I always locked it when I left; there were exorbitantly abundant records and files in that office, most of them for my eyes only. I pivoted and caught a glimpse of Karen, who had seen

60

what had caught my attention. She had a look of apprehension on her face. I shrugged to show nonchalance
and forged ahead, nearing the door. With each step it
felt like my legs were filling with liquid metal. A warning, perhaps?

My hand made contact with the metal door and I
exerted only the tiniest pressure, easing it open. I was
anticipating something horrific, something wrong—
and I was prepared to pounce to protect myself. Though
how do you fight blackness? That *thing* could take me,
hands down.

I peered into my office nervously.

It wasn't the blazing eyed creature from before. It
was Sally, leaning over the open box on my desk and
gingerly handling the chest within. The box-cutter was
lying on my desk, next to the box.

"What hell are you doing in here?" I barked, completely exasperated and a little relieved.

She jumped in surprise at my voice, her red hair
whipped around, and the chest went flying out of her
hands.

I watched as the dark wooden chest somersaulted,
as if in slow motion, through the air—and I caught
sight of the symbol on it for the first time. In that
instant, I knew I didn't want the box to break open.
Ever. Despite not wanting to touch it, for the second

time that day I dove through the air, torpedoing across the floor to try to catch the chest before it hit the floor.

But it was Karen, seemingly from nowhere, who seized it. Her fingers snatched it from the air with force. I hadn't even seen her come into the office.

She stood with the chest in one hand—cool, calm, and collected—staring at us. I had skidded across the floor after my failed dive to catch the chest (another one for my old baseball coach), and Sally was standing by my desk with a look of shock on her pale face. The moment felt almost comedic.

"Good God." Sally put her hand above her heart, like she was trying to restart it. "You scared the hell out of me!"

I scared the hell out of her? "What are you doing in my office?" I snapped, getting to my feet and straightening my suit.

"I—well . . . I was just . . ." she trailed off feebly.

"Out," I ordered, pointing furiously at the door.

Sally sprinted for the door, humiliated at being caught. *And that is exactly why I keep my office door locked*, I told myself. Security may be excellent from the outside, but once in the depths of the building, things seemed to be easily accessible. *Maybe firing Sally should be on my to-do list*, I thought angrily. I had considered firing her in the past, but had not gone through with it because of the time it would take to find someone else.

As the door clicked shut behind her, I turned around to see Karen eyeing the chest. The dark indigo sky, full of rain clouds, dulled the room's brightness.

"The craftsmanship is remarkable," Karen said, delicately holding the chest away from her body. "I've never seen anything like it. Is it old?"

"Um," I mumbled, walking towards her. My hands reached out to take it from her. They trembled like I had had twenty cups of coffee. But it wasn't the coffee that made me so nervous to touch the chest; it was the images burned into my eyes. Blazing eyes, darkness, a black creature—*warning me*.

Karen didn't notice my shaky fingers. Actually, she didn't seem to notice me at all. "Very old . . ." she mumbled to herself, frowning as if she had seen something she found very disturbing. "*Tenebre, io scaccio fuori*," she whispered.

"Italian?" I asked, a little worried. *That's it! I'm crazy. Now I think I am hearing people in a foreign language.*

Her eyes shot up from the chest. They were blue, like the ocean, but they burned into mine like fire. "Yes." Her fingers roamed over a symbol on the chest. It was the exact same symbol I had seen downstairs on the necklaces; the circle with a shield in the middle. The aged wood, a rich brown color, was worn on the edges. "Shadow of the Sun," she whispered.

"The what?" I was utterly bewildered. She was really starting to freak me out. I had no idea what was going on, but she obviously knew something I did not.

"Not what—*who*."

"Karen," I said tentatively. "You are beginning to . . . well, scare me a little. What does *Tenebre* . . . whatever you said, mean?"

Again, her eyes met mine. They were full of benevolence and oddly her face suddenly appeared ancient. "Darkness, I cast you out."

Darkness . . . A dreadful blast of realization hit. My legs moved without conscious thought as I backed into the wall. A framed photo above my head almost fell before I reached up and steadied it. I was reliving the feeling of the velvety darkness wrapping itself around my body, swallowing me whole. I shivered.

She knew.

Karen placed the chest down and rushed toward me, her face full of concern and worry. "You've seen it?" she said, delicately taking my hand. She must have seen the look of fear in my eyes. "There goes protecting you," she muttered to herself.

I yanked my hand away. Words just exploded

out of me. "What are you talking about? Protect me? Shadow of the Sun? Speaking Italian . . . *Who are you?*" It's all a practical joke, it has to be. *April fools, Gabriella.* Except it was October.

"Gabriella," she sighed. "I'm so sorry. I was supposed to be here earlier. Weeks ago, truthfully." Karen's fingers traced my face, looking me over like a mother tending to their kid who's just fallen off a bicycle. "You aren't hurt, are you?"

I couldn't help it; I exhaled in relief. Her touch brought warmth—a calming force I so desperately needed. Inside this office, people didn't really know who I was; but I struggled more than anyone around here could understand. It was hard to make friends when everyone my age was just beginning their lives, and I was already living mine. The only person who has never held my intelligence against me was my sister, Jenna. Work was my life. Whenever I tried to live outside the bubble I had created, I failed miserably. And here was Karen, taking this giant weight off my shoulders just by her touch, as if she were healing me. And honestly, I trusted her.

Why did I trust her?

"I guess we need to talk," I mumbled.

"No time now," she looked over her shoulder. The chest was still sitting on my desk. Tension rolled through my body. "It can't hurt you. Not anymore," she soothed, as if reading my mind.

I nodded.

Karen moved back to my desk. Her finger tips fluttered over the chest again. "*Rivelano.*" The chest flew open.

I wanted to fall back, to run and hide from whatever was within. I waited for an explosion, or for the room to turn into a dark mist. I waited, and waited.

Nothing happened.

My vexation was far from gone, but it had lowered from a boil to a simmer. My heart began to beat steadier as I moved towards the now open chest. I watched Karen as she loomed over the box, looking into the depths. Her hand reached out, but met resistance.

"What did you say?" I barely whispered.

"Reveal."

"Oh," I said. My anxiety grew as I approached the small object. It seemed such a mundane object to cause such a stir in my brain. The area associated with fear and panic was hit hardest. Inside the box lay two tarnished-silver keys, each with a symbol I hadn't seen before: two spearheads crossing in a circle. But the circle looked familiar. It was the one I had seen on the necklaces. The braided motif was intricate—the design flawless.

I don't know why I did it, but I reached out and seized them both. Just like with the necklace, I needed to hold them.

Karen gasped, a look of dawning wonder replacing her careful composure. "I thought the necklace was a fluke . . . but now, the keys . . ."

I sighed as she looked at me with a new light feeding her blue eyes. "Listen, Karen. If that's your real name . . . *Karen*. I have no idea what you are talking about. I'm clueless about everything that has exited your mouth since we entered my office. Who are you?"

"I'm an angel," she stated simply, like it was obvious. *Did Sally drug my coffee this morning?* "My kind are known as The Light of Heaven."

"Heaven?" I asked with nonchalance.

"Well, I wouldn't know. I'm immortal. Haven't died . . ."

Her words fell oddly upon my ears. I was lost in frantic speculation about how to best approach the subject. Instead of wording it in my head, I just gave in and blurted out, "*An angel* . . . God's creation?"

"An angel, yes. That is true. God? I've never met His holiness. The whole angel story in the Bible is just a myth."

"A myth?" I interjected. "You don't know God? You have to understand that is hard to believe."

She sighed, exasperated, as if she had explained this a million times before. "No. We aren't some mythical creature sent from God. That was just some of my kind being full of themselves, so to speak. Ours is an ancient people who were deeply involved in magic."

I scoffed, disbelieving.

"We were called *Senza Tempo*. Translated, it means timeless." She ignored my pursed lips of incredulity. "When my people were taken by a king and turned into slaves, they met in the evenings and finally decided to combine their magic to become truly timeless, just as their name foreshadowed. Immortals, as you know them."

"So," I said. "Let me get this straight. No God? Just a bunch of old people turning into immortals?" I needed to lie down.

She nodded. "But I never said 'no God,' just that I have never met Him."

This was all so much to take in. One day I'm plucking feathers from a dead man—who had sewn them into his skin to make people believe he could fly—and the next I was speaking to an actual, live angel. I must be dreaming. *Ugh! Or I'm going crazy!* And why the hell would she just come right out and tell me? "How did the angel thing come about?" I asked, skeptical. This had to be a practical joke. It had to be!

"Well, some of my people became arrogant," she said. "When Christianity was on the rise, they took advantage of many souls. Because of our magical abilities, one could seem god-like to a mortal. But flaunting power in front of those without it is dangerous. You see, while each of us has our own special abilities, we also share many of the same. You can blame some of my brothers for the tall tales of angels and God. The name sort of stuck, though."

"So," I paused, reeling in the information she had freely poured for me. "All the knowledge we have about angels is a fib that your brothers . . . *made up*?"

"Sadly, yes. We pre-date Christianity, and even Jesus. In the time when I was only a mortal, people prayed to the Olympians."

I sat, my mind soaking up the information like a flower soaking up the rays of the sun. My thoughts were too unwieldy to form any kind of coherent response. I believed her, and yet I barely knew her. *Was this the divine intervention that I had fiercely begged for?*

"Should I even ask where the cameras are hidden?"

"You saw the dark one," she knelt before me, taking my hands in hers, completely ignoring my camera joke. "Yet you survived."

My heart skipped a beat. "People usually don't?"

I choked.

"No. And no one, human or angel, has ever been able to break the bindings of the Shadow of the Sun. Yet you . . ."

"Did?" I offered.

"Precisely."

"So the 'dark one' is a member of this Shadow of the Sun?"

"Not exactly." She stared at the keys in my hands longingly. "It's not like a club. There is no membership. They are what they are. Part of the sun—the light— cast out to forever to be shadows of blazing light."

I raised my eyebrows. "You know, that's an oxy-moron if I ever heard one."

Karen giggled. The sound was like tinkling bells. "Yes, I'd say it is. But you saw one. They are dark as charcoal, yet their eyes blaze like the sun. They can play with fire, but it remains contained inside of them— no longer part of the sun. They're doomed to be held in shadow."

"Oh . . ." I said, as if I totally understood. I didn't. Not really. But I had always wished for the supernatu-ral and now I had it . . . in my office . . . talking to me.

Karen rubbed my arm, her eyes boring into mine. The blue seemed to intensify until I was calm, as if I had drunk some extraordinary tonic and was tingling with a secret magic.

"Did you do that?" I asked.

"How do you feel?"

"Peaceful."

"Yes," she said fervently. "That was me. I'm an empath. It is one of my many magical abilities. Empathy is a more precious gift than most."

"But that's ficti—" I cut myself off. I had to remember this was what I had wanted, and it was in my life now. The supernatural—the weird and strange and unexplained. *Get used to it*! I ordered myself.

Her hand patted mine gently. "I wanted to reassure you, send you the feelings I thought you should be feeling; but I didn't want to intrude. It seems I can only change your moods when you wish for me to. I've already tried to steer you in other directions during our conversation, but you deflected all of them."

"I did?"

She smiled and nodded, her long gold-brown hair bounced lightly. "It's rare that I'm sent by the Elders to protect someone, but I show up and you already have three angels in custody. Then I find out you lived through a meeting with a Shadow, and that you are able to penetrate their barriers and shield yourself from me. I have to say, I'm highly impressed and a little speechless."

My mind did a little spin as I took it all in. Why would someone be here to protect me?

Oh! The thought hit me suddenly, and if I were a comic book character you would have seen the light bulb above my head. *I must be in danger*.

"Why are you here?" I pondered aloud, feeling more stupid by the minute—a feeling I wasn't used to but continued to come across today.

"Well, I'm sworn to protect you. I'm your Guardian angel, of course."

6

SUMMONS

To say that I was bewildered would be illuminating the obvious. I was bordering on overwhelming incredulity. Angels . . . All my preconceived notions about the mythical creature went up in a puff of smoke. I had thought they were fairytales. My mind was in a whirlwind, and I couldn't seem to turn off the insane wind that was causing the uproar. Life would be so much easier if some things, including facets of my brain, came with an off button.

Karen had left me in my office to give me some time alone to adjust to everything she had told me. It felt like she had dropped the equivalent of an atomic bomb in my head, and left me to sift through the debris. I took several deep breaths and began to make a list in my head. One, I've lost my mind. Two, there are now *four* angels in this building, *that I know of.* Three, I've completely and utterly lost my mind. Four, a Shadow of the Sun tracked me down, yet I survived. This was perplexing, to say the least—even according to Karen. And five, I have a Guardian angel, sworn to protect me, probably because I was in some life-threatening

73

danger.

My head fell into my hands. I was overwhelmed. Why me? Of all the people on this planet, why did the Elders pick me to be guarded? I felt my life as I knew it slowly slipping through my fingers, like water. This meant more secrets and lies. Didn't I already have to keep a majority of my life a mystery to those I met?

Men came and went in my life, realizing I would never divulge the secrets I learned about in the lab and feeling my secrets created an emotional barrier. Of course, they also felt an "emotional barrier" when I wouldn't sleep with them either.

I didn't have time for them anyway.

There was a tapping on my door, and I jumped so high out of my chair that it nearly rolled out from underneath me. My fingers clutched onto the arm rests.

"Who is it?" I asked shakily. I really needed to get a grip.

"Sally."

My legs wobbled when I stood, all my jittery nerves rushing down my legs like small electric shocks. I opened the door without any expectations. As soon as it cracked open, she pushed her way through. She looked . . . apologetic. It wasn't a look that suited her well, or one I had ever seen on her before.

"I'm so sorry," she spluttered. "I don't know what

I was doing in here—you know, earlier."

"Sally, calm down," I said softly. She was nine-teen and sometimes I couldn't help but feel motherly toward her, even though she was rude and acted like she was better than everyone.

"I can't explain it," she said in a shaken voice, her eyes not meeting mine. "One second I'm sitting at my desk and the next thing I hear this voice . . . I don't even know how I got in here." She stared at me, expecting me to say something; but I was speechless. She looked back down at the floor. "It was beckoning me to open the box in your office." Tears spilled down her cheeks and onto the floor.

"It's okay," I soothed. "I believe you."

Her eyes snapped up to meet mine. "You . . . believe me?" she asked, disbelieving.

"Absolutely," I said sincerely. "Listen, we have no time to talk right now. I'm heading to Washington D.C. and I need a familiar face there with me. Go home, pack your bags, and I'll have someone pick you up in one hour."

She wiped the tears from her face and nodded before backing away and leaving my office. I had a feeling I was going to regret this immediately.

Rain splattered across my windshield while the wipers

worked furiously to clear the glass. It was that time of year again in Oregon—not quite cold, not quite hot—when all the trees turned a brilliant orange or red and the leaves covered every last inch of the ground, giving it a golden look. It was Darren's brilliant idea to build the Zelko Corporation out in the middle of nowhere, but the isolation was slowly growing on me.

Regardless of the fall colors, it was warmer outside than I expected, a rarity for this part of the country. The sky was dark and angry; the trees danced from side to side. Branches and leaves began smacking my windshield violently. The day was rounding on noon and visibility was minimal between the rain and the fog that had begun to rise from the blistering asphalt. Pine trees littered the area until the road broke out of the encroaching forest and ran along the ocean. Oretown was a small coastal town. The population was so small, in fact, that it wouldn't have surprised me to find it didn't register on some maps. But it was my home and had been for the past five years.

After turning off the main highway, I began driving on a narrow road, barely wide enough for one vehicle in some places. Sometimes I wondered who built the roads. It was like the city planners had thrown spaghetti at a map and decided to follow the pattern of loops and curves, resulting in roads that were dangerous to the extreme. During a two-mile stretch you could easily find the road doing a one-eighty, and then another. One second you're going east, the next you're going west, and suddenly you're facing east again. Anyone who wasn't used to the abrupt curves had a high chance of having an accident. So I drove slowly and with caution.

On the ride home, I called my sister to see if she and her daughter Jules would stay at my house while I was gone. Of course she said yes. They both loved the beach house. Plus, it was perfect timing—fall break. I had been exceptionally pleased when I first moved here to be so close to where she lived in Portland.

Jenna had recently dumped her loser boyfriend after being in an emotionally abusive relationship, and I knew she needed the break. Jules' father had died before she was born, in the Iraqi war, which was why Jenna was constantly on the emotional cusp of break-up no matter who she was dating. No one could ever live up to her dead husband. And I could understand that; he was an exceptional man.

Unlike most people, I loved the rain and found it peaceful. During the calming ride, I continued to review the day's events. There were angels—seriously, *ANGELS*—in my lab. Benevolent beings, creatures of light: whatever else one would wish to call them. "The

Light of Heaven" as Karen so eloquently put it. Either I was going crazy, or I really had stumbled upon the supernatural. I should be skeptical. Right? That was my job, to ask questions and demand proof. The dark creature, the glowing bodies, the angel in my office telling me she was an empath . . . it was all too much, yet also exciting. A terrified excitement, but it made me giddy all the same. What was going to happen next?

When I finally pulled into my driveway, the rain had slowed to a mist and the air had cooled marginally. Only one-hundred and fifty feet from my house, the ocean provided a hypnotic rhythm of waves. There wasn't another house in sight. It was my small slice of paradise.

The sky was still ominous with rain and somehow my house looked eerily quiet and dark. I shut my car door and listened for my Shar-Pei, Hercules. Normally he would be trying to claw through the front door to tackle me. Not today though, not even a peep. Goose bumps rose on my skin, and I wanted to turn around and leave. Instead, I braved the foggy mist and approached the door.

When I looked in the window I saw Karen inside, with Hercules curled up in a comfortable ball next to her. With his wrinkled skin, he looked more like a walrus than a dog when he slept. I sighed, relieved. Or was that Karen sending me those feelings? Who knew?

When I went to turn the handle, the door was locked. Did she lock it behind her—or maybe she could magically appear and disappear too? Perhaps go through solid objects like a ghost?

Or maybe she just locked the door behind her, Gabriella.

I fought with the lock and got the door open. Hercules awoke and came sliding across the wood floor, turning slightly to try and stop his impending crash with me. He might as well have been fighting gravity, because in the next second he almost knocked me over. He began wagging his tail so vigorously that his body was bending in and out of a kidney bean shape. I smiled at the greeting, one I always enjoyed. No man could ever love as unconditionally as a dog.

Karen rose from the couch and greeted me.

"You know," I told her, "Hercules never lets anyone inside the house when I'm not here. Especially someone he doesn't know."

She smiled brightly. "I'm sure it helps that I'm not a human. And don't forget, I'm an empath. It works on animals too."

"Right."

My voicemail machine on the kitchen counter was blinking. Karen followed my stare and her eyebrows knit together. "Gabriella, I don't know if you want to listen to that."

"Why? Who's it from?" My interest was piqued now. I rarely received calls on my home phone. I reserved it only for emergencies, or for taking messages from men when I first begin dating them. I preferred to let the machine answer so they couldn't get upset that I wasn't sitting by the phone, waiting on their beck and call.

"I don't know," she said, her voice apologetic. "He didn't sound too pleased, though." There was a strong resentment in her tone.

"He? Oh great," I said sarcastically and pressed the play button.

"You have one new message," the mechanical female voice said. Then the message started. Immediately, I knew it was Adam, a guy I had broken things off with because we never saw each other. He lived an hour away, but had rarely made time to see me and constantly made excuses. We had been friends for a few months, and after he saw me dealing with one screwed up "relationship" after another, he had asked me to give him a chance. I wasn't sure at first, because of the risk of losing our friendship. So I told him exactly the things I needed from a relationship—one of them was time. In my book, it's impossible to have a functional, loving relationship if you rarely see the other person. Long distance is not my cup of tea, so to speak.

"You know," his words slurred. "You can't just break up with me like that. Anyways, you're fat!"

I raised my eyebrows at that statement and looked down at my small waistline. *Okay . . .*

I heard giggles in the background and my face flushed. Karen grabbed my hand and held it.

"Yeah," a girl whose voice I didn't recognize said into the phone. "I saw your picture. You're a fat, ugly cow." There was a pause, and then Adam burped into the phone. *This is so embarrassing.* "Besides, it's best we aren't together anymore. I was cheating on you the whole time."

"Real mature, idiot. Get drunk, call the ex," I said scathingly.

Karen reached out and pressed the delete button for me. "You don't need to hear the rest."

There's more? "True," I muttered. "Though I can't say his words really bother me. One, he was drunk; and two, I know I'm not fat. He's just angry I broke up with him. Some men have their pride."

"How old is he, anyway?"

"Twenty-six. Divorced twice. I should have taken that as a sign, but we were sort of friends for a while. I always believed it was the women's fault, and not the other way around." I shrugged it off. I was old enough to learn not to waste my time on trivial things like scumbags.

"Well, he acts like he's fourteen. Though age doesn't really have the same meaning to me as it does to a mortal." She grinned, and dragged me to the couch. "Sit," she ordered.

I obeyed.

"There are some things that need to be discussed."

"I'll say."

"Well, it's been more than a hundred years since I was ordered by the Elders to guard a soul." She said the word *soul* with benevolence. "You're not like other humans. Some of the things I have witnessed make me wonder if you are human at all."

"Not human?" I scoffed.

Karen sighed deeply. "It's not a bad thing. But we do need to get this sorted out. We need to know what we are dealing with. The limo won't be here to pick you up for another"—she looked down at her watch—"forty-five minutes. I'm going to summon the Elders."

"The Elders?" I stuttered. She mentioned them earlier and they sounded important. "Maybe I should change?" I looked down at my dress suit which was wrinkled.

"You think the Elders are into fashion?" Her lips

twitched up. "Trust me when I say you look beautiful."

"Thanks." I could feel I was blushing.

Karen moved to the floor, sat cross legged, and closed her eyes. Her head snapped back, looking toward the heavens (of course I knew better now). Her skin began to glow a luminous gold color. Her mouth and eyes opened, light flooding from them like spot lights. Her hair began turning gold, and when she looked at me again her eyes glittered like blue sapphires.

Abruptly, five angels appeared before me. They popped into existence as if I had flipped a switch. They were a vision, with long white flowing robes and fluorescent eyes all boring into mine. Each of them was unique in appearance, but all had the same look of authoritative power. The spectacle made me want to kneel before them, though I resisted the urge.

"*Darkness Illuminator,*" they all whispered fervently at me.

elders

"What did you just call me?"

Six pairs of eyes all stared my direction, each with a different expression on their faces.

Hercules didn't make a single noise, not even a small huffy bark. He sat quietly—patiently—as if he could understand their words.

The Elders surrounded me, their power pulsing through the air like an electrical current. They were all striking regardless of their different ages—something I guessed went with the territory of immortality. Their splendor wasn't about their looks, though; it was about their presence—and they had an abundance of that. They contrasted oddly with the interior of my home. Though my house was beautifully remodeled with high beamed ceilings and intricate wood flooring, the angels made it all look dull and unimpressive.

"Darkness Illuminator," they all said together, their magical voices sounding like a song.

"Guardian, you have done well," an older woman said to Karen.

Karen bent at the waist and gestured for them to

sit. "This is Gabriella," Karen said to the Elders.

"Greetings," a woman with black hair down to her waist said. Her voice was like honey. "I'm Carmela. We've come bearing news." Her face was long and her eyebrows were arched perfectly above her diamond eyes. She looked young, though her presence overpowered her looks.

"Carmela," I greeted, though I continued to stand.

"Hello, my lady," a handsome man said. "My name is Leonardo." He took my hand and kissed it. I felt my cheeks flush and wondered if I had turned a brilliant shade of red. His eyes lifted under his tousled bronze hair to find mine, and he smirked. He looked to be in his mid-twenties. "We have not lost many of our kind through the ages, so finding out whose bodies you stumbled across did not take much research."

"Just jump right in, Leonardo," a taller man said sarcastically, yet playfully. "Don't give her time to breathe or anything." He turned to me. "I'm Lucio. You can call me Luke, Miss Illuminator." He looked more like he was thirty and had a five o'clock shadow on his face. He looked sturdy, like a construction worker. His hair was a dazzling auburn, his eyes glacial blue.

"Illuminator?" I questioned. "Why do you keep calling me that? What does it mean?" I had to stop myself before more queries could exit my mouth on my slippery tongue. I had too many questions and not enough time.

"We'll get to it, but first we must speak of the three lost immortals," said a woman, her face lined with age. "I'm Eleanor, the eldest of the Elders."

"Only by twenty-five years," chuckled Leonardo.

Eleanor looked like someone who wouldn't have any sense of humor, but her silver hair bobbed as she giggled like a little school girl. "This is true, Leo. I suppose it is only a small fraction of our immortal lives."

"Enough joking around! We have business to attend to," said the fifth angel. He looked as if he were built of stone and had black hair down to his shoulders. His face was hard, and he didn't seem to know what it meant to smile.

"There is no reason to be rude to the Darkness Illuminator. She could be our savior," Luke said. "You know, *Shadow of the Sun*." The stone man ignored him.

"You *did* forget your manners, Paolo!" Carmela pointed out. "I'm very sorry, Gabriella. This is Paolo."

I nodded, realizing that unless I was spoken to, words were not worth speaking in his presence.

"The name of the Shadow spreads panic to the angels, so eventually we quit talking about them," Eleanor informed me. "And we stopped talking about the three missing immortals, Andrew, Ehno, and Lucia.

We thought that they were gone forever."

Luke's eyes trailed across the room and bore into mine. The golden tint was unsettling, until I realized it was from tears forming in his eyes. "My twin sister," he whispered.

Carmela patted him on the back. "No worries my friend. That is why we're here." Then she turned to face me. "You have the power to save them all."

I blinked. "*I* have the power to save them all?" I tasted the words in my mouth, trying to swallow them. *Darkness Illuminator* flashed in my head, and then comprehension dawned on me. "Wait, you want me to battle the Shadow of the Sun?"

They all nodded.

"Are you insane? I barely made it out of my office alive the first time!"

"That's exactly why we know you've been chosen," Paolo said firmly. "No human has ever survived an encounter with a Shadow. Even some angels haven't survived."

"No *human* has survived . . . my point exactly!" I said. "You *aren't* human. You're *angels* with supernatural powers. Why put this kind of duty upon the shoulders of a human? Especially one who just today found out today that angels exist? I only just learned that all the tales I've read about angels are works of fiction made up by Karen's brothers." I was furious. "I am not supernatural in nature, but you all are." I barked.

Luke chuckled and elbowed Leonardo.

I ignored them. "I'm not some pawn in a game you are playing," I added defiantly. This was all so abrupt, like a car accident in which the devastation of the catastrophe was lasting much longer than the actual events that caused it. Maybe one of them had the power to erase memories, so I wouldn't have to remember any of this. *Or maybe,* I thought crisply, *I have lost all my marbles and this isn't really happening to begin with.*

Karen placed a hand on my forearm. It tingled slightly, and I wondered if she was trying to use her powers on me. I frowned at the air between us. "It's not going to work."

"Please, Gabriella," begged Leo. He got to his feet and then dropped to his knees before me, taking both of my hands in his. His violet eyes were shockingly bright and pleading. "Hear us out." *Great, he was begging—literally, on his knees.*

"Yes, please," whispered Carmela.

When they looked at me that way with their beseeching eyes . . .

Paolo—or stone man, as I thought him—sniffed

the air snobbishly. "This is a waste of our time."

"It can't be," Karen argued, talking over my head like I wasn't there. "I saw it with my own eyes. She pulled the Nebulous Sun off of Ehno, and two keys from the Shadow chest."

"And how do we know she isn't a Shadow herself?" argued stone man.

I took in a deep breath to retort, but I was beat to it. "What a ridiculous assumption, Paolo," Eleanor said. "Are her eyes like fire? Is she dark as charcoal? No! She is the opposite of a Shadow. She's got sea-green eyes, and her skin is beautifully tanned. How do you get one of those if you are a Shadow?"

"Thanks," I said.

Eleanor nodded slightly, still staring at Paolo with a threatening glare. Power radiated off of her unfaltering, inhuman force.

"It could be a trick," stone man muttered, but he was obviously forfeiting. I didn't blame him; Eleanor clearly had supreme authority in this group of immortals.

"*Enough*," ordered Luke. His eyes had a hard and determined gleam in them. The gold tint of his tears only added to their depth. His true age seemed to resonate through the sound of his voice. "This isn't about her supernatural status; it is about saving those angels."

I was so frustrated! I had so many questions, and I could barely get a word in. "What is a Nebulous Sun?" I practically shouted, trying to get a word in edgewise.

Carmela pulled a tissue from the box on the coffee table and drew a pattern with her finger. When she passed it my way, I saw there was now a drawing on the soft paper. It was the same pattern and shape, the intricate design of flawless beauty that I had seen before. "The necklace?" I asked.

"It's more than a necklace," Carmela said. "It's a symbol for the Shadow of the Sun. The circle represents a halo of sun; the shield is the darkness that binds them. They use it to hold us to the earth. When wearing these, we become almost helpless to their magic—as you have seen with our three family members."

"And what about the other symbols?" I turned to Karen, pulled the keys from my jacket pocket and held them out for her to examine. She didn't even look down at my hand.

"Yes, that is the angel's symbol. The halo of the sun with spears crossing in the middle is a sign that we protect the light from the Shadow," she explained. "It's called Definitive Sun."

"Why did the Shadow chest contain two keys with the Definitive Sun?" Now my interest was piqued. It was a wild mystery, intriguing yet terrifying at the same time. What did this all mean?

"That's what we're going to find out," Karen gestured toward us. Already, I didn't like this idea. The angel universe was unique and strange—fascinating, even—but it felt as if they were thrusting me into a war.

"I don't see how I could be of any service to you," I said confidently. "The angels already looked as if they were alive. Every minute, they seemed to be doing the opposite of dying." They all stared at me, mouths gaping open—all except Karen, of course. "So..." I continued when no one said anything. "If they *are* regenerating already, then why do I need to help the process? It seems they are doing just fine on their own."

"Lucia looked alive? She wasn't a— a corpse?" Luke asked hopefully, another golden tear escaping his eye.

"She looked like a corpse five days ago, but now she looks like sleeping beauty," I replied, smiling.

Now that I took in Luke's features, I could see the resemblance between him and Lucia. Their hair was of the same deep auburn color. I wondered if her eyes were the same shade of the shallowest of oceans.

"What could this mean?" Carmela piped in, her voice high pitched in incredulity, bordering on outright shock.

So many things had left me shocked and disbelieving today that when I saw the faces of the angels around me showed the same overwhelming jolt of surprise, I began to worry.

"It's the prophecy. Zola said she'd come, centuries ago," Eleanor whispered. "Don't you remember?"

A few of them nodded.

"She's never been wrong," Luke informed me.

"Never," whispered Carmela.

Karen wrapped her arm around my waist, I supposed in fear that I would faint. "Well," I hesitated. "What did this prophecy say?" The words tasted funny in my mouth. Only hours ago I was complaining about cold coffee, and now I was talking about prophecies and being completely serious about it. Any second I expected people to come in with a straight jacket.

Eleanor looked sideways at Paolo. He scowled and then nodded.

"The prophecy says,"—Eleanor's lips twitched down—"that three among us will perish to the earth, bound by shadow and fire. An Illuminator will extinguish the curse and save us all, for those three hold the key to the knowledge of light. Angel guards and Shadow barriers will not hold her back, as she will have access to both sides of the realm. Beware of encroaching danger, as the Illuminator will be surrounded; but she is not thy enemy.

"As the dark ones approach, the Illuminator should be set free, uninhibited by all Guardians. She will show us all who the enemies are, and how to defeat them. Until the Shadow's approach, protect her above all others, even from our kind.

"Blood does not hold the key to light and dark. Only our souls hold that power, as the Darkness Illuminator will prove."

I eyed Eleanor for a considerable amount of time. Many heavily weighted minutes passed. The silence in the room was full of meaning. Luke put a finger under my chin and pushed up to shut my jaw. His touch snapped me out of my haze as his eyes seized mine, the blue holding my gaze—searching.

"Shit."

Luke nodded and squeezed my hand. Karen's arm still clung to my waist, her grip firm. It took me a second to realize that she was actually holding me up. She guided me to the nearest chair. This time I welcomed *any* emotional climate change, yet she offered none. I sighed heavily as I regained my bearings. "How do you know this Illuminator is *me*?" I mumbled.

"Because you smashed through the Shadow's barriers like you were putting your hand through thin air," Leo said enthusiastically, his violet eyes lighting up.

"And because, well, *'Angel guards and Shadow barriers will not hold her back, as she will have access to both sides of the realm,'*" he repeated. *"Plus, you're a female, as the prophecy specifies."*

There are a lot of females in the world, I wanted to say. *But how many of them had angels in their living room?*

I sighed. "Oh." That was all I could think to say. The silence in the room was deafening. "So," I said after several moments, my voice slicing through the quiet air. "How did you find me?"

"That's easy," Karen grinned happily. "When the angels were unearthed in Italy, a huge power surge shot out through Oretown. The electricity went out for hours. The FBI became aware of it, but came to the conclusion it was just a power surge.

"However, the Elders knew better; and then we found you when Zelko Corp. called about the bodies. It wasn't until I was in your presence that I knew it was you. You're very powerful, which doesn't make any sense . . . because you're a human. It was like the angels were calling out to you. Your body responded by sending a beacon out to all the angels to come find you for help."

Ignoring her human quip, I said, "Oh. That was me?" It was embarrassing, though I didn't know why.

I remembered that night clearly. Hercules and I had been relaxing on the couch when suddenly everything became really noisy, as if someone had turned up the volume on a humming fridge—and then the power went off all down the coast. Now I knew it was all my fault.

"The problem was that the Shadow of the Sun *also* felt the growing power here," Karen said. "That's why I was delayed. A small group of angels were dispersed to protect you, and I was a part of that group. What I didn't expect was for Jeff to show up in Oretown. He's a Shadow. I would have cast him out then and there, but we had to keep our cover with all the humans around."

"Wait—what? Jeff is a Shadow?" I had my suspicions about him, but I would have never thought that. Nothing was what it seemed to be anymore.

Karen nodded. "A very well disguised one. He is very old and his power is great."

I remembered back to the incident in the office, the dark one squeezing the life from me—warning me. I found it odd that she said *cast him out* instead of *kill him*. "If they are so awful, why didn't you just kill him?"

"Because," Carmela spoke up, her eyes anxious. "He is—was—a double agent."

"I never trusted him," Karen interjected.

Carmela continued. "He spied on the Shadow of the Sun for us. That was why we left him alone—he gave us pertinent information."

"I thought I saw fire blazing in his eyes," I whispered to myself. Even now, Jeff bothered me. My wrist was still sore from where he had gripped it. I would have loved to have taken him down in some boxer-like style. Bite his ear and knock him out.

Karen giggled, pulling me from my thoughts. "Yes, he wears sunglasses a lot and the humans give him a hard time over that. He has a difficult time controlling his anger." Her voice turned sour. "He was fired after he grabbed you—"

"Wait a minute. You said he 'was' a double agent? What happened?"

Karen nodded. "The Elders and I took care of him."

"He disobeyed our orders," Paolo interrupted, his voice deep with loathing. "I knew it was a bad idea to begin with."

I shuddered. "When you say 'took care of him' you mean . . . ?"

"We didn't kill him," Paolo said, his voice hard as stone. The tone was fitting. "We can't *kill* them. We can only bind them or cast them out to another dimension for a while."

"Dimension?" I choked on the word. It should be hard to astonish me by now. "What do you mean you send them to another *dimension*?"

It was Luke who spoke to me. He had yet to let go of my hand and gave it another squeeze. "Your world is not what it seems."

Duh, I wanted to say.

He smiled at my expression. "I know you have many questions and we will answer them, but for now you need to pack your bags. Now that we know who you are, you need to be with the angels on that plane." I nodded. "Karen will travel with you, as she has been appointed to guard you. She swore an oath. And now that we know your significance, we will be assigning another guard when the angels awake."

"But what if I can't do this?" My voice was pleading and I was slightly embarrassed by the sound.

"I know you can." One golden tear dropped from his blue eye. And with that statement, they all faded from my living room.

It was just Karen, Hercules, and I left in the house now. "Karen, what do the Elders do?"

"They are protectors of knowledge."

That sounded really important. She smiled at me, leaned in to give me a hug, and then she was gone—as if she had fizzled into thin air.

8

My bedroom was fairly basic compared to the rest of my house, with simple sand-colored walls and a high ceiling. I'd never done much to it since I lived alone and I rarely had visitors—especially not of the male persuasion. But it was still a cozy room. My large king-sized bed, opposite the dresser, dominated the space. The walls were full of paintings—purchased from the amazing unknown artists I had come across during my travels—as well as photos of my family and I doing the vacation thing. There were French doors that opened up to the sandy abyss outside, and from where I was standing I could see the waves crashing wildly around.

My salary wasn't huge, but I'd always been extremely good at saving and finding deals. This very house I had purchased with very little money, even though it was beautiful beach-front property. My adoptive mother had been a great bargain hunter who always told me when I was younger that there was no need to pay the full price for anything, and her advice served me well in finding this house.

In my closet, I could see my business suits, lab coats, and all my other incredibly boring attire. I was in desperate need of a new wardrobe. Because I never really went out, there was usually no reason to buy anything dressy or fancy. I wondered if I would have the opportunity to shop in D.C.

I had no idea how long I'd be away, so I piled a huge, towering stack of clothes in my suitcase just in case. I stared down at it, hoping that sitting on it would help me close it, and wondering how I would fit a bunch of *new* clothes in there too.

My mind didn't linger long on those humdrum thoughts; I kept catching myself musing over what it must have been like in the time when angels were around, flaunting their talents to humans. The angels all seemed so young and beautiful—mystical, divine, and maybe even god-like—but not at all ancient.

I had an overwhelming urge to read the Bible and find the stories about the angels. Would I laugh at the fact that some of them were Karen's brothers? For the first time, I was actually disappointed I didn't have the Bible in my house. I wasn't a religious person and had never felt the need to read the holy book.

I was having trouble concentrating on packing my suitcase. How could I worry about whether or not I would have time to shop in D.C., or worry that I was running low on toilet paper and Jenna would need to buy some more—how could I stand in my ordinary bedroom, around my ordinary things, trying to have ordinary thoughts—when I knew that there was an extraordinary race of angels out there?

Or had I just imagined everything that had happened today—from the angels who just left my house to the three bodies sent to the lab. That was still a possibility. I began to feel deeply bothered by the turn of events. Just yesterday I was a normal human woman, interacting with normal, everyday people, living a normal life—well, as normal as one's life could be in my profession. Now I knew better. I had been wildly thrust into the supernatural, the *real* supernatural, not any of that stuff that I had previously dealt with.

There was an exceedingly faint ringing sound from my cell phone, snapping me out of my musing. It had always bothered me when people made their ring tones into songs or weird noises, and as technologically advanced as I was, that was one strange habit I refused to succumb to. It rang again, though I could barely hear it; the sound was muffled. I had no idea where I had put it.

It rang again and I began throwing clothes around, hoping I'd find it under one of the piles. I quickly searched the floor and the bathroom. As I entered the kitchen, the ringing became louder before it stopped all together.

Sighing, I sat on a bar stool at the island. I snatched up a banana from the bowl of fruit in the middle and began to devour it. I was starving; I hadn't eaten since yesterday. I completely forgot about my phone and began thinking about how empty the house felt without the angels present. It was as if all the warmth they had brought with them had been sucked into a black hole when they left.

Hercules sat on his haunches and looked at me, his tail wagging furiously. He was my only company and had been following me all through the house as I packed.

"I'll miss you too, buddy."

He pranced on his front paws and moved closer so I could pet his head.

Absently, I stared at the answering machine. The screen display showed zero messages. That, and the message I had received earlier from Adam, was just another reminder of my very non-existent love life. And even *that* relationship had just been an additional attempt to connect with another person. But again, I had failed miserably. As old as I was, I was still fairly naive about love and men . . . and relationships, period.

Of course I had dated, but each time it had ended disastrously, as Karen had witnessed earlier.

My whole life, besides the support and love of my family, I had been alone. When you are several feet smaller and several years younger than your peers in school, they seem to shy away from becoming friends.

I had graduated from high school when I was twelve; how was I supposed to relate to a bunch of hormone-enraged kids when all I was interested in was riding bikes with my sister or thinking of new science experiments to try out. My family and I were living in Ohio at the time, and they did everything they could to help me advance in life. Yale, among other prestigious schools, accepted me without question, and Yale just happened to have the programs I was most interested in. My family uprooted so I could go to school there and were as encouraging as ever. They had faith in me and knew that I would someday make them proud. But since my move to Oretown, I hadn't really seen my parents as often as I'd like; though I received emails from my mom on a weekly basis.

When I moved away, they were finally able to move wherever they wished and begin living their lives unhindered by their genius daughter. After they had followed *my* dreams for so many years, they were now able to follow theirs. My mom started up a business in Charleston, South Carolina, where she helped restore old buildings in the historic district. She loved to include pictures of her current projects in her weekly email. My father began boating and gave tours out on the water. It was great to know they were happy and living *their* dreams at last, instead of mine.

There were only two other important people in my life. My cousin, Nicole, who was my age and never held my genius against me. We met when I was first adopted, and she held my hand through some tough times when I was trying to remember my past and move on into the future. The other person was Jenna, my sister. She was adopted only two years before me and was four years older, but she treated me like I was the same age. I always respected her.

As far as friends went, I didn't have any. As an adult, I had been able to achieve some casual relationships with people, mostly co-workers since I didn't create opportunities to meet people outside of work, but I never did find a true friend. After being alone most of my life, I accepted it and filled the void by diving into the world of fantasy, wishing it to be true.

I'd come full circle. My wish had come true. Now I had angels in my life and a mission—to defeat the Shadow of the Sun. The way the Elders had talked to me . . . it was as if they thought I had known about them my whole life. They hadn't hesitated in revealing themselves or pleading openly for my help—the help of a *mortal*. They seemed to expect me to accept everything as they went ahead and pushed me into this new world.

I was freaking out about the whole thing, but probably handling it better than a normal person would have. I had spent my life constantly reading stories about the supernatural, and I'd always desired those stories to really be true. It was easier to believe them when I wanted them to be real anyway. Regardless, it was a lot to take in, and as I sat at the island I tried to come to terms with it. *This is your life now: the divine intervention that you begged for. Wasn't this what you wanted all along?*

The faint sound of my phone ringing again startled me and I jumped, nearly toppling over the bar stool. It rang again, and I searched the clean granite counters; but there was no sign of it. By the next ring I was getting frustrated. I stared at the stainless steel fridge and then, curious, I opened it. My keys and my phone were lying on the top shelf next to the milk. Feeling like an idiot, but somewhat amused, I snatched the phone up and answered it before it stopped. The metal was cold against my ear.

"Hello?"

"There you are!" Jenna exclaimed on the other end. "We're just down the road. Are you still at home?"

"Wow! That was quick. Yeah, I'm still here."

"Well, I was having a bad day and was ready to get out of town."

I caught myself nodding into the phone. "I understand. I'll meet you outside."

Jenna pulled into the driveway only seconds later. Jules unbuckled her seatbelt and tried to open the door, but the child-lock was on, so Jenna had to open the door from the outside. I could see Jules' impatient frown deepen as she waited to be released.

Finally, she bounded out of the car and attacked my leg, wrapping her skinny arms around me.

"Hi, sweet girl! You want to help me pack?"

She jumped up and down in excitement. "Yes! Yes! Please!"

I helped my sister grab her things and gestured for Jules to enter the house. Hercules came sliding across the floor, and I seized Jules and held her in the air momentarily to avoid the inevitable collision before putting her back down. She shrieked with happiness as Hercules greeted her.

I walked down the hallway to my bedroom and they both followed me.

"Aunt Gab-ella," Jules tugged at my pants, "What

are we going to do?"

I laughed at her attempt to say my name. "I'll show you," I said and pulled her into my arms.

I placed her on top of my suitcase. "Jump," I insisted.

Her grin grew wide and mischievous. This would obviously not be allowed at home. She began jumping on my suitcase until I was able to close it all the way. When I placed it on the floor, she continued jumping on my bed with Hercules dancing alongside her.

"Gabby!" Jenna shouted from the living room.

I hated that nickname, but I let it slide because my name could be a mouthful. "Hey! I want to visit with you before you leave. Get your butt in here."

"Be good," I mouthed to Jules, who only giggled and hugged Hercules to her chest.

As I rounded the corner into the living room, Jenna asked, "So why are you going to D.C. again?"

"You know I can't—"

"I know," she said with a smirk. "It's all some super secret. You know, sometimes I think mom goes crazy not knowing what you do."

I shrugged. "I do research in a lab."

"Supernatural research. Whatever *that* means," she said in a patronizing, but playful, tone.

"Well, I don't have a lot of people to hide those

secrets from. One of these days I'll be able to tell you. It's not like I have ever disc—" I cut myself off. *It's not like I have ever discovered anything groundbreaking.* Those words weren't true anymore. "It's nothing you would be interested in, anyways," I continued, trying to save myself.

By the look on her face, I knew she didn't believe me for a second; but she didn't pressure me. She never did. That was one of the reasons I loved her so much.

"How's Adam?" she asked.

"I guess I forgot to tell you—"

"That you broke up with him," she cut in, smiling. "I figured as much. You'll find someone one of these days, I'm convinced."

Jenna knew me too well. Men never broke up with me; I always got to it before they could. Sometimes they didn't want to break-up at all, especially the men who still held on to a shred of hope that they'd get me in the sack, but I couldn't stay with them. It was a curse: I couldn't find a man worth my time, and I refused to waste my time on duds. Deep down, I believed in true love and refused to settle for anything less.

As a peace-offering for forgetting to tell Jenna about the end of another of my doomed relationships, I didn't bring up *her* recent break-up.

Her hand on my forearm brought me from my

thoughts. "Maybe you'll find some hot guy in Washington. Aren't you working with the FBI?"

I nodded.

"Well, I bet there have to be some hunks around!" She winked at me. "Isn't being tall, dark, handsome, and sexy a prerequisite for joining the FBI?"

I sighed, not wanting to stay on this subject any longer than necessary. Delving into my personal life was not high on my priority list right now. "How's your job in Portland?"

Her smile brightened. "It's amazing! I love working with all the kids. Plus, I get to spend my days with Jules now that she is going to school."

After the tragedy of her losing her husband before their daughter was born, it was great to see her happy again. For a long time, she and Jules had stayed isolated. We all worried about her, but she went through the grieving process and decided to move far away from the military base in Augusta, Georgia. Now she worked at an elementary school as a first-grade teacher. But even though it had been five years, she still had her down times. I was just grateful that we had both ended up in the same state, at around the same time. I knew that we would always be there for each other.

"You can stay here for as long as you want. I'm not sure how long I will be in D.C." I patted her leg and she gave me a huge hug. There were so many unspoken words that went in that hug. She knew I was worried about her.

"If you're not back by the time we leave, I'll take Hercules with us. Jules will love that. I just hope she doesn't get any brilliant ideas about a puppy." We both laughed. "A trained dog is one thing; a puppy is another."

There was the soft purr of an engine pulling into my driveway and I grabbed my jacket and suitcase and gave Jenna another hug. "Thanks for doing this. You are the best sister in the world."

"Don't go! Don't!" a squealing Jules said, sliding down the hall in her socks.

"I'm sorry, sweetie, I have to. Give me a big kiss and I'll come back soon . . . with presents."

After many hugs and kisses from them both, I was on my way to the airport.

9

heights

y the time I arrived at the airport, the rain had
abated and the sun began to peek through the
shadow of the clouds. The grounds were blinding as
the water covered asphalt gleamed and shimmered,
reflecting the bright orb in the sky like a huge mirror.
I put my sunglasses on as I exited the limo, trying to
deflect some of the brightness. When my eyes focused,
I noticed there were roughly thirty people in the immediate area, many of them FBI agents.

Karen was among them. The FBI agents were
watching the airline workers lift the angel's boxes
and carry them into the cargo area of the plane. Karen
wasn't happy about the situation; a frown dominated
her features. The look didn't sit right with her face. I
didn't blame her, though. Who would want one of their
own to ride in the cargo area of a plane?

She must have felt my eyes on her because she
turned to face me, her frown instantaneously twitching
up into a very affectionate and welcoming smile. It was
effortless, beaming back. It seemed almost impossible

111

not to feel cheerful in her presence.

As the airport employees loaded the many boxes, I continued to watch. Karen turned to bark orders at one of the guys, and he actually cowered in fear. I just smiled at her exasperated face. I wondered if she was stressed. Did angels feel stress? I knew they could feel sadness. Luke's golden tears ran across my mind. I couldn't imagine the loss he must have felt at losing not only his sister, but his twin.

The limo driver placed my suitcase next to my feet. "Doctor Moretti," he tipped his hat.

"Thank you," I said before he turned to get back into the driver's side. The limo pulled away as I popped up the handle on my luggage. I dragged it across the tarmac toward the plane, hoping it wouldn't pop open after everything I had shoved in there. The stairs to the plane were down, but this was not some small puddle jumper; it was a huge Boeing 787.

One of the FBI agents came my way. He was tall and very handsome. Maybe Jenna had it right about the whole FBI requirements. His earpiece bobbed as he scampered my direction.

"May I help you?" he offered, shooting me a dazzling smile.

"That would be much appreciated," I said gratefully and grinned at him.

"My pleasure."

He lifted my suitcase effortlessly, as if it was as light as a feather. Instantly my mind began daydreaming about the muscles that must be hidden under his suit. Maybe I could introduce him to Jenna later . . . *or keep him for myself.*

"Ladies first," he said. His hand rested gently on the small of my back as he led me toward the stairs.

The inside of the plane was not set up as I was used to in a typical commuter plane. There were couches with coffee tables, big screen TVs, and a bar. Most of the couches were facing the front of the plane. Was this how the FBI traveled? Maybe I had gone into the wrong profession.

A hostess smiled at me genially and offered me a drink before I even had the opportunity to sit down. I declined.

The FBI agent helped me put my suitcase in one of the overhead bins and then smiled at me again, his teeth straight and white. "It was a delight to meet you, Doctor Moretti."

For some reason, it didn't surprise me that he knew my name. "You can call me Gabriella." I could feel the blush snaking its way up my cheeks. "I'm sorry. I didn't catch your name?"

His smile brightened. "Agent Carter."

"Will I see you on the flight, Agent Carter?" I couldn't help it, I was flirting . . . or I thought I was. He was delicious in his black suit with light brown hair and his dark-brown mysterious eyes. Plus, the voice-mail I had received earlier made me want to venture out. No more drunk, burping men on my voicemail. That was a promise I was making to myself—starting right now.

"You will, Gabriella." His eyes twinkled. "You can call me Joseph, by the way."

He paused to touch his earpiece. I thought it was funny how they all did this when someone spoke to them over the tiny device.

He frowned. "I've got to go, but I'll see you back here shortly." He threw me another grin before descending the steps of the plane.

Well, so far this day was faring well—except for all the mystical forces and prophecies being thrown around like beads at Mardi Gras, and the Shadow coming to my office to warn me. I bent to retrieve my book from my purse under the seat, and when I straightened Karen was sitting next to me. "Gah!" I screeched.

"I'm sorry. I didn't mean to frighten you." Her voice was magically engaging. Must be an immortal thing. "Good book," she murmured.

I put my hand to my chest to soothe my speeding

heart. "How do you do that?" I gasped.

"Now is not the time," she said, patting my hand. "Not while there are so many humans around us." Her eyes darted around the plane suspiciously. Maybe she forgot I was human too.

"Is there a . . . a *dark* one here?" I whispered.

Her head snapped in my direction. "Of course not! Did something happen?" Her eyes were wide with alarm.

"No!" I said hastily. "No, I didn't see one. But after what the Elders said about Jeff . . . well, I didn't know if . . ."

"Thank God!" she exhaled in relief. "You scared me for a second. Anyway, I talked to the Ladies of Light before I arrived at the airport and they placed a charm on the airport to protect us from any Shadows." Karen put a hand on my cheek. "You are the imperative one now. You *can* save us from our never-ending war with the Shadow of the Sun. Maybe those keys will lead us to the answer." Her eyes searched my face. For what? I did not know.

"Who are the Ladies of Light?" I wondered aloud. "I have the keys, but . . . where do they go? Where's the lock?"

She looked over her shoulders and her eyes darted around the plane, then she sighed. "Okay," she said, her voice lowered. "I can't tell you everything now, but this is what I can tell you. The Ladies of Light are the protectors of the immortals. They are fierce and all angels look up to them and follow their rules. They are bringers of light. Even the Elders answer to them." Once again, her eyes flashed from one side of the room to the other. "And those keys,"—she pointed to my pocket—"I am hoping we can figure out what they go to by waking the—"

"Hey guys!" Sally interrupted.

My earlier fondness for Sally disappeared in that second. Karen had been about to tell me something important, I just knew it.

Karen put her finger to her earpiece. I didn't think anyone was calling her over the device, though. I think she just wanted to leave. "I've got to go." She placed her hand on my arm and gave me a stare that seemed to say: *keep this between us*. I nodded and she stood up to leave.

"So," Sally said cheerfully, turning on her phone and angling it so I could see the planner on the screen. "One of the FBI agents gave me the itinerary for the next two days." She paused, but when I didn't say anything or react, she carried on. "Anyway, looks like we have a really busy schedule . . ."

She described the plans for the next two days, but

it was lost on me. Her voice just a low hum in the air as many more people began seating themselves on the plane. The keys in my pocket were distracting me. I could feel them there, like they were calling for me. What had happened to those three angels? Why was the Shadow of the Sun symbol placed around their necks? What kind of power did the Nebulous Sun hold? And why was the Definitive Sun, engraved on the keys, also inside the chest that was marked by Shadows? I wondered if the Shadow chest was in the cargo hold with the angels. My mind seemed to be on repeat as the questions continued to spin wildly in my head, though none of them seemed to be resolving themselves. I needed answers, but Karen seemed just as clueless as me. Okay, maybe not as clueless, but she probably had just as many questions, if not more.

I thought about Luke and his glacial blue eyes filling with golden tears. I wanted to stop those tears, make them go away. The Elders had told me I could fix this—that I could stop their war. And I wanted to, if only for the sake of seeing Luke's tears disappear.

". . . and I'm dating Bigfoot. There is just something scrumptious about big hairy men," Sally was saying, scowling.

"That's great," I said absentmindedly.

"And I have eleven toes . . . Are you listening,

Ella?" she snapped.

"Oh, yes. Wait, what did you say?"

She sighed heavily. "Since I'm on this trip, are you going to tell me what's going on? Something major must be brewing for the FBI to be swarming the place like they were. But that one FBI agent . . . Joseph? *Meow*!" She clawed at the air.

"Ladies," Joseph laughed.

Sally's expression turned from feisty kitty to outright mortification. She didn't look over her shoulder to where Joseph—tall and handsome—stood. Instead, she closed her eyes and bowed her head. I watched as her neck fluoresced red.

"Can I speak to you, Gabriella?" he asked, his brown eyes holding mine.

"I'm just going to . . ." Sally pointed to something in the opposite direction of Joseph and sprang from her seat as if she had been electrocuted.

Joseph and I both burst into laughter.

"It's always a good day when you get clawed at," he chuckled. "That happens more often than you'd think," he joked.

I laughed while he settled into Sally's seat. He didn't say a word, just sat quietly, comfortably, next to me. There was something about him that made me want to be near him. I couldn't put my finger on it, but he was different. Maybe he was an angel too. Who knew at this point? Were there any humans left?

As I was looking at him, I noticed over his shoulder that the window was white with clouds and then sat up straight in surprise. I hadn't realized how engrossed I had been in my thoughts.

Joseph must have sensed my shock. His gaze went to the window behind him also, and then he turned back to me. "Gabriella? What's wrong?" His features were calm, though his eyes were fierce, ready to spring for attack. Must be an FBI thing.

"When did we take off?"

He smiled, biting his lip as if to suppress a huge guffaw. When he got his composure back, he said, "We've been airborne for *seven* minutes."

His dark eyes bore into mine and many expressions flitted across his face. He seemed amused, yet anxious all at the same time.

"What did you need to talk to me about," I asked, changing the subject.

"Nothing in particular."

He smiled at me, his teeth gleaming against the sun that shone through the windows of the plane. *Well, he's not a vampire.* He leaned back in his seat, his head resting against the headrest, his smile still in place.

I raised my eyebrows.

"I was trying to rescue you from your assistant. I could tell you weren't paying attention, so I thought I'd pretend I needed to speak to you." He shook his head, laughing. "The few minutes I talked to her were . . . interesting and I thought you might need a conversation rescue. Though, I didn't realize what kind of conversation I was walking into."

"Me either," I mumbled.

"I've heard a lot about you," he said out of nowhere. His deep eyes looked sideways at me.

"Oh yeah? And what's that?" *This should be interesting.*

"You're a skeptic. That your job is to find the supernatural." He cocked his head to see my expression. "I heard it is almost impossible to fool you."

I just nodded. Maybe that was all about to change.

He became abruptly serious. "This might be the real deal, huh?" There was something about him that made me want to spill everything that had happened to me. I didn't know this man, yet his deep communicative eyes were constantly searching for something in mine. It might have made someone else uneasy; but to me, it was effortless to stare right back and get lost.

"Could be," I said as doubtfully as I could manage. What I wanted to say was *you bet your ass it is.*

He nodded, as if he could read my mind.

We were silent then, and it was a very relaxed quiet, one I didn't mind in the slightest.

I picked up my book to start reading. Right before I delved into the novel, I looked over the pages and saw Karen twisted around in her seat watching me. She smiled, gave a little wave and turned around in her seat. Even with her back turned, I knew she was looking out for me, protecting me.

Several pages into my book, the hostess padded on by. "May I get you anything to drink?"

"Cranberry juice?" I requested. I thought about asking for a shot of tequila, or maybe a shot of vodka in that cranberry juice, but decided that wouldn't be very professional of me.

"Sure thing," she said sweetly. She put ice in a cup and poured the drink into it. "Here you go, hon. And for you sir?"

"Nothing for me," Joseph said dismissively. She went on by, asking other people if they needed anything.

"So," he turned to look at me, "what exactly do you do in the . . . fishbowl, was it?"

It seemed he had been fully briefed on Zelko Corp. "Yeah. The fishbowl was kind of from a joke." I laughed. "On a normal day—if there is ever a normal day for me—I do autopsies on bodies that are suspected, or deemed 'supernatural.' We have some very rich, *very bored* investors who pay us a lot of money to tell them 'no, he wasn't a demon, he just had a really bad skin disease' or 'yes, he was very hairy, but sorry, he was *not* a werewolf.' This is the first time that I have been completely baffled. Those . . ." I almost said angels, "*bodies* are different. I was actually scared for the first time since I started working at Zelko Corp." I wanted to put my hands over my mouth because I was shocked that I had just admitted that to this man who I didn't even know.

"Really?"

"Oh yeah, the only other time I was remotely freaked out was by the feather man," I admitted with a twitch of my lips, trying to figure out why I was spilling my guts to this man.

Joseph laughed. "Feather man?"

His reaction surprised me. So, I continued. "Oh yeah. This moron had the brilliant idea to stitch feathers into his skin to make it look like he was a bird, or an angel . . . or who knows what actually goes on through a person's head like that?" I shook my head. "And it wasn't like he was scary—but removing hundreds of long emu feathers from the guys back was horrible. To think that someone probably helped him with it or to think of the poor bird missing its feathers . . ." I shuddered. "Never a boring day in the fishbowl."

"That sounds . . ." he made a disgusted face. I nodded in agreement.

"So, Agen—Joseph, what do *you* do at the FBI?"

"I over see our P.I. lab in Washington. For the most part, I stay out of the labs. They creep me out, especially the experimental ones." He shook his head at some thought he must have had. "I mostly work in the field, overseeing the majority of our investigations. Usually my cases involve horrific deaths that have been suspected to be of the paranormal persuasion."

"Like?"

"In Georgia, one year, there were several deaths that the Christians were presuming were the devils work. I had the 'pleasure' to speak to some very . . . *interesting* people." He laughed at the thought. "Even the coroner, *a scientist*, refused to work with the bodies, afraid he would be infected. Infected by what? I have no idea. When it was all said and done, it was two kids who had joined a cult and took it too far."

"Really? A cult?" I asked.

"Stupid, I know." He shook his head again. "They thought they were following the devils orders. If you believed in that stuff, perhaps they were."

"Perhaps." I looked over his shoulder again to see the clear blue sky stretching for eternity.

"I could really use a vacation," Joseph sighed. "Do you like to ski?"

My eyes shot back to his face. "I do, actually. I love it. Last year I went to Snow Bird in Utah. They have some amazing slopes."

"Really? I've never been. There are some places to ski on the east coast, but I've never had the opportunity to go. My brother lives in Colorado and invites me up every winter. My sister-in-law and their kids come with us. They are young, but they are very enthusiastic about skiing. It's a joy to teach them some of my *totally awesome* tricks," he laughed, using a surfer-dude voice.

I giggled at the thought of him showing off for his family. Then my thoughts went back to the last time I was skiing. It was an adrenaline rush, and at the same time, it gave me clarity about my life. Sometimes I hated the fact, that no matter how hard I tried, I was unable to remember a single second of my life before I was found outside the adoption agency. Every time I went skiing, I hoped that something would return to me, but it never did.

I looked down at the book which was still open and read one of the lines of the book, "Just because he was a creature of the night—of darkness—didn't mean he was evil. As he stared at me, all I could see was his benevolence, his light."

"Good book?" Joseph asked. I looked up. Again, his mysterious eyes seized mine. "Earlier, your eyes were moving so fast I didn't know if you were actually absorbing the information or not." He gave me a half smile.

"Yes, it's great—about a vampire." I closed the book so he could see the cover.

"Vampires, eh?" He raised an eyebrow. "The skeptic reads books on the supernatural?"

"Sometimes fantasy is better than reality," I mumbled.

"Maybe we should change that. I could show you the sights while you're in D.C. Your schedule doesn't bind you to the lab all day."

I wanted to scream "yes." All I could think about was getting lost in his eyes. He was perfect, from what I could tell, and I could tell him things I couldn't tell another man. He had to keep just as many secrets as me. Hell, I wouldn't even be able to pay attention to the sights. I'd be too busy staring at him. "How do you know my schedule?" I said instead.

He looked sheepish for a moment. "I gave the itinerary to Sally. And I was kind of curious about you. You aren't upset, are you?" He looked slightly anxious.

"No," I said too quickly.

He grinned. "I wish that we could just know the truth. All this secrecy is rather annoying when you're the one seeking answers." He shrugged.

"Then I would be out of a job," I said, laying my head back.

"True, and then I would never have met you. So maybe all these mysteries will end up being a good thing—"

The plane shook with turbulence. I looked out the window and saw massive, towering storm clouds ahead. I gulped and gripped the armrest on the couch-like seat.

"Anxious, are we?" Joseph asked, glancing at my death grip.

The plane shuddered again, and my fingers only dug in deeper to the fabric.

"Scared of flying?"

"Nope."

"Heights?"

"Nope."

The plane shook again and I closed my eyes, trying to take deep breaths.

"What is it, then?"

"I have a fear of falling from heights," I said, my voice cracking with panic as the plane dipped slightly. It had finally flown into the storm cloud.

Joseph gave a very musical laugh. "I don't understand the difference?"

My eyes opened to see him staring at me quizzically. "Put me in a plane, strap me up, or let me repel from a cliff—or hang me from a thirty story building—and I'm fine. It's when I'm not safe that I freak out. Heights are fine, until there is a risk of falling from them."

The plane hit some more turbulence and I jumped slightly.

"Maybe I could distract you," he whispered.

His hand softly pulled my fingers from their iron-clad grasp. That was a distraction enough, to have his skin on mine. Our eyes rose from our hands at the same time to meet each others. Was he flirting with me? *I really think he's flirting with me.*

My mind started to panic. It felt nice, but at the same time I wanted to pull away. He was sweet, funny . . . and damn, he was good-looking; but did I really want to get involved with another man so soon? I hated myself just then. There was a perfectly fine man sitting next to me, *obviously* flirting with me. *Don't be a dope!* I yelled at myself. It was my automatic reaction when I felt myself getting closer to someone—pull away and run.

Joseph opened his mouth to speak, but the pilot's

voice came over the speaker. "Ladies and gentlemen, we are entering into some really nasty storms. I'd like everyone to please buckle your seatbelts."

If it weren't for the terrifying jolt that ran through my body at the pilot's words, I'd probably have been grateful for the interruption. I gulped when the plane jerked again and hastily began to search for my seatbelt, taking my hand back into my own control. When I couldn't find it my heart began to pound furiously in my chest. I had a bad feeling about this—very bad indeed.

My fingers were busy scattering this way and that across the seat. Joseph leaned over and found my belt effortlessly. He buckled me in. My savior.

"No worries. We'll be fine," he said softly to me, his voice soothing.

That's when it all happened. That's when he *jinxed* us. The plane jolted, as if another plane had hit us. That wasn't the case though; I saw what happened—lightning. The plane spun around once before instantly dropping down through the storm cloud. Suitcases appeared everywhere. My drink flew to the other side of the cabin and my book lodged between piles of bags. The oxygen masks popped out and I reached for mine, arms flapping though the air until I reached it and placed it over my mouth and nose. Joseph's actions mirrored my own.

I squeezed my eyes shut, hoping beyond hope that we weren't all going to die. I thought of Karen and my eyes snapped open like window shades wound too tight. The plane began a nose dive, and all the debris slid forward. I spotted Karen. Her brown hair was in a mess, but I was relieved to see that she was all right. What I didn't expect was to see her suddenly unbuckle her seat belt and head my direction, literally climbing up the aisle.

Joseph's hand seized mine and I saw the horror-stricken look on his face. He could probably see the panic in my eyes too. If I was going to die, at least I was able to stare at the magnificence of his face in my last moments.

Karen reached us and the plane jolted several times as it fell. I wondered if the pilots were still trying to save our lives.

"Are you all right?" Karen yelled through the noise.

I shook my head back and forth against my seat. "You're an angel," I shouted back. *"Can't you do something?"*

Her eyes nervously looked over at Joseph. At that moment in time, what did it matter if he knew? We were about to die. Maybe I was fulfilling his dying wish, to know a semblance of truth.

"I must save you, but I don't know how," Karen yelled back.

"Can't you fly?" It seemed obvious to me.

She shook her head, and it was then that I looked out the window and saw that our view was no longer clouds, but the solid ground below. We had seconds.

Karen was sending me waves of tranquility. It didn't matter at this point. Nothing did. This was it. This was the end. I looked toward my Guardian Angel, and she wept golden tears.

crash

For once in my life I had thought I had found meaning, a purpose to exist. And then it was all being taken away. *Is this what happens when fantasy becomes reality?* The perfect man beside me held my hand as his eyes filled with tears. He and I were just humans; we both knew we were going to die. But I didn't think that was why he was weeping. It was my confirmation about the creature before me: the angel. Her face was filled with golden tears, her lips moving at an unreadable speed, and her skin glowed like the sun. She was radiating power, though her eyes were full of panic.

Through the window I saw the buildings take shape as we rocketed toward the earth. I closed my eyes and began to beg for help, *any* kind of help. If there was a god, I didn't think he'd answer me. And he didn't.

The plane continued its journey toward our doom and shook violently as another bolt of electricity slammed into the side of the cabin, as if Zeus himself was angry it was in *his* sky.

"I wish I could have helped," I cried out to Karen. "I'm sorry."

Her hand came up and she traced the line of my face, her deep eyes showing only hopelessness. The air whistled around the plane as the ground beckoned us below, the outlines of the town threateningly clear. My eyes closed to greet the end.

But it wasn't the end.

Warm arms wrapped around my body as electricity shot through me. It was a feeling I had never felt before, strangely calming. I could sense the seatbelt around my waist fall from me. Still, I kept my eyes closed. The seatbelt wouldn't save my life now anyway. Then the oxygen mask was pulled from my face. I didn't care. The arms around me felt protective, comfortable, as if the plane was no longer about to crash to the ground. I gripped the only fabric that clung to the warm body and my arms found their way around the neck. This must be my subconscious, giving me something of comfort before my final moments. I'd take it and be grateful.

But those arms, they felt so real; the electricity was still coursing through my veins. My eyes opened and I felt hope for the first time since our descent. Four angels were in my view; the one holding me had liquid gold eyes and long black hair, the same angel I had first approached in the boxes in the lab. But now he was alive—*real*—and staring right at me.

"Clear the path," he instructed, looking up.

The blonde male angel ripped the emergency door off its hinges, his red eyes staring at us expectantly.

"Karen, out. Now," my angel ordered. I didn't see what happened, I was holding on for dear life.

Another second passed and we were out the open door, the humans in the plane staring in wonder as we leapt from the opening. My heart broke—what about the other humans?

I thought we would tumble toward the earth, but we only floated there. There was a loud explosion below us, and then fire flew up into the air and surrounded us. The heat was overwhelming, though the angel did not seem to notice.

My heart broke and tears descended my face as I thought about all those who had just been killed in that one second. Tears were such a rare concept for me, but Joseph's face flashed in my mind and I shook fiercely at the thought of his death. I'd never lost anyone before. Tears only made sense at this point.

The whole time, the angel never looked down at me, though I couldn't keep my eyes off of him. His skin was a rich brown color, his jaw a perfect square shape of beauty, and his black hair was plastered on his cheeks from the rain that washed over us. I leaned my head against his chest, trying to control my sobs, giving in to all my fears. This *was* real. No dream, no funny drug slipped in my coffee. This was true, brutal and hard.

Then the angel's finger gently wiped away the tears on my face and lifted my chin. He looked directly at me—the depths of his eyes were amazingly golden, like treasure. It wasn't like looking at Joseph. This angel was different. We were linked, connected somehow. How I could know this in only a matter of seconds was beyond me. Suddenly, everything else seemed ordinary compared to him. The current continued to burn through me, though it was painless.

"*Siete al sicuro*," he murmured. I melted into his embrace.

I had no idea what he said, but the words soothed me. "Thank you," I barely mouthed.

He must have understood me, because he gave a small nod of his head.

We floated in the air for another moment before we began descending slowly. Below, there was chaos. Screams could be heard along with sirens. Lights flashed all around, coming from every different direction, all trying to find a way to the crash site. Fire flared from the middle of the cluster of trees where the plane had hit. From the twisted metal and downed trees, smoke rose rapidly into the air. It was like a beacon to the rescuers. *Good*, I thought. They needed to find the wreckage quickly.

We submerged into the trees, only a few hundred feet away from the crash. When we landed on the ground, the angel gently put me on my feet. The only thing I could think of was to get to Joseph and Sally. Maybe they had survived . . . though deep down I knew it was impossible. Not unless they were immortal, like Karen.

I ran toward the fire, splashing in the mud, and heard the sound of rushing wind over head. The angel dropped into my line of sight. He had flown over my head.

"You cannot help them," he said, his accent deeply Italian.

I tried to pass, but his warm arms wrapped around me again, this time constricting me and holding me to his chest. "I cannot allow you to go. You could get hurt." His voice was deep, firm, and final.

"No!" I cried out, but didn't fight him. It was a cry to God for taking those souls. I went limp, though the angel held me up until I regained my balance.

"Thank God you are all right," I heard a deep voice behind me.

I whirled to see Joseph. I blinked in the rain, not believing.

"I thought we were all dead," he said, a distraught look on his face.

"Joseph!" I ran toward him, hugging him as if I had known him my whole life. He embraced me back just as fiercely, and that same electric current ran through me and into him. It wasn't like before, this was almost painful. When I stepped back, I could tell he had felt my jolt of electricity, though he seemed to be okay. "How did you . . ." I trailed off, seeing three angels behind him *and Sally*.

Joseph smiled his brilliant smile, which I had thought I would never see again. "They saved us. I don't know how, it was all a blur. One moment we were plummeting to our death, and then a hole opens up, and the next moment we are on the ground."

I didn't have time to think about what that meant because I felt weak in my knees again—this time from relief. The angel who had saved me caught me as my knees buckled, and there was another undercurrent between us—this one pleasant.

"I think we need to get her some medical help," he said over my head to Karen.

"No," I insisted. "I'm okay." I tried to smile, though it was hard. The day was still a disaster, many lives were lost.

"Gabriella," Karen sighed.

"Really," I persisted.

The angel released me and I sank to the forest floor, overwhelmed. I took several long deep breaths, trying to regain my composure.

We survived.

Sally—her red hair tangled in her face that was darkened with ash—was crying, which left more streaks through the soot that was slowly being washed away by the rain. Joseph's face was also blackened with the ash, though his dark eyes showed a weird mixture of grief and relief. Karen was staring at me, concerned. But what interested me most were the now very *alive* angels—the ones that had once been corpses in those wooden boxes. The same ones we didn't know how to awaken.

"Andrew?" I canvassed. I remembered the names the Elder's had spoken of.

The angel who rescued me lowered to the ground. His golden eyes searched mine for a second. "I am Andrew," he stated. Then he said over my head, "This one is special."

"Yes," agreed Karen and also dropped down next to me. "Gabriella is the Illuminator."

"This one is the Darkness Illuminator?" another

angel asked. I guessed it was Lucia; she looked identi-cal to Luke. Her eyes were also pools of frosty blue and her hair was the same deep auburn.

I nodded slowly.

"What is a Darkness Illuminator?" Sally asked. They all ignored her.

"The Illuminator? You are sure of this?" Ehno asked. Karen nodded. "She is special indeed," he said in awe.

He bent to grasp my hand, but when he touched me electricity shot through me again—more powerful this time. I yanked my hand back and could see the electricity crackling between my fingers.

"What was that?" I gasped. *Had I been struck by lightning?*

"Your gift," Lucia said, like it was obvious.

"My gift?"

Ehno stared at me expectantly, his blonde hair rounding his perfectly angular cheeks. His red eyes were glowing. When I didn't speak, he turned to Andrew.

Andrew nodded as if they had just communicated with each other.

"Yes," Andrew confirmed. He seized my hand in his. The current raced between us. I didn't let go because it was different this time, like it was mixed with something else: patience, concern, anxiety, affection. "You are very strong. I can sense your power."

"How did she get these powers?" Karen asked.

Lucia stared at her like she was from another planet, which perhaps she was. "The Halo of the Sun have always given those who are worthy their powers," she said matter-of-factly.

"Who is the Halo of the Sun?" Karen looked at her with her eyebrows raised. "And Gabriella is a *mortal*. How could she have the strength of mind and body to possess powers?"

I stared at them, waiting for the answers. Sirens continued to blare in the background, though I was too engrossed in the conversation to be thinking about the scene behind me.

"Are the Halo of the Sun no more?" Ehno gasped.

"*They* never were," Karen said.

"What?" Andrew flew to his feet, leaving my hand cold. "The Halo of the Sun have been around long before we were immortal. Has your memory faded?"

Karen looked outraged. "No! My memory has not faded. There has never been any grouping called Halo of the Sun."

I was upset that no one answered Karen's second question. That was the one I was most interested in. Why did I have this . . . power? Or whatever it was.

Joseph and Sally just stared between the super-natural beings with out-right disbelief in their eyes. I didn't blame them. It was a lot to take in, and even I had remained somewhat skeptical until Andrew had saved me from impending death. Now I was a firm believer. There were no more doubts.

"No time to argue," Ehno said hastily. "They're coming."

"You've seen this, Ehno?" Lucia said gently.

"I have."

Before anyone could say another word, FBI agents swarmed around us. Their stance was not friendly; it was hostile. Their guns were raised and pointed at us. Andrew turned from Karen, his golden eyes finding mine, and then he raced towards me and seized me in his arms. We shot up into the air like a punctured bal-loon, maneuvering in wild patterns. He held me close to his chest as his skin absorbed the bullets that were being shot at us. He didn't even flinch. My mouth was slightly ajar in shock.

The electric current was back, and it felt like a warm fire was burning from within. The feeling was surprisingly pleasant, almost making me forget entirely about the bullets. I shook my head and focused my mind.

"What about the rest of them?" My eyes searched

below us, but all I saw were the tops of trees and the ever billowing smoke of the crashed plane. "Drop me off somewhere and save them," I demanded.

"Mortals cannot hurt immortals," he said gently.

"But there are two mortals down there!" I shouted.

He must have been able to sense my panic. The current between us twisted and changed—I was sending my feelings through it. "Gabriella," he sighed, "please, calm down. They will be fine."

"How do you know?"

"Ehno and I are connected psychically. All Halo of the Sun are." His voice was firm, straight-forward.

"They're safe?"

He was silent. He didn't look down at me, only forward as he raced through the sky.

"Oh no," I whispered.

"Gabriella," he sighed heavily. That was all he said.

The current between us intensified as anxiety gripped me. I closed my eyes trying to will the tears back. No more tears, I had to get a grip and start acting like an adult.

Our journey ended shortly after that, though the day was long from over. Would it ever end? He landed in a small meadow and placed me on my feet where I fell immediately to the ground.

"What happened to them?" I whispered, looking at the grass. Here I was, so happy that we were alive—and now they might be . . . *dead.*

Andrew's shadow loomed overhead. "They have been taken into custody." He didn't offer any assurances.

"Why?"

"They're the only survivors. There are suspicions."

"Terrorism," I said darkly.

"Yes."

I looked up at him. His hair was a black-blue in the rain and his eyes seemed to melt as he stared into mine. He was beautiful, mighty and powerful. Strength radiated from him.

"We're wanted suspects now," I said blankly, not fully comprehending.

"Yes," he repeated once more.

A small bit of anger flared through me and electricity shot from my fingers like a live wire. "Is yes the only word you know?"

Andrew grabbed my hand and I let the electricity shoot through him. His eyes closed as if swallowing something large. His grip tightened on mine as another round of electricity raced between us. "You hold the key," he whispered.

"Two, actually," I said crossly.

His eyes snapped open, his grip still firm. "What do you mean, two? I was speaking figuratively."

"Oh."

He made a face as the bullets seemed to be working their way out of his skin. His teeth smashed together and he reached over his shoulder to pull one of the bullets out. He was on his knees only two feet away from me. I got up and walked over to him, and gently pulled another bullet from his skin. There was a slight gold tint around his wounds. He looked at me gratefully as I helped him.

"Does it hurt?" I barely whispered. The storm above us seemed to have made its way east; the rain had finally stopped.

"Not much," he grunted as he yanked another bullet free.

I noticed that he was barely wearing any clothes—he still had on the same attire that he was wearing inside the box.

"Aren't you cold?" I wondered as I began to shiver in my soaked clothes.

He grabbed my hand and pulled me close to him. "No, but you are freezing."

I shrugged. "I'll survive." If I could live through a plane crash, I could live through the cold.

He looked down at his clothes. "I'm sorry, I have nothing to offer you to keep you warm."

"That's okay," I said, trying to give him a warm smile. I sat down in the soaked grass and sighed.

Andrew leaned in until he was only two inches from my face. His warm breath surrounded me. "What keys do you have?"

I didn't answer. His arm snaked around my waist and pulled me to his body. He was so warm. The current intensified between us. All my anxiety and fear were momentarily forgotten. I thought he would close the distance between us. I *wanted* him to, more than anything on this planet. I wanted his lips on mine. I heard the electricity crackle in the air. He pulled me tighter. I gasped. He quickly let go and stepped back, releasing all of me. I was disappointed and felt a little rejected.

"They know," he said furiously. His voice became rough as he cursed the area around us in a different language. The sun was almost below the horizon and the area was growing dark quickly. "They are taking them all to a secure facility."

I grimaced. "What do they know?" I said in a flat voice.

"That they aren't human, and that two of them are different." His voice was indignant. "They went freely

to keep up the façade, but it wasn't until after their capture that Ehno realized what was planned. Now they
have been taken away in some kind of metal contrap-
tion."

"A truck," I offered.

"A . . . truck?"

I sighed. "A lot has changed in this world."

run

We were on foot, running through the under-growth in the woods, the light fading too quickly. Andrew wanted to fly, but I told him times had changed and the skies weren't safe anymore. He didn't answer, only followed in my wake silently—so quietly that I had to turn several times to see if he was still there.

He eventually took my hand, realizing I couldn't hear his soundless steps. Electricity buzzed between us. He didn't pull away. His hand was warm and dry and very agreeable compared to the soaked nature of my skin. But he was an angel and I was just a lowly human. Why did I want him so much, even though I only just met him?

A road came into our view. I stayed in the cover of the shadows, my back to a tree. Headlights appeared on the road and a large semi-truck came barreling down the road. Andrew gasped and his hand squeezed mine in surprise. He was strong; it felt like my fingers were going to be crushed.

"It's just a truck," I assured him, my voice inflecting my pain.

His grip relaxed instantly.

"That is not what they took them away in." His gold eyes were wide, though his voice was firm. His head turned to look at me.

"Truck is kind of a relative term."

He nodded. "Ehno is anxious. He doesn't understand this world. Are we in another dimension?" He asked this so confidently, with such seriousness, that I couldn't laugh. It was clearly not a joke.

"No. You've been . . . dead," I said slowly.

He didn't react the way I thought one should—knowing that you were dead and now you weren't. His golden eyes roamed the wooded area as if searching for any threats, before they landed on mine. "How long?"

"Maybe two thousand years," I squeaked.

"What's the year?"

"Two thousand nine."

"Not two thousand years," he said with certainty.

"Oh," was all I said as I leaned around the tree to see if any police were driving in our direction. The road was only two lanes, but it was evidently a state highway. "So, how many years then?" I asked distractedly.

He was only inches from my body. I could feel the heat radiating off of his skin. A current zipped between my fingers and I hid them behind my back. That was going to get embarrassing.

"A few hundred, give or take," he shrugged.

My curiosity was piqued. He'd only been dead a few hundred years? How was that possible? Didn't his "corpse" date back longer than that—at least two thousand years? Carbon dating was not so flawed that it would be off by eighteen hundred years. Perhaps an angel's genetic makeup did not conform to normal scientific standards.

I wanted to keep asking him questions, but I knew that we needed to leave; soon this place would not be the safe haven it felt like now. My eyes closed briefly as I took in a gulp of air and then slid out from between Andrew and the tree. "Follow me."

He did, without question.

"We need to get away from here. Especially now they know you are alive." I paused. Something had just hit me like a ton of bricks. "Hey," I stopped mid-stride. "How did they know you were alive to begin with?"

Andrew looked down at me, his body towering over mine. He was probably well over six feet tall to my five feet six inches. "Ehno says they were tipped off."

My eyes narrowed. "And how does Ehno know they were tipped off?" It just didn't make any sense.

The plane was in mid-crash when the angels awoke and came to our rescue. Who would have had the time—or the thought—to call the FBI? "It just doesn't make any sense," I whispered beneath my breath.

"Ehno is very gifted," Andrew's voice was gentle. "Some would call him a psychic. It is an unusual talent, and he does not have any control over it. Sometimes he just . . . sees things, or knows things. Past, present, and future."

"Did he see your death?" I blurted out without thinking, and then mumbled, "Sorry."

He looked lost in thought, his concentration deep. "I . . ." he deliberated for a minute. "I cannot remember."

"Now is not the time to talk, anyway. We need to find a way out of this small town."

We walked beside the road, staying in the shadows of the trees. Sirens were still blaring in the background, and now and then a police car raced by, their lights illuminating the area.

"Can I fly now?" he asked. His expression was a mixture of excitement and terror. I didn't blame him— it was a lot to take in.

I pointed toward the sky. There was a helicopter flying overhead, a spot light shooting back and forth. "Probably not a good idea."

He watched the chopper as it disappeared over the trees. "Is that some kind of bird?"

I choked out a giggle. "No. That is a helicopter. It is sort of like a truck, but it flies."

His eyes shot down to mine. I tried to stifle another giggle and look serious so he would know I was telling him the truth. He just nodded.

We kept walking. Soon the town came into view, and I noticed that it was not much larger than Oretown. "Andrew?"

"Hum?"

"We need to get you some clothes," I pointed out.

"Oh." He lifted his torn and ragged clothes.

They were old and halfway disintegrated, but through the holes I could see a physique that was drool-worthy. Our eyes met and I felt my face flush with embarrassment for being caught ogling.

"That might be best," he said.

"Wait here," I ordered. He didn't listen and followed me.

"Andrew, you can't walk around looking like that." I gestured up and down his body.

"Gabriella," he whispered. "I don't know why, but I feel I must protect you."

"The clothing store isn't going to bite."

He raised an eyebrow.

"Just stay here," I instructed. I began to walk towards the small outlet store that was closest, but he gripped my hand and pulled me back to him, his arms wrapping around me.

"Be safe," he breathed into my hair.

I rolled my eyes but couldn't help but think that I might explode with the electric current racing around me. His affection surprised me. Maybe it was just an angel thing—Karen was just as affectionate.

"It's just a store," I repeated.

He let go and I sprinted across the street to the building. I patted my pockets and pulled out my debit card and some cash. Whenever I traveled, I always kept my money on my person, and today I was grateful for it.

It only took me seven minutes to find clothes and boots for both of us. I had to guess his pant size, but I was pretty sure they would fit. Before returning, I eyed an ATM machine and went for it. We would need cash later.

As I raced back across the street, I saw Andrew leaning against a tree in the shadows. He looked distressed, worried. When he saw my face, his expression changed to relief.

I handed him the bag after pulling my clothes out. "Put these on."

He took the bag from me and examined the material of it.

"Plastic," I said. "It was invented while you were . . ."

He nodded, pulled the clothes from the bag, and began stripping out of his. I turned my back to him; sure my face was flushing a brilliant shade of magenta. I quickly scrambled out of my clothes and had to practically peel them off my soaked skin and then I replaced them with dry clothes. I shrugged a jacket on and it was such a relief to feel warm that I didn't even think about the fact that I just stripped down while not only a man was standing there, but a man who was an angel that I didn't know in the least.

"How do I look?" he asked and I whipped around.

He turned around. *So he didn't see me strip?* My eyes roamed over his body appreciatively to see him in the plain grey T-shirt and blue jeans I had picked out. They fit perfectly. "You look great. Don't forget the shoes and socks."

His hand dove into the bag and he pulled out the socks and shoes. "These are very nice boots," he said, admiring them.

"Yes. I figured you would need something decent on your feet now that we are on the run." I looked down at my new black boots under my jeans.

He tried to tie his laces and looked frustrated. I came to his rescue, and he watched me intently as I made the loops. When I backed away, my eyes roamed over his body again. He was magnificent, even in jeans and a plain T-shirt. He handed me his tattered clothes and I stuffed both of our clothes back into the plastic bag.

"The lady in the store told me there was a bus station only half a mile down the road." I pointed toward the north.

"Let's go." He put a hand out to lead the way. "What is a bus station?"

I shook my head and only smiled at him. He seemed to be okay with that for an answer.

We strode silently through the undergrowth of the forest. The bus station came into our view shortly after, and I dumped our old clothes in the first trash bin I could find.

"It's our lucky day," I said, grasping his hand and yanking him forward. "Come on."

I checked the highway, both ways, looking for any conspicuous vehicles. I felt like a criminal in training. The highway was clear, and we dashed across the road to the station.

As we reached the small building, the door automatically opened for us. I went to stride in, but Andrew yanked my hand free of his, creating a noise like static electricity. When I turned around, he was standing at the threshold, staring at the door in wonder.

"It's just a door," I whispered and reached for his hand again. He obliged and let me lead him into the building.

We studied the map on the wall, and I realized we were in Burns, Oregon. We hadn't even left the state yet. "Pick a place."

"On this map?" he pointed. "It's very detailed."

I nodded for him to go ahead. He studied the map for several minutes. "Ehno says he's never heard of these towns."

I laughed. "You know, it's incredibly strange when you do that."

He kept staring at the map.

"Have you ever been to America?" I asked.

"This is America?" he asked brightly, his lips twitching up into the first almost smile I'd seen on him.

"Yup."

"I remember seeing it on a map for the first time in 1507."

My eyebrows rose.

"Well," he frowned in thought, the smile gone. "Okay, how about here." His finger stabbed Boise City, Idaho. For a second, the horrible blue football stadium at the university there popped into my head.

"All right," I agreed. "As long as we don't have to watch a football game while we are there. The color of their field kills my eyes."

This time he raised his eyebrows.

"Don't ask," I mumbled.

I decided to pay with cash for now. I'd paid with my debit card in the store, but it would be better if they didn't know which direction we were going from the beginning—or that we had even left in the first place.

I walked towards the counter to purchase our tickets. The woman had a tragic expression on her face.

"Did you hear about the plane crash? They are saying there were no survivors," she wiped a tear from her eye. "Terrorism," she hiccupped.

"Oh, no! That's horrible," I tried to say as convincingly as possible. It wasn't hard to be genuine; I wasn't completely heartless and I knew many people died in that crash. *Hmm*, I contemplated, *isn't that strange that no one survived?* Fancy that. "Can we please get two tickets to Boise City?"

"Sure," she mumbled and began clicking the mouse and typing information into the computer. "The bus will be here in ten minutes. Good timing."

I nodded. "How about that?"

Andrew and I sat on a bench in the back of the station, out of sight of anyone passing by. "What is a bus?" he asked.

"Kind of like a truck, but for multiple passengers."

"I wish I knew more about this world," he muttered. "I feel lost and confused."

"I know that things are strange right now," I said consolingly, "but I promise you I will try to help you out the best I can."

"Thank you." He took my hand in his. "You're cold," he frowned.

"It's that autumn air. October is always chilly when the sun goes down." The light above us flickered threateningly, as if it planned to go out and take the light away from us.

"Everything is so strange," he pointed toward the light. "It provides light, but not warmth."

"They are not meant for warmth," I said simply. An idea struck me then. "If you want, Andrew, I can take you to a library in Boise."

He straightened. "Books?"

"Yes. You can read . . . right?" And for a moment, I really did wonder if he could even understand any books, even if they were in English. He was from Italy, and a few hundred years ago English was very different than what it is now.

"I learn quickly. And yes, I can read English. We've been around for several centuries and I have lived in many countries."

"Great," I said happily.

The bus arrived, and a few people exited and unloaded their bags from beneath. I hoped that the bus driver didn't think it was odd we were going without any bags. Maybe he would just think that we were going to the city for an evening out.

The driver was short and round, his head balding, and he was incredibly polite. I handed our tickets over to him, and he checked them over—not too thoroughly—and then gestured that we should enter. "Another driver will be taking my place this evening," he told us. "He'll be here shortly."

"Thank you," I said, smiling as genuinely as I could. Things were going much smoother than I had anticipated, and I was starting to wonder if there wasn't something fishy going on.

"Ehno is jealous," Andrew said into my ear.

I shivered under his warm breath.

"They have trapped him in some super-jail." He indicated with his hand that I should sit down near the back, and I did. My lips turned down at the thought of the others being locked up. Maybe there was something we could do . . .

"Good evening, ladies and gentlemen," an older man said as he entered the bus. "I will be your driver this evening. My name is Albert." He smiled around the bus. There were only about seven people accompanying us on our journey east.

The driver climbed behind the wheel and fired up the engine.

Andrew tensed beside me.

"He's just starting the bus," I explained. "It runs on gas and oil."

He relaxed, deep in thought. "Interesting."

The ride was an estimated five hours. During this time, I planned to ask as many questions as I could; but it was a failed attempt. My sleeping schedule was all kinds of screwed up, and it had been almost thirty-six hours since I had last slept. My head rested on the back of the big seat, and soon after we were underway, I could feel my eyes drooping.

"You look tired," Andrew pointed out. His finger came up and traced the dark circles under my eyes. "You should sleep."

I shook my head. "I need to be alert."

His warm fingers traced my cheeks until his finger was under my chin. He lifted my face to meet his golden eyes. "This is no good," he shook his head. "I'll watch after you. I am a Guardian angel, after all. And you—you are in need of a Guardian, especially since Karen has been taken."

I bit my bottom lip. "Don't remind me. They are probably taking them to a lab like the one I work in."

"Lab?"

"Yes. I prove or disprove legends and myths using scientific research . . . basically, facts."

He wrapped his arms around me and put a hand on my cheek to move me towards his shoulder. "It'll all be okay. Sleep, Gabriella."

The current grew as he held me, but he only gripped tighter in response. I finally relaxed in his arms, thinking about how wonderful it was to be treated with respect. He was caring and protective, and I had only known him for an hour. And to add to the list, he was also incredibly thoughtful. I'd never experienced the warm feeling growing deep within me before, and knew instantly that there was something special about this angel.

"Andrew?"

"Hum?"

"What do angels do . . . you know, in their spare time?" I asked, undeniably curious.

His chest shook with light laughter. "I worked on a few farms with some very lovely families. Sometimes we took the horses out to go on long trips through the canyons around Italy. But mostly, I worked constantly with the Halo of the Sun to provide protection for those worthy of a Guardian. Though once, I worked with a blacksmith. Very interesting."

I yawned. "How do you know to protect someone? Does Ehno tell you?"

He chuckled. "Sometimes. We can talk about this later. Please rest. I'll keep watch over you."

The events of the day seemed to hit me all at once, and I realized for the first time that I was now considered a felon, on the run. Of course, I knew I wasn't a criminal, but that didn't stop them from thinking that immediately. "I'm . . . scared," I barely whispered.

Andrew didn't respond for a long time and I almost thought that maybe he didn't hear me. When he finally replied, he breathed into my hair, "I know," and pulled me closer to his body.

His fingers twirled in my hair. It was unbelievably relaxing. How could I deny myself something that my body needed so desperately right now? I closed my eyes obediently and was soon drifting toward sleep. Andrew hummed lightly under his breath. I couldn't make out the notes, but the vibration in my ears was comforting, and I was soon asleep in his warm arms.

journey

urking in the shadows was a pale face, his blazing eyes on fire. His glare was aimed toward a woman who seemed to be glowing a pearly white: her eyes, her hair, her skin. Everything about her was sparkling and shining.

The two were communicating, their mouths moving; but I heard no sound. A man stepped from the shadows to show a strong build and black hair. He wore the Nebulous Sun around his neck, which rested on his chest. His jaw was tight, his features strikingly handsome, but his clothes were from another time period— an ancient time. He was not like a Shadow that had seized me in my office; his features were human.

They were obviously arguing, each of them transmitting the intensity of their power and skill, I could tell just by the set of their faces. Light flashed between them and magical shields flew up as they both deflected the energy. Another woman, luminous and authoritative, joined the other. Now it was two against one. More light flashed between the group, yet I was unable to see the outcome.

My focus was fading.

"Abelie?" My head snapped to the left to see who was calling my name.

It was Andrew, terror in his eyes. "Run!" he shouted. His face was lined and grief-stricken.

The women turned to face me, their white eyes macabre. I stepped back and fell to the ground, tripping over something. My hands slipped on a wet substance, and when I looked down I saw golden blood leaking from the body I had fallen over. It was like a molten river.

My heart pounded in my chest so violently that I thought it was going to jump out of my throat. The women swept sinuously toward me, their stance threateningly close. Andrew flew through the air like a bullet, his eyes thundering his rage. The women turned on him and struck him down.

"NO!" I screamed at the top of my lungs. I could feel the tears descending my face, leaving saltwater stains on my white dress. Andrew's hand reached toward mine, but I couldn't grasp it, I was too far away. A force pulled me backward, away from the dying angel.

"Gabriella," a soft, frantic voice sounded in my ear. "Gabriella? Please come back to me. You're all right.

We're safe."

Suddenly I was in the dark, my eyes closed tightly, the tears still finding their way out from under my lids. Warm arms were around me, a steady hand sweeping my hair from my moist face. He was speaking light and fast, a liquid language spilling from his tongue. I took a breath as if I'd been holding air in my lungs for an hour and then blinked my eyes open.

Andrew's face was only inches from mine, a tortured expression displayed on it. His hand swept along my chin and up to my ear. "I was worried," he whispered. "You were sending sparking jolts through my body. I'd felt them from you before, but this was intense. I could feel . . . what *you* were feeling."

He hugged me to his chest before lessening his grip so I could see him again. "You *screamed* and it was as if lightning blew from your finger tips."

I realized the bus was quiet and craned my neck to look around.

"The bus is not functioning anymore." His eyes darted up toward the front of the bus before swinging back to my face. "It seems your gift has disabled it."

I sat up quickly and felt my head spin. "Ugh," I made a noise and put my hand to my forehead as if it would stop the spinning. It felt like I had drunk half a bottle of alcohol. "Where are we?"

I looked out the window, the darkness spreading out like a creeping shadow.

"Nowhere," he answered. "The man said another bus is on its way to take us to Boise City."

I stood and quickly lost my balance. Andrew steadied me. My breath whooshed from my mouth, and I fell back toward my seat.

"I didn't mean to frighten you," I mumbled. In the dream, it was as if I had been someone else. I tried to remember the name I had heard, but I couldn't grasp it. "My dream was so real . . . and I thought you were—" I cut myself off.

"Thought I was?"

"It's nothing. Just a nightmare." I looked down at my hands twisting in my lap.

His hand seized mine to stop the movement. Voltage shot between us, as if he were taking some of my tension away.

"I may not know this new world, but humans have not changed since I was last around. It's something," he said with certainty. "You can trust me, but I understand if you don't want to tell me."

"That's not it at all." I looked into his golden eyes. "I do trust you, more than I have trusted anyone in my life." I could hear the conviction and awe in my own voice. "You . . . *saved me*. I thought I was going to die, and you jumped from a plane with me in your arms."

Somehow, in the plane, he had woken at the last second and flown in like the angel he was—and saved me. What made me more deserving than the others who didn't make it? I didn't see the difference—but the angels did. I had to make sure he knew that because of his bravery, I trusted him. "I owe you my life," I murmured as I looked back down at my feet.

He was silent. I wanted him to say something. *Anything.*

His finger lifted my chin to his angelic face. "No, I owe *you* my life." His smoldering eyes only backed up his proclamation.

"But I didn't do anything."

"Yes, you did, Gabriella!" he exclaimed, exasperated. "Don't you understand? I was dead until you came around and released me. You saved me from my tomb."

"How is that possible? Tell me. What happened on the plane?" I needed answers. Not even Karen and the Elders had known how to wake the angels, and yet here was Andrew telling me that it was *I* who had woken them all.

He sighed. "You don't see how amazing you really are."

"All I did was nearly plummet to my death."

He held my chin again so I was looking directly into his eyes. His grip was firm. "Your cry to save Karen's life—to save your friends—overwhelmed any thought to save yourself. Whatever spell was on us broke immediately, shook us from our prisons, and brought us to you. We all knew instantly that we were meant to protect you, save you—make you safe again." He grabbed both of my hands and brought them close to him. "I was so afraid, so utterly scared that we'd be too late. We were falling out of the sky and all I could think about was getting to you. It was as if my existence would have been worthless if I didn't stop you from . . ." he trailed off. He seemed unable to say the word "death."

"So it was me who woke you?" I whispered under my breath. "I still don't understand how."

His lips twitched up into a knowing smile. "Your . . . death was coming to light. You are *the* Illuminator. The one who will stop the darkness—the one who will save us all. It was foretold long ago that the Halo of the Sun would protect the luminous one—you," he pointed out. "And my coming back? Well, I was meant to protect you. No spell could bind us from our sacred duty to you.

"But that is not all that brought us back. It was your selflessness that did it. You had to *prove* you were worth saving." His smile grew and he kissed the tops of my hands. His lips lingered there for a few seconds longer than I would have expected, and he looked up to gauge my reaction. I shivered, and he let go.

I shook my head, first to shake off the feeling that his kiss had given me, and second to make sense of everything he had said. Sometimes he seemed to have trouble telling me things in a way I could understand. "If you say so," was the only coherent thing I could come up with.

"You were worth saving," he said as he leaned his head back against the seat. "Ehno informs me that the next bus is near."

"That's a relief."

He lightly laughed. "Which statement?"

"Both, I guess."

Lights flooded through the windows of the bus and for a second my heart began to flicker uselessly in my chest. Was it the FBI finally coming to capture us? Would we be taken away and placed in the same prison cells that Ehno and Lucia were in right now? Andrew saw my stricken look and said, "It's the bus."

My heartbeat slowed.

"Are you worried? Your heart was fluttering like humming bird wings." *He could hear that?* Heat filled my cheeks.

"You are new to this world," I said. "Those people—the FBI—they are a very powerful force to be
reckoned with. They have military weapons, spies, and
undercover agents. This isn't like a few hundred years
ago. Technology has advanced to the point where one
small weapon designed by a few could level a city of
millions." I realized I might have gone a little out there
with my explanation for him, but it was all true. Things
were different. This wasn't the world the angels had
known before.

Again, he was silent. For a moment I thought I
saw fear flash in his eyes, but when I looked at him
more closely there was nothing but compassion and
loyalty. His bold features were stark in the illuminated
bus, the lights made his jaw look chiseled, as if from
stone, and his eyes were molten gold. *He* looked like a
force to be reckoned with.

But when his words came out, they were nothing
more than a nervous whisper, "Millions?"

I nodded. "Not only that. We have all kinds of
technology. Now we can talk to someone on the other
side of the planet, and see their face as if they were two
feet away from us. People can fly to any country in the
world in planes, and most of us have our own cars too.
They're like this bus, but smaller. We have cell phones,
so we can talk to anyone we want, anytime—no matter

where we are." I watched him engulfing the knowl-edge. "They're great; you know, when you are at the grocery store and you forget if your sister wants the baked chips or the Cheetos." I smiled, knowing he had no idea what I was talking about.

"We were on a plane when I saved you," he stated, as if working a problem out. "But it was falling from the sky and that's when I awoke." I nodded. "And you can really see someone on the other side of the world, and talk to them?"

"Yes." I had always wondered what it would be like to meet someone who was completely oblivious to technology. Here was my first glimpse. "And we've discovered things too. We found out the world is round . . . or a geoid, to be more accurate."

"I can fly," he said simply.

Like I wasn't aware of that fact. "I know."

"Well, I could tell that the earth was not, in fact, flat. Some people were idiots back in the day," he remi-nisced, grinning.

"Excuse me," the old bus driver said over the light chatter of the nine people on the bus. "The other bus has arrived. Thank you for being patient."

We watched as the others stood to exit the bus. Andrew got to his feet and held out his hand. I grasped his palm and that same current raced through us. He raised an eyebrow at me as I lifted myself up.

"What?" I whispered.

He tried to hold back a smile. "Nothing."

"Uh huh," I said, looking at his striking features. It was hard not to be aware of his absolute beauty. "It's something."

"That's what I said."

<hr />

We sat in companionable silence during the rest of our journey to Boise City, which was not far off from where the bus broke down—thanks to my new gift of electricity.

We got out of the bus, and Andrew stood staring at the city, which was lit up like a birthday cake.

"We need to find a place to stay," I whispered.

"Surely there is an inn around here?" he asked.

"That's easy enough," I said, walking toward the bus station. "There should be all kinds of travel magazines and information in here."

He lifted one perfect brow. "I'll follow." His eyes seemed to race around the area in one quick swoop, as if scoping out the place for Shadows lurking in the darkened woods behind the station.

Inside, I found a table full of brochures and magazines, free for the taking. I picked up one and began sifting through information about the city, restaurants, activities, events, and eventually the hotels.

"This one looks decent," I pointed at the picture. "And look, there is a coupon for ten percent off."

Andrew didn't say anything and I looked up to see him touching one of the pictures on the cover of the magazine. His eyes were far away, like he was thinking of another time.

"Andrew?"

He didn't look up. "This painting looks so real."

I tried not to laugh. "That's not a painting; that's a photo."

He looked over at me, questions in his eyes. "You know—a visual representation . . ." I said slowly, and then trailed off. "It comes from a camera. They're devices that can capture a moment in time, and then be printed onto paper."

"There are a lot of devices in this world."

"I agree," I said and showed him the magazine I was holding. "Tell me, does this look like an okay place to stay the night?"

He seized the magazine right from under my fingers. "It's beautiful. Won't it be expensive? I don't have any money."

I sighed. "I do. It's only sixty dollars for one night, and look," I stabbed the coupon. "It says if we bring this in, we get ten percent off . . ." My eyes scrolled down to see the fine print below. I should have known, always read the fine print. ". . . rooms with one king-sized bed."

I thought Andrew would offer something like "I'll sleep on the floor," or "We'll put pillows between us," but he didn't.

His eyes grew wide. "Sixty dollars? That's pre-posterous!"

"No," I whispered. "That's normal. And we have plenty for the room. I took a few thousand out of my savings before we left Burns."

"Thousands?" His eyes grew wider in shock. "I've always had money; it's just part of being alive forever. But women—" he cut off. "To have that much money, you'd have to be rich!"

"No, I'm in the medium income level in America." I said in as matter-of-fact tone that I could give him.

"And that would be?"

"I believe the average yearly income for a house-hold in the U.S. is roughly fifty thousand."

His mouth dropped, but now he was on another subject. "The U.S?"

"The United States of America." I sighed. "I can't wait to get you to a library."

"Take me tonight," he suggested. "I read swiftly."

"Okay, if I can find one open this late. It's almost

ten in the evening. If there is a campus nearby . . ." My eyes roamed the many flyers, magazines, and brochures around the table before I saw one with a university in the background.

"Ah hah!" I exclaimed and snatched it up. "Boise State University. Why didn't I think about this before, I knew the university was here. We'll call a cab and go see if their libraries are still open. When I was in college, the libraries on campus stayed open all day and all night." I would know from the many hours I'd studied instead of making friends.

"A cab?"

"Andrew, quit asking questions and just go with the flow," I snapped, and then realized I'd been rude to the angel who saved my life. "I'm sorry. I didn't mean to be impolite. I'm not used to someone who doesn't know anything about living in this world."

He smiled his wonderful smile, completely unaffected. "Gabriella, the only way you could hurt me is by not existing anymore."

I knew that I was flushing a slight pink color. "I'll call the cab company."

"Of course. Go with the flow," he said in his Italian accent. He just seemed so . . . *innocent*. I laughed and seized his hand in mine, letting the electricity flow between us. The feeling was extraordinarily amazing.

13

Library

The library towered over us—its lights shining like tiny beacons. We stood outside the door, reading the sign displayed there.

"They're only open until midnight," I conveyed to Andrew, exasperated. "We don't have much time, maybe an hour."

"I read fast," he reminded me ostentatiously, gazing at the towering building. "I've lived a very long life and have read over a million books. Literally. I can assimilate information from paper quickly." He motioned us forward. "Watch for yourself," he offered.

He pushed the doors to the library open and gestured for me to enter. The aroma of old and new parchment hit my nose. Rows of books lined the walls, placed neatly in succession and towering up to the ceilings. One of the student employees greeted us with a little wave of hello before sitting back down behind the counter to keep reading her book.

Andrew walked along the shelves of books, his fingers tracing the spines of each of them. "This library is remarkably immense." He took in a deep breath.

"Don't you just love the smell of books?"

I smiled at his face. He looked like a kid at Disneyland, though his vocabulary proved to be of an exceptionally—and possibly excessively—educated adult. *Join the club.*

"This is only the first floor. There are eight more above us."

He looked up automatically.

"Do you still think one hour is long enough?" I challenged, my voice smug.

He moved to the second long row of books. "No. But for the important things—yes." His fingers lingered over the bindings of the new row, and then he reached for a book. "I'll start here." The book was *Chemistry Methodology and Mathematical Models.*

This place was a titanic mine of information, so I just nodded, thinking *Good luck.*

"Take a seat," I said instead, pointing toward a table not far away. "I'm going to go upstairs to look through some of their *non*academic books for something to read."

He gave me a solemn look. "Maybe I should go with you?"

"Andrew," I answered dismissively, "I'll be fine. It's just a library."

He surveyed my face for a few seconds and

grinned. "It won't bite," he said, mimicking my phrase about the clothing store, except in his wonderfully deep Italian accent.

"Exactly."

As I walked toward the stairs I looked over my shoulder to see him staring at me intently—his expression growing more somber by the second—before he reluctantly opened the book in his hands. He leaned over and began reading, flipping past the first two pages before I had even started up the stairs.

On the sixth floor, I thumbed through several science-fiction and fantasy novels, wishing I could take them all home with me. I loved reading, and if I had it my way I'd blow my whole pay check at the local bookstore. I found a book I had never read and skipped back down the stairs, taking two of them at a time. When I finally reached the first floor, Andrew was at the table leaning over a pile of books so large it partially blocked him from view. I gasped and dropped my book, the shock so outrageous that it rooted me to the spot.

Andrew leapt to his feet, practically flying across the room, which I knew he could have if he wished. Within seconds, he was at my side, picking up the book from the floor. His eyes were uneasy.

"Gabriella? What's wrong?" He led me toward the

table and helped me sit down.

"How many—" I paused to lift some of the books off the table. My shock turned to awe. There were physics, chemistry, geography, geology, biology and many other scientific books splayed across the table. Half of them were open. "How many books have you read? I was only upstairs for fifteen minutes."

I checked my watch to make sure I hadn't gotten carried away looking at the books, which happened more often than not at any bookstore or library when I wasn't careful.

"Yes." He looked pleased. "I read through twenty books, and I must say they were astonishingly fascinating. Science has enhanced tremendously over the past few hundred years."

"Twenty?" I mouthed, trying to recover from the shock of the books piled taller than Michael Jordan.

"When I was young, I read as fast as you," he informed me, "but age, time, and my magical abilities have given me the opportunity to gain knowledge by reading quickly, and to keep the information stored perfectly in my mind."

"I'll just stick to my single book right here." I lifted up my book on werewolves. "You know, this is my kind of scientific research," I teased.

He laughed and pulled out his chair, grabbing

another book off the table. "Aerospace engineering is a fascinating subject."

"Werewolves," I countered, "are equally intriguing."

"But completely fiction," he pointed out.

"I'm not sure. I haven't had the opportunity to disprove that yet." I grinned at him.

"Or to prove it."

"Anyways," I said, "angels are supposed to be a work of fiction as well. Okay . . . to most people, anyway. But here you are—positively, solidly here." I poked him and he grabbed my finger and laughed.

"If you say so."

"I do." He let go of my finger. "Now get to reading. We don't have much time." I pointed toward the clock on the wall. "Librarians are very strict."

"I know. I used to be friends with one."

At that moment, someone *shh'd* us. We both fell silent and pulled our books to our faces, our smiles spilling over the pages.

He flipped through the pages of his so quickly I thought he was just looking for pretty pictures. I tried to tear my eyes away from him and read my book on werewolves, but for several minutes all I could do was watch this angel rapidly slicing through the pages. He was more engaging and enchanting than a man who turns into a wolf.

Andrew looked up when he noticed I wasn't reading. "Something wrong with your book?"

"No. You just surprise the hell out of me."

Hell. At that word, a thought came to me—one that I hadn't had much time to consider or think about since we'd been on the run. I felt worse and worse as I tried to digest the appalling thought, like an invisible hand was twisting my insides. I began wondering how the other angels in their prison cells were doing.

He must have seen the look on my face because he raised a perfectly arched eyebrow. His dark hair fell perfectly around his face. "What is it?"

I became abruptly serious. "Do *you* believe in hell?"

He looked slightly taken aback for a second before his expression cleared. "Why should I?" he shrugged with dispassion. "I am immortal. Death constantly eludes me. The Olympian gods were who we all feared when I was a child. But, as you've seen, even being in the ground for a few hundred years hasn't stopped me from living."

He did not elaborate on how he ended up there in the first place.

I didn't want to continue with my line of questioning; it reminded me forcibly of the dream of the dead angel and the golden blood. They were unbidden, unwelcome thoughts. Were angels really as immortal as they believed? Even Paolo had said that some angels didn't survive attacks by the Shadows.

I tried to rid myself of the image. It was hard to resist asking questions; there were so many answers that I wanted to know. We had only a little time left for reading anyway. He must have interpreted something in my eyes, because he bowed over the book again and began flipping through the pages.

Silence fell between us.

I immersed myself in the werewolf book, beginning to enjoy the main character's struggle with self-denial. Those were always my favorite kinds of stories—probably because I had never had the opportunity to be in a position to self-deny.

My eyes flickered up toward Andrew, stealing another glance. His long dark hair fell to his shoulders as his golden eyes raced across a page. He was reading a book on popular culture and I watched as his lips twitched up several times. The line of his jaw was perfectly straight and twitched with each smile, and his nose was perfectly proportioned for his face. I studied his arms and the well-formed muscles. I'd almost bet my life savings that he had a six-pack under that shirt. Add wings and a halo, and I'd believe he was an angel from heaven.

Then again, I was using my life savings to keep him safe, so I was already betting on him being the real deal. I flipped the page of my book distractedly, but couldn't help but continuously peek up at Andrew.

He was studiously reading through another book. The title was half covered by his long fingers, but I could see that the basic subject was medicine—surgical practices, to be exact. I watched as he took in the information. Sometimes his facial expression would change from incredulity to out-right fascination. Watching this process became more enjoyable for me than reading the now forgotten teenage werewolf on the pages before me.

Abruptly, he got an excited gleam in his eyes and jumped up to grab another book, completely unrelated to medicine. He tossed it aside and grabbed another. The title on that one was *Environmental Epidemiology*. For a second, I wondered why he was reading about epidemics in the first place. Whatever he was looking for, he must have found it, because his eyes gleamed with triumph at his discovery. After a moment, he went back to his book pile and pulled a book out from the bottom, which he had left opened to a page. His eyebrows flew up at something he read. He plopped another book on top of it and continued reading a while before the amused skeptical look left his face. There was still a ghost of a smile on his lips.

For the last thirty minutes at the library, I watched him go through several more books, ranging from astrophysics, cellular biology, and botany to bioengineering and world culture. Instantly, I felt like my entire college career and all of my degrees were useless. He was soaking up this information as easily as a snake soaking up the warmth on a sunny day. I had struggled, studied constantly, and never attended any parties all throughout school. I was an outcast for my intelligence. But then I felt immediately better. The one person who everyone would look up to—an angel—was the one who reveled in education.

I felt a jolt of pride, in myself and in Andrew. In that moment, I just knew he was *my* angel.

As if he heard my thoughts, his eyes shot up to mine as he sent me a smile.

"We have to go," I sighed.

"Ten more pages," he said, and his eyes went back to the book in his hands.

"Done?" I asked after less than a minute. He had flipped through eleven pages. I was counting.

"Yes," he said, looking up at me as if the book had bewitched him. "This world is . . . different. I feel overwhelmed and enthralled all at the same time."

"I can't imagine what it would be like, taking so much in at once like you just did." I looked over his pile of books. "Let's go, before the librarian breathes fire at us."

Andrew raised an eyebrow at me. How does he do that? "Let's," he said.

We swept out of the building. Outside was chilly, the deep hour of the night making the air feel absolutely frigid. The sky was dark, and I could barely see the tiny stars with all the city lights blocking them out.

"Looks like we're going to have to walk," I told him.

Without conscious thought—or so it seemed—he grabbed my hand and pulled me forward. The familiar electric jolt shot between us. He squeezed my hand in reassurance.

Big, round yellow lights lit the sidewalk for us as we walked, but that didn't stop the shadows from looking terrifying. I started to feel a chill in my stomach that had nothing to do with the temperature. It felt as though someone, or something, was following us. I shivered at the thought of what could be in the dark of the frosty October air. My thoughts weren't helping the situation.

Our footsteps echoed in the silence. There was a far-off hoot of an owl. *That wasn't creepy*, I thought sardonically. Shadowy figures seemed to loom in and out of view as we continued down the sidewalk, though Andrew seemed oblivious. Maybe it was all in my head. Despite the strange feeling I had about the night, for some reason I really couldn't feel completely afraid with Andrew by my side. He radiated some indefinable sense of power that immediately made me feel safe, guarded.

Still, it was hard to suppress the suspicion.

I took up a more brisk pace.

A thunderous clunking came from an old truck behind us. It backfired as it passed and then wheezed on down the road. Its headlights briefly illuminating the area and showed that there was nothing in the shadows, just trees and quiet houses—exactly what I should have expected. I felt slightly reassured at this knowledge, but still, something seemed creepy.

"You're freezing," Andrew stated simply, looking at me with deep golden eyes, full of concern.

He wrapped his arm around me and began rubbing my arm with his palm to produce heat with the friction. Sparks shot from the contact. I didn't know if I should feel embarrassed or not, but for several seconds there, I didn't care; the feeling was amazing. The cold seemed to have no affect on his warm skin and his simple embrace was like wearing a space heater.

"Thank you," I murmured, not meeting his eyes.

We passed a stretch of blank wall, which momentarily blocked out the shadows. "We need to find a place to stay," I said after a minute, anxious. We were on the run, after all. What if a police cruiser drove by?

"Yes. This way." He pointed with his free hand and smiled down at me knowingly. His gold eyes pierced through me and made me melt.

I shook my head, trying to dispel my slowly growing feelings for this angel. He may want to protect me, he may be charming and breathtaking, but he was not mine—no matter how much I felt the need to claim him. He was an angel; I was human. He was immortal; I was mortal. He wasn't just some vampire, where I could beg him—the man of my dreams—to turn me into the deplorable creature he was so we could stalk the shadows for eternity. This was a genuine angel, full of radiance and love—something I couldn't reciprocate in full because I'd get old and die, while he stayed young and eternal. Any ideas of loving him had to be dumped right now. For the first time ever, I had no expectations.

"Here it is." Andrew stopped in front of a three-story hotel. Its outside looked like any three-star hotel—nondescript. The parking lot was packed, so people had parked their cars on the road, blocking off part of it. There were large trucks and jeeps parked in the grass. I was sure the management loved that.

"We have a reservation," he said.

"How did we manage that?" I stared up at him in shock.

"When you were upstairs, the librarian was very helpful. She said this was the most popular hotel in town because of the restaurant and bar."

"Oh," was my ingenious response.

"She told me that they stay open late. We could order some food perhaps?"

We? I thought. So he *does* eat food. I hadn't been sure if he did or not. Suddenly, I felt like a dunce. How else would he sustain his life? He wasn't a vampire, so no drinking of blood or other concoctions, nor did I think he fed off the life force of humans. I felt like a simpleton for even having questioned it in my mind.

"Is that all right with you?" he persisted when I didn't respond.

"Food, that sounds nice," I said faintly. The day's events were starting to weigh on me. "And a shower would be even better."

His face brightened. "I read about those. Who-ever came up with sewer systems and water treatment plants was exceptionally clever."

We continued to trudge through the brightly lit

parking lot. There were no bugs circling the lights like they would have been in the summer months. Winter was only around the corner and once again I felt the chill in the air.

As we approached the hotel, for some unknown reason, I felt reluctant. But I knew I'd rather be inside than out in the cool misty darkness. An odd chill ran up my spine, emphasizing my thoughts. I cast a quick look over my shoulder. The parking lot was empty, besides two men walking to their truck.

When Andrew reached the door, he didn't hesitate; so I didn't, either. The door slid open automatically for us, and he didn't even flinch—just continued on through like this world all made sense to him now. Maybe it did. It was nice to see that his face wasn't so bewildered and completely apprehensive about all of the new technology surrounding him anymore.

The woman behind the counter looked up from her computer screen to greet us with a bright smile, though her grin was not for me, but for Andrew. I'd be in awe, too, if I were her. I leaned over the counter.

"We have a reservation," I said calmly, though I was full of nerves. I knew the FBI were still looking for us, and I knew it would be a risk to use my name, but all modern hotels demanded ID.

I turned to Andrew, realizing I didn't know whose

name it was under. "Andrew, did you put it under my name?"

He nodded. "Yes. Doctor Moretti."

I gaped at him for a second before turning back to the girl, who was focused on something on the screen. I'd never told him my title or my last name. "It should be under Doctor Moretti."

When the girl looked up from her computer, she had a strained smile on her face. She seemed suddenly tense, alarmed. "Of course, Doctor Moretti. How would you like to pay for your hotel stay?" she asked with a bite of vehemence in her voice. "I'll also need to see your ID."

I handed her my driver's license, which was already in my hand. "I'll be paying with cash," I answered apprehensively.

"You have to leave a credit card at the front desk," she barked, her words punctuated by her quick slap of my driver's license on the desk—another show if edginess.

I flinched slightly at her manner. She was starting to make me nervous; yet, at the same time, there was a twinge of annoyance growing in me. I wondered why she was being so hostile in the first place. Had I not been polite to her? It couldn't possibly be because Andrew was with me, could it?

My card was in my back pocket and I put my hand behind me to reach for it. The girl, watching me, gripped the counter so hard I thought she would cut off the blood flow to her fingers. When she saw the plastic card come out of my back pocket, she relaxed.

She was acting especially peculiar. I slid the card toward her, across the space between us. She snatched it up and practically threw our room keys at us. "Room 310," she said dismissively.

"Thank you?" It came out more like a question than a statement.

A vacant silence greeted my words, so I wheeled around, puzzled by her open enmity. I started to stroll towards the stairs, which were next to the elevator. "Our room is on the third floor," I said, grabbing Andrew's hand.

When I reached my hand out to push the door away from the stairs, he stopped and pulled me back. "Can we take the elevator?" He pointed his head to the right. "I read about them . . . and I want to ride in one."

I laughed, I couldn't help it. He really was like an excited three year old. "Okay—but don't press all the buttons." He had already pressed the button to call the elevator down to us. "I'll try not to," he smiled mischievously.

The room was just as boring as any other. Tan walls with horrid flower wallpaper around the edges, matching curtains, and comforter. There were about a million lamps and no light on the ceiling. Typical, I thought. The small flat screen TV on the dresser was more or less a surprise. I was suddenly distracted from the normalness of the room by the bed. To my bewilderment, we had only one bed—a king-sized bed—but still only one. I thought him choosing a different hotel from the one on the brochure was to make sure we *had* two beds. Apparently not, seeing as how Andrew wasn't acting like this was any big deal.

There was an upsurge of noise as the heater turned on.

Andrew, his eyes roaming over every fine detail of the room, threw himself onto the comforter.

"I don't ever remember a bed as comfortable as this!"

Hesitantly, I perched on the edge of it and gave it a little bounce. "It's not nearly as nice as my bed at home," I noted under my breath. Here I was, already talking about my bed to Andrew. *Pitiful.*

He sat up, his golden eyes full of delirium at this revelation. "Really? It gets better than this?"

"It sure does."

14

The shower was very refreshing. No, more than that, really—it was divine. Though we were on the run, it didn't feel like it. After every misfortune that had occurred, it was incredible to be able to stand under a hot stream of water and feel as if all my troubles were draining away. My muscles were tense and the heat helped me relax. I never thought I'd be so ecstatic to see hotel shampoo and soap. The whole process seemed so necessary for me—so critical. Even though I had to put my dirty clothes back on, it was still wonderful to have clean skin.

Andrew, on the other hand, found the whole experience more entertaining than rejuvenating. After I explained the concept of the shower, he played with it for a good thirty minutes before the novelty wore off and he actually showered. When I checked on him, the curtain was pulled and the bathroom was soaked in water. He was humming brightly. I bit my lip to stifle my giggle. It was hard to believe, in that minute, that he was an ascended being.

When he finally came out, with his clothes sticking to his skin, he looked like he had just climbed out of a swimming pool. All I could do was laugh.

It was nearly one in the morning when we were finally dressed and presentable, but the hotel's restaurant stayed open until two, so we were safe.

D'oliva Lounge was mainly a bar, but there were tables and booths away from the loud music and away from the gyrating of the highly intoxicated patrons. We enjoyed watching them in our sober states from afar. When our waitress came to our table, I ordered a hamburger, fries, and a soda for each of us. It wasn't as though this place had fancy food, especially at this hour of the evening.

"Andrew?"

He had been watching the men playing their guitars on stage, but when I spoke over the music, his head snapped in my direction, as if I was much more appealing than everything else around us. "Yes?" He bent forward.

"Tell me, what it was like before . . ." my voice trailed off feebly.

"Well," he began, "things were definitely different from the way they are now. My brothers and I protected and guarded mankind, and the Ladies of Light protected the two thousand angels in the world."

This was news to me.

"We gave assignments, along with the Ladies of Light, to protect humans. That is how we claimed the title of angel. We were always saving the day in flamboyant ways, something we quit doing as the world aged."

I felt a great wave of remorse for him, losing his life for so many years, unable to see the world grow old.

"My rankings were high and I trained Guardians for new tasks. As the talk of angels died down, we had to become more covert."

"What about family? Were you in love or married?" I asked as nonchalantly as possible.

He shook his head. "I have my brothers and my friends. My parents died when we were mortals." He frowned, deep in thought. "I tried courting a few angels, but there were none that I could live with for forever. There was one human who I loved deeply, but she aged and eventually died. After that loss, I have never tried to love again. It is too difficult to lose someone you sincerely love and care for."

We were silent for a few seconds. "I've never really found someone to love, so I wouldn't know how that feels," I mumbled.

He placed his warm hand over mine. "Well," he replied, smiling, "I really care about you."

I was surprised he had even heard me over the music. I giggled—literally giggled.

Trying to alleviate his penetrating gaze, I asked, "So, where do angels live when they aren't out saving the day?"

His smile grew. "We live all over the place. The last place I remember was Italy—back home. But before that, it was Africa and then Russia. I stayed in Greece for quite some time. It's easy to go from one place to the next, so angels don't always have to live together. Being around each other for thousands of years can get highly irritating after a while." He chuckled at a thought he must have had. "We suggest to Guardians and other angels that they mingle with humans, to have human experiences and enjoy life as much as possible—which most do, immensely so."

I nodded, taking in all of the fascinating information.

"You were part of the Halo of the Sun?" I prodded, remembering the quick argument he had with Karen before the FBI took them away. I'd been brought into this mysterious world of awe and terror all in a matter of hours, but finally, I felt like I might get some answers.

He nodded slowly. His eyes were staring into mine, but he seemed to be off in another universe. "We were trusted," he reminisced, "and loved by all. It was a great honor to ascend to that level." He heaved a great sigh of regret.

"Tell me about the Shadow of the Sun," I requested. The memory of the Shadow looming over me, *warning me*, still sent shivers down my spine.

His face grew grave, his eyes hard. "It had always been a myth among my kind. Before we became immortal, the story was told to us at bed time, when we were children."

"But you believed it?" I canvassed.

He raised an eyebrow. "Gabriella," he said against my ear as he placed his hand tenderly over mine on the table. His breath in my ear sent my body into sensory overload, while his touch sent electricity shooting through me—a warming, tingling feeling. Was he trying to be seductive? If so, it was working.

I snuck a peek at his face. He didn't appear to be intentionally seducing me, but any second I was going to melt into his touch. We were now leaning close to each other. Perhaps he was just leaning in to keep our conversation private and to hear me over the blaring music. He didn't have to move far, we were sitting right next to each other at the small round table.

"Listen," he continued, completely oblivious to my incoherent state. "It must be a lot to take in—being

195

the Illuminator—but I'm here to help you in every way possible. I'll protect you on your journey."

I pulled backed to look him full in the face before I swooped like a bird of prey on his words. "Journey?" I felt so lost. This whole world, and everything he said, was just so *new*.

"Do you have those keys on you?"

My fingers automatically reached for my pocket. I felt a small bump. I nodded and put my hand in my pocket.

"Wait," he protested. "Let's eat first."

Fabulous, I thought sarcastically. *That wasn't anti-climatic at all.* I didn't like the idea of eating first, but just as I was about to voice my opinion, the waitress returned with our food and drinks.

Andrew gave the waitress a half smile and she blushed brilliantly before turning and scuttling away. I could understand how she was feeling. One look at his angelic smile and I had melted too. He grabbed a fry and held it up, staring with a flicker of curiosity on his face. "What is this?"

"Fried potato."

He looked as though the idea was ludicrous, but he didn't hesitate before he stuffed the whole thing in his mouth. He chewed a few times before looking at me, his eyes wide. "It's amazing!" he exclaimed and then he grabbed three more.

I laughed at his expression. "Slow down, you're going to choke."

With a little nudge, I pushed his soda toward him without thinking. He ignored the straw and started drinking swiftly. Then he stopped, put the glass down, and stared at me with a genuinely eccentric expression on his face. He covered his mouth and burped.

I burst out laughing at him, unable to keep a straight face.

"*Scusami*," he said in his flowing Italian. He paused for a second before he did anything else and then grabbed for the drink again, this time with even more pleasure. You'd think I had given him a small sip of liquid heaven.

I watched him devour his food for several minutes, but there was definitely a sense of jittery anticipation in the air. Finally, I couldn't take it anymore. I had so many questions building up behind my lips, begging to be answered. Words just burst from my mouth. "What journey?"

Andrew stopped mid swoop for another french fry. Ignoring my question, he asked, "How did you find out you were the one? The Darkness Illuminator?"

"It's sort of a complicated story," I said, and then told him all about how he and the other two angels had been sent to my lab for critical analysis, and about how Karen had arrived, infiltrated within the FBI. I told him about the necklace, the chest with the Shadow of the Sun symbol, the keys, and the fact that it was supposed to be impossible to remove them. Then I mentioned that a Shadow had attacked me in my office. "I was so scared. His eyes were on fire . . . and though his hands weren't touching me, it was like the darkness had collapsed around me and was squeezing the life force out of me. It was terrifying—" I broke off, remembering the Shadow's warnings. Earlier, I hadn't been able to tell Karen; but for some reason, I knew I could trust Andrew with my life. He wouldn't betray me. "He spoke to me—*warned* me. He told me not to wake the angels."

Andrew had dropped the hamburger and was giving me a calculating stare, as if he was measuring me up. "This isn't good." He looked aghast, even slightly unhinged.

I blanched at what he might mean. "What isn't?"

His face quickly changed to a serene mask. "It's time we go back to the room. We need to talk, without all of this noise."

Lamps sprang to life around us as if giving us permission to leave; it was the last call for alcohol. We pushed aside what was left of our food. I placed money on the table, not waiting for the check. Andrew seized the twenty-dollar bill and stared at it with great interest for a moment before replacing it and seizing my hand. This was becoming a habit. That same zing of electricity shot between us. He didn't even flinch. Instead, he just looked at me with a smirk on his lips—a little amused, a little pleased.

The silence on the way back up in the elevator was deafening, and continued to coil for several immeasurable moments before the doors slid open and the third-floor hallway spread out before us. We quickly made our way to our room.

Inside, Andrew sat on the bed, looking at me expectantly. He knew I was about to bombard him with questions. I thought I had every right to ask those questions and to receive the answers. Honestly, after everything that had happened today, I wondered if it was all just some joke the universe was playing on me.

So that I wouldn't distract myself by being so close to him, I took a seat on the swivel chair at the desk. "I'll try to be good," I conceded, "but there are things I have to know." Actually, questions were exploding in my mind like fireworks. Getting answers would be the only antidote.

"Let's start with the Shadow of the Sun," Andrew said. He was sitting up straight, as if propped against a wall.

I was immediately rapt with attention.

"Shadows have always been a myth," he said. "But from the small amount of things that I can actually remember from before I . . . ended up here . . . there had always been rumors of attacks, of Shadows consuming angels."

Horror rose inside of me. For some reason, I liked Karen's explanation better, the one I couldn't understand. This one was all too clear. "What do you mean by 'consume'?"

"Well, they turn those full of light into Shadows. It's a horrible way to end a Guardian's existence. But, honestly, I'm not even sure I believe any of those stories." Regardless of his words, his eyes showed a deep grief, and I wondered whom he had lost. "They aren't the same once they are changed." His voice was soft, quiet—*sad*.

"What do they want?" I asked quickly, trying to move over whatever it was that he was seeing in his past.

"Their warnings are never clear," he whispered. "Usually, they only cause harm. Angels are not afraid of the dark, but we are creatures of light. We enjoy the sun. To be a Shadow is a curse."

"Maybe you could try to remember why you,

Ehno, and Lucia all had their symbol around your necks." I thought for a second, crinkling my eyebrows together. "The Elders called it the Nebulous Sun."

"Their *symbol*? I don't remember them ever having a *symbol*. What did it look like?" He seemed honestly inquisitive.

I swiveled in the chair to grab the complimentary pen and paper and drew the symbol: the halo of the sun, with the shield in the middle of it. It was impossible to get the shape as flawless as it was in real life.

I scooted the sketch across the desk, and he leaned over to snatch it up. He stared at it for a moment, and I couldn't quite get a good read on his face until rage seemed to propel him to his feet. He was still looking at the paper. His eyes widened wildly, dramatically, before turning into a hot molten gold. He seemed to be swelling with some inexpressible anger.

"This,"—he pointed furiously at the drawing, his tone like a whip cracking—"is not the Nebulous Sun!" His teeth came together and for the first time I saw the extent of his great beauty and overwhelming power. He practically glowed with it. "This is the Guardian's symbol!" His voice seethed with his incandescent rage—deadly. The sketch crumpled in his hand and he dropped it unceremoniously to the floor.

During his out-burst, I had shrunk back into the

chair and had become rigid, frozen with fear. I was frightened, for the millionth time today. It was getting old. The day had not been faring well at all.

His skin still glowed with his rage. When he looked down at me, his eyes seemed to cool suddenly, his expression turning into horror. "Oh, no!" he gasped, a note of anxiety in his voice, as he knelt down in front of me. "This is not your fault, you are innocent." All his fury dissolved into alarm. "Maybe this is why you are here, now. Why I was sent to you."

He looked down at the maroon carpet. When he spoke again, his voice was dark, cryptic. "Someone has been telling lies." In the silence that followed, his shoulders moved with his breathing, which was slowing to a normal pace. "I'm not sure who is doing this—but there is something very wrong. I knew it when Karen said there had never been a Halo of the Sun. And I knew it when I found out you were the Illuminator."

I didn't respond, letting him think. He took in a deep breath and let it out before finally looking up to meet my eyes. The golden irises were hard, but his voice was soft—calming and soothing. "Let me see the keys now." He held his hand out. His expression was carefully cultivated into a tranquil expression, though I could easily see through his charade.

I reached into my pocket and pulled out the two

keys. The symbols on the ends glistened beneath the lamp light. They spread out on my palm. Andrew leaned over to see them for himself. His finger smoothly traced the two crossed arrows. An electric current grew between us.

"This," he whispered, pulling his finger away when the current intensified, "is the Definitive Sun. It symbolizes angelic protection against our enemies. It is the symbol of the Ladies of Light. The Halo of the Sun bestows the Guardian symbol to the males who are protectors of mankind. The shield represents the protection of the light—the sun—from all who wish to diminish it."

"Does Karen have one of these?" I pointed toward one of the keys. "You know, because she is my Guardian?"

"She is your Guardian angel," he stated simply, as if that answered everything. "Normally, you would be guarded by a male, since all Guardians are male, but I suppose you are different—special—and you deserve protection from someone more powerful. But sometimes the symbol isn't on a key or on a necklace. Sometimes it's branded into your skin."

When I didn't reply, his golden eyes shot up to see my expression. For a moment, I just let the silence spiral. "You mean . . ."

"If she was branded," he jumped in, "then she is your Guardian for life. That is very rare. But she would gladly have accepted a gift as generous as being the one to protect the Illuminator. It's a great honor."

For a second I swelled with pride before swallowing it down. "So," I curled my hand around the keys, and then placed them on the desk, "what do these keys unlock?"

His dark hair fell forward some, and he pushed it back so he could see me clearly. His jaw was square. "A library."

"That's all?" I was highly disappointed. "Is it like some super library that holds all the worlds' secrets? Because I'd love to know who shot Kennedy."

He coughed out a laugh. "It holds our history. It is the Divine Library."

"The Divine Library," I said in awe. Now I was interested. "Since the beginning?"

He nodded slowly. "It's odd that you would be sent these keys. They should have been kept safe by the Halo of the Sun, but if we have diminished . . ." he frowned deeply, as if he were having some sort of painful internal struggle. "And how the Shadow of the Sun could have been attached to the chest . . . well, I can't fathom what that means."

For a second, I struggled not to interrupt; I was

interested to hear what he had to say, and I didn't know how to put my question without angering him again. He was beautiful and mighty when angry, but also terrifying. "Why would Karen and the Elders call the Guardian's symbol a Shadow of the Sun symbol?" I prompted apologetically. My question sounded a little more pointed than I meant it to be.

For a second, I could see that same rage flare behind his eyes, and then he took a steadying breath. "I don't know, but I plan to find out." His voice was laced with threat. If I were the one responsible for all of this confusion, I knew I wouldn't want to be on the receiving end of his wrath.

"Now that we covered the basics—"

"Your journey," Andrew cut in, knowing exactly what I was going to ask, "has never been known. Zola, the prophetess, never explained much about the Illuminator's journey. But there are pages about the Illuminator, and I'm sure that now there are many more than the last time I was around."

"Pages? In the Divine Library?" I asked, my curiosity absolutely running on high.

"Yes, but the Divine Library is hidden deep within the mountains of Italy, near our old home. There are more precious treasures there then just books, but you have to possess both keys to enter."

"I *do* have both keys," I pointed out.

"No, you don't," he stated matter-of-factly. "One is for the library; the other is for something else."

"And that would be?"

He picked up one of the keys I had placed on the desk. "I don't know. This one is not for the library, but it is definitely important if it was sent to you."

I leaned my head back against the chair. "And why did you say 'this isn't good' when I told you about the Shadow's warning?"

Andrew pulled a strand of my hair away from my face. The gesture was sweet. Each second I seemed to be falling in deeper.

"You're tired. We should sleep." He was trying to distract me.

"We will, after you tell me what you meant."

"I'll tell you if you get ready for bed. I won't look," he assured me, turning around.

Of course he wouldn't; he was the perfect gentleman. And, of course, now that I had finally met a man who treated me how I deserved to be treated, it turns out he's an angel—and completely out of my league. I sighed under my breath and pulled my slacks and shirt off before slipping under the covers in my underwear. The sheets were freezing and little goose bumps rose on my skin, but I knew that in a few minutes my body heat would warm them.

"Tell me," I prompted.

He turned on his heel, facing me now, and peeled his clothes off, all the way down to the boxer briefs I had bought him. Immediately, I meticulously surveyed every glorious inch of him. His skin was a lustrous golden color, and I was right – he did have a six-pack. I blushed, sure that I must be turning an unflattering shade of magenta. I could feel the heat warming my cheeks.

He pulled a blanket out of the tiny closet and lay on the bed next to me, on top of the covers. My head was on the pillow and I had already curled up into a little ball. He propped himself up on his elbow and looked down at me. I was momentarily basking in his infinite glory.

He took a deep breath, as if he were about to tell a very long, complicated story. "The Ladies of Light come in cycles," he began in a serious voice. "The cycle disperses power evenly throughout the years so that no single group of angels gains control for eternity."

I nodded. "Like how the president only gets a four-year term, and can only be elected for two terms in a row?"

"Yes," he said approvingly. "Exactly like that.

When the cycle is up, the Halo of the Sun and the Ladies of Light join together to help vote in the next leaders. This happens every one-hundred years, for both groups."

I yawned. "That's fascinating, really, but it doesn't explain your reaction."

His hand traced the side of my cheek, and electricity shot between us. For a moment, I wondered if I would ever again be able to touch someone who *wasn't* an immortal. Would my handshake burn someone to a crispy critter?

You're delirious, Gabriella.

"Gabriella, you are tired, I can tell. Rest. We can talk about this tomorrow." He looked at me with quiet desperation.

It was tempting, but I thought I could hold my eyes open to hear this. Why was he trying to hold back on the information? Maybe it was something so bad he couldn't fathom putting it into words. Like my death? I shuddered. Andrew mistook the reason and spread out his blanket to cover me too.

"Please, tell me, and then I'll go to sleep," I promised, full of determination.

He reached above my head and flipped the lamp off. We were plunged into darkness. We stayed in motionless silence for a whole minute. I thought he wasn't going to tell me, but finally he whispered, "When new leaders are chosen"—he took a deep breath, as if bracing himself—"they are *awakened*."

The shock of his statement, that the Shadow might have been warning me about *other* angels, lodged in my throat like a big rock. Everything that had seemed permanent and unquestionable was now thrown into doubt.

A wave of piercing cold broke over me. "Oh."

15

dreams

Why would the Shadow warn me that I shouldn't wake the angels, when I didn't even have the power to do it? Andrew, lying next to me in the dark, was quiet. The complete silence was suddenly broken by the whirring of the heater.

My mind still wasn't working; my thoughts were an incoherent babble in my brain.

"Gabriella," Andrew said in a delicately inflected voice. He reached out and tucked my hair behind my ears. "Please, say something."

"I—" I didn't know how to respond. He waited patiently, something I was not used to. "We . . . Well, we need to find the others." What other options were there? Something was afoot, and it seemed we couldn't figure this out on our own, prophecy be damned.

Again, there was nothing but silence between us. The dark was like a velvet curtain over my eyes.

"How do we do that?" he whispered gently with benign interest.

"We, um . . ." I knew what we had to do, but at the same time I was highly against it, and I knew he would

210

be too. "We let them capture us."

He sighed, a long heavy breath. When he spoke, his voice was calm, serene. "We'll talk about it in the morning. Sleep," he said, and suddenly, unexpectedly, he brought his warm lips to my forehead. There was a spark that lit between us—a tiny bolt of lightning.

"Sorry," I mumbled, not thinking.

His body shook with silent laughter. "Goodnight, sweet Illuminator." His tone was as smooth and rich as melted chocolate.

I was still aching with curiosity, however. "Andrew?" I asked, my voice almost inaudible. "Are you going to sleep? I mean, *do* you sleep?" I'd never known an immortal before. *The possibilities*, I thought wryly.

His laugh was low and throaty. "Of course I do, but I've been *asleep* for years. I'm not tired."

This time I was silent, barely acknowledging his explanation with even a yawn. I was anticipating the sleep that was finally about to dominate my greater senses. I was exhausted and knew I needed rest. As I faded toward a dream state, I could feel Andrew's warm arms wrap around me, his warm breath in my hair. He kept the blanket between us. Perhaps he was just trying to soothe me, and honestly, he was. I never wanted him to let go. So I didn't object, but fell comfortably into his shoulder, tucked beneath his arms . . . and soon I was asleep.

Flowing auburn hair glittered against the sun like molten copper. A knife tucked securely into a holster around a leg. Glacial blue eyes turned toward me over a perfect shoulder, staring, *cautioning* me. Her face was that of an angel; her body was that of a goddess. The tattoos that covered every last inch of her skin was intricately woven in a pattern that seemed to have no beginning or end.

She turned away from me, her short white dress billowing in the wind. It was silk-like, so thin I could see through it. Her tattoos went beyond her arms and legs; they continued snaking up her back to circle around the shape of two arrows crossed together.

Automatically, my hand reached out to trace the symbol. It was familiar. As I took a step toward the goddess-like warrior, another hand reached out and yanked me back. The skin was dark brown and beautiful, just like the angel before me. My head moved, as if in slow motion, to see whose face belonged with the hand.

He was tall, roughly six-four. I had to look up and up.

"Luke?" I whispered. He was not threatening,

though his light-blue eyes bore into mine. The hair falling toward his face was the same shade of auburn as that of the woman's.

He was scared, anxious. Naturally, my eyes scanned the area around us to see if there was any threat. Behind me, in the distance, I saw a small army, a moving sea of leather. Weapons were strapped to sheaths or in their hands. I felt my eyes widen. But when I turned to share my distress with Luke, he was staring in another direction. There was no mistaking his feelings. He trembled with stress. *What could be worse?* I thought with dread.

My movements felt dream-like—as if I were sleep-walking. I turned toward what was causing his unease.

I felt myself suddenly tense in alarm. Two women, dressed all in white, were standing at the top of a small hill nearby. Their dresses were identical to that of the goddess, who now stood only feet below them. Their eyes were pure white. It unsettled me. They were warriors, their eyes fierce, their skin intricately marked. And though it didn't make sense, I could feel that the large army behind me was absolutely frightened of the two women. For some reason, I could feel the womens' power too, and I shook with fear.

Everything was silent, even though the wind

continued to blow around us. The sun was low in the sky, casting long shadows from the beautiful women. Squinting, I shielded my eyes from the light.

Suddenly, the auburn hair of the angel flew up in the air, her dress clinging violently to her body. Luke staggered sideways and fell to his knees, golden tears wetting his glorious face. The goddess below the white women turned to look at him beseechingly, and I saw a single tear escape her ice-blue eyes, eloquent with despair.

It made sense then.

"Lucia," I breathed with difficulty. My voice sounded distant, echoing. Her eyes closed, the tears seeping from beneath her long lashes, as if nodding in acknowledgement.

One of the women in white pulled a long knife from her leg-sheath and held it in the air ceremoniously. It only took me a second to realize what was happening. I was paralyzed with fear.

"No!" I screamed an inarticulate yell of rage and took the first step to run towards her. An indefinable sense of power pulsed through the air and stopped me dead.

Lucia looked behind her again; she wasn't staring at me, but at Luke. She whispered something, her lips moving inaudibly. Luke, already on his knees, fell forward on all fours. He put his head to the grass and began tearing at it, shaking with grief.

The army behind us didn't move, but stiffened with terror. Why weren't they fighting? I wanted to scream at them, "Fight back you cowards!" Tears began rolling down my face and I wiped them away with my fingers. The wetness was gold against my skin. But, for some reason, that didn't matter.

The woman with the knife held it at an angle, a perfect position for stabbing. Luke looked up, his face glittering with gold. There was cold fury in every line of his face.

The knife sliced through the air and plunged deeply into Lucia's chest. She bent over with the force. The shock rooted me to the spot and a sick feeling of nausea rose in my throat. The knife slid into her as if into butter, and she lifted her head to the heavens as a scream of unendurable agony tore from her lips. The noise pierced the silence like a bullet. She writhed and shrieked, and then fell to the ground.

I tried to look at something else, *anything else*! Her dress was no longer white but a sickening, dripping scarlet that spilled wastefully onto the grass—the crimson liquid spread over the white like a disease. Iron bands seemed to tighten around my chest as I tried to digest the horrible image before me. Her blood wasn't gold . . . and this made me realize that this *really* was her ending.

I didn't hesitate this time as I tore past Luke, sprinting toward Lucia. *Someone, help her!* I pleaded silently. Two men rushed past me, though I didn't see their faces. All I could see was Lucia.

I approached and stared down at her, transfixed, as if my will could force her to mend. She stared back at me without seeing. Her head lolled to one side, blood trickling from her lips. She didn't move, and her chest was no longer rising.

I looked behind me, toward Luke, begging him to tell me it was a lie. His eyes only sparkled with golden tears. It wasn't a lie. Horror rose in me, quick and rough.

A pair of hands seized me. I screamed and there was suddenly a hand over my mouth—suffocating. I grasped at the fingers. Then, it was as if I was ripped from my body.

"*Shhh!*" whispered a deep, frantic voice in my ear. I blinked in the velvety darkness; it seemed as though the sun had just given up on the earth and plummeted away. Darkness pressed in all around me. I fought against the hand over my face, the hot body pressed over top of me. I couldn't breathe and I began kicking—anything to move, to get oxygen. Each attempted breath tore at my lungs.

All I could think about was Lucia and how I desperately needed to get to her, to bring her back, although deep down I knew she was lost. I ached with the thought. My throat was becoming sore from the constant scream trapped in my esophagus.

"Please, Gabriella," the distressed voice pleaded. "Quiet."

All my breath had gone from my body. It was then that I realized I wasn't breathing through my nose and that was why I couldn't get air. Immediately, I took in a shuddering breath, gasping like I'd been doused with cold water.

"Yes, good. Calm," said a soothing tone of a voice I recognized. "Breathe."

Andrew. Instantly I relaxed in his grip, my whole body going limp. I felt wilted—numb—after what I had seen. In my head, I was chanting that it was all just a dream; but it had been so real . . . too real. I shook my head, trying to rid myself of the vertigo-inducing image. It didn't work.

He removed his hand from over my mouth and reached over to turn the lamp on, bathing the room in a blinding golden glow. I blinked in the sudden brightness; the light left an imprint in my eyes. Squinting, I could see Andrew hovering over me, like a tiger about to devour his prey—except his eyes were pleading, anxious...

"The FBI are here," he breathed. "Be very quiet." His voice was unearthly, the most beautiful sound in the world, though his words stunned me into silence. I'd been optimistic to the point of foolishness; of course they would find us.

Despite the danger of the men on their way to capture us, I felt the urge to hug Andrew to my chest. I was so happy to be away from the horrible nightmare. Instead, I nodded. I could hear the rustling noise of many footsteps echoing in the hallway. There was no time to run or escape.

Andrew pulled on his jeans, but left his shirt lying on the floor, discarded. He was just as shockingly beautiful as he was the first time I saw him. I was immediately ashamed of myself for thinking about him that way, considering our distressing situation.

The doorknob jiggled and I jerked up, pulling the covers over me to protect my exposed skin. Andrew's eyes zoned into the movement like a homing missile. The door flung open and at the same moment Andrew pulled me from the bed in such a lightning quick movement that I was standing behind him before I knew it. One arm held me there, as if protecting me. I blinked, confused for a second. Men in bulletproof vests swept over the threshold and flooded into the room, guns raised, all pointing at Andrew.

I dug my fingers into his side, frightened. His heart was racing. Deep inside me, I could feel a profound surge of electricity building, coiling around my insides, growing. When I gripped Andrew tighter, it shot through him—rough, hard, and hot. He jerked, but held his ground. The oddest thing happened then. I could feel my thoughts and feelings rising up and flowing out of me and into him. My shock, fear, distress . . . all of it swelled in me like venom, compressing my lungs, and then it flowed between us.

His fingers found one of my hands and yanked it from his skin. A blue stream of electric thoughts flowed through the small distance. For a second, I thought he was going to pull me away from him; instead, he wrapped my arm around his body, hugging me there. I didn't know what to think about this connective current that had been created between us, but I knew if there was anyone I could share my thoughts with in this way, it would be Andrew. He was special.

"Let the girl go," ordered a short and stocky man with an almost shaved head. He was a deep, thundery guy. "Now," he seethed, punctuating my assessment. The malice in his voice was unmistakable. This was a man who got off on his job.

"We're not armed," I croaked, leaning my head over to get a better view. "Please."

A blank silence met my words. The man's tiny, beetle-like eyes never left Andrew's face. The blackness in them reminded me of a misty window, full of chill and emptiness. He surveyed Andrew like an enthusiastic collector who was about to claim the gold piece of his collection. "Doctor Moretti, are you alright?"

"Perfectly fine," I cried out, my voice choked but growing stronger by the second. I was still trembling from my dream.

"I could fly," Andrew breathed, too low for the others to hear. He sounded like a gambler, contemplating his chances. My fingers tightened their grip, his pulse picking up its pace. "Yes?" he pressed.

I shook my head and another jolt of electricity burned between us. He stiffened, rigid as a waxwork. I tried to send my thoughts to him, concentrating with all my being in increasing desperation. *They think I'm a victim. They won't harm me. This is our chance to get into their secure facilities.* I tried to focus, hoping he would get the message.

This time he shook his head. I could imagine him eyeing them all malevolently. "No, I won't be able to protect you," he whispered, with a plea in his voice.

It almost broke my resolve; but after my dream,

I knew we needed answers—and help. I refused to be resigned to this unsolvable mystery. Plus, he knew there was a grain of truth to my words.

"Will someone throw me my clothes?" I asked the room at large, though I was speaking into Andrew's back. "He'll let me go and come peacefully."

The tension in Andrew's body was palpable.

The tiny black eyes of the agent flickered to mine for a second, surprised out of his preoccupied longing. He motioned to someone, and they kicked my clothes towards me. My grip on Andrew slackened so I could reach for them, but he only doubled the strength of his grip on my arms. Anticipating trouble, several guns in the room clicked as the men prepared for him to do something. He let go immediately.

I dressed hastily, feeling better at once. "Who's in charge?" I demanded, though now I was feeling a certain reluctance in my plan.

The man who demanded my release used his radio to summon someone, though it was hard to understand their radio-speak jargon. The reply was fuzzy and even more difficult to make out.

Only minutes passed before a man, perfectly polished in a black suit, stepped through the sea of men still guarding the door. They parted as if he were Moses. I recognized his tall form and light-brown hair,

shiny with gel. Dark eyes peeked out beneath his perfectly arched eyebrows.

"Joseph!" I practically fell over myself to get to
him. "Tell them to be gentle. He's harmless!"

Before I knew it, Joseph had pulled me into a
giant hug. It was effortless, embracing him back, like
I belonged there. In my ear, he whispered, "Karen's
been beside herself with worry, and so have I."

There are just some events, like almost dying
together, that bring you close to someone. I gripped
him closer for a minute before he released me and
turned toward his men. "Agents? Do as she says," he
ordered.

The men surrounded Andrew and he looked over
them—at me—a man of uncertainty, barely clinging to
reason and restraint.

"*Please*," I mouthed.

He closed his golden eyes once, slowly, as if
acknowledging my plea, giving in without a challenge.
His face was stricken.

It felt like an ice cube was sliding down into my
stomach.

"He'll be fine," Joseph whispered in my ear. "Kar-
en's waiting at the lab."

At least they aren't taking him to jail, I thought
dryly. They threw his grey T-shirt at him and he put it

on. They were even nice enough to let us put our shoes on.

They still cuffed him and held him at gunpoint as they set off down the corridor, leading him to the stairs.

We descended in silence and stepped into the cool misty darkness. The girl who had checked us in earlier was standing outside, her back against the brick wall, police lights reflecting off her pale skin. She had a cigarette in one hand and was puffing away like a train. When she caught sight of me, she looked smug, her eyes gleaming with triumph.

Now I understood her hostility earlier. I shot her my most brilliant smile and showed my wrists, which were cuff free. She choked on the smoke as her eyes bugged slightly in disbelief. I resisted the urge to stick my tongue out at her. *So there,* I thought back, just as smugly.

underground

During the ride, I felt anxious, nervous. Andrew was in another truck and I knew the small stocky man was with him. Of course, Andrew could escape if he wished, but he would do this for me and for those angels trapped in their prisons. The windows to the large SUV were tinted so black that I couldn't tell if it was night or day, or where we were going. Not that I'd ever want to find this place again.

"He'll be fine," Joseph said to me, pulling my attention from the window that I had been staring at for nearly two hours. I couldn't see anything, but I wasn't really looking—I was thinking. "I promise." There was a slight note of jealousy in his tone, which almost made me blush, but I had other things on my mind.

"And the others?" I whispered. Who knew who could be listening right now? I had every right to be suspicious.

He nodded slowly. "We called in Director Halistor. He refused to help until we found you and brought you safely to the lab. Even my superior requested that it be you who does all lab work. You're the best in your field."

I breathed out a sigh of relief. "What happened to Sally?"

He chuckled. "Director Halistor sent her home." His smile grew in width and amusement lit his features. "She accidently set off two alarms in one day. She's rather nosey."

I smiled back without effort. "I can understand that."

"I bet you could. Why did you ask her to come along in the first place?" He raised his eyebrows.

"Karen revealed some information to me that . . ." I trailed off, realizing he would understand what I was talking about. "Anyway, I needed a friendly face in the place. I'm sorry she was a pain. Normally she is my pain and I can just send her away on an errand when she becomes overbearing. As I see you did."

"I learn quickly," he smiled knowingly at me.

For an instant, I wondered exactly how much Karen had informed him about. Surely she didn't keep him completely in the dark. It felt incredibly pleasant to now have another person aware, even if his information was limited. I wasn't alone in this anymore.

The vehicle took a turn and I slid in my seat slightly. The driver acted as though he wasn't paying attention, but I had seen his eyes flick to the rearview

mirror more than once. Joseph made this same obser-
vation to me in a low voice, and we both laughed. It
was as if the huge stress bubble had finally grown too
thin and burst.

We soon came to a stop, and the driver rolled
his window down to speak with some men standing
guard outside. From what I could see, they were heavily armed. They made several security checks before
admitting us. I made sure to remember everything I
could about this facility to help with our escape. But
with Joseph, Karen, and Andrew on my side, I hoped
that it wouldn't be a problem breaking Lucia and Ehno
out.

Once we were on the other side—behind enemy
lines—I watched suspiciously as the vehicle holding
Andrew turned to the right. We turned left, and I began
protesting immediately.

"I have to stay with the subject," I ordered.

In response, the driver merely pressed a button,
and a sliding glass window rose between us. Anger
boiled up in me. "You take me to him right now!" I
demanded, banging rapidly on the dark glass. I was
taking a deep breath, planning on arguing furiously
through the glass.

Joseph gently, yet firmly, grabbed my arms and
brought me back against the seat. Electricity zapped

him, making him jump back slightly.

"Calm," he said, shaking his hand and looking dis-comforted. "We must act normal. If they suspect that you see them as more than subjects in an experiment, they will toss you out of here so quickly your head will spin."

I huffed and crossed my arms against my chest. "Of course," I said crossly, "you're right." My instincts disagreed.

He put two fingers to his lips to suppress a smile, though I could easily see through it. "Don't worry. Karen will be waiting for him." He shook his wrist again. "And wow, you seriously have some juice there. Be careful with that."

I stared at him. "I don't know how to control it yet. I mean . . . I hope I can learn to manage it."

The vehicle stopped and the doors automatically unlocked. Joseph reached over me and opened the door. "After you."

When I stepped out, I took in several things at once. There were buildings lined up perfectly in the ghostly moonlight, all of them the same size and type of structure. I could see key-card readers and palm readers, similar to security at the entrance of Zelko Corp., except there were armed guards at every corner here, constantly walking back and forth, their eyes suspiciously flying to every movement or shadow. And at this time of night, it was us that they found interesting.

Several guards turned our way, watching. On top of the buildings were satellites, radio towers, and other equipment that looked important. Spotlights lit the main road between the buildings. Beyond the lights, all I could see was inky blackness. I wondered where we were.

Joseph walked ahead of me and pulled out his key card, which had a gold strip on it. He swiped it and then put his hand on the screen on the door. It welcomed him in, and the door opened with the suction-noise of something airtight. My heart was pounding furiously in my chest as I followed behind him.

Suddenly a short woman, shorter than me by almost a head, scampered up to me with a lab coat and a key card in hand.

"Doctor Moretti. Hi, I'm Susan and this is your lab coat and key card." Boy, she got to the point immediately. No reason for pleasantries. "This color here," she said, pointing to the orange strip on the back, "is what your security clearance is. You can only open doors that have the color orange, green, or yellow. Blue, red, and gold are restricted. Follow me." She marched off down a hallway.

Joseph looked over his shoulder and had a huge

grin on his face. I shot him a *what's that look for* kind of stare, but he only turned to follow Susan, his shoulders shaking with mirth. I wanted to whack him across his shoulder blades.

"We need to scan in your right hand," Susan called. I approached the desk she was standing at. Before I knew it, she had yanked my wrist out and put my palm against a screen. She began typing furiously across a keyboard, and then yanked my wrist and scanned my hand twice more.

When I freed myself, I put the lab coat on. They had already embroidered my name and title on it, "Doctor Gabriella Moretti, Supernatural Specialist." When had they had time to do that?

Susan turned back to me when she was done. "All right, now that everything is in order, we have some business to attend to. Agent Carter," she shot her head in his direction, "did you want to come with us?" She raised her eyebrows almost to hairline level, her voice extremely sarcastic.

I sent him a pleading look that I hoped spoke the words I couldn't say aloud: *please don't leave me alone with this woman!*

"Ms. Joy, I am here to assist and protect Gabriella. We, at the FBI, believe that she is in danger," he said, straight faced—more straight than mine at least. I was biting my lip in laughter. "I'm her shadow until we feel the threat has been eliminated."

Susan stared him up and down, all six feet plus, as if she were looking down on him instead of up. "Fine," she bit. "If you feel that's necessary."

"I do."

I sighed in appreciation for his lie. Her ranking was not as high as his, and she had to take him at his word.

We reached the end of a hallway, which was all in white: the walls, ceiling, and windowsills. There was an elevator which needed an orange security-level key card. Susan looked over her shoulder after we stood staring for a minute. "Are you going to scan your card and your palm?"

"Oh. Sure." I had thought we were waiting for the elevator. I frowned and swiped my card, which was accepted, and then I placed my palm on the screen. It took a few seconds to scan, but then a robotic female voice greeted me as if we were old buddies. I had a feeling that we might just become that way if I had to stay here for long . . .

The door opened with a ding and we all got on. I wondered where we were going. There had seemed to be only two floors on all the buildings I had seen from the outside.

When we stepped inside and I saw the options, I understood then. This really *was* an underground facility. There were at least seven levels below ground level. Immediately, I was impressed. At Zelko Corp., there was only one floor below ground, which contained the highly sensitive labs, including the fishbowl. I speculated on how many labs they might have under this building alone, and wondered whether all the other buildings were also equipped with underground levels, and whether they were connected below ground—so many questions, so many possibilities. Breaking out was going to be more problematic than I first realized.

Surprisingly, elevator music was playing. My expectations of what a government installation would consist of were obviously inaccurate. I felt tense and alarmed, but I tried to hide this from Susan and her prying eyes. I didn't trust the woman as far as I could throw her. And she was really plump . . .

Without my permission, my mind wandered. Where was Andrew? I felt a sudden desire for his comforting hand to be in mine and his arm around me—with our current racing between us. We had an undeniable connection. I mentally sighed. It was in that moment that I realized how attached I had grown to him. Stupid hopeless longing; I was already doomed to heartache. An old commercial ad about drugs flashed through my head. *This is your brain on Andrew.*

When the doors slid open on the fourth level below ground, I was immediately blinded by the bright lights. The whole place seemed suffused in mysteries and secrets. By the look on Joseph's face, he had never been down here before either. We both shot each other curious glances as we stepped out of the elevator and followed Susan. She was walking like one of those mall walkers, and we had to pick up our pace to catch up with her.

I tried to take in as much as I could as we walked down the hall. There were labs to my left and right. The walls were made of glass, and I could see many scientists working on experiments.

When we passed the doors to the first two labs, I noticed a symbol displayed on each door. It was two snakes in attack positions against each other. Around the image were the words: "United States of America Copperhead Project." The first lab to my right was the cancer research department, which was full of animals in cages ranging from monkeys to mice. A woman was holding a clipboard in her hands and writing something on a chart as she observed one of the monkeys.

Across the hall, the lab on my left was full of chemistry and biology experiments providing medications and treatment plans to the lab rats—or so said one of the signs on the lab wall. There were culture tubes, some of the latest microscopes, fume hoods, and different color liquids. Across one of the counters, a man was measuring something out into a beaker.

I nodded my head in approval at what I saw. Joseph was suddenly at my ear. "We're not as bad as you think," he whispered.

My eyes shot up to meet the deep depths of his dark eyes. "I didn't think that!" I protested. "But these . . ." I lowered my voice. "These angels are alive and breathing. What we are doing is inhumane, and you know it!"

He held his hands up in surrender. "I'm on your side."

I lowered my voice to the point where he could barely hear me. "So, does that mean you'll help me?"

He shot me a dazzling smile. "Oh, Karen and I have already been planning an escape."

"So she told you about—"

"Yes. She did. Now if only she would keep her eyes off Darren, we'd be farther along in our plans for Operation Liberate Angels."

A smile spread across my face. "Operation Liberate Angels, huh? That's an interesting title." I wondered how much they had investigated in a few hours time.

233

"Do you like it?" He waggled his eyebrows.

"Absolutely." I giggled like a schoolgirl with a crush, and my cheeks must have turned fluorescent pink.

"Good! I was the one who came up with that. When others are around, we call it Ola—like a name. If someone asks, we say we are talking about Karen's wild older sister who became a stripper in Vegas."

I shook my head in disbelief, but the smile was still squarely on my face. "You're joking, right?"

He looked at me in faux scorn. "Absolutely not!"

"You're full of it."

He bumped me with his shoulder, and we continued to walk down the hall. We passed a bathroom on the left, and then took a right turn down another hallway. Again, there were glass walls showing labs fully in operation. Lab technicians were working furiously on both sides. To my right, it looked as though they were building some type of fully functional, human-sized robots. To my left the door said: "Bioengineering." I couldn't even imagine what they were doing in there.

"We're here," Susan said crisply, with an obvious case of resentment. Her eyes roamed over Joseph again before she turned to me. "This is strictly your lab. You have the right to revoke privileges. Karen will show you how to do this if you wish."

I nodded to show her I understood, and she stepped out of my way and went back down the hall without even a good-bye. The click of her heels against the floor grew fainter until I couldn't hear anymore when she cut the corner.

I turned back to face the door and read the title across it, which said "Supernatural Beings Department."

"It's like we're on the geek squad," I joked, and Joseph chuckled beside me. "Well, let's hope this works." I swiped my key card and then placed my right hand against the scanner. Just like in the elevator, a female voice welcomed me, but this time by name. The door clicked open with the now-familiar sound of a sealed vacuum being opened. "Talk about special services," I smiled at Joseph.

"You have no idea. I heard that if you have top clearance, the machine brews you a cup of coffee exactly how you like it," Joseph said, absolutely serious. Something flashed in his eyes.

"I don't believe you for a second."

"Why?"

"Because you have top clearance, and I don't see a steaming cup of coffee in your hands yet."

He seemed to realize I had observed his key-card

clearance earlier. He smiled again, his wonderfully warm smile, "You got me."

Before I pushed the door all the way open, I turned around to face him full on, all joking aside. "Why doesn't our lab have glass walls?" Maybe I was just being paranoid.

"Isn't it obvious?" he asked.

I shook my head and he sighed.

"They don't want the others knowing what goes on behind this door, especially now that we have *live* subjects. Most of them don't care to know, anyways. These people are scientists. The supernatural is . . . well, un-provable."

"I'm a scientist," I scoffed. "I received my PhD by the time I was nineteen from Yale. I was on the top of all my classes!"

He didn't even question me. "It doesn't matter to the guys around here. Surely you didn't take classes on *this* at Yale?" He raised a single eyebrow and gestured to the sign on the door.

"Well, no. Of course not. But you wouldn't need special training for this, if you had my credentials," I growled, pushing the door open. "It's just a little ridic-ulous—" I stopped in my tracks at the sight, my argu-ment completely lost as I felt a spasm of horror and a small angry cry of shock left my lips. Joseph put his hands on my waist and pushed me forward so he could shut the door behind us. Ignoring Karen, I rushed past her. My hands went straight to the glass wall between me and my angels. "Andrew!"

He placed his hand on the glass where mine was. "Gabriella," he said devoutly.

Tears sprang into my eyes, and I tried to blink them away but there were too many.

"No. Please, don't cry," he pleaded.

I searched him over. My gaze landed immediately upon his hair—the only obvious difference in his appearance. They had cut it, but they had done it haphazardly, as if they had taken shears to it and shredded it off. In the craziness of the situation, I couldn't help but think the wild haircut suited him and his personality. He was still in his jeans and t-shirt.

"This is all my fault. I am so sorry, Andrew."

"It'll be okay," he soothed through the thick glass. I choked a little. I couldn't believe he was the one soothing me. It was like he always had some strong impulse to comfort me. My heart jumped.

There was a warm hand on my shoulder, and I looked behind me to see Joseph, his face no longer the smiling man I had seen only moments ago. Even his eyes were darker. "You need to move away from the glass."

When he caught a look at my expression he abandoned his look of poker stiff disapproval.

"Why?" I cried out. "You expect me to ignore the fact that they are in here?" I looked around the room and noticed there were five cells like this one. Ehno and Lucia were separated in two of them. I lowered my voice. "They're angels!" Each breath was sharp in my chest. I was livid.

Several lab technicians looked up from whatever they were doing to see what all the fuss was about. Joseph ignored them and leaned in closer to me. "I know," he whispered patiently. "But there are cameras everywhere. Remember what I said on the ride over here. You can't let them know you are as close to them as you are. I can promise you that we can speak freely, but your actions are being watched."

No reason to be paranoid, I thought sarcastically. My eyes looked swiftly to all the corners. They really were watching our every move. I backed away from Andrew, distressed. My mind just couldn't comprehend what I was seeing. Andrew, *my* Andrew, and the other beautiful angels all locked away, caged like animals. I couldn't stand to see them like that. The very thought burned and caused a dark flush to creep its way under my skin. Irritation and a heavy vexation choked me. I knew what I had to do, if I was being honest with myself. It was time to fight back.

Hardly able to tear my eyes away, I turned toward the lab techs who had stopped what they were doing, staring at me. My temper flared, but I had to remember what Joseph had said to me in the car. Be calm, assured, like this was no big deal. But it was and that was why I was feeling so troubled. The most heavenly, unearthly creatures, who only *saved* human lives, were now contained by the very people they protected. It made me sick and ashamed.

With significant effort I controlled my expression. *Smooth, calm, serene.* I had to make them believe that I was on their side, though I knew I'd lose brownie points once I spoke. Everyone was still frozen, staring at me expectantly, but I was unable to give them any orders they'd want to hear. Tough!

"Out!" I ordered with assured authority. It was time to get down to brass tacks.

Smiling, I just stood there, enjoying the effect of my words. Everyone, I saw with some satisfaction, turned to leave—even Joseph and Karen. In this tense moment, I had to fight a mad desire to laugh. It was like I was some queen they had to obey. One lab technician, whose nametag read "Sue," sent me a look of utmost loathing and disbelief as she passed. I didn't have time to care as I watched her swell indignantly and march out, her brown hair pulled into a tight bun at her neck. She was probably wound just as tight as her hair. I glowered at her backside.

"Not you or you," I said and grabbed both Karen and Joseph from behind at the same time. Joseph jumped with a slight spasm in his face, as if I had shocked him and I grimaced. I probably had. Oops.

Karen's face displayed the same startled look, as if she could feel my electrical power; but she seemed to just shrug it off as if it was no big deal. It probably wasn't, for all I knew.

The technicians flooded out of the room. When the door shut behind them, I turned to the two remaining allies and to the three imprisoned angels. "It's time to get busy."

scheming

"So far, we have no effective strategy," Joseph explained while leaning over one of the lab tables. "There are cameras at every corner and guards at every exit. This place is locked tighter than Fort Knox."

"Cut the electricity." I shrugged. It seemed pretty obvious to me. The men inside couldn't see and the men outside would no longer have the spotlights to light their way. There would be no cameras to watch our every move and the doors would open—

"Then the doors would be sealed with us inside!" Karen muttered as if she could read my thoughts.

"Oh," I whispered.

"True," Joseph said thoughtfully. "But we might also be able to use that against the guards. If we accomplish getting outside and turning the power off, they will be stuck inside."

I nodded earnestly to the superior plan. I could see Andrew leaning against a wall in his cell, watching us intently. His golden eyes seemed to be glued to my every move. The glass couldn't be that thick, and the door . . . why couldn't he just rip it off like Ehno ripped

241

the door off in the plane? What kind of metal or material were the FBI using for the cells the angels were in? I found it extremely unusual that the angels couldn't just rip the doors off; I'd seen Andrew's muscles first-hand and knew he could do some damage if he wished. Though it should have been the last thing on my mind, I couldn't help thinking about him in action, his muscles rippling with the effort. My face flushed at my thoughts.

I glanced at Karen—wondering if my feelings were easily displayed on my face—who was looking pensively at the door I had entered. My thoughts turned another direction—back to my scheming. Karen had just magically appeared in my house and so had the Elders. Why couldn't they do the same? Suddenly, I became suspicious. Of what or who I wasn't sure, so I didn't voice my internal thoughts, afraid to alert them to my suspicions. There was no time to worry. We'd only been underground for minutes and I was already geared up to get the hell out of there.

"Okay!" I sliced through the silence. "How do we get on the outside and cut the power?"

"That's the tricky part." Karen pulled up a stool and sat. "If we go into the cells then it will look like we are working, but if the angels *leave* their cells then it looks like we are rescuing them."

"What happened to 'Operation Liberate Angels'?" I asked, pursing my lips. It was funny just a few moments ago, but now I just felt disappointed at the lack of a plan. The name had given me hope, and now I had none. "It seems there is no 'operation' to speak of." My voice was bitter, and I immediately felt guilty at the look of reproach Joseph shot me.

The room grew silent then as we all just stared at each other.

My mind was working furiously towards a solution to our predicament, but I didn't know anything about the facility. Palm scanners, key cards . . . who knew what other type of security clearance you would need to get into the more secure places.

I caught Joseph staring at me and was about to ask the questions that were formulating in my head, but as soon as I opened my mouth Ehno spoke up. "We could fight!" he said through the small holes in the glass. When I looked his direction I noticed that his hair was cut much shorter than Andrew's had been. I wondered if Andrew fought with them and they just gave up.

"With four angels we could easily take them out," Ehno continued.

There was a growling noise coming from Andrew's cell and all of our heads snapped his direction. I didn't know a person could make that kind of noise. *Well, he isn't a person now, is he?*

Andrew pushed off the wall he was leaning on and I could see that his jaw was tight with anger. "That is not an option! Gabriella could get hurt."

"It's true," a soft soprano voice came from the farthest cell. Lucia's voice was that of a calming ocean wave; soft and smooth.

"We must protect her above all others. The prophecy speaks of keeping the Illuminator safe. She must be protected at all costs. Fighting is not the answer."

I shot Lucia a grateful look. I didn't think they should fight either, though the reason she gave seemed kind of silly to me. I was worrying about their safety more than mine.

"So that's out of the question," I said.

Joseph sighed and rubbed his eyes with the palm of his hands. "Brute strength isn't going to help us get out. We are going to have to be clever."

"So we manipulate the system," I barely whispered. They all stared at me expectantly. I was the super-genius, after all. So, of course they thought I would have all of the answers—which instantly ticked me off.

"Any ideas?" Joseph prompted when I didn't continue. "Because I think we are all anxious to hear what you think we should do."

Great.

"You two are FBI agents—don't you know more about this place than I do? More about *missions*? I'm just a scientist."

"Gabriella," Karen sighed, "this is a different facility than the one we work in. You were supposed to be flown to D.C. But now, with the angels . . . alive, they decided to not travel any farther than necessary."

"We're all in the same boat," Joseph said. "So, any ideas?"

"Um . . . Anyone recently watched any James Bond movies or Mission Impossible? Could give us some insight," I joked nervously.

Joseph sighed, though his smile was blinding. "That wasn't exactly what I had in mind—"

"Yeah, you all thought that because I am super intelligent I'd have all the answers. Right? Well, I didn't graduate with a degree on escape or take *Getting out of a Secret Government Facility Alive 101*. Maybe if I had detailed plans of the building, more information to go on . . . but I've only been here for a few minutes. My knowledge base of this facility is limited at best."

Joseph's smile vanished and I felt ashamed at my rudeness immediately. I hated that I was here, putting everyone in danger.

There were so many new people in my life and though I'd barely knew them, I'd felt an immediate bond to all of them. It was strange that this was happening all at once. I kept to myself my whole life, pretty content at being alone. The only constants in my life had been school, my job, and my family. Although my adoptive parents sacrificed a lot and always provided for me, we never truly emotionally bonded, but Jenna and my cousin Nicole were always there for me. They were better than any friends I could make at school or work.

"We know it's not up to you," Andrew said behind me. I turned to see his golden eyes. "We are all in this together." He sighed in frustration. "I hate being behind this glass, unable to keep you safe."

In the reflection of the glass I could see Karen's lips twitch, almost as if she were suppressing a smile. It bothered me that she would be suppressing any emotion that resembled contentment.

I sighed, circled around the lab table, and walked toward Andrew's cell. Though I was facing Andrew, watching every smooth stride across the small space, I spoke over my shoulder to the two FBI agents. "Joseph, get me the blueprints to this place or something similar that will give me the layout. Tell them it's about security for the lab or something convincing.

Karen, I need you to write down any and all information about the guards, security and anything else you can think of enlightening me with. Flirt if you have to. It's time to illuminate the Illuminator." I stepped closer to the glass that was keeping my angel and me apart and put my hand against it. "We're getting out of here," I promised.

There was nothing but silence behind me as I continued to watch Andrew. His gold eyes were smoldering into mine. Just one look into his golden depths made me weak in the knees. No one had ever had that kind of effect on me before and more than anything I wanted to be behind that glass. When I turned around to see if they had left, they were both arguing silently to each other and stopped immediately when they saw me looking at them.

"Can I go in there?" I yanked my thumb over my shoulder.

Karen frowned. "It's your lab, Gabriella." I looked at Joseph for confirmation and he nodded silently.

"Well, how do I get in there?" I couldn't see any doors. Maybe the glass just slid away?

"Go on, Karen. I'll keep an eye on Gabriella." Joseph pointed toward the door, just in case she didn't know which way the exit was. I wondered what their small tiff was about, because they both looked pretty upset with the other.

"You are Gabriella's Guardian," Lucia said harshly through the glass cell. "You are not supposed to leave her."

"I told you," I heard Karen say to Joseph under her breath.

"No, Lucia. I'll be fine. What could happen?"

"I'll keep an eye on her," Joseph promised.

Lucia's blue eyes narrowed fiercely for a second.

"Lucia! Really! I'll be fine. I'm about to go into Andrew's cell, anyway." She deflated at my words, though the piercing look she was shooting Karen didn't falter.

"So . . . can you help me into the cell?" I asked, eyebrows raised. Joseph nodded and we both watched Karen turn around, put her palm on the door and slide her key card. The door popped open and she strode out, the door sealing back in place like we were being locked in a large Tupperware container.

Joseph waved in the direction I should walk. I saw a door to our right and walked towards it, his warm hand on my lower back. It was strange how comfortable I felt with him being this close to me.

If it weren't for Andrew, I'd probably fall right into Joseph's capable hands. Tall, dark, and handsome didn't even cover the small glimpse of the personality that I'd seen. I never thought I'd meet anyone like Joseph, and I most definitely never thought I would meet someone like Andrew. Everything had happened so fast! But no matter how generous, kind, and sweet Joseph was, my brain seemed to revert back to the golden-eyed angel that saved my life.

The door opened to a small hallway with five doors to the left. That was actually the first door that I had gone through where I didn't have to go through some kind of security check. "Each door opens into a cell. I'll give you some privacy." He turned around and the door shut behind him.

I breathed in a steadying breath and walked toward the first door, which I knew was Andrew's cell. The door after that was Ehno's and the third was Lucia's. Standing outside Andrew's cell door, I tried to gather my thoughts, but there was no fixing that disaster. His door, though, did have security. After the appropriate checks, the door popped open like it was sighing in relief. There was a tanned arm that reached out and snatched me up. Andrew hugged me to his chest and I comfortably put all my weight on him. He didn't seem to mind. The thought of cameras, glass walls, or people watching our exchange completely slipped my mind. I didn't want to pull away from his warm embrace but we needed to talk. He didn't object, but still held me close to his face, his eyes searching mine. He closed his eyes and put his forehead against mine.

"I can't figure it out," his hot breath filled the air between us.

"What?"

His eyes opened. "This . . . *connection* we have."

I nodded in understanding, our faces still only inches apart. As his words sunk in, the electricity flowed through me in rough, hot waves and my hands, which were on Andrew's forearms, gripped him tighter with the shock. All I could think about was how wonderful it felt to be this close to him. He didn't shy away from the electricity, but only pulled me into another bone crunching hug.

"I never thought I would feel this way again," he whispered. "Especially for a human."

There it was again, the reminder that I couldn't have him—that I'd age and die. There was a warmth growing in my cheeks because I had a feeling he'd probably heard my thoughts through my touch. Now I wasn't so sure if I liked this gift of mine.

"Andrew?"

"Hum?"

"Why can't you get out of this cell?" I barely whispered into his chest.

"I . . ." Andrew pulled me from his embrace to just

an arm's length away, his fingers around my wrists. "I don't know why, but this place weakens me. Ehno is having the same problem, as surely as Lucia is. I have a bad feeling about this place. The sooner we get out of here, the better."

"Does that mean you have a plan?"

"No," he sighed. "But when you find the blue-prints, bring them to me. We'll figure something out."

"I'll do that," I answered confidently. We definitely needed someone else on our side. After watching him in the library, I was sure he would be able to spot the best avenue of attack—or escape. Preferably escape.

His fingers traced under my eyes. "My sweet, you're in need of sleep." My stomach did a somersault at being called "my sweet."

My experience with men was slim to none, and it probably showed. "Not yet. I will soon, though. I promise."

"Go on. I'll be here." His lips twitched a little at his words. He kissed my forehead. That was the second time he had done that and it surprised me just as much as before. There was a small spark that lit between us and I was sure that I just blushed a deep shade of red for the millionth time today.

the sight

My pen was tapping the paper as I slouched over in my chair across from Ehno, inside his cell. He was perched at the edge of his cot in his cell, his back ram rod straight. The white scrubs the FBI had made them change into made his red eyes even more shocking. They were like an albino's, which contrasted dismally against his now short blonde hair that used to reach past his shoulders. You would think that this being was wicked, but he wasn't. He was otherworldly, no doubt, but he was divine, too.

The line of his jaw twitched. "I cannot remember," he stated. He cocked his head to the side as if he were listening to something. "Andrew cannot either."

Their strange way of communicating might come in handy later, I thought out of nowhere.

Ehno continued, oblivious to my thoughts, "We have both been trying. It is as if the last moments of our life have been wiped away. There really is no time frame I could compare it to."

I sighed and looked back down at my paper which was blank. "Ehno, I'm going to get you out of here. I promise." I looked back up at him, pleading with my eyes. He gave me a sharp nod. "Tell me about your psychic ability?"

He raised a perfectly arched eyebrow at me. "I wouldn't call myself psychic."

"Oh," I said intelligently. "What would you call it, then?"

"I'm intuitive." His rigid posture relaxed some and he leaned towards me. "You are the Illuminator. You have the power to get us out of these cells. I've seen it."

My head did a nose dive right into my palms. "I'm sorry! I don't know how to do it," I growled, frustrated.

I felt his warm hand on my shoulder. "I know it's hard—you don't know how to control your power right now, but we *will* teach you." When I didn't look up I heard him take a deep breath and sigh. "Do you trust us?"

"What?" I looked up to his strikingly red eyes.

"Do you trust us?" he repeated.

"With my life."

"Then listen to me. We will teach you what you need to know." His face was serious, though I could see his lips twitching as if they were itching to spread into a wide grin. "Andrew has taken a particular liking to you." He finally smirked; the look really suited him, much better than his previous rigid posture.

"Really?" I was curious. Was I like a little sister? A good friend? Who knew? I was hopeless—condemned to heartbreak.

"Gabriella, you don't see what you truly are." His posture was back to the firm position it was before. The more relaxed Ehno disappeared as quickly as he had emerged.

Reflexively, I looked out through the glass to see Joseph leaning over at a desk, his cup of coffee only inches away. His eyes were closed and I could tell he had slipped into a somewhat uncomfortable sleeping position. He looked so peaceful.

When I looked back at Ehno he hadn't moved an inch. "I'm just a human who happened across an ancient race of angels," I said cynically.

"You're wrong," he disputed smoothly. "You're more than that. So much more . . ." he trailed off in thought.

"How's that?" I challenged, hoping to get more information. He didn't respond. He only looked at me with a curious gleam in his eye. I looked back down at my blank paper. "Ehno, people are watching. I have to act the part—"

"I know," he cut me off. Of course, he must have known what I was going to do next. "You won't hurt me," he promised.

Turning in my chair, I reached for my supplies. I was going to draw blood. After snapping my latex gloves on, I reached for the alcohol swabs and tourniquet. He automatically placed his left arm out for me and I wrapped the tourniquet above his elbow and watched as the vein swelled. I patted it a few times before finding the best angle to draw the blood. I was extremely nervous. From my training I knew that I needed to insert the needle as smoothly and as swiftly as possible to prevent pain. I'd done this a million times before but this time I faltered, unsure if I could truly continue with this façade. Was I really going to do experiments on these angels until I came up with a way to release them? *Or*, I added in my head, *a plan of escape*.

Ehno noticed my hesitation and tried to smile at me, reassuring. "You won't hurt me," he repeated. "It's okay."

With a smooth calculation, I inserted the needle. He didn't even flinch, so I felt some relief. I added the blood specimen tube into the holder while keeping the needle as firm as my anxious hands would allow, and watched as the tube started to fill with blood. I gasped and pulled the tube out before extracting the needle from his arm. It looked as though I had sucked molten gold from his veins. My eyes studied the rich color for several seconds as a dream came rushing back to me. Two white angels attacking . . . tripping over a body . . . *golden blood.* I thought any second that I would get sick so I leaned over, putting my head between my legs and breathed in deep breath after deep breath, trying to stabilize my frantic heart and quick intakes of air.

In a flash—literally—Ehno was at my side, his hand on my shoulder again. He seemed to not know what to do to comfort me. "What's wrong?" he asked, concern laced into his words. I didn't answer.

And that was when it happened.

I snapped, completely.

Tears burst from my eyes and I tried to wipe them away furiously, ashamed at my behavior. I was usually calm and collected. It had been a really *long* day. Instead of the sobs lessening they seemed to double and intensify until Ehno was no longer at my side, but banging on the glass. *What was he doing?* I didn't know or care. Tears continued to spill onto the floor and suddenly someone was yanking me from the chair and into their arms. The scent was familiar. *Joseph.* He stroked my hair and wiped the tears from my cheeks, mumbling nothing coherent but it was soothing, nonetheless.

When I looked up to apologize to Ehno he had

an expression on his face that I couldn't quite place. It was somewhere between apprehension, concern and discomfort. "It's just been a lot to take in," I tried to explain. There just weren't any words that would express exactly how I was feeling.

He was pinching the bridge of his nose, as if he had a headache, before he noticed me. "I'm sorry, Gabriella. Andrew's sending me *maddening* thoughts in a stream of *constant* shouting, figuratively." He sighed heavily, as if struggling internally.

Joseph helped me back into my chair and sat next to me, holding my hand firmly, yet tenderly, in his own. It was comforting to feel his pulse against my skin. He was alive because of these angels. Instantly, I was grateful all over again. Ehno's normal charade was gone and he was soon next to me on one knee. "You've seen our golden blood before, haven't you?"

I nodded slowly. "In a dream."

In a movement of inhuman speed he was standing, pacing back and forth in the confined space. "*I knew it*," he said between his teeth, muttering other incoherent words. He began rubbing his chin in irritation. "Someone has given her the sight," he muttered, obviously to himself or to Andrew.

"The sight?"

He pinched the bridge of his nose again. "Sometimes I forget you have not been around all these years."—not like he had been around all of these years—"The sight is something an angel can inflict upon another angel to see their past—like their memories are implanted in your head. Some angels were forced to give up their memories for disciplinary action when they broke our laws. It's true, raw, evidence."

I didn't like the word *inflict* one bit.

"You first start to see glimpses in your dreams. They can be confusing—your thoughts mixed with the angel's. As time goes on you will revisit past events that have happened to the angel who has given you the sight. It might feel so real to you that you don't realize you aren't actually there." He turned once he had paced to the end of the small cell and started walking back again, a fierce look piercing his eyes. I might have seen them glow. "It's forbidden to do this to a human," he growled.

"Can they take it back?" I barely whispered.

"Yes, but if the angel who did this to you doesn't reverse it—*and soon*—things could get dire and fast." He stopped his pacing and his jaw tightened. "I know, Andrew," he answered tersely, out loud this time. The mental argument must have become explosive for Ehno to lose his calm composure.

"What is it?" *Could I take any more bad news?*

He shook his head. "Why would someone do this?" he muttered to himself. He started his pacing again.

Joseph had remained silent by my side, my hand still in his. Surprisingly, there was no electric current. Was I controlling it, after all? I knew that he might think our skin pressed together like that meant more than comfort, but honestly, I needed that support. Joseph was wonderful, but it was Andrew with whom I wanted to be.

As if he knew I was staring at him, he leaned over to me. "We are beginning to act suspicious. We need to leave his cell. If anyone asks what happened in here you tell them that you were exhausted and fainted. Do you understand?" Could my out-burst of remorse really be explained by "fainting"?

Ehno had stopped his pacing and stared down at us.

"I understand." My eyes roamed up the white scrubs to the red eyes gazing at me. "Please, forgive me."

Ehno sighed in utter exasperation. "There is nothing to forgive you for. You need sleep; you're exhausted."

"Thank you, Ehno. Like I told you before, I will get you out of here."

"It's hard to tell . . ."

Psychics! I wanted to say. Instead, I nodded.

"Gabriella?" Joseph said, providing his hand for support. "It's true. It's late and you need rest if we are going to make plans to get these angels out of here."

"Goodnight, Ehno," I whispered.

Joseph placed his hand on the hand print reader for the door to open and then slid his key across the lock. As the seal broke, Ehno spoke up, "Gabriella?"

I turned around. "Yes?"

"Have I been in any of your dreams?"

"No, but Andrew and Lucia have."

He was silent then, so I turned back around to leave. Joseph was waiting patiently in the door frame.

"Joseph? Don't let her sleep alone," Ehno barely murmured. Goose bumps ran up my arms and down my back. I didn't look back as I walked past Joseph who only nodded toward Ehno.

The lab was quiet and our footsteps echoed loudly in the extremely bright room. Expensive equipment was covered with protective covers and the steel of lab tables gleamed in the fluorescent lights. There was a desk with several cups of coffee on it, where Joseph was previously sleeping.

"Would you want to . . ." Joseph trailed off while pointing toward the door. I knew he was offering a place to sleep.

"No—no. That's okay," I protested, sitting down at the desk. He raised his eyebrows. "I'm going to stay here and analyze Ehno's blood work before this place starts to crowd in the morning," I clarified.

He looked at his watch. "You know that is in less than two hours?"

I nodded. "I know, but I don't want the others to see this."

He sighed and leaned over the desk. "When was the last time you slept—and I mean *really* slept?"

Right now, sleep was the last thing on my mind. "It's been a while—but Joseph, it doesn't matter. Getting them out of here is what is important now!" I pointed toward the thick glassed cells.

"How are you supposed to be your best if you are exhausted? You could make mistakes, and they will suffer for it," he countered.

"Touché."

"I'm going to take Ehno's warning seriously," he said sincerely, ignoring my attempt at joking. "The Paranormal Investigations sector hasn't quite set up a room for you yet. Of course, I have a room at most of these types of facilities. Plus, the FBI were thinking that you would be staying in D.C. instead of our Nevada branch—"

"We're in Nevada?" I asked, surprised.

He smirked. "Yeah. I guess the tinted glass did its job."

"My mind was elsewhere," I mumbled. *Wasn't that the truth?*

"That doesn't matter. What matters now is that you get some rest. You can stay at my place, I'll take the couch."

"Okay, but I'm going to finish this blood work first. If you want to come back here in"—I looked at my wristwatch—"one hour, I'll be ready to go to bed, if not, I'll make myself comfortable on one of the opened cell's cots."

"Don't be ridiculous!" Joseph scoffed. "Of course I'll come back. I'm not going to make you sleep in a cell where your coworkers will see you when they arrive to work in the morning."

"Thanks," I said. "Now go relax some while I finish this up."

"Okay, I'll be back here in one hour and you're coming with me whether you like it or not."

"Yes sir!" I snapped to attention like a soldier.

He rolled his eyes and left the lab.

The silence was oddly peaceful and creepy all at the same time. What Joseph didn't know was that I didn't plan on doing any lab work whatsoever on

Ehno's blood. And neither was anyone else. I pocketed the tube with the golden liquid and rose from my seat.

Lucia was staring at me through the glass of her cell. She had on a pair of white scrubs identical to Ehno's. Regardless of the shapeless outfit, she was still overwhelmingly breathtaking. I walked over to the glass, put my hand on it, and sighed. "Lucia?"

She walked over to the glass and placed her hand where mine was. "You'll know what to do." Her voice was a perfect soprano.

"I'll do whatever I can to keep you safe," I said pointedly.

She smiled, though it didn't reach her eyes. "I know you will."

The perfect memory of my dream came flooding back to me. Now that I knew these images were of the past, I wondered what exactly happened to her. Whatever it was, I was determined to find out.

She removed her hand from the glass, sat on the cot, and pulled her long auburn hair into a tight knot before lying down. "Goodnight Miss Illuminator."

Stupid nickname.

Sighing, I stepped away from the glass. I didn't know Lucia and she didn't know me, but there was some bond linking us. I could feel it deep in my soul. As I watched the knife plummet through the air and strike her in my dream, I knew there was a reason why I saw that particular scene—and now I was going to find out. Whatever the hell this "sight" business was, I had an odd feeling it wasn't about someone trying to hurt me, but someone desperately trying to give me the truth without being caught. Who was this mysterious person trying to warn me?

As I walked past Ehno's cell, I noticed that he was sleeping soundly already. He looked peaceful again, just as he did the first time I saw him in his coffin prison. And in the last cell I passed, there was Andrew, in all his beautiful glory. Though I felt connected with all three of the angels—more than Karen, even—there was just something undeniable between Andrew and I. Ever since he flew me from the plane, I knew I was meant to be with him. And I hated that feeling because we *couldn't* be together. Hell, he might not feel the same about me, anyway. The immortal-falls-in-love-with-a-mortal story has been around for ages. What those stories seem to fail at explaining is that only one of them is able to live forever while the other ages, withers, and dies. I'd be the one dying in this one—not the happiest of thoughts.

Andrew's eyes never left mine as I slid down the wall beside the glass. He sat on the floor opposite me and put his forehead against the glass where there were small holes for communicating. "Gabriella—"

"Don't, Andrew. Please. I know you didn't want to do this and I'm sorry." The guilt was really starting to settle in when his fingers started playing with the holes in the glass. "I just need to know you can forgive me for getting us into this situation."

"I wasn't worried about me when I disagreed with us being captured," he explained, unabashed. "There's this pull . . ." I heard him say through the tiny holes. "It's like I can't get close enough to you. I have this overwhelming instinct to protect you and keep you safe." He was staring down at his hands as he said this and then looked up into my eyes. "I honestly don't know what I'd do if you were to die. If anyone hurts you—" his fists clenched tightly.

"Andrew," I barely whispered. "We can't . . ." *be together*, I finished in my head.

He nodded, understanding what I meant.

"You're immortal and I'm . . . not."

He looked down at his hands again. "That Joseph really cares about you," he noted.

"That's funny," I muttered. "I've never been able to find a man who really cared about *me* instead of . . ." I trailed off. I wasn't sure if Andrew got it. He nodded like he did, so I continued. "Now I've got you and Joseph—who both just want the best for me—

all within forty-eight hours." I knew I was probably blushing brilliantly at this point at his declaration and my need to ramble on about more information than is necessary.

"You're important and you're special. We're no fools," Andrew murmured and then sighed. I noticed he didn't deny my words. The heat in my cheeks intensified. "You really *do* need to get some rest. When you were sleeping in my arms . . . it wasn't peaceful."

"What did I say?"

"You didn't say anything. But you cried and shivered and clung to me like you were falling from the sky. Ehno's right."

"About?"

"You should not sleep alone. Those dreams are only going to become more vivid. You need someone to anchor you—to keep you grounded." His fists clenched again. "Since I can't do it, you need Joseph to help."

I frowned deeply. "He offered to let me sleep at his place, he'll take the couch."

The line of Andrew's jaw tightened, turning into a straight and severe line. "That's not good enough, and though it kills me to say it, you need to be close to him. I've seen what these dreams can do to someone. Immortals can handle it, but you are human. If you act out anything you are witnessing, you could kill your-self."

"Oh." I didn't realize it was that bad . . .

The look on Andrew's face was so tortured that I wanted to break through the glass to comfort him. Angels should not have to endure the heartache that was evident on his face. Did he look this way because he knew how close Joseph would be to me tonight? Could he be jealous? Ehno *did* say that Andrew had taken a liking to me, *but why*? I was just human. Or was it the thought of me possibly killing myself while dreaming that had him so heartbroken?

"Please," he begged, "I couldn't live without you."

I didn't quite understand where his intense feel-ings were coming from, and I most definitely didn't understand where my own mutual feelings were from, either. Imagining a world without Andrew . . . well, that wasn't a world I'd want to live in.

I was in love. It seemed stupid to deny it at this point. I didn't realize it would happen so suddenly. I put my head back and it hit the wall with a slight thud.

Ugh, why did I have to fall in love with an angel?

19

prophecy

My eyes were firmly shut. The chilly night air was softly blowing over my skin, as was usual for November in Italy. I just couldn't sleep in this confused haze. Not here, not now. The ground was too hard, and I just knew that I needed to be somewhere. There was something important I was supposed to be doing. What was it?

"Abelie?"

The haze disappeared.

My eyes snapped open. The sky was dark, though the stars could be seen like tiny beacons. *This* was *where I needed to be*, I realized.

My hearing was great and his footsteps—no matter how hard he tried—were easily heard behind me.

"Abelie? Where are you?" He knew where I was—hiding behind a large boulder.

"*Shh*! Keep your voice down, Aiden."

I turned when I knew he was going to attack. His arms wrapped around my body, sending warmth through my skin. His eyes were on fire, and I'd like to think they were on fire for me. His skin was dark and

his appearance was one we were told to fear—but I did not. Our lips met and the heat seemed to intensify until we were both out of breath. Still, our lips continued to mold together out of fiery passion. He was my love—he was my life.

He was forbidden.

When our lips parted he smiled, pulled me into his arms, and spun me around wildly. "Abelie! I missed you so much!"

"How much?" I murmured.

His lips slammed into mine again. It seemed like we never had time to see each other anymore. It was so wonderful to be in his arms again. I hated lying to everyone, letting them think that I was at the Divine Library—where I was *supposed* to be.

"Aiden?" I mumbled, our lips still together.

"Yes, love?"

"We have to go to the library tonight."

He groaned in my mouth and pulled away. "That place is so dusty and smelly. Completely unromantic."

"I think we could find something romantic to do in there," I purred, and brought his mouth back to mine.

He snatched me up into his arms and took off toward the library. We were lucky that Camellia had already unlocked the door—all we needed was my key to gain access. Immortals weren't allowed in the

Divine Library without both keys. Two keys were always required. And honestly, I didn't know why she wanted me to be there this evening, anyway. It was late and usually there was a motive to be at the library. As an Elder, it was my job to protect knowledge, but I didn't understand why tonight I was commanded to come here without *any* reason.

He raced up the stone steps to the library, though my mind didn't comprehend when we were finally inside. My thoughts were too focused on Aiden and our lips firmly placed together. It had been weeks since I'd been able to see him and now he was in my arms. Our bodies molded together like two pieces of clay. Our passion could have been felt for miles as we danced between the book shelves, completely oblivious to the towering books around us. Aiden had picked me up and held me to his chest as I wrapped my legs around his torso. We slammed into objects and many things rained down around us. Still, I didn't care. I was too wrapped up in the moment—Aiden finally in my arms. He began kissing down my neck, all the way to my collar bone. It was pure bliss. He slammed me against a wall and books came clattering down. I didn't care. Neither did he.

Things were growing intense between us. I practically tore his shirt off his body, which was blackened like charcoal. I didn't care if he was forbidden—I had to have him. His hands slammed down on either side of my head and fire sprang from his finger tips. I gasped in his arms and pulled him closer to me, thrilled at his enthusiasm. He spun me around and threw everything off a nearby table. I could hear glass crashing and books thudding as they hit the ground. He threw me onto the table and began sending a trail of kisses down my neck again. I was in heaven.

"Abelie," he moaned under his breath against my skin. He yanked my small, white robe off and threw it to the floor. I was exposed. The way his eyes roamed over my body made me blush. He was staring at me like he couldn't get enough. He pulled my long brown hair away from my shoulder and started kissing down, down, down until he reached my navel. I was about to explode. But his light kisses on my exposed stomach brought me back to reality.

"Aiden," I said, out of breath. "Wait. Stop."

His eyes shot up to mine, the fire blazing fiercer than before. "Is there something wrong, love?" He straightened, looking concerned.

I sat up on the table and began crying. I didn't mean to be so emotional, but it seemed like everything made me cry now-a-days. He wrapped his charcoal arms around me, mumbling that it would be okay. He

271

didn't know what was wrong with me—if he did, he'd know things were *not* okay. Far from it. I was with child, an impossibility with our kind. It was either a miracle, or a curse. I was about to tell him about the baby growing inside me when we heard voices. He threw my robe toward me, yanked me into his arms and we hid behind a bookcase. My back was against the old musty bindings, Aiden's chest firmly holding me there. His breath was hot in my hair.

"*Shh*," he whispered.

"Aiden," I choked out, "if they find you here, they will cast you out. They think you're *evil*." Right now, I hated the immortals. *Angels*, as they liked to call themselves. They were far from it.

"No baby, I'll be fine," he breathed in my ear, soothing me.

"I love you." The tears rolled down my cheeks and I hated for him to see me like this, but if anyone were to find us, he'd be sent away, so far that I couldn't get to him myself.

There were footsteps echoing through the cave-like library. Voices followed in low-hushed whispers. Immediately, I recognized the voices. "Oh, no!" My fingers clawed into Aiden's blackened skin. His eyes roamed over my frightened expression and he pulled my face into his hands and put his forehead against mine.

We were silent then, trying not to give ourselves away. The Ladies of Light were circling around the building, their footsteps growing louder. They were probably checking to see if anyone was listening. My grip tightened on him when the footsteps came frighteningly close. He pulled me into his hard chest—his heartbeat tattooed against my skin and I knew he was just as tense about our predicament as I was.

"The place is clear, Mimi. The doors were locked and it is late," I heard Liz say. I was thankful that Aiden remembered to do that, because I hadn't.

Was this why Camellia wanted me to be here? To witness their meeting? It was all incredibly confusing because Camellia was a Lady of Light, and I had yet to hear her voice. Were they meeting without her? Suspicion rolled off me in waves and I was sure Aiden could feel my muscles tense. He was holding my head against his chest, lightly pulling his fingers through my long, brown hair—soothing me.

"Good," Mimi replied. Her voice was stiff. "Because it's time."

There were three sets of footsteps, though the only voices I heard were Liz and Mimi's. I wondered briefly if Camellia was the third party.

"Zola's prophecy?" Liz asked nervously.

I'd read the prophecy and remembered it perfectly. It spoke of the Darkness Illuminator, and about how she would show us who the enemies are and how to defeat them. The name "Darkness Illuminator," and Zola's cryptic words, implied that Shadows were our enemy. Immediately, I didn't like this meeting. How could anyone believe that the Shadow of the Sun were evil when one of them could love me as deeply and passionately as Aiden? Did Camellia know about Aiden? Was this her way of warning me that there was trouble afoot?

"But there have been no signs of the prophecy coming to light," Liz argued. I could only guess that Mimi had indicated that Zola's prophecy was *exactly* what they were talking about.

"The assassin has been chosen," Mimi countered.

"And this is?"

"The Soul Stalker. She will find and kill the Darkness Illuminator. She'll be using the pseudonym Karen."

I gasped and Aiden placed a hand over my mouth. They didn't notice the sound.

"And what about the other angels? Don't they remember?" Liz wondered.

"The Soul Stalker has been thought to be dead for more than three thousand years. The Elders have had their minds altered—they won't suspect the lie."

When I heard the name, I almost couldn't believe it. The Soul Stalker had been forced out of society thousands of years ago for her ruthless behavior. Everyone knew the stories of the Soul Stalker's brothers, and many people believed her to be the enforcer of their actions, even after her death. It was rumored that she influenced them to act like fools and to speak lies to humans. We were not the celestial attendants to God, as they liked to tell humans.

Before Soul Stalker's downfall, she would stalk humans and torture them—without ever touching them—by manipulating their feelings. "Empath," they called it—she had *no* empathy. No one knew why she acted the way she did, but it wasn't long before she was nicknamed "Soul Stalker" because she was believed to be devoid of a soul—constantly stalking those who possessed the one thing that she couldn't. It was common knowledge that she was defeated three-thousand years ago. And now—here in the Divine Library—the Soul Stalker and the Ladies of Light were planning on killing the one person who could bring us our salvation.

There was loud shouting all around me. My mind was in a fog and my eyes were securely closed. Through the thin skin of my eyelids, I could see lights flashing. There was the sound of glass cracking on my right. I was too tired to find out what was going on and soon I was drifting back toward sleep . . . back to that strange dream . . .

The door shut with a loud grating noise. Aiden refused to let me go. "Abelie, we're safe, everything is okay."

But everything wasn't okay. They were going to kill an innocent girl—the Darkness Illuminator. Though I feared that she would destroy the Shadow of the Sun, and ultimately Aiden, I knew she wasn't evil, she couldn't be. This must be what Camellia wanted me to hear, but *why*?

Aiden reached for my hand and led me out from behind the bookcase where we had been frozen for thirty minutes. As we rounded on the table that the Ladies of Light had just vacated, I noticed a book that I had never seen before. It was opened and the pages looked yellow, old and worn. It wasn't surprising to see an old book in the Divine Library but I felt compelled to read it. I bowed over the book and read swiftly across the page.

The Darkness Illuminator will

be born during the lightest day
of the year when the Ladies of
Light will kill one of their own.
The Illuminator's mother will be
of the Light of Heaven and her
father will be a Shadow of the
Sun. Angel guards and Shadow barriers will not hold her back;
as she will have access to both
sides of the realm. Until the
Shadow's approach, protect her
above all others, even from our
kind.

Even from our kind . . .

I quit reading.

This was different. Before, there had never been any mention of where the Darkness Illuminator would originate from, or who her parents would be. For some reason I always thought it was just another immortal. This was *not* the same prophecy immortals had been reading all these years. My hand automatically touched my stomach where I knew a baby was forming. A child created by an angel—or Light of Heaven—and a Shadow of the Sun. It all made sense now. I felt weak and then there was nothing but blackness.

The lights flashed through my eyelids again.

"Joseph"—I heard Andrew say—"wake her up!

277

Now!"

"Gabriella? Please! Wake up!" My shoulders shook slightly and I could feel fingers over my cheeks and forehead. "Andrew, she isn't coming to."

Images came flooding back to me—a dream trying to be remembered. A library, a Shadow with *compassion* . . . the Ladies of Light . . . *Soul Stalker*. Anger flared and electricity shot through me in hot waves, more violent and dangerous than ever before.

"Ouch!" Joseph exclaimed. "Andrew, I can't help her when she uses her ability."

"Put something between your skin and hers," Andrew demanded through his glass cell.

My eyes snapped open. I was finally regaining control of myself. Everything seemed fuzzy, dizzy . . . faint. My mind had never felt so confused and clear all at the same time. Oxymorons were becoming part of my life.

Ignoring Andrew's demand, Joseph loomed over my head. "Gabriella? Are you all right?"

"Why do people keep asking me that?" I said faintly. I could hear a nervous chuckle through the glass wall and looked over to see that the glass was cracked down the middle as if someone had been trying to kick through it. Everything was cast in a bluish tint and yellow lights were continuing to flash in my vision. "What happened?"

"You fell asleep," Andrew explained. "Your dream must have been wild because you started shooting lightning bolts. It was intense for some time. I tried to call for you—wake you. Even Ehno and Lucia were trying to find some way to reach you. The electricity shut off and lights have been flashing since then—a warning, I suppose. It took Joseph fifteen minutes to *finally* get the door open."

My eyes shot to the door where it looked blackened as if it were on fire at one time. *Did I do that?* I looked down at my hands and could see bruises covering my arms. "What did I do?" I asked quietly.

"I don't know," Joseph looked behind him at the door. "But you blasted that thing open for me."

"Oh."

"You were acting out your dream," Ehno spoke through the little holes in the glass. "What was it about?"

I stood up and realized that my body ached everywhere. Emergency lights were lighting Joseph's face and I could see the concern obvious in his eyes. Tears descended my face and Andrew gasped in shock. I didn't know why, I was too busy reeling in the information from my dream. Joseph pulled me into a tight embrace. Over his shoulder, I said, "My parents."

 the clock is ticking

They were all gaping at me. Joseph's mouth was ajar while Andrew's eyes burned into mine, the color of melted treasure. His expression was one I couldn't place. Astonishment? Shock? Disbelief? Ehno and Lucia had their faces practically plastered to the glass walls, their expressions just as unreadable. The emergency lights barely lit the lab and the flashing yellow lights made the whole scene look surreal—dream-like. But this was *reality*.

Andrew opened his mouth as if to speak, but then closed it after a few seconds of silence. That was okay. I was still trying to comprehend everything that happened in my dream. I felt a little faint and sat on a stool at a table, leaning over the countertop for support. As the tears slid down my face, they dropped on the stainless steel lab table before me. If I thought my level of bewilderment was reached, I was incredibly wrong. The two small droplets were like tiny beads of hot gold. Immediately, I began brushing at my face, wiping the tears from my eyes. When I looked down at my fingers they were wet with golden tears. Gold? Why were they gold? This was a first. I turned back to the angels.

"Wha— what . . ." I stuttered.

"You're an angel," Andrew whispered in awe.

"I'm a . . ." I trailed off. Images of my dream came slamming back into my consciousness. Bam, bam, bam. One by one; Abelie, Aiden, the Divine Library, the Ladies of Light, the Soul Stalker, the prophecy . . . *the prophecy.* "I'm a hybrid," I realized aloud. Suddenly, I looked over my skin to check for the charcoal color of a Shadow. There were only bruises, most of them already turning a faint yellow color. If I had a mirror I would have searched my eyes for the fire blazing behind them.

This is too much. All too much! I couldn't handle this. I gripped the table for support as the room swayed at a funny angle. Was the table always tilted sideways or was I leaning that way? Each passing second felt weirdly sluggish as everything seemed to shift sideways.

"She's going down! Catch her!" shouted Andrew.

Before my body fell into unconsciousness, I could see the ground swirling up toward my face. Then everything was black.

Warm fingers were on my face. "Please wake up," murmured a soft tenor voice. "Gabriella . . . please."

Without opening my eyes, I asked, "Did I faint?"

"Thank you," whispered a voice. "Yes, you fainted. How do you feel?"

I blinked, the lights hadn't returned and Joseph's face was cast in shadows. "I feel . . . well, I'm not sure if there is a single word in any language that could describe how I feel."

He let out a breath of relief. "I was so worried."

"We all were," barked Andrew.

I sat up, a little too quickly. My head felt like it was swimming in an ocean. "Is the Sou—Karen here?"

"No," several people answered at once.

"Thank god!" I sighed and leaned against the bottom of the lab table. Andrew raised his eyebrows at my reaction. "She cannot be trusted," I explained simply.

"I don't understand," Lucia said from the farthest cell to my left. "She's your Guardian; *of course* you can trust her."

Ignoring her words, I looked straight at Ehno whose eyebrows had come so close together that they almost made one single severe line. "I know who gave me the sight . . . and now I know why."

"Who?" he asked.

"My mother."

"What?" exclaimed Ehno.

"Your mother?!" Andrew bellowed.

Lucia stared at me in complete disbelief. "Angels don't have children . . ."

"Maybe you knew her?" I shrugged. "Abelie."

My words were met with silence.

I tried to get to my feet, to move closer to the angels in their darkened cells. Joseph held out a hand to help me up. Once I was standing, I moved toward the glass cells which were reflecting the yellow flashing lights. "Do you?" I asked. "Know her, I mean."

"She's an Elder," whispered Lucia.

"We all knew her," Andrew finally said. "She was the librarian at the Divine Library."

There were too many things going through my head, too many aspects of my dream that they needed to know, but all I could do was stare at them. I'd finally found my mother, so to speak. "What was she like?" My fingers came in contact with the glass of Andrew's cell. The glass vibrated as electricity shot through me. A small crack formed beneath my finger tips and began a spider-web effect through the glass until it touched all four corners. Then the glass wall crumbled to the ground in tiny little pieces as they all scattered every direction. Instead of jumping back in shock, I stepped over the pile of reflective crystal, glad the barrier was finally gone—and so were the camera's intrusive eyes because there was no power. I felt relieved at once.

Words weren't necessary. I fell into Andrews arms.

"She is beautiful, like you," he said while stroking my hair. "She has the kindest heart of any angel I ever knew. But I am confused as to why you think you are a hybrid. Abelie was deeply in love with her *angel* husband, Aiden. If she's your mother—*an impossibility,* I might add—then you would be an angel . . . you *are* an angel . . ." his voice lowered to a whisper until it trailed off.

His words surprised me. I didn't want to pull away, but that was what I did—quickly—jerking my way free. "*What?* But that doesn't—in my dream he *wasn't* an angel."

From the cell next to Andrew's, I could hear Ehno's noises of impatience before he spoke. "Maybe you could use your powers to let us out, too. I know you can. I can see it."

Andrew nodded at me.

"Yeah. I suppose I could try, right?" I stepped over the fragments of glass. Joseph still hadn't said a word; he just continued to look at me as if he were seeing me for the first time.

As I turned to go toward the glass, I could see Ehno's almost excited expression. I sighed and shook my hands a little before placing them on the glass. I noticed that there were no bruises on my arms anymore and gasped, startled. At the same, time electricity shot through me so fast and violent the glass didn't just crack and crumble to the ground, it exploded. Joseph dived behind a lab table. Ehno, red eyes wide, smirked. I bit my bottom lip, unsure of what to say. He stepped over the pile of shards before tracing a spot on my arm. I looked down to see small droplets of golden blood escaping a deep gash, a piece of glass sticking out. Speechless, I yanked the glass free and watched as my skin grew back together, leaving the golden droplet on my arm. My heart beat rapidly as I saw this. When I was younger I had skinned my knees up, I was in a car accident once and every time my blood was red, *not* gold!

What does it all mean? I thought, flabbergasted.

"It's true then? You really *are* an angel," Ehno breathed in wonder. "You'll become very powerful." He nodded at some thought.

I wasn't sure if that was a statement or his psychic ability. When I turned around I almost ran right into Andrew who was staring over my shoulder at Ehno. It seemed like they were having a silent conversation.

"Hurry," Andrew said to me then looked back at Ehno. "While the power is out, we might be able to break free of this place. Ehno can't quite see the outcome yet."

Behind Andrew, Joseph was staring at us, his eyes as big as silver dollars. It was now or never; I rushed over to Lucia's cell and didn't hesitate as I put my fingers on the glass.

Nothing happened.

Ehno and Andrew were standing on either side of me. "What's wrong?" Andrew asked.

I stared at our reflections in the glass. They were waiting for me to free her—to break the glass as I did before. This power was still new to me, and I wasn't quite sure how to control it. I tried to will the electricity to come. Again, nothing. When I thought about it, I realized that the previous two times electricity had exploded from me was when I was feeling an overwhelming emotion. In my attempts, I was getting a little frustrated, but that emotion was not strong enough to wield any results. I tried to think about my dream, but nothing happened.

"There's no electricity," I said angrily.

Andrew and Ehno started having another one of their silent conversations, I could tell just by the changing expressions on both of their faces.

"The clock is ticking," Andrew stated. I turned around and stared between the two, waiting with much impatience at their silence.

All of a sudden, Ehno's eyebrows shot up. "That might work!"

I exhaled a deep breath, ready to demand to hear what they were saying to each other in their heads. "What might work?"

Both of their eyes snapped down to me before they looked back at each other knowingly. I opened my mouth to demand more information when Andrew's face descended to mine until he was only an inch away. He took me completely by surprise. I began breathing heavily at the feeling of his face being so close to mine.

What was he doing?

His rich, warm scent swirled between us. My back was pressed against the glass wall. He hesitated so close to my lips I thought I was going to explode with anticipation. We stood like that for several *long— too* long—seconds. Butterflies assaulted my stomach and sent a wave of bliss rushing through my throbbing veins—my veins that were now full of golden blood. *You really are an angel*, Ehno's words repeated in my head.

I closed my eyes and Andrew finally closed the distance, his hands on the glass beside my head, trapping me. I didn't care. His lips were warm and soft against mine as I responded to his mouth. The taste of him was much better than I could have ever imagined. He was like honey. Desire raced in my veins; desire for him, his body, his lips against mine. Each time he moved his mouth away, I brought his lips back with my own. Everything around me melted away—there was only us. And in that moment, I knew that he was *my* angel. And would always be *my* angel. I would refuse to give this up—to give him up.

A strange, new and exciting sensation rippled down my spine. Electricity began building inside me. I could feel it gathering at my core, growing hotter. Andrew pressed his body against mine, pressing me firmly against the glass. His body was hard and sexy as hell. And though everyone was here to witness this very intimate moment, I didn't care. All my worries seemed to vanish. I was melting in his capable hands as his fingers roamed over my cheeks and got lost in my hair. As I was reaching toward his face I could hear the electricity crackling between my fingers and quickly put my hands behind me. Andrew's hands went to my back and grabbed my hands. Before I knew what he was doing, he was pressing my palms flat against the glass and pushing into me even more with his spectacular body.

Unexpectedly, I was falling backward, but I didn't have the chance to fall far. Andrew seized me, pulling my waist to him as he pressed his lips firmly against mine, becoming more eager. I wrapped my arms around his neck. Someone cleared their throat. We pulled apart as if we were both being yanked back with hooks. His chest was heaving, as was mine. *Was I blushing? What does it look like now that my blood is gold? Do I glow? Was I glowing?*

"I'm sorry . . ." Andrew looked ashamed.

I shook my head. "Don't be." *Do it again!* I wanted to scream. *Didn't he feel what I was feeling? Was it bad for him? Did he not enjoy himself?* I hated that I felt so insecure, but I'd never felt a connection like that with anyone before; the electricity, the rushing of my blood through my body, warming every inch of my skin. All of a sudden I felt extremely vulnerable. He could really hurt me if he wanted to. In the past, I had never let myself get to this point with another person. I was fully clothed, but I suddenly felt naked, my comfortable layer of protection gone.

Lucia stepped past me, patting me on the shoulder as if she was sympathizing with my thoughts.

"Can we quit with the theatrics and get the hell out of here before the power comes back on?" Joseph snapped, standing on the other side of the table that had acted as his shield earlier.

Theatrics? Was that what that kiss was? An act? I had forgotten that he was here after that kiss. I didn't have time to think about it. He was right—we needed to get out of there and fast. I brushed some glass off my clothes and began walking forward with the angels and Joseph.

Karen—or should I say *Soul Stalker*—came running into the lab, her eyes wide with distress. She was a good actress, better than good, really. Instantly, I didn't trust her look of concern.

She was nicknamed "Soul Stalker" because she was believed to be devoid of a soul.

With everything that was going on, I still hadn't had time to tell the angels of exactly what it was I saw in my dream.

"Are you all right, Gabriella?" the *Soul Stalker* asked. "I knew I shouldn't have left!"

"I'm fine," I said, trying not to let my resentment leak into my voice.

"Thank God!"

I gripped Andrew's hand, letting the electricity flow between us. Before, I was able to communicate through the current, and I was hoping now more than ever that he would be able to hear the thoughts that I was screaming at the top of my mental lungs. *She's not who she says she is! She has come to kill me. She is an assassin. The Soul Stalker. We need to get away from her. Please! Andrew, please!* His grip tightened on mine, but I wasn't sure if it was because of my frightened thoughts or if it was just a reassuring gesture. I hated that he couldn't talk back to me through that same current. *It was the Ladies of Light! Everything is their fault, I just know it. Karen's bad. B-A-D. Do something, anything. Just let me know you hear me.* I gripped his hand with all my strength.

Several images from before, when we were in the fishbowl together, flooded back to me. My need to take the necklaces off the angels—the necklaces that were actually a symbol of good and not evil—the pull to take them off was intense, strong, and now that I thought about it, it was probably Karen's doing. Did that mean those necklaces held power or did she just want to strip them of their titles? I had no time to think, though.

Andrew looked sideways at me and lifted his hand to my cheek, his face out of view of the Soul Stalker and gave me a tiny nod. The breath I didn't know I was holding came out in a rush. When Andrew moved, I could see Karen walking over to me, as if to assess my well-being. It looked more like a lion preparing to pounce on its prey. I didn't want her anywhere near me. Her acting wasn't going to work on me anymore.

I had believed her this whole time, trusted her. I felt sickened.

Anger swelled up inside me and I could feel it burning just beneath the surface of my skin. I put my hand up to tell her to stop her movements, that I was fine. When I did this, electricity shot from my hand and hit her hard, fast and rough. She shook with the voltage, which was more electricity than I had ever felt inside me before. She collapsed to the ground and the rest of the angels turned to look at me. The Soul Stalker was out.

"In my dream, the Ladies of Light were meeting about Zola's prophecy." The words were tumbling out of my mouth as quickly as I could speak them. "During the meeting they were talking about how the assassin had been chosen. She was hired to kill the Illuminator. The assassin was the Soul Stalker," I finished in a rush.

Andrew stiffened next to me. Joseph looked just as confused as ever, the look of bewilderment scrunching up his forehead. Ehno and Lucia were staring at me like I just told them I was a mermaid.

As if we didn't already have a pile of trouble, Darren came stumbling into the lab.

Shit! I shouted in my head.

"Karen!" he gasped and knelt beside her. "What happened?"

He looked straight at me, and for the first time in my life, I lied so smoothly you would have thought I was a professional fibber. "I don't know! She just came in here and fainted."

Darren looked back down at the Soul Stalker with affection. Bile rose in my throat. "Oh baby, please be okay." If only he knew.

"I'll go get help," I offered.

"You can't. All the doors are locked. If it weren't for the engineers, I wouldn't have been able to get this far," he said, his eyes never leaving Karen's face. I was grateful for that much because if he even took a second to put things together, he'd understand that we were trying to escape. The room was completely destroyed, three glass cells were broken, and the angels were out, one of them holding my hand. Master of the oblivious—that was Darren.

"Then we'll all go. You can take care of the So— Karen, right?" I asked.

Darren nodded. "Yeah. Go. Hurry!"

He didn't need to tell us twice. We began running down the hallway as if a fleet of dragons were behind us, lighting our asses on fire. As we turned the first corner, the lights flared to life. We all froze.

"That's not good," I muttered.

21

Liberation

id-stride, frozen in the funniest positions . . . the deer in headlights, glazed-eye look just wasn't accurate enough in describing how we all appeared when the electricity came flaring back to life.

"Bathroom!" I pushed Andrew as hard as I could through the door that was only feet away from us. In doing this, they all fumbled through the tiny entrance into a one stall bathroom. I turned the lock and slammed my back against the door.

"Good thinking," Joseph nodded in approval. "There are no cameras in here." *Sheesh, I hope not.*

Lucia, looking at the toilet with mild apprehension, raised one eyebrow. "What's a camera?"

I had totally forgotten that she didn't know these things. Because of Andrew and Ehno's psychic link, I just assumed that Andrew shared the information he had learned with Ehno, but I had not even considered that Lucia would still be in the dark about this modern world. Regardless, she was in control of her emotions and showed no signs of distress. She had more guts than me.

Joseph opened his mouth to answer her. "No time," I interrupted. "If they haven't realized we are gone already, it won't be long until they do. We need to get out of here quickly and *quietly*." They all stared at me for the answer, and for once, it just came to me. "Joseph, you need to leave. If anyone asks what happened—*you don't know*! Go above ground and find us a car. Wait for us outside the building we entered. I have a feeling people won't ask you questions, considering your clearance."

He nodded. "Go!" I ordered. After unlocking the door, Joseph peeled out of the bathroom like he had wheels attached to the bottom of his shoes.

"Okay—here's the plan," I said while I bolted the door again. "We are going to walk out of this bathroom like it's no big deal. You three don't say a word to anyone. If someone asks what's going on, I'll tell them that I am taking you for testing. "Hell," I rubbed my neck, anxious, "I don't really know *what* I will tell them. Maybe I'll just shock them. I'll try my best not to. We need to keep attention off of us."

"And what about the cameras?" Andrew asked.

"Keep your wrists together behind your backs at all times. They'll think I've captured you and will never know the difference." Or so I hoped. "Once we're on the surface, I need you to fly Andrew. Just take off into the sky."

"Not without you," he argued resolutely.

"There is no time for this! We have seconds before guards show up and start shooting us! We need you in the sky to let Ehno know if anyone is behind or in front of us once we get off this property. Plus, Ehno and Lucia will be with me." The words were rushed. I had to stop to take a breath. "I'm not even sure how we are going to get out of here. Please, Andrew, I need your help."

He closed his eyes as if he were praying for patience. Then he looked at me in defeat. "Let's go."

"Okay!" I turned around and unbolted the lock. "Let me look, first." Opening the door slowly, I had a moment of déjà vu. This was sort of how I felt when I was opening the bathroom door to my office right before the Shadow attacked me.

I peeked out of the crack I made to see two armed men walking down the hall. I shut the door and put my back up against it again. "Crap, crap, crap!" I whispered furiously. I took a deep breath and slid the door open a little bit farther.

"Doctor Moretti?" A deep voice said.

"Oh, hi . . . ?" I slipped out of the bathroom, trying to do my best to keep the door shut as much as possible as I closed it behind me and put my back to it. "I'm sorry—"

"Agent Kowski." The agent was tall, with a full head of gray hair. "We're just down here checking on all the labs. Are you okay?"

"Oh yeah—yeah. I'm fine," I said nervously, hoping he couldn't hear the unease in my voice.

Agent Kowski stared at me suspiciously for a few seconds before he gave a curt nod and walked into the bioengineering lab, which was only two feet from the bathroom.

I looked quickly around the corner and noticed that no one was in the supernatural department's lab yet before dashing back to the bathroom and flinging the door open. "Let's go!"

The three angels flooded out into the hallway and sprinted toward the elevator. Their movements were fluid and sinuous, and surprisingly, so were mine. There was no time to think— I slid my key card across the lock and put my palm against the screen as it read for my print. The female voice greeted me, just like it had earlier. After a few seconds the doors opened to admit us.

"All aboard," I ordered.

Ehno and Lucia entered and Andrew grabbed me around my waist to push me forward with him. Warmth spread through me at his gentle touch. The doors shut and I let out a breath of relief . . . until the doors opened on the next floor. There was a man in a suit, roughly six-four with dark brown hair. He was facing away from us but turned around when he heard the *ding* of the elevator.

I breathed out a high sigh of relief when I recognized the dark brown eyes. Joseph seemed to deflate some when he saw me, too. "Oh thank God!" I exclaimed. "What are you still doing underground?"

"I thought I'd never get away from that guy." He shook his head back and forth. "I ran into one of the scientists on the elevator and he asked for my help."

"Wait . . . that means you haven't been on the surface yet."

"No," he confirmed. "I haven't."

"Crap! What are we going to do now? We can't just all wait around until you pull a car around," I bellowed, frustrated.

He stared at me intently for several seconds as the elevator continued its ascent up the shaft before he groped in his pockets. He pulled out a tiny device that I recognized as an ear piece. He turned it on and put it in his ear. "Agent Jackson?" There was a pause. "Pull a car around building four, leave it running." Another short pause. "No! Right now. Yes. Yes. Okay." He turned the device off and shoved it in his pocket.

"There will be a car waiting."

"Good," I sighed. "Andrew is going to take to the sky immediately. He'll be able to communicate with Ehno in the car to let us know what's going on ahead and behind us." Andrew shot me a conspiratorial look.

"Are you sure you haven't done this before?" Joseph smirked.

"No. But since the only thing you could come up with was a cool name, I had to act rashly when we had the chance to escape," I scowled. "Operation Liberate Angels . . . Ola," I grumbled.

"Hey," he said, raising his hands in defense, "we had only an hour here before we were shuffled back out to capture you. I still can't believe you used your actual name at check-in." He shook his head and *tsked* at me. I was about to reply with some witty and funny comment when the doors popped open on the ground level. Susan and Sue, two of the lab technicians that I kicked out in the wee hours of the morning, were standing there, like they had been waiting for us.

"Ah-hah! I knew we'd find you trying to sneak out of here with the subjects," Sue said triumphantly.

Dammit! I shouted in my head, cursing myself up one side and down the other.

Susan was already holding her radio, about to call for back-up. I panicked. Everyone else was still; their expressions were all frozen in a thinking stupor. The angels were protectors so they were probably struggling with what was right and what was wrong while Joseph did nothing—probably so he could say we captured him. I didn't blame him if he didn't want to fight back—just to save face. But who really knew what was going on through their heads? They could be thinking about the price of tea in China for all I knew. Plus, they were two women and I knew that men had a hard time thinking about hurting women. Well, I wasn't getting caught; I wasn't going back down into that lab so they could experiment on these angels—the very creatures who saved my life and Joseph's. I was the Illuminator, here to save them all. Save them *all*.

I reached out and seized Susan's wrist. The anger had boiled up inside me and I knew she was about to get shocked. Andrew grabbed my wrist gently, but didn't pull me off of Susan. I didn't know what he was doing. "Susan," I said through gritted teeth. "Put the radio down."

Her short stubby finger pressed down on the talk button as she looked at me with the smuggest look I think I have ever seen grace anyone's face. She opened her mouth to talk. Though the voltage building up inside me wasn't anywhere near what I had shocked the Soul Stalker with, it was definitely a dose that would really knock a person to their knees, or possibly even kill a human. There was a tiny part of my brain that was screaming, *this is a bad idea*, but the other part of it was shouting at me to do it, because freeing the angels was more important than one human life. Oh, who was I kidding? I could never take a life.

The current grew deep inside me, and for some reason I was able to control it this time. Andrew's warm breath was at my ear, the whisper barely heard, "I've got you."

The rush of emotion; anger, passion, desire, and outrage all burst through me at once, like the past two days events just kept hitting the wall of a dam until it cracked and burst open. The current raced to my finger tips which were wrapped around Susan's fat wrist and discharged. Andrew yanked my hand back as soon as Susan went down. Immediately, I felt horrible and dropped to my knees to check for a pulse. She was alive, just knocked out.

"You—you," Sue spluttered. "What did you do?" Her hand was placed over her heart, a look of shock on her face.

I stood up quickly and reached out to grab Sue's upper arm. She recoiled from my touch, so I just leaned in more until I snatched her in my grip. "You're coming with us."

"A hostage?" Joseph asked, eyebrows raised. The look on his face was merely amused. "This will be fun."

"Ehno?" I called. His glowing red eyes shot to mine. "Can you see the outcome? Will we get out of here?" I should have asked him this before, but I was too busy thinking about how we were going to get out of here.

"I do not know what will happen," he said calmly. "Andrew and you will be safe, but I can't see if we will *all* get out of here."

His words only made the fear dominate my system again. *What to do, what to do!* My mind began working furiously toward an outcome where we would all survive. Plan after plan raced through my mind. Though I'd always been a quick thinker, my brain seemed to be working at twice its normal speed. The layout that I'd seen of the property here was burned in my memory and it came up in my head as if I were playing a three-D game.

"Joseph! Grab the radio," I commanded. "Give it to Sue."

Sue's eyes narrowed at my words and her cheeks sucked in a little with her anger. "I'll call for help," she threatened. Then she puffed out her sucked-in cheeks, like she was trying to make herself look bigger and braver than she really was. Almost like a blow-fish.

"You'll do no such thing," I snapped. "Get on this radio and tell them that you and Susan saw us . . ." I tried to think of where, but I didn't know this place any better than I knew the underground tunnels between Mexico and the US.

"Under building six, level four," Joseph filled in for me. "We were trying to break into the atoms lab and you have us trapped."

"I won't do it," she sniffed.

I stared up at the camera above our heads, knowing that they were capturing all of us on the screen until I noticed that the little red light that indicates it was on wasn't working. Joseph was staring at me, waiting for me to continue. He had a slight smirk on his face. He was enjoying this much more than he should. Lucia and Ehno waited patiently behind him, an unreadable expression on their faces. Andrew was right at my back, his warmth radiating from his skin as he gripped my hips, ready to pull me away from possible danger. I tried to shake off the wave of desire, the longing for his lips. *Focus,* I had to tell myself. *Focus!* I nodded toward the camera and Joseph turned toward it.

"It's not working. You must have done a number on their system," he said fondly.

"Great!" My plan was going to work better than I

thought. My eyes came back around to land on Sue's. Her upper arm was still in my firm grip. If she radioed in our false location before anyone noticed that the lab was a disaster scene, then we'd be alerting them to our presence, but if she didn't and they *did* know, then they'd be heading this way any second. Also, if the Soul Stalker woke up she might come after me. She was the assassin meant to kill me. How long would Darren stay at her side before he went to go get help for her himself? "Joseph, get on your little do-hickey thing and see what's going on. Find out if they have they been down to the supernatural department."

It only took him a second to understand everything I was just thinking. He popped the tiny earpiece into his ear and we waited. "Most people are still in bed. There are a lot of guards and FBI agents still unaware of the power-outage." He paused for a few seconds. His eyes grew wide as he pressed the earpiece against his ear. "Run," he shouted.

He didn't have to tell me twice. Completely forgetting Sue, we all ran down the extremely white hall. As we were turning the corner, I noticed that Joseph was far behind us. We were moving too quickly for him. "Andrew!" I gasped, slowing down some.

"Gabriella, he can take care of himself. You are the most important one of all. We must get out of here,"

Andrew pleaded.

"Not without everyone!" I demanded, almost coming to a complete stop. Joseph rounded the corner and almost ran right into me. I began to run again, but I kept my pace steady for Joseph. As we came to the door that led outside, we all came to a shuddering stop. There was no window; no way to tell what was on the other side of that door.

"She's coming," Ehno hissed. "Karen."

There were no questions asked, no one yelling at me not to open the door, I just placed my palm right on the scanner and slid my key across. There was a large *boom* underneath our feet and the floor shuddered, making my whole body vibrate. *That wasn't good.* The sound of metal being ripped apart could be heard down the hall. Andrew yanked the door handle and grabbed my waist. I didn't know if there were guards waiting outside or if there were unicorns prancing around—all I saw were pink clouds as Andrew yanked me into his arms and shot like a bottle rocket into the sky. The sun had almost fully risen, I noticed, as I clung on to him.

"The others!" I pleaded. "We can't just leave them there."

"Look below us," he said soothingly.

I did. Below was a black Cadillac moving swiftly toward the gate that surrounded the government installation. "What's going on?" They had come to a stop at the guard's station and I wondered what in the hell Joseph was going to tell them so he could leave.

"There's no one there. Joseph says that everyone has gone to stop the terrible creature that is attacking." He let out a long, bereaved sigh. "I'm so sorry. Karen said she was your Guardian. I just assumed she was tattooed since you are the Illuminator. I should have demanded to see the Guardian's mark. She could have killed you—"

"*Shh,*" I said soothingly. I placed both of my palms on his face. "I'm fine. I'm right here in your arms."

He closed his eyes and nodded before opening them back up. "Thank the heavens for that."

As we seemed to just be floating above the car below us, I almost went limp in his arms, finally feeling a tad bit relaxed. I should have known that my relaxation wouldn't last for long, because I heard squealing tires and the sound of crunching glass and screeching metal. I knew what that sound entailed. I didn't dare look at the scene below. My heart jumped in my chest and slowly, I could feel it break.

Please, I begged whichever entity was listening. *Let them be okay. Let them all survive.*

22

Ladies of darkness

The air was bitingly cold as we flew through the early morning sky. But it wasn't the cold that made the chill bumps rise up my arms, it was the horrifying cacophony. The images in my head were of the dreadful devastation that lay below. I hadn't dared look as I clutched onto Andrew, my eyes closed in absolute fright at what I would find if I were to open them. Andrew was silent, but I could feel his body tense around me— his muscles hard. The noise of metal crashing against asphalt rang in my ears, like someone was throwing pieces of the car around. *Maybe that is exactly what is happening.*

Did Soul Stalker finally catch up to us? And why didn't Andrew see it coming? Wasn't that what we were here for—to watch the ground for possible attacks? The guilt I felt only seemed to grow like a venomous bubble in my chest. *Andrew was too busy paying attention to me . . .*

"Please don't feel guilty," Andrew said as we flew over the accident. I could feel the heat rising in my cheeks—embarrassment and partial anger—because he could read me so easily when we touched. My skin glowed an electric blue in all the places that touched him.

"Put me down," I ordered, trying to focus my mind.

"No," he said softly.

I took a deep breath and stole a glance over my shoulder to see what was happening beneath us. I gasped at the scene, unable to form any kind of coherent phrase for a second or two. Finally, I shouted, "Put me down *now*!"

"Please!" His eyes searched mine pleadingly. "I can't. It's too dangerous. Ehno and Lucia can take care of themselves."

I could read the lie and the conflict in his eyes. Of course he was doing it to calm me down, but it actually had the opposite effect. Gritting my teeth, I looked down below us again. Joseph was ducked behind the now mangled car, his back against the door, while Ehno and Lucia fought against Soul Stalker, who had apparently acquired back-up in between the underground facility and the wreckage site. Two new angels were dressed in all white, billowing robes and fought alongside Soul Stalker. *Damn—if only they were on* our *side.*

"You are nothing but betrayers!" Lucia shouted toward them. "Your treachery is disgusting!"

There was a flurry of light, like a tiny star burst in between them.

If Andrew doesn't put me down so I can help— so help me god I will scream! What was the point of watching? Andrew could fly and I had the power to manipulate electricity. *We could help.*

"I'm not asking, Andrew. I'm telling you. Put. Me. Down!"

He looked down at my incredibly severe face before he lowered some in the sky in concession. "Stay with Joseph," he demanded. His facial expression made it clear that this point would not be negotiable.

There was a scream from below along with the sound of crackling, like fireworks were exploding underneath us, piercing the cold morning air. I didn't say anything. He must have taken my silence as an agreement because we dropped so quickly that one second we were high above the trees and the next we were on the ground, behind the destroyed car. The vehicle was bent almost in two, as if the Soul Stalker herself had run into it. The tires were bent at a funny angle and the glass was shattered out of every window. Andrew put me on my feet and I turned toward Joseph who was leaning against the bent door, his head bleeding. It was crimson against his skin. He was definitely human.

"Crap, Joseph! Are you all right?" I said as I bent down behind the car and ran over to him. The noise on the other side had become explosive. You'd think a nuclear war was being waged in the middle of the street—with huge bursts of light and large booming sounds vibrating below our feet.

Andrew stared at the two of us for a second. *What is he waiting for?* "Please—help them!" I pointed through the broken window of the car, pretty sure that no matter where I pointed, devastation followed.

He gave me a small nod, his eyes full of some emotion that I couldn't read, and then literally flew toward the scene of chaos on the other side of the car. How even was this fight? Who were the other angels? I shivered at the thought of what would happen if our side didn't win. Why was all of this happening? Was Andrew's flying ability going to keep him safe?

Joseph coughed, bringing my attention back to his wounds.

"Joseph?" My fingers flailed uselessly around his injury.

He turned his head my direction. "Hey, Gabriella." He put his hand to his forehead and brought his fingers to his eyes. The color was a brilliant red, fresh from the gash. "I'm bleeding. Is it bad?"

My eyes roamed over his forehead, down his cheeks to the back of his neck—analyzing every last part of skin I could see. "No. You're okay. Maybe a concussion. Are you dizzy?"

"A little."

"Don't close your eyes. Don't you dare go to sleep," I ordered.

The car shook with the mass of something, as if someone just threw a grizzly bear at it. It made me jump a few inches off of the ground in surprise. "What was that?" Joseph asked sluggishly. His eyes blinked slowly.

"I don't know." Gradually, I picked myself off the ground so I could peer over the edge of one of the broken windows. Andrew, Ehno and Lucia were moving so quickly I could barely tell what was going on. The only thing that I seemed to be able to discern, was that my angels were fighting furiously for their lives while the white-eyed women were carelessly throwing curse after curse toward them. My breath caught in my throat and I dropped back down to the ground. I started cursing under my breath—a nice long stream of insults. "We need help!" I exclaimed to Joseph, who was still looking around, his eyes a little hazy.

It was the Ladies of Light—the ones who had

tried to kill Lucia. My dream slammed back into my memory; the warriors all ready to battle—all shaking with fear at the two women at the top of the hill—their white dresses billowing against the wind, their skin intricately marked. Whoever came up with the name *Ladies of Light* needed to be shot . . . twice. They were more like the *Ladies of Darkness. If an army of warriors were scared of these women, what kind of power did they have?*

"We're going to lose," I whispered aloud, my gaze staring at nothing. The tree by the road cracked under the force of a spell . . . or maybe a body . . . I wasn't sure. It perfectly emphasized my words of our imminent death.

Joseph moaned beside me, his head lolling to the side. My eyes snapped his direction as I reached out to shake his shoulder. "Wake up! Don't go to sleep. Please," I begged. His eyes popped open and shot to my face. I felt a little relieved. "I'm going to help them. Will you be okay? Can you stay awake?"

"Yeah. Save the world, Gabriella." He smiled then, a very painful smile. I patted his arm fondly, hoping that this wouldn't be the last time we would see each other.

The sun started warming my cold cheeks as I moved into the light and out of the shadow the car had cast. Trying to gather strength, I concentrated with my mind on the electricity that was flowing in my veins. I closed my eyes to focus on the burning in my core, like there was a small blue ball of power inside me. In my head, I was manipulating the ball of power. Though I had now shocked two people, it was obvious I didn't know how to control it enough to do the right type of damage. Ehno told me they would show me, but we never had that chance. I was going to have to learn on my own. The image in my mind was one of power, strength and brute force.

You can do this—

Something landed on top of the car as if it had fallen from the heavens above, the velocity too fast— the collision too violent. I stood, looking over the top of the car. How ironic, it was Andrew—the angel— his body perfectly dented into the black metal, his teeth gritted in anger, as if he wasn't hurt at all. The woman on the other side of the car narrowed her eyes at me. Andrew hadn't noticed that I was no longer hidden behind the safety of the pile of metal. Instead, I glared at the woman in white—the one that haunted my dreams—more like nightmares. This was the same one who advocated murdering an angel, the same one who tried, and the same one who failed—the one who would fail again.

Andrew began peeling himself off the car, as if he were stuck into the metal. The woman's white eyes stared at me as if she wished to pick my bones clean, which only made my anger burn more fiercely than before. We were fifteen feet apart, but I knew the distance didn't matter. I put my hand out towards the white-eyed woman and just willed the current to obey—ordered my body to respond to the revulsion inside me. *To make her feel pain.*

As Andrew sat up, crouched to spring, he noticed that the white woman's glare was no longer on him, but on something else. He whipped around and his eyes locked on mine. He flew toward me, trying to yank me out of the way. It was too late; my body obeyed my wishes. It was more power than I had ever felt before. Fifty times more than the high voltage shock I gave the Soul Stalker. It was as if lightning was shooting out of my palms and right into the white woman's chest.

Andrew stopped mid-swoop to look behind him at what I had caused. The white woman didn't go down like I had hoped (and prayed). Her head snapped backward and her chest rose until her feet no longer touched the ground. She hovered like that for several seconds. I wished someone would cut off her head already. I felt the power slowly draining from my body. She lowered back to the ground until she stood on her own again.

The electricity crackled and spluttered as if it were going out. The white woman put her lips together like she was going to whistle and then blew at the stream of electricity like she was blowing out a candle. And that was exactly what happened—the blue current went out like a flame in the wind. The white woman's face only seemed amused.

Why didn't she go down?

She raised her hand as if calling the elements to her. Her voice was low and vicious—the Italian words lost on me—before a violet light flashed from her palm.

"NO!" Andrew dived for me and we both fell to the ground. His eyes searched me over for any damage before he jumped to his feet, hovering over me protectively, then he shouted something in Italian. It was as if a bubble formed around us. He reached down and pulled me up from the ground, turning us so he was between the white-eyed women and me. "This won't last long. Are you okay?"

I nodded. "Yeah," I muttered while dusting off my pants—like that would do any good. "I'm fine. Just feeling a little juiced out."

His face grew grave. "I thought I told you to stay with Joseph."

"Well," I rushed out, "I saw that you were fighting against two Ladies of Light. That one was the one who tried to kill Lucia in one of my dreams. Or visions . . . or memories."

"What do you mea—"

A blast of violet light slammed into the small balloon around us. It rippled and then burst open as if it were a soap bubble. In the distance I could see Lucia and Ehno fighting side-by-side. It looked like they were dancing; their movements were fluid and graceful. The other white-eyed woman struck Ehno with a flash of white light and he fell to his knees, his hand across his chest as if he had just been stabbed before his arm went limp at his side. I watched as droplets of golden blood dripped sickeningly to the asphalt, coloring the black ground in a river of gold. He fell forward and I screamed out for him. This couldn't be happening . . . not Ehno. Not now! I had only just found the angels!

"It can't be," I cried out and sprinted his direction. Andrew shouted something at me but I was too focused to hear his words. Something hit my side so forcefully that my breath was knocked away. It was rough and hot and painful. *Did I just get run over? Because that is how it feels.* I reached for my side and noticed gold dripping from the bottom of my shirt. "Dammit," I whispered to myself stupidly, furiously. The injury ached and burned as my veins gradually lit on fire. A sound left my lips, though it wasn't discernable. It was a cry—a scream of unbearable pain. The ground swirled up to my face, and I realized that I was no longer going to be able to fight. We were finished. And all I could think about was how I didn't get the time I wanted, the answers I needed or the love I desired. Life wasn't fair.

Andrew was suddenly scooping me into his arms, cradling me there. It hurt when he moved me, but I didn't care. The small amount of spark I had left tingled beneath the surface of my skin. "Please! No! This can't be," he cried. Andrew put his head to mine and golden tears leaked from his eyes and dropped onto my cheeks. I wanted to soothe him, but I couldn't gather the strength.

The Soul Stalker's clear voice could be heard only feet away. "Get away from the Illuminator and we will leave you be."

Though I couldn't see Andrew's expression when his head yanked toward the Soul Stalker's voice, I bet it was colorful. She said a string of words in fluid Italian before a stream of silver light came cascading down on us. Andrew put his hand above his head. "*Proteggere,*" he whispered and another shield formed around us.

"I'll keep you safe," he murmured to me.

My mind was too hazy to pay attention to the scene around me anymore so I closed my eyes. The pain was excruciating. The noise around me suddenly turn to silence and I felt like I was drifting away, like I was on some sailboat in the warm pacific waters.

"Abelie?!" Aiden shouted from across the field. "Run!" As he dashed toward me, I wasn't sure what was going on, but I noticed that his movements left burn marks in the grass. "Run," he screamed again, and this time I could see the distress in his face and in the distance, a Shadow running after him. The dark creature's silhouette was cast sideways as the sun began to fade in the west.

So it has finally come to this? I thought to myself as I spun around to flee. Aiden had finally caught up with me. He took my hand and fire burst from the contact. It didn't burn; it only gave me a powerful strength. Shadows were faster than angels and I knew that he would catch us because of my slow pace.

"Why is he after us?" I cried out.

"He found out about us. He followed me. He knows about the baby." Aiden turned to look behind him and yanked my hand forward as if it could make my legs move quicker.

He wasn't after Aiden, he was after my child—our beautiful daughter growing inside of me. She was the Illuminator. Though the prophecy I read, and the one that was known to all the rest of the angels was very different, for some reason I had a feeling he knew all about the parents of the one who would destroy the dark ones.

All of a sudden, Aiden was yanked free of my hand, as if a black hole had sucked him up into oblivion. I whipped around wildly to see the dark creature standing in the blackness of my oddly cast shadow. The fire blazed viciously behind his eyes. It was hard to believe that there was such evilness in these creatures because, though Aiden was also a shadow, he loved me and protected me. I fell backward and caught myself with the palms of my hands. The pain was nothing in relation to the baby kicking inside my belly. The thought of my child—the chosen one—being murdered before she took her first breath was worse than any physical injury. I began chanting spells, protective ones to keep the Shadow away. He inched closer, and when he looked down at me, the fading sun lit his blackened face. It was Jeff. He was fiercer than any of the other Shadows. He'd killed two angels already. Was I going to be next on that list?

"The Illuminator must be killed," he growled.

Where is Aiden? Here I was, a protector of knowledge, at a loss for words. They just wouldn't form. Either he had bound my tongue or I was literally speechless. Where were those words that would cast him out—sending him to another dimension far, far away from here?

"Ombra, ho gettato fuori," Aiden's voice sounded behind Jeff, a little breathless.

Jeff growled in fury. "This isn't over," the Shadow yelled, absolutely livid, as he twisted and turned until he curled into a ball and disappeared all together. I sighed, grateful to hear the most beautiful words on this earth: *Shadow, I cast you out.*

My baby was safe—we were both okay. It was in that second that I knew the life growing inside me had more meaning to this world than what some ridiculous prophecy said.

Piercing noises sent me rocketing back to reality. A horrifically painful feeling also came rushing back to me. It felt so much better being out of it, in another world—another mind. Soft hands pulled my hair from my face.

"Sweetie?" The voice was musical—beautiful—a little frantic. "Please, honey. Open your eyes."

It was too fatiguing to do that. Too excruciating.

"I told you, Abelie. She was hurt quite severely. That spell should have killed her—who knows how much time we have left," I heard Andrew say, his voice heightened. That really didn't sound good. "We need to get her out of here! It's too dangerous."

Wait . . . Abelie? Was I still in my dream, or was I back at the battle? I was so confused. Was Abelie here? I mean, *really* here? Ehno did say that my dreams would become vivid, that I might even start acting out things while awake . . . but I'm not Abelie, I'm me, and she's here.

There was the sound of wood crackling in the background, as if we were near a campfire. Through my eyelids, I could tell that the sun was pretty high in the sky now. The sounds of a battle could still be heard in the distance, and it was even louder than before.

My head felt fuzzy and dizzy. There was movement beneath me and my eyes shot open in pain as I bit down on my tongue to stop the scream from escaping my lips. Above me was the most beautiful woman I had ever seen, like she was in some strange fog—or in my imagination. She had long brown hair that was curtained around my face; her eyes were large, round and the most brilliant green I had ever seen—very similar to my own. She had a small nose and a dazzling smile. She was an angel. No, she was more beautiful than an angel. *Am I in heaven?*

"Abelie?" I breathed.

"Hi, sweetheart. It's so wonderful to see you." Her

smile was blinding. Her eyes were full of rich, golden tears.

All of a sudden the pain didn't matter, the battle around me disappeared and the only two people that existed were me and *my* mom. The sun was against her back, making a perfect halo of light around her stunning features. Tears streamed down my face, a mix between bliss, terror and the pain from the throbbing ache at my side. And though we were all in danger, I felt comforted by my mother. I tried to sit up but Abelie held me down against her lap. There were several loud crashes to my left, but I was unable to see.

The fog returned, though I tried to wade through the mist. I grasped and clung to reality, but I was so exhausted. My body wanted to sleep, but I couldn't— not while everything was happening around me, and most definitely not with my mom holding me in her arms. This could be the last time I ever see her—I could be dying. Or this could all just be an illusion— one I didn't want to go away.

"Aiden, grab Joseph!" Lucia shouted in the distance. *Aiden? He's here too?*

"Andrew, it's time we get out of here. I don't know how much longer we are going to be able to hold up our shields. I'm growing weak." Lucia's voice sounded strangled.

What about Ehno? I wanted to ask. It felt like someone had given me morphine lollipops. My head was spinning and everything seemed confusing and disorienting. Andrew reached down and pulled me from my mother's lap. Her smile was still in place as she rose to my level. I tried to return it, but I'm sure it came out more as a grimace than the loving smile I wished.

As the seconds passed, I could feel myself falling back into the blackness. Andrew's fingers were on my cheek, his voice murmuring his beautiful Italian words in his deep accent. Every time I thought about speaking my throat would spasm like it was willing me to scream my discomfort. No—tripping in public is uncomfortable. This was unspeakable torture.

Suddenly, an ear-splitting noise rebounded off of every surface and made me want to cover my ears. There was shouting, yelling and more loud crashes and bangs. I closed my eyes and buried my face in Andrew's chest, not wanting to see the outcome. Everything happened so quickly.

"Aiden! Behind you!" someone yelled.

"Ehno—use your shield," Lucia called out.

"*Proteggere!*" Ehno shouted. I breathed a sigh of relief at his voice. *How is he okay? Why wasn't I okay?*

"*Ombra, ho gettato fuo,*" one of the white-eyed

323

women chanted.

"*Deflettere!*" Abelie commanded musically.

"Thanks, baby," I heard a man's voice say, probably Aiden.

The white-eyed angels began chanting a long, fluid stream of Italian words. It sent chills down my spine.

"We have to get out of here!" Lucia screamed. "Now!"

Andrew gripped me tighter in his arms. Pain shot down my legs but I didn't care. Getting out of there was the best plan I had ever heard in my entire life.

Afraid of what I would see, I debated for several seconds about whether or not to open my eyes. I gave in to my better judgment and chanced a look.

Aiden was there—truly and really there. I still wasn't sure if I was dreaming or not. He was literally on fire, his skin blazing with his viciousness. But he wasn't vicious; I knew that from my dreams. He was fighting against the two white-eyed women at the same time, his palms shooting fire. *Human flame-thrower*, I thought dazedly. But I knew better—he wasn't human at all.

Abelie, my mother, was standing between Andrew and the white-eyed women, protecting us. Her long white robes blew out as she sent a spell flying into the madness.

Ehno, covered in a molten gold was radiating a reddish light, his power pulsing from his body. Every spell the white-eyed women threw at him, he deflected. He closed his eyes and expanded the red light to surround us. I couldn't see Joseph, and assumed he was behind us—I hoped, for his sake.

In the distance, a tree was on fire, the branches hanging crookedly from the trunk. Lucia was the farthest from me; her long auburn hair was tangling in the rush of wind that came out of nowhere. Her back was to me, but I could see her raise her arms out, her palms flat, as if she were pressing against a wall. The wind picked up and her hair went flying up into the air. There was a disturbance in the space between her and the tree in the distance.

The two white-eyed women put their arms out, palms down. They continued their fluent Italian chanting. A silver mist descended upon Ehno's red light.

"Run!" Abelie commanded frantically.

Police sirens could be heard far off, though they were quickly growing louder. Andrew took off toward Lucia. We rushed en route to the disturbance in front of Lucia. She beckoned us forward and he took a step into the strange air before us.

Everything disappeared.

fatality

It was as if we tumbled into a painting. Maybe I was dreaming again? *Was this just another memory?* Rolling hills spread out around us, the towering trees in the distance were a rich golden red. The sun was low in the sky, and the moon could already be seen in the twilight. Far off, there were gigantic snow capped mountains. Clouds were hugging the top of the mass.

"Where are we?" I barely mouthed. The small amount of strength I had was fading away. The pain in my side was only getting worse.

"Italy," Andrew murmured. He placed me on the soft grass. It was incredibly cold, but it could have just been from blood loss.

How did we get here? I wondered dreamily, still in a fog-like daze. The sun was lowering in the sky and I began to shiver, making my muscles knot, causing a piercing pain to shoot through me. One by one the angels appeared around me. First Abelie, who was at my side in an instant, and then the others. Ehno was last, Joseph's arm around his shoulder. Now that I knew everyone was okay, I wanted to sleep. Exhaustion began to overtake me as I started to tumble through a cold blackness.

"Gabriella?" Abelie whispered. I blinked. I didn't realize I had closed my eyes. "I'm going to help you, but I need you to do me a favor." I barely nodded my head, just a small little nod. "Hold still," she commanded. Like that was going to be a problem, I could barely lift my head. "Andrew?" Abelie looked up and soon Andrew's silhouette came into my view. "Do you mind?"

"Anything." His voice sounded desperate, pleading. I actually believed that he really would do *anything* for me. I was lucky to have found him.

Andrew held out his hand and Abelie grabbed it. I wondered why that was. She placed her other hand over the wound, her palm warm against my cold skin. Maybe I'd lost more blood than I realized. She closed her eyes and bowed her head. I wondered what they were doing. Suddenly, Andrew jerked but he didn't let go of Abelie's hand. I had no idea what was going on. Soon, her face was lighting with a golden glow. It was then that I realized it was the reflection from the light being emitted from her palm.

I didn't realize how cold I had really become until warmth spread through me like a wildfire. It felt amazing.

"Take it slow," Aiden cautioned, placing a hand on her shoulder. "We can't heal you if something happens."

As I lay there, I had to see for myself what she was doing. Each second I could feel my strength coming back. I sat up. The torturous ache was almost completely gone. The deep wound at my side was healing. I couldn't see it, but I could feel it. Abelie began to take in deeper breaths until she collapsed backwards.

"Are you okay?" I gasped and got to my knees to check on my mother. *My mother* . . . My mind was spinning uncontrollably.

"Yes, baby. I'm more than fine." She smiled up at me, a little breathless. She reached up and her fingertips trailed along my cheek. "You are more beautiful up close than you are from a distance."

"What did you do to me?" I barely whispered in awe, more to myself than to anyone. I realized I was being rude, but I wanted to know.

Ehno and Lucia came to Abelie's side and helped her up. "You were going to *die*," the word sounded sour on her tongue. "The wound was a magical one— the Ladies of Light are more powerful than all other immortals. I did the only thing I could—I healed you."

Maybe I didn't hear her right. "You *healed* me?"

A gusty wind whipped my hair up and around my

face. Abelie caught a few pieces and put them behind my ear. "Yes. Not many know about my ability. My whole existence I have feared that someone would use it against me. I am a Healer, and always have been. But I was surprised I was able to heal *that* wound." She placed her palm over the torn spot in my clothes for a second and then looked into my eyes. "It is one that would kill an angel if not treated correctly." She paused for a moment. A pained look flittered across her face. "It would only take minutes for the magic to flood through your veins like poison and kill you. We were lucky I was able to do as much as I did. I was so afraid I wasn't going to be able to help you. It's impossible to completely heal that wound, but I did my best."

My palm automatically went to my side where I could feel the scar there. I still felt weak, but amazingly better than before. Then I looked back up at the face of the angel who saved my life. For several short seconds I just stared at her in wonder, comparing our features. The same sea-green eyes, the same nose, even the same color hair. She was fantastic and the first person I had ever met who *looked* like *me*. And no matter how much I resented the person who left me all those years ago; she wasn't someone I could begrudge. That was when I began to cry the happiest tears I had ever cried…and then I tackled her. She hugged me back and

we sat in the cold damp grass like that for several minutes—the sun fading in the background. We cried and
laughed and smiled and felt each other. She was real
and she was my mother. I was part her and . . ."My
father?"

She pulled me away, but still held my arms. "Aiden
is your father, Gabriella."

"So it's true then? I *am* the Illuminator?" Even
though angels popped into my house and tried to
explain this to me and even though I saw the prophecy myself in my dream—I needed to hear it from my
mother.

"Yes, baby. You're the chosen one—the one who
will light the darkness." She didn't sound upset, she
only sounded proud.

Aiden put a hand on my shoulder and I watched
Andrew flinch behind Abelie, like he was nervous
about the Shadow being so close to me. In my head,
I remembered Andrew saying he knew Aiden as Abelie's angel husband—not the dark creature before us.
I wondered briefly if this was the same being Andrew
remembered.

I looked up into the face of the dark creature—a
creature that I had once feared. There was no horror in
his presence. And just like with my mom, I practically
leapt into his arms like a four-year old jumping up to

meet her daddy's embrace. His arms burst into flame when he grabbed a hold of me. There was no heat from the fire, only an enormous amount of love engulfing me, as if the cool flames held his feelings. He spun me around and placed a kiss on my forehead. "My sweet Gabriella," he whispered in relief.

When he put me down I looked between my parents and a million questions went flying through my mind. But the one I wanted to ask the most, the one that I had been trying to find the answer to for years, came bounding out of my mouth. "Why did you leave me? How—"

"Sweetie," Abelie cut in, getting to her feet and putting her palms on my cheeks. "We didn't *want* to leave you. We tried to keep you hidden for five years, but one day a Shadow found you. His name was Jeff— a nickname he acquired after seeking out and killing twenty-seven mortals named Jeff. He wore the name like a trophy. We fought him off, as we had in the past, before your birth."

The images came bobbing to the surface. When I was in pain and the blackness consumed me . . . they were running from a Shadow. *Jeff* . . . I *hated* him. How many times does an angel have to cast one of them out? But even as the images unfolded before me, it was hard to tear my eyes away from my parents. *My* parents.

"I met Jeff," I barely whispered.

"What?" growled Aiden and Andrew at the same time. Watching the two of them, their faces angry, was for some reason funny to me. I swallowed the giggle before it could surface.

"He was disguised as an FBI agent."

"Wait," Joseph interrupted. I had almost forgotten he was here. When I turned to look at him, he had dried blood on his face and down his neck, making his appearance look brutal. I was surprised he hadn't freaked out by this point. Hell I was surprised *I* hadn't freaked out. "Jeff was a Shadow?"

"Yes," both men answered. Joseph's face distorted into a grimace.

"Anyway," Abelie continued, "we didn't *want* to give you up. We cried over you and fought against the whole unbelievable idea, but we *knew* if you were to survive, you would have to live a life far away from angels and the supernatural. We've watched you grow up when we were able to get away," Abelie explained. "We knew you were safe and happy. Your adoptive parents did a wonderful job in your upbringing."

That brought me to my next train of thought. "How was I human and now I'm . . . and my memory?" I mumbled.

"You were such a smart little girl," Abelie reminisced fondly. Now, more than ever, I wished I could remember the time before. "It was amazing how resourceful you were, even at such a young age. Your memory was perfect." Aiden wrapped an arm around Abelie as she began crying. "We—we cast a spell that turned you human. Your blood ran red and then you couldn't remember a time before that. We didn't realize that would be the side-effect, but we were happy that it was so, because we didn't know how we would explain the situation to you." Her shoulders shook with her quiet sobs. "And we knew that the angels couldn't find you, and if they did—they would not know you were the Illuminator. The whole world would know you as human, not angel. We did it to keep you safe. It was the hardest thing I have had to do in four thousand years.

"What we didn't even think about was that you would one day possess a gift. Everyone felt the shockwave you emitted. I knew how smart you were and so I sent you a chest, with a key."

I nodded, stunned. "Two keys," I corrected.

"Two?"

"Yeah."

"Huh," she said, bewildered. "That is . . . very strange."

"No, the Shadow was *very* strange."

333

"There was a Shadow?" she gasped. "I left you a message with the key to the Divine Library, explaining what it went to—just in case something happened to me or Aiden."

"There was no message—only a Shadow." I paused.

"Wha—what happened, did he hurt you?" Abelie's hands flailed around my body, searching for any signs of harm.

"No, I'm fine. Apparently all the damage happened in my head. He tore my office apart, but when he left everything was normal again."

"Gabriella, I'm so sorry. I had no idea. I was only trying to provide a way for you to get some answers about your life."

"Why didn't you just come to me?"

"We were afraid that we would lead the Shadows or Ladies of Light to you. They both knew you weren't dead, but they couldn't find you. We had to be careful. But," she hesitated for a second, "who could have tampered with it?"

I shrugged.

"Well," she began and then paused, "did you at least understand that the key was meant for you?"

"Yes, though it was pretty cryptic, if you ask me." I smiled.

"I was trying to warn you about the Ladies of Light—that they could not be trusted, no matter how wonderful they seem."

"Okay . . ." I placed my hand on my shirt which was still wet with my golden blood and pulled it away. I placed my palm toward them and asked, "But why did I turn *back* into an . . . *angel?*"

Abelie sighed and Aiden answered this time. "We don't have the answer to that. But I am pretty sure it is because you are the Illuminator. No spell or powerful charm will keep you from becoming who you were meant to be. Deep down, I think we knew that. It was still incredibly hard to . . . let you go. It was for your protection, you have to understand that."

"I do."

Everyone was silent around me. Everything whirled around in my head. There was so much to take in. "How did we get to Italy?" I blurted. The question was reasonable, I thought.

Lucia laughed—an enchanting sound. "My dear Illuminator, I am able to manipulate dimensions. I opened up a portal and sent us all somewhere else for a second before I sent us here."

I shook my head, trying to comprehend what she just told me. Did she really just tell me she opened up a portal—sent us to another dimension—and then sent us here? "Come again?"

Lucia smiled at my bewildered expression. "It must be hard for you to understand our world, being so new to it, but you should know that you were made to live as an angel and you will adjust better than anyone else."

Andrew put his arm around my waist and pulled me to his side. "You're freezing," he stated. "Let's get you inside."

"Inside where?" I said, looking around. Was I missing a building or a house? I glanced over my shoulder and back around me again. There was nothing but rolling grassy hills and small rocky precipices for miles, and mountains in the distance.

"The Divine Library."

"Really?" Again, my eyes scanned the surrounding area. The sun was almost completely behind the horizon and I couldn't quite see that far. As I did a second sweep across the tall trees to the east I saw something move within the shadows. I jumped and electrocuted Andrew, who then looked around suspiciously.

"Let's go," he said to everyone. "We are not safe out here."

We are not safe out here, I repeated in my head. Ehno nodded toward us and we walked the opposite direction of the line of trees. Chills ran down my spine and I couldn't help but look over my shoulder again. It was too dark, I couldn't make out anything. That didn't stop the goose bumps from rising on my arms.

The sky was lit with a purplish tint as the sun finally made its way West. Instantly, everything started coming into focus. Shapes that were blurred were now clear and sharp. And that's when I saw them—a line of roughly thirty Shadows. They were dressed in black robes, which billowed in the wind; all of them except for one who was dressed in a black suit. Even at a distance I could see their eyes glow. The two at the end of the line stomped their feet and fire lit between them, illuminating the Shadows in the middle. My heart started racing ahead. I didn't know what to do, and it seemed that the others didn't either. We were all frozen in place. When I looked at my angels, their eyes glittered with the reflection of the fire. The scene was eerily like my depiction of hell.

One of the Shadows stepped forward from the fire. He was the only one not wearing black robes and I could tell by his black suit and that same cold glare that it was Jeff. There was no reason for him to be wearing his glasses when he was among his own kind. He still looked more human than the others, but the façade was gone—his appearance just as wild looking as the Shadows around him. Their skin was dark and cracked.

Inside the cracks it looked like a river of lava was flowing. They looked like demons.

Were we going to fight them? Were they here to capture me? How would we survive? My heart began to beat faster. Instead of staring at our enemies across the way, all I could do was look at the angels and the very human Joseph who would either be a witness to my death or die alongside me. I couldn't allow that. He was innocent and good and didn't deserve that fate so young. We couldn't fight against them all. They were strong . . . *too* strong.

As the Shadows converged upon us, their robes rippled across the ground like flowing waters by the wind. I could feel the electricity burning within me, begging to escape. My heart was pounding so fast in my chest that I thought it would jump right out. As the line of fiery Shadows moved closer, all I could think about was protecting those I had grown to care for. Instead, the angels circled around me, keeping me from the view of the Shadows. I hated how they felt obligated to protect me. This was a battle I didn't want them to fight for me.

Jeff stepped forward through the fire as if it were air, a manic gleam in his eyes. "We don't need to fight," he said viciously, a grin spread across his charcoal face. Whatever magic he was using to conceal himself when

I first met him was gone. "Just give us the Illuminator and we'll leave you be."

Andrew growled and pulled me closer behind his back. If it wasn't for the situation, I might have raised my eyebrows and asked "Did you just growl?" and laugh. Instead, I gripped onto his skin right under his shirt, letting the current flow between us. *Let them take me*, I thought, sure he could hear. His head jerked to the side and I could see the look of disbelief and pain in his eyes. *We can't fight them. We can't win. And I can't lose any of you*—especially *you*.

Ignoring the fiery Shadows, Andrew spun around and put his warm hands on my shoulders. He looked down, his eyes pleading. "I won't allow it."

"It's not your decision."

"We are not going to hand you over," he said firmly. His eyes surveyed my face for several seconds, like he was looking for some answer that I couldn't give him.

"Just let me go," I petitioned.

Andrew frowned and brought me into a comforting embrace. "Please don't ask me to do this," he barely whispered against my ear.

I took in his magnificent scent—kind of like honey and the most delectable cologne I'd ever smelt. The electricity burned within me, strong, hot and fierce. I knew in that moment he could feel my emotions—hear my thoughts. He pulled me away and put his hot hands on my cheeks. This time there was no reason for him to kiss me, no ulterior motive. His lips pressed firmly, yet gently against my own and everything around us disappeared. My arms snaked around his neck and he let go of my face and put his hands on my lower back, pulling me to him. I was in heaven, right in the middle of an oncoming battle. And no matter the small amount of time I had known him, I loved him. We broke free of each other, breathless. His forehead was against mine and he looked content and distraught all at once.

"I love you too. That is why I cannot allow you to give yourself over to the Shadows." Andrew's gaze was intent.

I sighed heavily. For a whole second I almost gave into his demands. Though his words were sweet, and unexpected, I had to make him understand. I repeated part of the prophecy, "*As the dark ones approach, the Illuminator should be set free, uninhibited by all Guardians.*" I went on in increasing desperation, "You must realize that I know that this is what I was meant to do. You need to let me go—it's the only way."

Lucia tapped his shoulder. "Andrew, she's right. Even though my mind and body are screaming for me to protect her, the prophecy states that we should not hold her back."

Abelie interrupted. "You can't seriously be considering this, Lucia. She's my daughter. I just got her back."

Her words were touching, and I knew how she felt, but I had to do this—not just for her, but for all the angels. It was time for me to protect her. "Enough!" I ordered. As I stated before, this wasn't their decision, it was mine. "Stop talking about me like I'm not here. Listen to me—I love you all more than I've ever loved anyone in my entire life, and I refuse to stand by and watch you all die trying to protect me." Unfortunately, I had no idea how I would defeat the Shadows single-handedly.

A soft tenor voice sounded from behind me. "Gabriella," Joseph said, "there is no reason to be self-less right now when we are all here to help. You don't have to carry this burden alone. Let us all carry the weight."

"It's true, we will all fight!" Ehno agreed.

Behind Abelie was Aiden, his back to all of us as he watched the Shadows' every move. "We aren't giving you the Illuminator," he yelled toward Jeff, his voice ferocious. "We didn't give her up when she was a child and we certainly won't do it now!"

Jeff laughed, almost amused. "She's going to kill

the Shadows—that includes you. The daughter that you continue to protect is the one who will kill you. Priceless."

Aiden growled and fire shot from his palms. The flames raced across the ground and circled around Jeff before they licked at him. Jeff merely stomped on the ground and the fire went out. Only smoke continued to linger in the air around him. "Then we fight," he smirked.

"No!" I shouted and sprang forward, out of Andrew's embrace, and tried to penetrate the circle of angels. Andrew yanked me back by my waist and the circle only tightened. "Let go of me!"

"I can't let you do this. Please Gabriella, please don't go . . ." Andrew pleaded, his eyebrows pushed together in frustration.

I struggled in his grip. "Please don't fight them," I begged, tears descending my face. "I can save you all . . ." I repeated the prophecy's words.

Andrew placed his hand against my head and pulled me to his chest where I continued to cry out.

"I don't care about the prophecy. I won't let them take you. I just won't," Andrew said.

I quit struggling and just let him hold me.

"Even if you went to the Shadows, I'd fight to get you back." Andrew lifted my chin to his face and placed his lips to mine quickly before he looked up toward Ehno and nodded.

Chaos erupted—just like a volcano bursting at the seams with hot molten lava. Though the sun had set, the area was alight with fire. The Shadows attacked and soon the circle was penetrated. Aiden had already broken free from our small grouping and he charged into the group of charcoal creatures. And then he was gone, as if a bunch of ants just attacked a piece of meat and swallowed him whole. Lucia battled against several Shadows, but I could tell she was wearing down. I knew that she had been weakened after the Ladies of Light attacked us, and I was sure she hadn't returned to full strength. Still, she continued to thwart her attackers. Ehno sent red light flashing into a group of the inky creatures and several of them went down, but not enough to make a difference. There were too many of them, and not enough of us.

Andrew stayed at my side, his voice low and vicious as he shouted many fluid Italian words, making sparks fly from his palms and race through the bedlam. My eyes shot around the battle, desperately looking for Joseph whom I had lost sight of. He was only human and I knew there was no way he would be able to fight against these black creatures. When Andrew looked over his shoulder at me, he pointed off in the distance, as if he could read my thoughts when we weren't touching. As my eyes shot the direction he was pointing, I breathed out a deep sigh of relief. Joseph was fine, as far as I could tell. He was on top of a Shadow, punching him mercilessly, his strength disproportional to his size. His powerful punches surprised me—he had extraordinary strength for someone so human.

As everyone fought against the Shadows, I tried to keep track of them. The pandemonium was too much. Lucia was down on the ground, hurt. I ran toward her, shouldering my way through the battle, and slid on my knees in the dew covered grass. As I went to her aid, a Shadow came out of nowhere and dove for me. He pushed me down on my back and held my arms above my head with one hand. He ripped at my shirt and I tried to electrocute him, but my strength had not fully restored since I received my injury from the Ladies of Light. The Shadow's hot, greedy breath was at my throat—like he was sniffing me. His fingers around my wrists began to burn my flesh away and odd little whimpers escaped my mouth before I writhed and shrieked, unable to cause any damage. Suddenly, the Shadow flew across the field and tumbled into a few others. They went down as if they were bowling pins.

Andrew leaned down on the ground and moved a strand of hair from my face. He had an anxious expression displayed on his face. "Are you hurt?"

I was, but there was no time to worry. The burns would have to wait until later. We were in danger. "No. I'm fine, really."

He helped me up and two Shadows came up from behind and yanked me back into the chaos. The Shadow's skin was rough and hot against mine. Andrew shouted something and sparks flew as fire flared in my view. I cried out for him—screamed for him. There were no answers. I couldn't see any of my angels now. There was a loud explosion and several of the Shadows flew into the air, their bodies limp. Abelie walked through the smoky remains of the grass and shot off spell after spell. As the wind blew the smoke away, I could see Andrew break free. But he was too late— three Shadows sent fire sweeping across the ground toward Abelie. My pulse quickened. I shouted for her to run, but she couldn't hear me through all the noise. As I watched, helpless, a feeling of horror rose like bile in my throat. The fire ran up her clothes. It didn't burn her like I thought it would, it only snaked slowly up her body, around her neck. The Shadow smirked and made eye contact with me. And, as if the whole loud battle ceased, I could hear the loud crack of her neck. I gave a small cry of shock. My stomach gave a sickening jolt and I felt as if my heart would fall out of my chest.

The raging battle before me disappeared and all there was—was my mother.

Andrew ran toward Abelie, catching her before she hit the ground. Her body was limp, her face empty as her green eyes, my green eyes, stared at me lifelessly. There was a chill in my stomach as I tried to digest the horrible image before me. Each breath seemed to become sharper in my chest. It was oddly disembodying, like part of me was being detached.

It's too late, a voice echoed in my head.

A scream of agonized fury tore from my lips. "No! Please . . . God! Not her! Not my mother. Take me instead!" I shouted at the sky. No longer was I paying attention to the battle. A Shadow could have struck me dead and I would have been okay with that— *anything* to alleviate this horror.

Aiden sprinted through the smoke toward Abelie. His whole body burst into flames, and for the first time they were blazing hot, just like his fury.

As the tears descended my face I could see Andrew leaning over my mom, or what was left of her. I took a step toward the woman who had done everything she could to keep me alive. Out of nowhere, Joseph sprang up and tackled me just as a violet light flashed over our heads. How was he still alive—a human—and my mother—an angel—not? *Abelie isn't here to heal me this time,* I thought abruptly. I thought my heart would burst with the overwhelming anguish I felt. And at the same time, it felt as though something was being ripped from my body. I crawled to her like a soldier, needing to hold her in my arms—those same arms that would never bring comfort to me again.

I gasped and knelt beside my mother. There was no puddle of golden blood, no marks—just a lifeless body. It was in that moment that I realized I'd never be able to speak to my beloved mother again. Though it killed me to tear my eyes from her, I turned to see Aiden sobbing molten golden tears. Regardless of his Shadow name—he was an angel. When I looked to Andrew, hoping he could tell me something different from what I already knew, he looked up to meet my gaze. To my surprise and shock, his eyes were like sapphires, the richest most electric blue I had ever seen— his face tortured. It was true then . . .

"Your eyes," I whispered and went to wipe away his tears. A fiery mist burst over our heads and descended upon us. Hadn't there been enough damage done? I could see Jeff in the distance, a gleam of triumph in his eyes and a smirk quivering on his lips. Hate and revulsion rocked my body.

It was then that the Shadow to my left gasped in shock and fear. The others followed when they looked my direction. I knew what they were afraid of. They were frightened of me and my glowing skin. The prophecy's words scrolled through my head, *"As the dark ones approach, the Illuminator should be set free, uninhibited by all Guardians. She will show us all who the enemies are, and how to defeat them."* I stood, more livid than I had ever been in my whole life. It was time to prove who was the most powerful. It was me.

My vindictive wrath acted as a stimulant. The waves of fury I generated could probably be felt by those around me. I welcomed the tide of anger that swelled within me. Powerful hatred swept through me roughly as electricity coiled at my core. I eyed all the Shadows malevolently.

"Ombre, è il momento di cadete," I said in a low and deadly voice, my arms outstretched, palms facing forward. There was no hesitation. I didn't know where the Italian words came from, but I understood them, "Shadows, it is time to fall." And fall they did, like sooty pieces of wood as electricity exploded from my luminous anger. Every Shadow in a mile radius was probably knocked off their feet. Even the dancing firelight was extinguished; only oily smoke was left billowing in the wind. The grounds were bathed in a ghostly moonlight and through the dim light I could see all around me the scenes of total devastation.

divine library

The cold night air ripped through my lungs and each breath continued to burn. The moon lit the vicinity with a silver radiance. It would have been a scene of beauty if it wasn't for the smoke rising from the smothered flames. Shadows lay scattered across the grassy hillside like large lumps of coal. As my eyes moved over the still body of Abelie, there was no preparation for what I would see. In those seconds I was fiercely accumulating more reasons to hate Jeff—to swear revenge. I looked away, unable to look at her any longer. I saw Ehno, who was assessing Lucia's wounds. She must not have been hurt too badly because she sat up without any help. The two were whispering softly to each other and for the first time I could see the love and tenderness of Ehno's fingers across her cheek.

"Sweetheart?" a voice breathed delicately. Everything seemed to be in slow motion, even when I spun around to see Andrew's now electric blue eyes. It was as if his soul could be read through the indigo, showing only concern, love, and devotion. His arms were outstretched, almost as if he didn't know what to expect from me. A powerful force pulled me toward him. His palms cupped my face as his thumbs rubbed away the onslaught of my tears. "*Shh*," he whispered and put his lips to my forehead. I melted like an ice cube on the hottest day of summer. Andrew caught me in his arms and held me firmly against his chest.

"Your eyes are blue," I stated, almost numbly.

"When an angel feels loss, it is shown by the color of the eye."

"Oh."

All of my rage and fury vanished when I was in his arms, and the only thing I could think about was my mother . . . she was dead . . . *gone*. It wasn't fair. It just wasn't. It was only moments—just a handful a minutes—that I had with my mother and now she was . . . lifeless. The quiet scene was disrupted by Aiden's piercing cries, the sound like a sorrowful requiem. Each shuddering breath he took in was echoed by the surrounding angels. I turned to look at Abelie, and once again, I jerked my head away from the limp form on the ground with Aiden kneeling beside her, not willing to comprehend her end.

They should have let me go. This was entirely *my* fault.

A Shadow moved in the moonlight and the same wrath and anger boiled up to the surface. I pushed my way free of Andrew's arms and walked toward the moving form. My breathing hitched, my chest moved up and down faster and faster. In the back of my head I noted that no one stopped me from my movements. Fire burst from the dark one's clenched fists as he started to get to his feet. The moon cast an odd shadow over the creature as I positioned myself over him.

"*Stay down*," I ordered with a flick of my finger. Rage boiled in my voice—my tone was that of cold fury. The Shadow fell instantly back to the ground. Italian words weren't necessary, electricity wasn't required—I just possessed the power.

I turned around to see the stunned looks on several faces. The eyes of the angels were all a liquid blue— even Lucia's eyes were more like sapphires than the shallowest of oceans I was used to. "They won't stay like this forever," I conveyed.

Lucia was on her feet—her posture exhibited the substantial beating she had received. Aiden brought Abelie into his arms, cradling her like she was a new born child. Joseph was covered in soot; his once pristine suit was now wrinkled and dirty. Again, I noted how well he was accepting his circumstances.

Or maybe he was just as frightened as I was.

Andrew walked towards me, his hand outstretched. "I think it's time we leave." He gestured behind me with a small nod of his head, where several Shadows were now reorienting themselves.

My hand stretched straight out in front of me as I turned to point at the lumps of charcoal, my eyes fixed threateningly upon them. "*Down*," I ordered. "*Freeze*." A couple of them dropped back down, one Shadow froze in place. But it wasn't enough. There were too many of them moving and soon we would be overwhelmed. My head whipped around to find Andrew only inches away, his expression was a wild mixture of grief, awe, and disbelief.

"It's time to go," he repeated. He outstretched his hand again and I grasped it. The electric current flowed where we were connected.

Several Shadows rose from their fallen states and then the darkened grounds began to light again with their fire. We ran. Aiden was ahead of us, Abelie's head bouncing from side to side against his arms. A sharp pain rose in my throat at the sight. It made me sick, but I couldn't look away. Each second, each breath, each excruciating emotion threatened to overwhelm me, but I knew I had to keep going. We had to get away before we were out-numbered again. Joseph followed in our wake as Ehno and Lucia brought up the rear—chanting in their liquid Italian.

"We can find shelter in the Divine Library,"

Andrew shouted to Aiden. "We can devise a plan once we are safely inside."

Aiden made no noise, he just lengthened his strides. He was amazingly fast considering he was carrying Abelie. *My mother.* She was the one person who had continuously saved my life when I could not save myself. From before I was born, all the way up to this day. All she did was make sacrifices for me, even when it broke her heart to give me away.

As the wind whipped behind me in our wake—the Shadows only yards behind us—the only thing I seemed to be able to think about was my heart, and how it had shattered into little pieces. The saying "life isn't fair" was more accurate than I would have ever imagined. I could feel the rush of anger leaving me.

As we approached a rocky precipice, I noticed a worn path in the stone. My dream-memory flooded back into my mind—a time when my mother was still alive. The worn, uneven steps were familiar and I knew, even from the faint memory, that this would lead us to the door. Reaching into my pocket, I pulled out the two keys, preparing to unlock the door. Suddenly I remembered that I didn't have the second key—you had to have two keys to enter the Divine Library. Andrew had told me he didn't know where my other key went to, but that only one of them would open the door here. I felt panicked. It was easy to pick up my pace and soon I passed Aiden. Maybe we could just break the door down. But I knew it couldn't be that simple.

"Hurry!" I yelled as we ran up the stone steps to the library. I was leading the way, Andrew on my heels. Joseph started to lag behind. As we reached the top I spun around so I could see what was happening behind us. The dark night had twisted into an inferno as the Shadows began to light on fire. Aiden held Abelie in his arms, her body limp in his grasp. Joseph ran to keep up as Lucia and Ehno brought up the rear, running backwards as they cast spell after spell, trying to prevent the Shadows from getting anywhere near us.

I jammed my key in the lock, hoping it would work. It didn't. "We need the other key!" I cried out when my single key didn't do the trick.

"It's in Abelie's pocket," Aiden said, his voice rough with his grief.

I just couldn't fathom putting my hand in her robes, not while her body was limp and . . . *lifeless* in my father's arms. Andrew could see the look of angst on my face; the tortured expression must have been clear as glass. He gently reached into her white robes and pulled out a key identical to the one in my palm. At the same time we put the keys in the locks, turned them, and shoved the door open. The stone made a grinding noise as we pushed our way through.

Andrew whispered under his breath and all the lights sprang to life. Every corner, every wall, from floor to ceiling, was covered with shelves of books or artifacts. It was amazing, with tall ceilings and towering bookcases, just like I had remembered in my dream. Any open space on the stone walls was covered in frescos. Andrew yanked me out of the way when I paused in the doorway and pointed toward a clear table for Aiden to place Abelie. I looked away as he pulled a drawer out and placed a silken cloth over her body. Joseph tripped up the steps, his breath heavy as he entered the library before he practically fell to the floor.

I bent down to him. "Joseph? Are you all right?"

He coughed and pushed himself off the ground. "Yeah." He looked at me funny. "You are one powerful woman," he coughed out before walking past me, a mingled expression of terror and awe on his face.

I stood and looked out through the door and wondered where Lucia and Ehno were. When I looked down the stone steps I could see them battling with the multitude of Shadows. Lucia, even with a slight limp, was holding her own. Without thinking, I left the safety of the library and stood on the top step. Andrew followed behind me and wrapped his arm around my waist, preparing to pull me back inside. I looked over my shoulder. "I'll be fine." That was a lie. He raised an eyebrow in disbelief, easily able to see through me. The look on my face was probably not believable—I couldn't gather the strength necessary to put up pretenses.

"Watch," I barely whispered.

I closed my eyes and let my head fall back as I took in several steadying breaths. It was odd—this new feeling that was growing inside me. It was powerful, and I knew that I could control it. Electricity flared between my fingers and began crackling.

"Ehno? Lucia? Duck!" I shouted. And they did. I pointed toward the stairs below them. Electricity exploded from my finger tips and the stairs crumbled away and the Shadows fell roughly fifteen feet to the rocky hill below.

Ehno helped Lucia up the stairs and Andrew grasped my hips and pulled me inside. Once Ehno and Lucia were inside, we pushed the door closed and then we both entered our keys to lock it from the inside. I placed my hand upon the door. "*Seal.*" Sparks lit at all the seams until there was no door there.

"How—"

I put a hand up to stop Andrew. "I'm not sure, I just know I can." He didn't respond, either he was speechless or had nothing to say. Though something amazing was happening to me, I had no room in my head for these thoughts.

My knees went out on me and my back hit the now solid wall where I slid down to the floor. I folded my arms and put my head down and to try and create a small amount of privacy for my anguish. My heart swelled with agony so forceful, so jagged, so *real*, I didn't know if I could move without crumbling to pieces. My sobs were violent, and I choked on the air, air that Abelie would never breathe again. My mind raced around as I looked desperately for some loop-hole, where she would live, come back. But as I replayed the scene in my head over and over—the fire wrapping around her neck, her lifeless body, Aiden's golden tears—I knew she was gone. And in that instant, it swept over me— the awful truth—more completely and undeniably: *my mother was dead.*

It was a brutal end to what should have been a new and lasting relationship with my mother. And it was just taken away.

The room was full of quiet despair. You could feel the emotions, thick in the cool air.

Karen's story of how they became immortals flashed through my mind. *"We were called* Senza Tempo. *Translated, it means timeless."* No matter what their ancient name might be, it was today that I found out immortality doesn't always mean forever.

Words wouldn't form and tears wouldn't even flow anymore. The restraint I was using to keep myself together was almost painful. My shoulders shook with my dry, silent sobs. Even though Andrew remained silent, I knew he was sitting next to me—silently soothing me. Still, I kept my face hidden in my own personal torture.

As the minutes passed, possibly hours, no one bothered me. I didn't blame them. What kind of words of comfort could they offer?

There were the soft sounds of muted conversations happening around me, sort of like a fly buzzing around my ear.

"So it's really you?" Andrew asked, not concealing his voice. "*Aiden*? *The* Aiden?"

I didn't look up; I only listened to their conversation in the echoing of the large room. The room I should be immersing myself in right now—with all of its treasures. The same room I should be enjoying with my mother.

"Of course," Aiden replied, his voice rough with sadness. "Why are you staring at me like that?"

"I'm sorry," Andrew barely whispered beside me. He reached up under my folded arms to hold my fingers. He didn't try to pull my arms apart, he just held my hand. Andrew continued, "Do you remember me?"

"No. Should I?" Aiden sounded confused.

"Maybe you aren't the Aiden I am thinking of," Andrew mumbled. "But if you are, you were an angel . . . part of the Halo of the Sun. We were friends. You were Abelie's husband before . . ." There was a long pause. When Aiden didn't answer Andrew continued, "How did you end up as a . . . a Shadow?"

"I . . ." Aiden paused. "I have always been a Shadow." His voice sounded really confused now. "Maybe I'm not this Aiden that you think I am?"

Andrew's hand disappeared and I could feel a slight wind as he stood next to me. "That is not true. You were an angel. I remember you and Abelie. We were very close friends." I could hear soft footsteps pacing back and forth. "You're wearing the Guardian's symbol right now, aren't you? Let me see what is on that chain under your robes."

Curious, I finally looked up to see Aiden pull a necklace from his shirt. "This is the Nebulous Sun." And it was—the same shield in the middle of a halo. The only reason I knew it really wasn't was because Andrew had told me differently.

"No," Ehno and Andrew both said at the same time.

"I've been wearing it for as long as I can remember. This is the Shadow's symbol. Those who wear it are cursed," Aiden disagreed.

Ehno pulled up the sleeve to his white scrubs he was still wearing to show the same symbol tattooed on his shoulder. "We are both telling you—it is not the Nebulous Sun. It is the Halo of the Sun symbol—the Guardian's symbol. Those who wear it are protectors of mankind—not the other way around."

Aiden's eyebrows knitted together, the powdery black color of his skin cracking as he did so. "I want you to be right, but I can't remember a time when I wasn't a Shadow." A golden tear leaked from his eye. "Abelie would have loved to have made our relationship public . . ." his voice constricted under a choked sob.

Tears leaked from my eyes again as a new shuddering sob hit me. Andrew turned around and saw my face. His eyes were still a luminous blue.

He leaned down to my level and placed a simple kiss on my lips. "Words cannot express how heart-wrenching these circumstances are. Please, let me comfort you," Andrew breathed in my ear. Another sob jerked my body and I wrapped my arms around his neck as he pulled me off the ground and just held me to him. And that was all I could ask for.

My mind wanted desperately to think about something else, to preoccupy my emotions. The fact that we were in the Divine Library reminded me of the prophecy Abelie read in my dream and I seized gratefully onto the new subject. After raking in my emotions, I whispered against Andrew's ear, "The *real* prophecy is in here somewhere. I want to read it."

"Already found it," Lucia piped in. She looked like she had recovered from her wounds already. I'd never recover from my emotional ones.

As we all sat around the table, the book of prophecies opened before us, no one wanted to read the words that would dictate my fate. Did it talk about my mother's death? Did it talk about mine? Was there a secret in there that would be devastating? Would I learn who my enemies were or who the backstabbers would turn out to be? The pages, yellowed with age, the sides softened with use—this was all about me and my life. Here in these pages was my past, present, and future. Did I really want to know those things? For the first time in my life I was going to decline reading a book.

On a desk, only three tables away, lay Abelie's body, covered with a soft silken drape. It was less than half a day ago that I was dreaming about that table, the same one my parents were about to make love on—probably the same one that the Ladies of Light occupied when my parents overheard their conversation. And maybe it was that exact chair that was pulled up underneath the desk that Karen had sat in when she was introduced as the assassin—the Soul Stalker. My heart was incredibly cold, my limbs almost numb.

"I'll read it." Aiden's charcoal fingers traced the cover of the book. "You are my daughter, Gabriella, and I will do whatever it takes to keep you safe—no matter what this book says."

"Go on, Dad." I hoped my smile came out right. It felt different—right to call him "Dad."

Aiden's lips twitched up into a sad smile in return as he placed his blackened hand over mine. The touch was full of peaceful serenity and I appreciated his warm touch. He cleared his throat before he opened the book and began reading. "A battle will be waged. Great heroes will be lost. But they will survive in another form—one of darkness and shadow. But blood does not hold the key to light and dark, only our souls hold that power, as the Darkness Illuminator will prove.

"During the darkest time for all angels, the Illuminator will be born during the lightest day of the year when the Ladies of Light will kill one of their own."

"Who did they kill?" I interrupted. My voice was thick with my anguish. Why did so many have to die?

Aiden had a confused expression on his face. "Camellia, one of the Ladies of Light, was killed by a Shadow—or so *they* said—but I have never heard of a Shadow defeating someone so powerful. The only immortal that could have done it was . . ." Aiden trailed off, knowing I'd understand the rest of the sentence.

"Do you mind?" Andrew asked, pointing toward the book.

"Of course not," Aiden conceded.

Andrew slid the book toward himself before he continued. "The Illuminator's mother will be of the Light of Heaven"—I glanced over my shoulder to the still form on the table—"and her father will be a Shadow of the Sun. Angel guards and Shadow barriers will not hold her back; as she will have access to both sides of the realm. Until the Shadow's approach, protect her above all others, even from our kind.

"As three among you perish to the Earth—bound by shadow and fire—do not be fooled by the warnings given to incite terror and mayhem. Those three who fought against the growing power will be laid to rest until the time comes—the time of light.

"Beware of encroaching danger, as the Illuminator will be surrounded, but she is not thy enemy. As the dark ones approach, the Illuminator should be set free, uninhibited by all Guardians. She will show us all who the enemies are and how to defeat them.

"When the time comes to battle, our Illuminator will come to save us all. Worlds change, lives transition, and everything will be turned upside down. Warriors are found—the fog lifted. The Halo of the Sun will keep her safe and the time of the Illuminator will come. She will rule us all."

Silence. It was as if we had all been struck dumb.

Andrew turned a page, then another. "The rest is blank, like someone erased it."

The words opened up a whole new vista of thoughts. My mind churned as images began clicking together in my head. So there will be a battle—or there was a battle. . . . *do not be fooled by the warnings given to incite terror and mayhem*, I repeated in my head. I took in a deep breath. "Tell me about the angel hierarchy, Andrew." I felt like the answer to this whole mystery—the Halo of the Sun disappearing, the Shadow of the Sun producing someone not so evil—Aiden—was just seconds from being answered.

"Some of this we have already talked about," Andrew began. "Angels were never 'ruled over,' per se, they were governed in a whole different way than a ruling class. Angels are usually ranked by strength and gifts. The Ladies of Light, which consisted of the three strongest immortal women, were angelic protectors.

They kept the immortals safe from those who wished to destroy us. As I've told you before, they come in cycles—every one-hundred years."

I nodded in understanding. "Why the tattoos?"

"They are proud of their title."

"Wait . . ." I turned toward Lucia. "Were you once a Lady of Light?" Her tattoos were beautifully woven across every inch of her skin in intricate patterns and symbols.

"I was," Lucia admitted. "But, of course, since my . . . death . . . my cycle has been up. Usually, one would go through a ceremony where her tattoos would be removed."

"But who would have the strength to bind you for hundreds of years?" I inquired.

She was silent then, her eyes darting from Andrew to Ehno. "That's . . ." she paused. "Well, that's a good question. It would have to be a Lady of Light or a whole army."

"It was," I informed her. She looked taken aback. I continued, "In one of my dream-memories you were stabbed by a Lady of Light while the other stood by and watched. In the foreground was an army." Lucia's eyes widened. I pressed on. "Your blood was red. And the women—they were the same ones who attacked us outside the underground lab."

365

Again, silence. When no one spoke, I knew I had to say something to pick up the gathering muteness, but no words would form.

"It can't be," Lucia barely whispered. "They wouldn't . . ."

"They did." The three angels looked back and forth between each other. Aiden and Joseph sat silently, only taking in the information. "Andrew?" I interrupted their staring. "Keep going . . . the hierarchy?"

"Oh, yes." His blue eyes shot to mine. "The Halo of the Sun consisted of many angels, all male. Though they are not as strong as the Ladies of Light, they are still very powerful. They are—were the protectors of mankind. Those worthy of saving are assigned a Guardian angel. Sometimes it is just for a day, but can last up to the lifetime of a human—which is rare."

"But from everything we know—the Halo of the Sun is no more?" I wondered aloud.

"Never heard of them," Aiden responded first.

"Something very strange is going on, indeed." Ehno shook his head back and forth.

"Continue," I prompted.

"Then there is the Prophetess, Zola. She warns the Ladies of Light of danger to the immortals and gives the Halo of the Sun assignments for those who need a Guardian angel."

"So," I interrupted again, "Zola, the Ladies of Light, and the Halo of the Sun are all equal in the angel world?"

"Yes," Andrew clarified. "The Elders rank below, but are still powerful. They are protectors of knowledge. Abelie," Andrew barely whispered, "was an Elder. She was the librarian I told you I knew when we were in Boise City."

I looked down at the table.

"I'm sorry," Andrew said quickly. "I shouldn't have said anything."

I looked up to his face. He looked worried. I scanned the table to see everyone staring at me with pity. Joseph's face was a mixture of sorrow, confusion, and a look of extreme discomfort.

"No. It's okay. Please, continue," I insisted.

He stared at me for a few seconds, but must have read the determination on my face because he continued. "The Elders consist of historians, librarians, teachers, or an angel with any kind of hobby or job that pertains to gaining or protecting knowledge. Then there are the Guardians. They are the lowest in the hierarchy, but are still respected—the elite, if you will. Sometimes you can have many titles. I am part of the Halo of the Sun and a Guardian."

There was something in my brain telling me the

answer was just on the tip of my tongue, but I just couldn't grasp it. I was exhausted, sore, and my heart was beating funny. And I realized that if I slept I would see her again—*I'd be her*—my mother. When I didn't say anything for several minutes Andrew grasped my hand.

I jumped. I looked back down at the table. "I miss her," I barely mumbled, not caring if they all heard this.

"Oh, sweet Gabriella. I . . ." Andrew trailed off. The other angels shared uneasy looks. They could probably handle grief better than I could.

The ache in my chest pulsed like an open wound. "It feels like a piece of my heart has been ripped from me—leaving me forever."

I saw Andrew's chest go up and down slowly, taking in a deep breath. "Come on," he finally said and held out his hand.

I grasped it and he pulled me to my feet. "She needs sleep," he announced to everyone sitting at the table.

As we passed my father, I reached down and encased him in my arms. "I'm so sorry," I barely whispered. He returned the hug and nodded his head.

Andrew and I walked through several rows of books without looking back until we came across a staircase. In silence, we ascended the steps. We passed a few floors before we reached the top of the library—the fifth floor. His hand was so warm and comforting . . . I didn't think I'd ever want to let go. We stayed silent as we passed shelf after shelf and bookcase after bookcase. Finally, we came to a dark wooden door engraved with more symbols, most of them I didn't recognize. He put his hand on the door knob but didn't turn it. He took in another deep breath, conveying sympathy just by the expression on his face and then turned the handle.

Inside the small room was a vanity, a small bed, and a tiny closet. "This," Andrew gestured with his hand, "was Abelie's room when she worked in the library."

Instantly I began absorbing the scene around me. Her hair brush was sitting on the vanity alongside a cold cup of tea, the spoon still inside. She'll never have tea again, or stare at her reflection in the mirror. It was like she was sitting here only yesterday, and now . . . she'd never sit in that chair again, or sleep in that bed, or have dreams or thoughts. My fingers traced her belongings, desperately needing to touch everything that had to do with her. And for those several precious moments, the whole world centered on her and nothing else existed.

"Wear this," Andrew said, bringing me from my

thoughts. He was holding up a white robe. "Your clothes are a mess and I know your mother wouldn't mind if yo—"

I snatched it out of his hand so swiftly he didn't have time to finish his sentence. "Thank you." I hugged the piece of clothing to me like he had given me the best present in the whole world. I breathed in the scent of roses and honeysuckle. I stepped on my tip-toes and gave Andrew a small kiss on his cheek.

He half smiled. "I'll let you change." He hesitated for a second before leaving and shutting the door quietly behind him.

I stood there and stared at the door. The room was quiet, so silent that it was deafening. I yanked my clothes off and threw the robe on, wanting Andrew back in there with me. It wasn't a good time to be alone—I needed his comforting hand in mine. In the mirror, I could see my reflection. There were dried golden tears on my face, and large dark circles under my eyes. The robe fit me perfectly, and fell just above my knees. The fabric was silk-like and smooth against my skin. And it was hers.

As I was making my way to the door, I noticed photos on the wall and quickly strode toward the far wall. There was a picture of me and my mother when I was only a child. When I was younger I had blonde curls, which later turned brown, but in this picture they were still platinum blonde. My fingers traced her face over and over. When I looked at the next few pictures I was really surprised. It was after my mother had turned me human. There were pictures obviously taken from afar that were of me during a baseball game, singing during a choir recital, and one of me riding my bike on the streets outside our house in Ohio. I didn't think I could look at them anymore.

I dashed across the room and almost pulled the door off its hinges with my urgency to be comforted. There was no one there. For a whole second I thought I would collapse from the emptiness—inside myself and outside the room.

"Andrew?" I called out, panicked.

"I'm right here." He moved from underneath a shadow. His voice was the most angelic, most welcoming sound I'd ever heard in my entire life. I leaned against the door frame, wilted.

He moved closer to me and his finger traced under my eye. "It's time you slept."

I nodded in agreement and he led me back inside the room. There was a soft click of the door as it shut and in that second I felt some relief at being able to hide from the world outside—at least for tonight. He pulled the covers back on the bed and gestured for me to lie down. When I perched myself on the edge of the bed, Abelie's scent wafted around my nose. Sitting on the bed—*her* bed—I didn't know if I could be alone. Not tonight and not here. I needed Andrew's comfort. He stared down at me, his blue eyes searching my face.

"Will you stay with me?" I breathed.

He let out a breath, one I didn't know he was holding. "Of course I will."

He took off his shoes and shirt. The image of him was the same, but still breath-taking. I scooted across the bed, sitting with my knees against my chest. He sat beside me, put his arm around me, and pulled me down onto the bed, holding me there. I clung to him because I knew this night would be the most difficult night of my life. Andrew murmured something in Italian and the lights went out.

His chin was on top of my forehead, and my head was in the crook of his neck. He was warm, and he was soothing me just by holding me. His palm was on my cheek while this thumb rubbed comforting circles on my face. I could hear his heart beat steadily in his chest, the one thing Abelie would never have again. She had left this world—she had left *me*.

"Why?" The word was almost inaudible.

"Why what, sweetheart?" Andrew murmured.

The sobs were back and my body shook with my

overwhelming feelings of loss. "I just don't understand
. . . *why*? She was immortal and now she's . . . *not*. And
I just don't know how that can be, why that is. It's *stupid* and doesn't make sense and I just can't . . . I just
don't . . . It just *doesn't make any sense* and I—I." Each
second I choked on my words, my grief threatening to
overpower me. My tears were coming at an alarming
rate. The words were incoherent and blubbering, but I
just couldn't stop them for fear that I'd lose any sanity
I had left. "She was my mom and those Shadows took
her away from me. And now she just can't get back
into her body . . . I can't accept that, I can't register the
fact that she will no longer breathe or talk in her sweet
voice or hold me. I only had minutes . . . *mere* seconds
with her and then she was taken. It isn't fair, it just isn't
and—"

"I know. It's not. It really isn't. *Shh.* I'll hold you
all night; I'll be here with you. I'll take care of you,"
Andrew's voice whispered in my ear. His thumb wiped
away the tears that covered my face. I was glad he had
the impulse to comfort me because I needed it now
more than ever. "Close your eyes. Dream about your
mother."

I obeyed and closed my eyes—begging sleep to
take me. As I lay there, I knew I was still shaking and
whimpering, but I wasn't embarrassed. It was neces-

sary. My world had crumbled all around me in the last forty-eight hours and now all I could do was try to pick up the pieces. But not tonight, not while each second brought on another round of earth-shattering thoughts and images. I was nearly at the end of my emotional rope. And I didn't know how I could have made it without Andrew there, holding me.

Somehow I slept, and my mother's worst moments flowed into my mind.

ancient battle

an you believe it?" I said through gritted teeth to
Aiden. "For thousands of years we have protected
mankind, guarded them, and now the Ladies of Light
think that it is okay to . . . to . . . *kill* them." I threw my
key to the Divine Library. It clanged against a golden
artifact and a chip of metal soared through the air,
reflecting in the soft light.

"Abelie, don't worry," Aiden soothed. "Everything will work out, I promise."

I sat down with a huff. "How can you say that?
What is it that you think *you* can do?"

"You *know* that the Guardians won't let them go
through with their plans." He placed his hand over
mine in comfort.

"Plans?" I snapped. "You mean the mass extermination of mankind? 'Plans' is just not a dirty enough
word for what they have in store. How about genocide
or massacre or . . . or *slaughter*?"

He sighed heavily at my disdainful look. "I know
you are upset, love. We all are, really. How could they
make that kind of a decision without conferring with

the Halo of the Sun? Andrew and Ehno are especially angry. *Trust me*, I hear their thoughts."

"Okay," I bit back, swelling with the deepest of loathing toward the Ladies of "Light." "What are the *Guardians* going to do about it? What if the Ladies of Light refuse to back down? You know how powerful they are, how easily they could strike an angel down. Their power sometimes *disgusts* me. They wear their title on their skin like they are gods. Haven't we already made that mistake in the past—you know, with the Soul Stalker's brothers? *Stupid worthless fools*," I responded in a tone of revulsion. I took my hand back and folded my arms angrily. I was so overwhelmed with irritation.

Aiden only looked at me with pure love in his eyes. He knew I was livid, but he knew I still loved him with all of my heart. "The Ladies of Light know not to do anything *rashly*. They will probably speak to the Prophetess. The Guardians are already planning a meeting." He leaned in closer to me and put his hand on my arm. "I can understand your anger. I am also enraged. What they have proposed is ludicrous."

I deflated some at his words. "Well, you aren't having any sort of meeting without the Elders. Count us in."

He smiled at me. "I wouldn't think anything different."

We were silent for several lengthy seconds. Unfolding my arms, I leaned even closer to Aiden; I'm sure the terror was evident on my face. "But what if this *doesn't* work out? What if they go ahead with their plans? The humans will be helpless. And what if they fight back against . . . *you*." I cringed at the thought. "I love you, and it would kill me, literally, if something were to happen to you."

He smirked, trying to lighten the mood. "Nothing is going to happen to me."

"You don't know that."

"I do," he insisted, rather smugly. "We are immortal, we will never die."

"'Never' is a word I wouldn't use when it comes to the inevitable fate even us angels possess," I countered. I hated how calm he seemed about the whole situation. What *were* the Ladies of Light thinking? "Are *they* going to be invited to this . . . *meeting*?"

He looked as though he was thinking deeply, but I knew he was probably just communicating with his brothers. "I suppose it's best if they do come." He rubbed his jaw in thought. "Abelie, please don't let this worry you, not until we talk things through—figure this whole ordeal out." He leaned in and cupped my face. His breath was warm on my lips. "No matter what happens, I will do everything in my power to protect you, and to protect mankind." When I was about to protest the fact that I didn't need him to protect me, he closed the distance between our lips. Just the warm, soft embrace was enough to make me forget about the threat . . . at least for the moment.

"Quiet!" a booming voice sounded in the crowded theatre. The small whisperings of the group died down immediately. There was a charge in the room as everyone focused their attention front and center.

There was not enough seating for all of the angels; luckily only a select group of elite were invited. We had not met in that place in several hundred years, but the Pompeii Odeum was the only place we could find at short notice. It was old, but useful.

"We've gathered to discuss an alternative proposal to our previous proposition," Liz, a Lady of Light, addressed us while she smirked unpleasantly. She was wearing her usual white, silk robes that formed perfectly to her body. Through the silk you could see the tattoos covering every last inch of her skin. She was tall and striking with her long white hair which matched perfectly with her white eyes. "After speaking with the eldest of the Halo of the Sun and the Prophetess, we have decided that mass extermination

378

is probably not the best idea." She looked displeased with having to agree with that fact. "Our alternative suggestion would be to enslave mankind." There was uproar in the crowed. Liz continued through the commotion, "*They* are killing this planet. Some are evil and murderous. They are filthy creatures."

I leaned over to whisper furiously into Aiden's ear. "And you agreed to this 'idea'?"

He turned to look at me, his eyes wide with innocence. He shook his head back and forth. "No, we disagreed."

"So why isn't anyone doing anything about it?" I snapped, wild with impatience. "Killing humans is probably better than making them into slaves! This is outrageous! You would think they would remember when *we* were *mere* mortals. Things weren't so wonderful when we were slaves of that repugnant king. But humans now-a-days don't even possess magic like we do. This just . . . I just can't believe . . . it's revolting!"

"...we will all come together to build a better, more peaceful world where angels and humans coexist," Liz continued, barely able to conceal her broad grin. There was another outbreak of muttering among the masses.

"Coexist?" I bit in a low, furious whisper. "How is slavery coexisting?" My voice had a note of hysteria in it. "It's sickening!"

Aiden looked absolutely nauseated at the words coming out of Liz's mouth before he turned to me and nodded in agreement. "It really is."

"Then why is no one speaking up?" I demanded in a strained whisper. "Why aren't *you* speaking up? *I* would but I am *only* an Elder."

"Because," he looked at me like I had lost my mind, "if someone speaks out of turn, or does anything to humiliate one of the Ladies then they might get struck down." His voice lowered. "They have killed immortals before. They won't stand for disobedience. We will need time to think of another strategy. We thought we had talked them down, but apparently this only opened them up to more brutal ideas."

"Obviously," I said angrily, looking back down at the three women with distaste, casting them a venomous look.

Liz looked rather smug that no one had stopped her from her from making her proclamation. Mimi, another Lady of Light, stood only a foot or so behind her. She closed the distance and leaned over to whisper something into Liz's ear. The superior look on Liz's face twisted as she broke out into a wicked smile. Shivers shot up my spine. *What now?*

"We will start the integration of humans into our

lives shortly. Mimi has already devised a plan to make things run smoothly," Liz continued in her horrible, honeyed voice while she smiled self-righteously. I wanted to slap that awful look right off of her face. And at that thought, I smiled.

Lucia, the other Lady of Light, was standing farther back. She had the same look on her face as I did: revulsion and abhorrence. I had always liked Lucia, and her expression only made me like her more. I wondered why *she* wasn't doing something to stop this. Of all the angels present, she had the most power. She was the number one pick for the Ladies of Light.

When the small murmurings of the crowed died down, Liz raised her arms in a gesture to let us know this meeting was over. There was a dubious smile stretching her wide mouth. "That is all. You are dismissed. We will gather again shortly to discuss our next move."

Behind the closed doors of the Divine Library, the Halo of the Sun, the Elders and even some of the Guardians gathered around in the confined space. The noise was heightened when Andrew, Ehno and Aiden stepped up on a small landing next to artifacts from ancient Greece. I sat next to Luke and Carmela. Of all the Elders, they were my favorites. I was quiet, but they both spoke animatedly about a topic I couldn't hear. As Luke talked, he would gently place his hand on her knee and she would lightly touch his arm when she leaned in to say something. Even after four-thousand years, their love had not gone any farther than the longing in their burning gazes.

Suddenly, all the Halo of the Sun quit talking. That was everyone's cue to quiet down and listen. Briefly, I wondered what it would be like to be a Halo—to have your thoughts shared when you wished.

"We have met with the Ladies of Light twice now, and they refuse to back down from their plans," Andrew said. "Mimi has already devised a well-thought out plan that will have Italy under our thumb in a matter of weeks." Angry shouts erupted from the crowd. "We can't allow it, but their cycle will not be up for another fifty-years. This is a problem."

"So what do *you* plan on doing about it?" a Guardian shouted.

"*I* don't plan on doing anything," Andrew countered. "But *we* can work together to strategize so we can stop them from making this horrific mistake."

"And when you say strategize you mean . . . what?" the Guardian shot back.

"We fight back," Aiden stated firmly. There was a murmur of general agreement. Aiden was a force to be reckoned with and the Guardian knew it. He backed down from his line of questioning. "They aren't going to let this go. Whether we like it or not—they are planning on enslaving mankind."

Luke and Carmela looked at me with wide eyes.

"Don't look at me like that," I whispered crossly. "What else would you have us do? Fight or go against everything we have always believed? Hum?"

Luke nodded. "Fight."

"Exactly." I agreed in triumph.

As the noise level grew in the enclosed space, I focused upon a small slit forming in the door of the Divine Library and peered over the onslaught of Guardians in surprise. A dim light glimmered through the crack. "Luke?" I shook his arm, never tearing my eyes from the goddess that had entered, unbeknownst to the angels inside.

"Abelie? What is—"

"What's your sister doing here?" Carmela asked in disbelief.

"I . . . well, I don't know, to be honest," Luke blubbered. We all gawked in her direction for several seconds before conversations started to cut off around us, several eyes followed the path of ours.

Immediately, Andrew, Ehno and Aiden welcomed her up to the make-shift stage. Ehno had gently taken

Lucia's hand and kissed it. They all then began talking feverously to each other, their voices too soft to be heard, even through the silence of the crowd.

Finally, Andrew stepped forward. "Lucia has come to join our cause. She disagrees with Liz and Mimi's plans and wishes to do whatever she can to help us."

It was silent for several deafening seconds as everyone continued to gawk at the tattoo covered goddess. She was powerful and respected and now she was my hero. I began clapping. It wasn't long before others followed my lead with a roar of approval.

Lucia, the most reserved of the Ladies of Light, advanced to the very edge of the small landing. Her presence was powerful and everyone had their full attention upon her as the clapping faded away. "I've tried to talk my sisters down from this outrageous suggestion that we are above mankind and deserve to enslave them." Her voice was smooth and authoritative. "They won't listen, and they refuse to have any more *meetings*. It's time we fight back."

A storm of catcalls and cheers erupted, the noise deafening.

❦

The sun started to descend over the horizon—the light momentarily blinded me. As I regained my sight, I noticed the two Ladies of Light at the top of a small incline. They were waiting for us.

They knew.

Behind me, hundreds of Guardians lined the horizon. Aiden shouted commands to them as they moved closer to the women. As the sun hit their bronzed metal armor, I turned back to see the two women stare at the scene with pure enmity in their eyes. When did the Ladies of Light become so hateful? What happened to the love and devotion they had always shown? When did they become so *corrupt*?

Ahead of me, I could see Ehno, Andrew and Lucia. Their heads were close together as they talked rapidly to each other. Andrew's golden eyes constantly darted up toward the Ladies of Light who just stood there, waiting patiently to see what we would do. Ehno had both of Lucia's hands in one of his as he reached up and tucked her auburn hair behind her ear. They were in love, you could tell just by the burning gazes they shot each other. Ehno pulled something from his sheath and placed it around her neck. It was the Guardians mark. Lucia nodded to something he said before she broke away from them and walked towards the other Ladies of Light.

Every muscle in my body became tense, as if someone had electrocuted me. My eyes darted around before I looked to my right were Luke and Carmela held hands. The other Elders were on my left. The fear was obvious in their eyes. For the first time I wished I were telepathic instead of a healer, just so I could hear what was going through everyone's minds.

We all watched as Lucia stopped only feet away from the Ladies of Light. Her long auburn hair cascaded down her back as the wind blew it behind her. She was beyond beautiful, she was more god-like than I had ever remembered. Her tattoos wove up and down her dark skin. You could easily see through the short, white, silk dress that was clinging wildly to her with every rush of wind. Around her leg was a knife. It had the Definitive Sun symbol on it, one that showed great power among my kind.

Mimi and Liz clasped hands together and immediately a white light glowed between them. Fear gripped me, coiled through my stomach and up to my chest where my heart gave a horrible jolt. What were they doing?

Lucia looked over her shoulder, her light blue eyes warned me to stay quiet. I put my hand out and was about to protest this but Luke grabbed my arm and pulled me back.

"Luke?" I whispered. "Let me go."

He shook his head; his eyes stared at me with a wild intensity. This was his sister, his *twin* sister and he was just going to let the Ladies of Light get away with this?

Lucia's head turned in slow motion to stare at Luke. "If it's a sacrifice I have to make . . . I'm doing it for you."

Suddenly, there was a loud explosion, like fireworks, as tiny white lights descended upon Lucia. She didn't move away, or try to protect herself. As each tiny light hit her skin, I could see her skin start to glow red.

"No," I barely whispered. In that second, I wished that Aiden weren't responsible for the Guardians behind me because I needed him to hold me, to tell me what I just saw wasn't true. "No!" I shouted louder this time.

The Elders all turned to look at me; their eyes begged me to stay quiet. They were scared.

They should be.

"No!" I screamed this time.

"It's too late," Luke whispered. His eyebrows scrunched together as tears pooled in his eyes. "She's human."

My eyes shot around the area. Why wasn't anyone helping? Behind me, the Guardians all stood with their weapons out. What was the point if they weren't going to use them? As I turned back to Luke, he stared off toward Lucia again. The pained expression had not left his face. Carmela held on to his hand with more fierceness, as if she were protecting him As my gaze followed Luke's, I took in the two women at the top of the hill all in their white, like they were pure. In that moment, I wanted to scratch their eyes out and paint them in black. I wanted to burn the tattoos off their flesh. They weren't worthy enough to wear such divine markings. We were protectors—we were not evil, yet these women, they were. I felt a chill start at the base of my spine and work its way up.

Twilight was upon us as the sun had almost been swallowed whole by the earth. The shadows of the Ladies of Light extended far beyond Lucia, almost as if they were consuming the place in darkness. No one moved—no one fought. What were we waiting for? This horrible crime was more than I could stand; I stepped forward, ready to fight, even if it meant my life.

Hands gripped my waist and pulled me back and I could feel Aiden's breath at my neck. "You can't fight them alone, Abelie."

Tears fell down my face. "Why are we sitting here watching this?"

His warm lips kissed my neck. "By the time they cast the spell, it was too late. If they have the power to turn her human, they would do it to the rest of us."

Carmela was no longer able to hold Luke up as he collapsed onto the ground. He sat on his knees as he looked up, the tears drowned his face. My heart broke for him.

"Lucia." Her name was like a sigh upon the wind. She turned toward me again, fear and confusion written all over her face. Tears escaped her eyes as she closed them before she turned back to the Ladies of Light. I realized then that they didn't turn her human because they couldn't fight her; they did it to show they were above her—that they were above us all. I'd only heard of that spell, never seen it performed firsthand.

Mimi stepped forward, pulled her long knife from her leg and held it up in the air. The knife that was meant as a symbol of angelic protection was now being used to kill one. I gasped. Fear gripped me, and all I wanted to do was run up there and save her, but Aiden held me tighter.

"No!" I screamed. Rage propelled me forward, though Aiden was stronger and only held on with a firmer grip. Liz turned her white eyes upon my struggling form and I froze. A mocking smile crept across her face. I wanted to slap that grin right off her face.

Then everything happened in a matter of a few seconds, as if someone made us move in fast forward.

Mimi put the knife high in the sky and then let it carve through the cool air as it plunged deep into Lucia's chest. Lucia went down, her head falling back as a torturous sound tore from her lips. I gulped, trying to swallow the bile as I watched her white dress turn a brilliant crimson color. Her head fell to the side and the red blood dripped from her mouth. Her eyes were strangely unfocused. It was in that moment that I knew it was her ending. She was dead—she would never return. And I couldn't handle that thought. Immortality didn't always mean forever, and today I knew that better than on any other day. Her eyes were lifeless as they stared at me, the glacial blue color tainted by the red blood in her veins.

Luke fell forward as his forehead hit the grass. He didn't use magic during his time of wrath; he used only his strength as he tore away at the ground. Each second his body was consumed with earth-shattering sobs. The tears were relentless as they tumbled down my cheeks. I wiped them away, only to turn my fingers gold with the action.

There was no indecision as I took off. I sprinted toward Lucia. Someone had to help her. Maybe it wasn't too late for my healing powers to help her. That was when all hell broke loose. I wasn't the only one that couldn't take the scene before me. Ehno took off toward the women, sending curse after curse their direction, unable to do any damage. His movements were swift, and he became a blur. Andrew tore after him. When they were both within ten feet of the Ladies of Light, they went down like two large sacks of potatoes. The same spell had turned them to humans and Mimi ran forward and stabbed the two in the chest, just like with Lucia. My screams of protest echoed around me. Now their crimson blood joined Lucia's, turning the grass a dark color. I felt sick as I dashed across the field knowing if didn't reach them in time it would be too late—my gift of healing could save them. Not many knew of my gift, but now was not a time to hold back.

Aiden caught up to me within seconds. He pulled me to his chest. "Let me go," I whispered frantically into his ear. "Please." His pleading eyes bore into mine and then he pulled me into a hug. "I can't lose you. I'm too selfish to let you go." He gripped me tighter. I pushed away from him some and saw the most pained expression I had ever seen. Tears rolled down his face.

I went limp in his arms, unable to hold myself together under all the unendurable agony that had gripped my body. He went down with me as he held me. Aiden no longer ordered the Guardians to attack; they were doing it of their own freewill. The movement below their feet made the earth vibrate.

The Ladies of Light ripped through the hundreds of warriors as if they were nothing more than air. It was all too much.

"Stop!" I screamed toward the women, the cry scratching my throat. It was as if a rock had decided to lodge itself there.

And that was when everything changed, when everything that was normal and made sense turned upside down and inside out and backwards. The Ladies of Light had joined hands again as they chanted their long streams of spells. I recognized the words that would be the end of them all—the Guardians—all the Halo of the Sun. They were the words of death, repeated over and over as the white glow expanded. And when it did, it began to encompass those attacking. When they were all enveloped in the light, Aiden let go and ran toward them and yelled at them to run—to disperse. They didn't listen and suddenly Aiden was under the light along with them.

"Aiden! No! Please!" I screamed in a storm of protests. I ran, going toward my husband, my lover. The only reason I had to exist in this timeless immortality. "*You can't leave me!*"

As I ate up the space between me and the light, two of the Elders reached out and held me back. "You can't, Abelie," Eleanor said.

"We can't let this happen. All the Halo of the Sun . . . all the Guardians—there will be no one left to protect mankind."

This isn't happening. This *couldn't* be happening. But it was. It *really* was.

The white light grew brighter and brighter, the intensity so vivid that I had to shield my eyes. The center, around the Ladies of Light, grew to a deep blue color. The sapphire light exploded out from the middle of the Guardians. It overtook them, rays of blinding light bursting from their every orifice right before we all fell to the ground from the spell.

My head hurt as the world spun around me. I stared up at a patch of starry sky, the moon full. Nothing made sense. Everything was wrong, different. Putting my hand to my temple, I sat up to see Shadows scattered across the ground under the pool of the dim moonlight, their skin black as charcoal. When I stared at the biggest one, it looked as though a flame started up inside him and burned through his eyes. The frightening stories of Shadows slammed into my mind. There had been rumors . . . but I never believed it. The Shadow looked at me as if we knew each other before he raised his upper lip to expose his teeth. A growl escaped from deep in his chest. I backed away in terror, my world aligning in an unfamiliar pattern.

26

There was a cold so penetrating I thought I would choke on ice. The scene before me burst into a million tiny wisps of smoke. My body trembled, a little unhinged, as I cried out. I jerked upright, silencing my voice.

"Abelie," I breathed. The infinite sadness resonated in my voice as my mind pulsed and churned.

I took in my surroundings. I was back in her bedroom—not on a battlefield. It felt as if I had just fallen back to reality with a thud.

There was a movement in the darkness and I jerked away, startled and a little frightened.

"It's just me," Andrew whispered as he lightly traced a finger down my cheek. There was a small spark of electricity that followed the gesture.

My chest still jumped up and down rapidly as I tried to regain my composure. Fear and grief were boiling in the pit of my stomach. Andrew whispered something and a lamp in the corner of the room sprang to life. I blinked, trying to adjust my eyes. My back was pressed against the wall, my knees pulled up to my chest. Andrew was sitting up, the covers still over his legs. I looked down at the top of my knees, Abelie's silk robe still covering them.

"Gabriella?" Andrew ran his fingers along my jaw. He had a pained expression on his face, his eyebrows knitted together. "Are you . . ." he trailed off when my eyes shot to his face. He examined my expression and must have seen the panic in my eyes. "Oh, Gabriella," he sighed. "What did you see?"

My breathing slowed some, but not my thoughts. They were exploding in my mind like a hammer slamming into a mirror. "Your death . . ."

"Who—"

"The Ladies of Light," I cut in. "It was them all along. From your death to the Shadows . . ." I shook my head. "It was them. Always . . . it was them."

I was looking over Andrew's shoulder, not really focusing my sight. He cupped my cheeks between his palms so I would look at him. His eyes were still a brilliant blue—just as somber as before.

"Tell me what was in your dream. Please," he pleaded softly. "Let me help you."

I took in a deep breath before speaking. "The Ladies of Light are after me. They are after the Illuminator." A blast of realization hit me, so hard and rough that it knocked the breath out of me. "And now I know why. It's because I know—because Abelie knows . . . knew."

"I know they attacked us before but—" I put a hand up to stop him. He needed to know the truth.

"It's more than that. I know why Karen . . . Soul Stalker didn't remember the Halo of the Sun. I know why Abelie wasn't married to Aiden like you remembered and why he is a Shadow now. It all makes sense. I understand . . . I know *why*." I blinked a few times, trying to rid my eyes of the pictures from my dream.

It was in that moment that I realized that names did not define good or evil, but it was the soul within. The Shadow of the Sun might have caused death, but their minds had been altered by those full of light. I saw it happen. The Ladies of Light wanted the power, they were hungry for it. *They* turned the Guardians into Shadows. *They* altered Abelie's mind. In the dream, I could feel what she was feeling, hear what she was thinking. She didn't remember Aiden when she stared at him after he turned into a Shadow. She felt terror. And in her mind, she didn't know why she was there, or who the Halo of the Sun were.

Andrew pushed a piece of my hair behind my ear, startling me from my thoughts. There was a faint frown line between his eyebrows. "Tell me. I want to know, I want to help," he begged. "What is it that you witnessed? I could sense your feelings while you slept—they were a mixture of emotions. You were angry and irritated, you were afraid, and you grieved. And all I could do was hold you, and try to take those feelings away. Please, just let me do that now. Let me be your peace."

I nodded my head slowly. I felt like I could cry again at any second, but I was dry—there were no more tears left in me. Plus, I was tired of crying. The whole concept was still new to me, and I didn't like it. "I saw it all," I breathed, my voice weak with tiredness. "The answer to everything."

"Which is . . ."

"It's best if I tell all of you together," I told him, my voice barely a whisper. "It pertains to you all."

He nodded and looked down, as if in deep thought. "I'll gather everyone together." He looked back up at me, a look of avid anticipation on his face. "Will you be okay while I . . ."

"I'll be fine." I gestured with my hand for him to go. "I will meet you down stairs in a few. I just need—"

"Some time alone." He stood up and grabbed his shirt. He shot me a small half-smile before he bent and kissed me on the forehead. "If you need me . . ."

"I know where you'll be."

He nodded once and opened the door to leave.

He hesitated for a second at the door, looked over his shoulder, and shook his head once before deciding to finally exit.

Sitting up, I tried to shake off the feelings from the dream. Abelie's grief was still overtaking me. It was weird to feel so upset over three deaths that I knew were irrelevant now. Those angels were alive and waiting for me downstairs. I knew that it wasn't only Abelie's anguish I felt. A lot of it was my own, because I knew that there was one angel that wouldn't be waiting for me downstairs—the one angel that would never have those memories of a time before the Shadows . . . the Shadows that were all just a lie—a trick.

When I looked in the mirror, I noticed the green of my eyes had faded into that same bright blue as Andrew's. Automatically, my hand rose to the large dark circles under my eyes. I was never going to get a good night's rest with these dreams. My eyes followed the line of the beautiful silk robe. It was more of a dress than anything. It was beautiful and even more stunning on Abelie; I remembered from one of my dreams. I went straight to her closet and opened it to see more robes just like this one, but in different colors. I put my nose to the first one I grabbed and drew in a deep breath. It was her scent—her lovely smell that I would never . . . I pushed the thought aside and closed the closet doors.

I dashed down the stairs and peeked onto each floor. I wondered what kind of mysteries this place presented. Voices wafted up the stairs and I started to take them two at a time, eager to reach the bottom.

When I peered through the entry way, I could see that at the end of the tunnel of books was Abelie's body. I made my way slowly toward the silhouette as if I were wading through deep water.

"Let's go this way," Andrew whispered in my ear, seemingly out of nowhere, as if I were fragile. He placed his arm around my waist and pulled me in another direction. "Everyone's waiting for you."

Aiden sat at the head of a very long table, the same one we had gathered around last night. Ehno and Lucia were beside each other on Aiden's left. Joseph was on his other side, an anxious expression on his face. Andrew and I sat beside Joseph as everyone turned toward me, all of them nervously waiting for me to speak. I was uneasy too.

I stared at Aiden, trying to look past the charcoal-like skin, the fiery eyes, the lava filled cracks in his skin. He was a Halo, a part of the elite.

"Aiden, how long have you been a Shadow? Where did Shadows even come from?" If the Ladies of Light altered the Shadows' minds, I wondered what they did to blanket their time of being angels, instead of Shadows.

Aiden seemed a little confused by my questions. "I have always been a Shadow," he stated. "If there was a life before this, I do not remember it. Ever since I can recall it has always been told that Shadows were from hell, cast out of the light to forever be tortured in fire. Of course, I can't remember any time in hell." He snorted.

"Whatever you think you know, it is a lie," I told him with a straight face, deciding to get straight to the point.

The fire in his eyes seemed to brighten. "I don't unde—"

"You are the leader of the Guardians," I said this as present tense because I knew no matter what, he was still a leader—one of the good guys. "You have *always* protected mankind. You were Abelie's husband before you were ever a Shadow. That was why you were so attracted to her, you always loved her, long before—"

"Wait," Ehno cut me off, "this *truly is* Aiden," he pointed at him, his eyebrows raised, "*the* Aiden that reigned over all the Halo of the Sun? But he's . . . and . . ." his speech faltered.

"What was the last thing that you can remember doing before you woke up on the plane, Ehno?" I wondered, curiosity had welled up inside me.

His expression hardened.

It just didn't make sense. If Andrew, Ehno, and Lucia were all "murdered" when I saw their deaths, then they would have known about the Ladies of Light. In my dream they knew of their plans and were preparing to stop them. It just didn't make any sense.

It hit me then, like a bright light bulb had turned on over my head: A consequence of being turned into a human was the loss of memory. I knew that first hand. But how did they know anything about the angel world then? And how had I been able to see the things that I have through Abelie's memory if her mind was altered? Was it because the lie had not been planted deeply enough into my mind either? My head was beginning to hurt from trying to understand everything.

"Andrew, Aiden, and I were all working with some of our new Guardians, explaining to them what their assignments were," Ehno explained. "Zola had informed us only days before that there was going to be a fire in Istanbul that would destroy ten-thousand homes. We wanted Guardians there to help save as many human lives as possible."

Andrew nodded in agreement. "I remember. Lucia interrupted to inform us of a meeting that the Ladies of Light had requested we attend. Of course, you don't argue with the Ladies of Light. After that . . . I can't remember a thing."

"It's true," Lucia chimed in. "But no matter how hard I try, I can't remember what the meeting was supposed to be about."

"Well," I frowned, "I *do* know what it was about."

They all looked at me eagerly, like I was about to disclose the solution to a mystery. I had no solutions.

I inhaled deeply before I spoke, as if I were about to say it all in one breath. "The Ladies of Light informed the Halo of the Sun of their plans to slaughter the humans—*all* of them." There were several disgusted sounds across the table, and Joseph, who had previously remained quiet, very visibly gulped. "Of course, the Halo of the Sun would not permit it, and you three," I pointed between Andrew, Ehno, and Aiden, "went to meet with the Ladies of Light in private to talk them down. They agreed not to kill the humans. Afterwards, there was an assembly of the elite angels; Halos, Guardians, and Elders. The Ladies of Light went behind the backs of the Halos, made a few choice decisions, and informed the angels during the gathering that killing mankind had not been a wise decision, but they had come up with a more 'brilliant' plan of enslaving them instead, saying that it would be more merciful."

403

There was a spasm in Lucia's face. "That's just ghastly," she spat.

"Intolerable." Ehno stood, exploding with anger.

"Are you sure?" Andrew looked at me intently as he rested his big hand over mine on the table. "That is what you saw in your dream?"

"That's only the beginning," I said in my desperation to make them all understand how dire this all really was. The dispiriting realization crept up my veins. Everyone was quite still as the impact of my words hit them.

Andrew's hand tightened over mine. He broke the silence first. "Of course not. I could feel your emotions. You were livid and aggravated. Next came . . . *fear*." He looked as though he just had a sudden rush of understanding. Then came the anxiety.

Ehno lowered back down to his chair, exchanging a dark look with Andrew and Lucia.

I barely nodded. "Lucia came to join your side because she disagreed with what Liz and Mimi had decided."

"Absolutely!" Lucia agreed. "How would I ever let them get as far as they did?" she shouted angrily, shooting up from her chair just as Ehno did.

"There was another meeting," I continued. "Except this time the Ladies of Light were left out." I gestured for Lucia to sit down. She did. I leaned toward her. "Lucia, you were there. Everyone had agreed and planned to stop the Ladies of Light before they were able to go through with their hideous plan."

Lucia folded her arms and huffed angrily, "I knew they seemed to be enjoying their power more than any one should."

"Well, the Ladies of Light won against the Halos, Guardians, and even you, Lucia." I stopped, not wanting to go on.

Ehno took in a deep breath and closed his eyes. "I can see it."

Andrew's head snapped away from my face to look at Ehno. I could see the thoughts crowding behind Ehno's eyes.

"It can't be!" Andrew said in a scandalized voice.

"What do you see, Ehno?" Lucia asked, placing her hand on his forearm. "Tell me."

"They came to battle against the Guardians," Ehno said, his eyes closed as if he were watching the scene in his head. "They wanted to kill them all. They were suddenly irrelevant to their plans—there would soon be no humans to protect, or none worth protecting. They didn't care—they converged upon the Halos and the Guardians." With each word, his voice began to rise furiously. "Lucia sacrificed herself for the greater good. The Ladies turned her . . . *human*. Then they killed her." Ehno's eyes snapped opened.

"How is sacrificing yourself an effective strategy?" Joseph asked incredulously.

"I don't know . . ." Lucia whispered.

We were all quiet for a moment before Ehno continued. "We fought back, of course." He stared at Andrew like they were communicating silently. They probably were. "It was chaos after that as the Ladies started to chant deadly words to finish the job. Their overwhelming spell didn't kill the Guardians and Halos; it turned them all to Shadows." Lucia made a funny noise and when I looked at her, she looked as though someone had just slapped her in the face.

Ehno's jaw tightened as he continued with the story that I had witnessed only an hour before. "The Ladies of Light were frightened when they realized that the Guardians and Halos didn't die—that they were Shadows. They panicked when the Shadows started to wake from the spell and that is why no one remembers—they altered their minds. All of them— Shadows, Elders, all the angel world."

"So," I said, "how can Lucia remember being an angel after being turned into a human? I thought that was a side effect."

It was Aiden who answered me. "Dear one, she

died . . . and then she came back to life. If her body could be restored after such an absolute death, surely her memories could be as well."

"It still doesn't make any sense—why can't they remember *everything*?"

Aiden sighed. "I don't know. I'm sure there is an explanation, I just don't know it."

I looked around the room to see if anyone else had the answers. None of them said anything for several painfully long seconds.

"We are in trouble." Ehno frowned deeply. He muttered horrible curses under his breath. Andrew turned his direction and then nodded in agreement.

"I know we are," I admitted, snapping them all out of their horror-struck gazes. "*It has all been a lie.*"

Ehno's muttering became more and more offensive. I ignored him as I watched everyone else struggle to comprehend what we both tried to convey.

"You mean . . ." Aiden looked down at his skin, his eyes opening widely, dramatically. Then, he got this look in his eyes, as if a light had just turned on in his mind. "I'm *not* a Shadow, and this is all just a . . . *a spell?*"

"Exactly," I said.

Aiden just looked at me like the idea was ludicrous. Then an alarmed expression spread over his face. I could understand; if I hadn't seen it firsthand I wouldn't have believed it.

There was nothing but stunned silence after that.

"So why are we in trouble?" Joseph cut through the dead air. Many emotions flitted across his face before he settled on looking politely puzzled.

"Because," Andrew said, trying to inject a note of common sense, "if the angels' minds have been altered, then none of them know the truth, not even the Shadows themselves. We are in this alone—we have no allies. No one would believe that the Ladies of Light are capable of such brutal means. What we know, and what the other angels know, are two different universes."

I pulled my hand out from under Andrew's and brushed my fingers against his cheek. I knew he could feel the electricity from the touch. His head turned my direction and his expression softened.

"If the Halo of the Sun *are* Shadows now, and the Guardians are too, then why aren't humans slaves?" My voice lowered with a determined calm. "Or worse—*dead*?"

We all turned our gazes upon Aiden for the answer. He was the only one who had been around this whole time.

He plunged immediately into his story. "The

Shadows have prevented angels from going through with their actions because we knew that with humans on their side—even if they were just slaves—the Shadows might be defeated. All we have ever wanted was to be left alone."

"What?" I shot up as if fired from a canon. Now *I* was irate. "You knew all along yet no one ever said anything?"

"We didn't know that it was *only* the Ladies of Light who wanted humans to be their slaves," he confessed. "We thought it was all of the angels. That was how I met Abelie." His eyes were reminiscent.

Pain seared in my stomach at her name. I was jealous of all the time he had to spend with her, when I had no time at all. Reflexively, my eyes looked over his shoulder toward her still form. The image of her death still haunted my mind. Her body, still and lifeless on the ground, almost overwhelmed me every time my mind replayed the gruesome scene.

Aiden continued, not noticing my distracted state. "My instructions were to try to gain access to the Divine Library to see if there was any information that could help us defeat the angels. After spying on Abelie and following her for weeks, I realized that she was *good*, moral. She didn't want to harm humans. She even loved them.

"Once I revealed myself to her she was terrified, but for some reason she didn't back away or cast me out. She just stood there in all of her beautiful glory." His lips twitched up into a small smile. "I spoke to her and she listened. That was then I stopped trying to destroy the angels—thirty years ago." He looked over his shoulder at the silhouette of Abelie's body under the silken cloth.

Andrew reached out and took my hand and pulled me back to my seat. I had forgotten I was even standing. "There's nothing we could have done," he said softly.

I knew that, I just didn't want to believe it. "Why?" I pleaded weakly, like an annoying child.

My eyes never left that silken cloth draped over my mother. Andrew put a finger to my jaw and turned my head to face his. The golden color hadn't returned. His eyes were still blue, just like Ehno's and Lucia's. For several long seconds he studied my face and then brushed his thumb over my lips.

"I wish I could make you smile and laugh like before." Though he continued to hold my face still, my eyes darted down, hoping that his words wouldn't make me dissolve into tears. "Please look at me, Gabriella." When I did, he only looked more desolate than before. "We couldn't have saved her—she was gone before any of us could have prevented her death."

"I still don't—"

"If it was anything else, she would have survived. But that was magic. That spell severed her soul from her body," he whispered, grief evident on his face.

My insides were boiling at what he just told me— that she was really and *truly* gone. I jumped and found myself on my feet, like I was a cork exploding from a champagne bottle. All the air had vanished from my lungs. Andrew pulled me back down to the chair again. I bit my lip trying to will back the tears, but just like earlier, I was dry. The pained expression must have still evident on my face because he hugged me to his chest.

"What do we do now?" I asked in a low, anxious whisper. He pulled away and looked at everyone else around the table.

Lucia stood, walked toward the other end of the table, and picked up the book on prophecies. She set it down in front of me, the dust floating up in a cloud at the action. "We find the rest of this prophecy. The Ladies of Light didn't go through all of this trouble to try and kill you if you weren't a threat to them."

"She's right," Aiden added. "We are in the Divine Library. There is bound to be something in here that could answer some of our questions—or possibly provide us with answers on how to stop them." He shot me a sad smile. "I have a feeling you are the one who will have the honor of restoring the minds of the angels. You are *my* daughter, after all," he said proudly. "And you are part Abelie."

I couldn't help it; I smiled for the first time in what felt like a decade.

"Let's separate," Lucia said. "We can cover more ground."

"What are we looking for?" Joseph wondered.

"I'm not sure," Lucia admitted. "But if you find anything that you think could give us answers, grab it. Whatever you find, bring it down here so we can go through it."

Everyone stood and made their way to the stairs. I stayed put and Andrew hesitated at the edge of the bookshelves. When I didn't look up from my death stare at the table, I saw out of my peripheral vision that he had nodded to himself, like he had made some internal decision. Then he turned and floated away.

When the room became quiet, I scooted my chair back which made a horrible noise across the floor. I didn't bother pushing it back under as I inched toward Abelie. My hand reached out without my permission to remove the silk cloth from her face. I moved it slowly, as if not to wake her—which was silly. Maybe I was just hoping in the back of my mind that she would come back to me. Her eyes were closed; her skin was almost as white as the sheet covering her. What happened to her was so horrific—it was hard to digest. All of the happiness I had left felt like it was being leeched out of me.

"I didn't have enough time," I whispered, afraid speaking loudly would ruin her paradise, because surely that was where she was now—paradise. But more than anything, I wanted to get her out of the Divine Library. I wanted to put her to rest. I leaned down to kiss her cold cheek. With much effort, I placed the cloth back over her face. My previously exhausted emotions seemed to be reviving. I closed my eyes and let a single tear escape and trickle down my cheek. In that second, I decided that I couldn't afford to let something like this happen again. I would protect those I loved, no matter what the cost to myself.

I followed the path to the stairs and ascended them, listening to my footsteps echo in the silence. On the third floor, I found the place absent of anyone and began to look through the books. The place looked like a large splendid hall full of secrets begging to be shared.

Hours passed, and no book seemed to jump out at me. As I walked through the shelves of books between the thirteenth and fourteenth centuries, my mind continued to wander from one line of the prophecy to the next. Andrew said there was more, but not in that book—the pages had been erased. The third floor was full of interesting books and information that I would have normally loved to have read, but not today. Not after Abelie, and not after reading that prophecy.

Every time I thought I had figured something out explained it, there was always that one thing that would come in and pull the rug out from under me, turning my life upside down and backwards.

As my fingers drifted between the Italian books, I noticed that my fingers had left trails. It was dusty. And as if to prove my point I sneezed.

"Bless you," murmured Andrew.

I spun around, startled. He saw the look on my face, the one that was screaming for him to hold me. He didn't even hesitate. He took two long strides and ate up the space between us. There was just something about his embrace that made me feel whole—like he was keeping the pieces of me together. His sturdy hands snaked their way around my shoulders and his warm lips pressed against my hair. "We will get through this."

"As long as we are together," I whispered against his chest. It felt odd for me to feel so weak when the power was obviously growing within me. His arms squeezed me tightly, and I was enveloped in his intoxicating scent.

As we pulled apart, he kept his face mere inches from mine. His breath filled the space between us. "I know you are eager to leave, but I am worried about what or who will be waiting for us when we unseal the door." He could read my emotions so easily. Abelie deserved to be laid to rest.

My hands were on his chest, his arms still holding me to him. By the look in his eyes, I could read that he was just as absorbed by our closeness as I was. "We can't stay here forever," I barely whispered. "Abelie can't stay here . . ."

"*Shh*," he murmured and pulled my hair away from my face with his fingers. His expression was one of torture. "Please don't cry."

I didn't know I was.

With great gentleness, he secured my face in his palms. I stopped breathing then. My heart thumped against my chest. He hesitated, but I continued to gaze into his sapphire eyes. He wiped the wetness away from my cheeks and then moved in closer to me. So many emotions raged through me at once: desire, passion, and ecstasy. He was only an inch away from my face. I closed my eyes and felt the electricity flowing between us. Every second that passed, a new emotion would flit through my body, sending shivers of pleasure through my veins. I trembled under his touch.

Finally, the very tips of his lips brushed lightly against mine. He pressed against me more earnestly until our lips moved with each other. And for the first time in my life, I could actually hear his heart hammering in his chest, along with mine. This kiss was more passionate than before; it had more meaning. There were deeper emotions—stronger desires. My skin warmed under his eager grip. I embraced him back just as fiercely. He knotted his hands in my hair and pulled me closer to him. We were both breathing heavily now. I parted my lips as he deepened the kiss.

The fireworks one would look for during a kiss were nothing in comparison to the bright explosions of euphoria I felt. Suddenly, my desire ignited, and I was immediately aware of the blood that had rushed to my cheeks. There was a peculiar sensation in my midriff. My fingers found their way to his hair and I pulled him even closer to me. I didn't think that was possible.

Andrew must have felt the change in my body because his lips quickly found their way down my neck as he kissed wildly around my throat. It was in need now. His heart pounded passionately against mine as we clung to each other.

We were approaching a precarious level. He continued to push my restraint to the limits. Normally I would have pulled away, demanded a breather. But I didn't. We fit together so perfectly, like puzzle pieces. And as cheesy as it sounded, it was true. He was my angel and I was his. In that second, all I could think about was how I had to have him—*all* of him. And I knew in that moment that we were destined to be together—there was no other explanation for these feelings.

My arms encircled his neck as I lifted myself up and wrapped my legs around his waist. All of my exercise in self control was slowly losing ground, but it just felt right. He pulled away slightly and stared at me with a look of hunger in his eyes. He searched my gaze for several seconds as his chest rose and fell rapidly with each of his breaths. "Are you all right, Ella?" he breathed with a look of pure adoration on his face.

I nodded. My heart leapt at my name coming from his mouth. Though I had been called Ella in the past, it had never seemed right, but on his tongue, in his rich accent, it was perfect. *He* was perfect.

"We won't go farther," he barely whispered. His face was so close to mine and I was ravenous. I had to have him.

"Of course not," I said breathlessly and brought his lips firmly to mine. And though his kisses were the best things I had ever tasted, I felt like I needed more. I deliberated kissing him fully, deeply, but then knew what the consequences of such an indulgence would be. I'd lose control; I knew I would. And I didn't want that to happen here, amidst the dusty shelves in the library.

I broke away from his mouth and kissed the line of his jaw up to his ear and then down his neck. A low growl rumbled in his chest and he pushed me up against the bookshelf. A book toppled down and Andrew reached out and caught it. Before he tossed it to the ground, I caught the title of the book, *Timeless*. Though the title wasn't what I had been looking for, something told me we needed to open it.

"Wait!" I barely choked out. "I think we need to read that."

power

ndrew held out the book to me. I grabbed it and rubbed my thumb over the title *Timeless* again. It seemed to be suffused with a mysterious glow. That was what angels were—living in their timeless immortality. Or that was what I thought until Abelie died. Even she thought that death was a fate the angels would eventually endure. She was right.

"There was a part of your dream you left out earlier," Andrew said, bringing me from my thoughts. "And I want to know what happened. You said you saw my death."

Without looking up, I responded, "The Ladies turned Lucia into a human. I can only guess that was the same spell that Abelie and Aiden used when she decided to turn me human. Anyway, this was the second time I had seen Lucia's death. She was stabbed with a knife with the Definitive Sun symbol on it by a Lady of Light." I finally looked up to see Andrew staring at me intently. "Ehno loves Lucia, doesn't he?"

He nodded. "Always has."

"You can imagine how livid he was, then," I

mused. "He ran after her and you followed, probably trying to stop him from getting himself killed. The Ladies didn't even hesitate as they turned you human and struck you both down alongside her."

"What did you see after that?" he prodded, not even a note of anxiety in his voice.

I didn't want to think about it, but he deserved to know since he couldn't remember. "A battle began. The Ladies of Light tried to kill the Halos and Guardians. Instead they turned to Shadows. In Abelie's head she didn't remember what happened; she just saw the Shadows and panicked. When she stared at Aiden, she didn't recognize him. That was when I figured out that the Ladies of Light had altered her mind. And they obviously altered the minds of all the other angels, including the Shadows." I shook my head back and forth in disgust. "You know what this means?"

"No—"

"*It means* that we have to change the Shadows back." I sighed. "We have to find a way to return the angels' minds. How else will we fight against the Ladies of Light?"

"We'll try to find the answers," he promised.

"Have you seen this book before?"

"It looks familiar," he said. His eyebrows knitted together. "Let's take it downstairs."

I nodded, my breathing still heavy from being intimate with Andrew. He moved in closer to me and I backed into the bookshelf again. He placed a kiss on my ear and then whispered against my skin, "We'll talk about this," he moved his hand between me and him, "later." My breathing hitched and he pulled away, chuckling.

He took my hand and we went back down to the first level of the library. Lucia was the only one down there, scouring through the bookshelves for something that could help. When she saw us she stopped poring over the books to join us at the table.

"What did you find?" she wondered.

"Have you ever seen this book?" I held it up for her.

She snatched it out of my grasp. "Yes," she breathed.

Andrew and I exchanged a look of surprise.

"It's about our history. It's been more than a thousand years since I've seen this. Where did you find it?" she asked, a faint crease between her eyebrows.

With a smirk, Andrew said, "It fell from a shelf above Gabriella's head."

I could feel the heat rise in my cheeks. "Andrew caught it before it could knock me out," I admitted. "I saw the title and, for some reason, I knew we needed to read it."

She nodded, but didn't look up from the dusty bindings. Without speaking, she handed it back to me. "If you have a feeling there is something in here that can help, then you should be the one to read it."

I raised my eyebrows.

"Because you might see something that one of us doesn't," she explained and shot me an inquiring glance.

"Right."

I sat down and placed the book before me as I stared at it like it would express words of comfort. The binding was hard and a dusty grey color. The only word on it was *Timeless*. There were no pictures, no author name . . . just *Timeless*. I blew the dust off the cover and opened the book to reveal yellowed pages that looked so fragile I wasn't sure if I wanted to turn them. I looked up to Andrew who smiled back at me. He placed his hand over the page. "*Proteggere*," he murmured.

Protect. It was easy to understand him, and that weirded me out a little. There was a slight gleam to the pages, as if an electric force coated the paper before it disappeared.

"Thanks," I said.

I flipped the first page over, looked at the writing

and squinted. "Um, this isn't going to work," I told Andrew as I pointed to the text. "It's in Italian."

He sat down beside me and put his finger to the first paragraph. "*Tradurre*," he mumbled.

Again, I understood the word. *Translate.* "It's weird that I can understand you when you speak Italian, but I can't read it," I told him with a half smirk. "But, I wonder, why is it that I was able to use magic without using Italian . . . you know, earlier?"

He smiled. "Because you are far more powerful than you realize. You are only learning about yourself. I personally believe it was your grief and anger that made you explode with power like you did," he rationalized. "Plus, you don't even have to use words to wield magic. With practice, you can just think it—will it to happen and it will. Not many people bothered to learn that skill, but it is one I would advise you to practice."

I nodded. "Because it looks like I have a battle ahead of me?"

He ran his fingers through his hair. "I hope not, for your sake, but it is better to be prepared than not."

I looked back down at the page and started reading.

```
It was easy to hide ourselves in
the mountains of Italy, away from
the cruel and corrupt. But as armies
became more powerful, they also
became more greedy. After centuries
of being left alone, an army finally
found its way through the mountains
to the small village of Divina.
```

This really was their history. Immediately, I became intrigued, pulled the book off the table, placed it in my lap, and leaned closer to devour every word. Andrew chuckled next to me.

"Try this," he barely spoke in my ear. He grabbed my hand and put it over the page I was reading. "Close your eyes," he whispered.

"I don't see how covering the page and closing my eyes is going to help me read this any better," I said, amused.

"Trust me," he breathed.

"I do. You know I do."

"Keep your eyes closed and will the story to be told to you."

"What?" I asked. My eyes flew open and I shot him a skeptical look.

"You can use magic to read this without ever look-ing at it. Trust me," he smirked. "All the books in this place have been infused with memories. Memories can tell you more than the words."

"More than the words?" I raised my eyebrows.

"Sometimes secret messages can lay hidden beneath the context of the words. My mother and father used to pass love notes to each other on the pretense they were making pottery when they were younger—before we became immortals. That was four-thousand years ago." His eyes seemed to blaze an even more radiant blue. "If one were to try to pull the images from the pottery, they would see the messages, or images, that they were passing back and forth to each other."

"What happened to your parents?" I wondered aloud.

"My mother became sick when I was twenty and she didn't survive the winter." His chest rose under a heavy sigh before he continued. "My father lived until I was twenty-six. When he was hunting, he was bitten by a snake. He was too weak to use magic and the other hunters did not get to him in time. He was dead by the time they found him."

I realized, all of a sudden, that I hadn't asked him how old he was. "What age were you when you became immortal?"

"I was twenty-eight."

"And so you've been immortal for four-thousand

years?"

"Roughly. I suppose immortality isn't all it is cracked up to be. Eventually someone was going to snap; I just didn't think it would have been the Ladies of Light." His fist clenched above the table. "They were pure and good. They saved millions of lives. That is what makes it so difficult to believe that the Ladies of Light would do those things." He looked up at the ceiling and shook his head. "Turning Halos and Guardians into Shadows? It just doesn't make any sense. You don't think that someone is forcing them to—"

"No one forces the Ladies to do anything they don't want to do," Lucia cut in. "We fought against them. And we both know the *Soul Stalker* isn't strong enough to control them." She snickered. "You saw what Gabriella did to the Soul Stalker—what she couldn't do to the Ladies of Light. It's obvious that they are doing this all on their own. They are not who they used to be."

I nodded in agreement. "I didn't see anything in my dream that would counter what we saw when they attacked us outside the underground laboratory."

We all relapsed into silence.

I closed my eyes and put my hand upon the pages of the old book. Who knew when this had been written? In the silence, I concentrated with all my being on trying to pull the words, the meanings, off the pages. And without warning, there was a sinking sensation. I felt like I was being squeezed into a small hole, or as if a big hand was pulling me down until I was standing in a small sand-colored room. There were five people who all stood around an elderly woman who sat like an ancient sentinel. Her eyes were glazed over as if she had cataracts and her face was radiantly wrinkled and dark.

"Welcome, Illuminator." She smiled at me. A few of her teeth were missing. "I am Zola, the prophetess."

"Zola?" I questioned, moving forward. It felt like I was in a dream; all of my movements were slow. Each tiny movement seemed to be magnified—like I was a sleepwalker. For a few seconds, I just stared at her in complete disbelief.

"I knew one day you would come." She gestured for me to sit down. The five others, all dressed in white togas, moved away to reveal a stone chair. I strode past them and took a seat, wondering why they all looked like Greek gods.

"Where am I?"

"*We* are in Greece, but this is only a memory, placed in the *Timeless* book for you to find," she explained in her throaty voice. Her face remained stony. "These are the Ladies of Light." She pointed to three stunning women, their hair tied in beautiful knots around their heads. Beneath the white of their heavy togas you could see their tattoos that snaked around their arms and neck. "And these two are leaders of the Halos and Guardians." Both men were tall and well built. The one thing that seemed to be the same with all five of them was the fact that their skin looked like it had been carved from wood.

They all bowed before me, low enough that they were horizontal at the waist, almost as if they were looking at their toes. "Illuminator," they greeted, then they rose.

"The prophecy you know of is a *lie*," the prophetess said, getting straight to the point.

"What?" I stood up, chest swelling. "Is *everything* a lie?" There was a trace of panic in my voice. Hadn't people heard of the saying, *honesty is the best policy*?

One of the Ladies of Light put her hand on my shoulder and returned me to my sitting position. She was tall and her hair was like liquid silver. She had a fair face and angled features.

"It wasn't always that way, bright one," Zola rasped, bringing my attention back to her. She leaned back on her perch with veiled eyes. "But some have not been able to handle the power with the grace we have always promised ourselves. You cannot trust those around you. Be cautious, always."

"Who *can* I trust?" The panic in my voice was more pronounced, my heart leapt in my chest. If there was anyone around me that I couldn't trust, I didn't know what I would do. I couldn't imagine Andrew, Ehno, or Lucia ever doing anything to hurt me, and I knew my father would protect me. I just knew he would. That's what fathers do, right?

"Illuminator, you can trust your kindred soul and those who died to save mankind." That answered one question: Andrew, Ehno, and Lucia were trustworthy.

"Kindred soul?" I asked, my eyebrows raised.

"Have you not met him yet?"

"Are you talking about . . ." *Andrew*, I finished in my head.

"Ah, you have met him." She nodded to herself as if I had answered her earlier question. "Confide in him. He will not lead you astray—he will do everything in his power to protect you. He will love you more than any human could ever love another."

I barely moved my head up and down in a nod. He cared for me, he obviously wanted to protect me, and I was pretty sure, even within a few hours of being with him, that I had quickly fallen for him. Normally, I could barely tell if I liked a guy within two dates, let alone love someone. My head felt like it was being weighed down with anchors and dumped into the ocean.

"And what about my father?" I questioned to try and quiet my mind. No such luck.

"He loves you dearly." She smiled her toothless smile at me. "You can trust him."

I already knew that—but I had to be sure so I could crush that small fragment of thought that he was not as perfect as I wanted him to be.

"And what about *other* angels?" I pressed. The thought of Karen being so sweet and nice to me and how I just completely fell for it made me feel sickened and angry.

"Their minds have been altered," she reminded me. "They know you are the chosen one, but they are easily manipulated. Until their altered minds are repaired, you cannot trust any of them. They are not all bad, but their minds are easily corruptible."

"Why are you telling me all of this through a book?"

"The Ladies of Light will capture me," she stated. "You'll need to find me."

Automatically, I turned to look at the three women. They didn't speak. They only gazed at the old woman, their posture so straight it was as if a steel rod had materialized in their spines.

"Find you?" There was a note of real desperation

in my voice.

"Oh no, bright one, not *these* Ladies." She coughed out a soft laugh. "Each cycle brings about new Ladies. The cycle I am speaking off will be the new Ladies of 1700. If you find me, I will be able to help you save them all."

"Um," I paused. "Do you mean A.D.?"

The prophetess sighed. "Yes, luminous one. But that is not why I have left this message for you."

"Why have you?"

"The prophecy." One of the Ladies handed her a clay cup. She took a sip before she continued. "You were born to illuminate the dark ones. But you have also been born to vanquish those full of shadow. This is one part of the prophecy the Ladies of Light have taken out of context so angels will believe you are here to kill the Shadows, when in fact it is to kill them." Her voice lowered. "They are frightened of you, as they should be. If you learn to control your power, you will be able to kill them."

I shot up like a rocket. "I am not a murderer!" The idea was repugnant. "Sure, I'll fight to save the Shadows, but I will not *kill* anyone." The thought was just ghastly. I couldn't fathom taking someone's life, like those Shadows who took Abelie's. Even though in the back of my mind I thought about how I was willing to hurt Susan to break the angels free. Deep down I couldn't really do it though, I knew that.

Zola's face stayed controlled and unemotional— completely unfazed. The only thing she did was raise her eyebrows in an irritating and superior way. The three Ladies of Light looked absolutely hawk-like.

"Not a murderer? What if it saved your kindred soul?"

That was the last straw.

Though I couldn't see the book anymore, I knew my hand was still placed upon the page. Livid, I yanked my hand from the book and the scene around me vanished in an instant and all I was looking at were the backs of my eyelids. When I opened my eyes, Andrew was gazing at me, waiting to hear what I would have to say. He stretched out a consoling hand. *Kindred soul* flittered across my mind. I let out a breath I didn't know I was holding in.

"I can't stay here," I said pointedly. Suddenly, everything came out in a rush. "I need to bury my mother and who knows what my family must be thinking. They probably think I'm some *terrorist*. We need to get this all worked out and I need to call Jenna." I took in a breath before I steamrollered on. "She is probably worried sick. And my dog, Hercules . . . and now I am supposed to be a murderer. *I'm* supposed to *kill* the Ladies of Light and I am *not* supposed to kill the Shadows," I went on desperately, my voice high-pitched and somewhat hysterical. "I am supposed to 'illuminate' them—*whatever that means*. And everything is a *lie* and I don't even know what is true and what is false and you are an angel . . . and I love you and you admit that you love me and I am just a little crazy right now." It was starting to become difficult to talk due to my hysteria. "And all I can think about is getting out of this place before I go absolutely nuts. And now here I am—"

Andrew silenced me with a kiss. I felt a rush of gratitude for his intervention. His fingers came up and lightly pulled me closer. Reflexively, my eyes closed and I let out a long sigh and relaxed under his fingers. It was only for a couple of seconds, but it seemed as if his touch melted away all of my hysteria. My frustrations seemed to disappear for a moment. But when he pulled away, it all slammed back with force.

"Like I told you before, we will get through this *together*," he declared with obvious sincerity. I wanted to tell him how much it meant to me that he was here for me, but words were not enough. He placed his hand on my knee and I seemed to deflate under his penetrating gaze. "Now, what did you see?"

"It was Zola. She said that the Ladies of Light will

capture her—which means that she is probably already locked away somewhere *and* she said that I am supposed to kill the Ladies of Light, *not* the Shadows. That I am supposed to save the Shadows by illuminating them." I took several breaths, the panic about to spill over at any moment. "She said that I was powerful and that the Ladies should be scared of me." Once I said the words, I realized how silly they sounded. I couldn't imagine being more powerful than the Ladies of Light—the same ones who tore through an army without a bat of an eyelash. I wish I knew where that power was, because I felt like I was greatly lacking.

Andrew nodded slowly and frowned in concentration. "That all makes sense to me."

I heaved a great sigh, though it sounded more like a roar of frustration. My nerves were wound as tight as guitar strings—you could probably play a tune on them. "I'm glad you found clarity, because I haven't. I feel just as confused as ever."

"We'll all be there for you. We will find the answers." He said this so firmly, so absolutely that it made me jealous that he felt so sure, because I did not feel very assured.

"Where are the others?" I wondered. "I don't think it is wise to stay here for long with all of those Shadows waiting outside."

Andrew turned toward the direction of the staircase and, abruptly, Ehno, Aiden, and Joseph emerged from the hallway of books. It was nice that Ehno and Andrew were linked—it saved time.

They all stared at me, waiting. When had I become this all-knowing leader when I still didn't know diddly about this world?

I took charge anyway. "I've seen angels just pop in and out of existence. Why can't we just do that now?" I wasn't sure if 'pop' was the right word or not. "I know that Joseph can't and of course there's Abelie . . ." I sighed as my thoughts rolled around in my brain like tumbleweeds. I shot a few covert glances towards Abelie. "Or how about a portal to another dimension, Lucia? And as a matter-of-fact, why couldn't you guys just do that at the underground lab?" The pressure, all the weight from everything, seemed to be weighing heavily on my shoulders.

Ehno, Andrew, and Lucia all exchanged uneasy looks. "It took me a while to figure it out," Lucia admitted. "At the lab, there must have been a spell over us to prevent us from leaving, at least leaving in a supernatural way."

Ehno nodded. "It makes sense, especially after we found out that Karen was the Soul Stalker out to murder you."

Each time I uncovered something, it was as if a knife were twisting further into me, refusing to let me solve this mystery.

Lucia walked over to me, her long auburn hair falling forward as she bent down to me. Her blue eyes seemed to search mine for several seconds before she spoke. "The Divine Library is infused with powerful magic to protect it from the outside world which ultimately keeps us inside. The only way in and out of here is through the front door."

Thinking about being on the other side of that door where all of those Shadows were sent a strange excitement through me. There was a burning fiery urge for justice that filled my veins.

"Well"—I stood and turned towards everyone—"I hope you are ready to leave because I'm unsealing that door."

28

Be at peace

It was all about being mentally prepared. Before, there were roughly thirty Shadows. Within the twenty-four hour time frame we had been inside the Divine Library, who knows what kind of crowd had accumulated. The Ladies of Light could be standing on the doorstep this very second—or possibly the Soul Stalker. I shuddered. My master plan of leaving the library suddenly felt stupid and idiotic, but I was hungry and Abelie deserved to be laid to rest.

The others stood behind me as I gazed at the wall where the door used to be. No one pressured or pushed me forward to unseal the door. Andrew was at my back, his key outstretched on his palm. I took in a deep breath before I reached over and grasped the key and held it securely in my hand. I knew we needed to leave. I had to keep telling myself that we were doing the right thing. For an hour I gave myself pep talks.

In my other hand was the *Timeless* book which I handed over to Andrew as I placed my palm against the smooth stone. I took another necessary deep breath and then whispered, "*Unseal.*"

437

Sparks lit around the edges, and then slowly the outline of the door began to form. It was like watching the door seal in reverse. Like a moron, I placed my ear against the crack and listened. The door was shut securely, so of course I wasn't able to hear anything except for the sounds of the rock, which were silent, of course. It was almost like putting my ear to a seashell. It sounded like the ocean, the air weaving in and out of the space between my ear and the rock.

"Did you hear anything?" Ehno chuckled from behind me.

I turned around to cast him a glare which made him laugh even more. "No," I said icily, but couldn't help but smile in return. "I couldn't hear any rock 'n roll, to my dismay," I deadpanned.

Everyone laughed at my very dry humor and Andrew raised his eyebrows to hair level.

"I'm not always sad." I shrugged.

"Trust me," Andrew smiled, "you can be quite witty and funny, too. We all understand why you would be feeling a little *overwhelmed* right now."

I saw Lucia and Ehno nod in agreement.

"You got that right," Joseph said, absolutely serious. "I'm not some 'special chosen one', so I know it has to be a million times more difficult for you than for me. Plus, you just lost your mother . . ." he trailed off feebly and my eyes automatically darted to Aiden who was standing over Abelie's body in the distance.

Andrew walked in my view. "Let's lay her to rest."

I nodded imperceptivity and turned to insert the keys. A reckless daring seized me and I put them both in their locks and turned them at the same time. A puff of dust rose from the cracks as the door scratched across the stone floor.

As I stood at the opening of the library, the violent wind whipped across my face. I expected to see the Shadows light the distance with their fire. There were none—no Ladies of Light or Shadowy figures on the horizon. But it was dark, and my vision was not as great in the inky blackness.

"I don't see anyone," I barely whispered to Andrew.

His eyes narrowed as he scanned the view. "Me either." He turned around. "Ehno, have you seen the outcome of this evening?"

Ehno shook his head. "No, but I think we will be safe."

"Grab the keys," I told Andrew who handed me the keys and the *Timeless* book. I held onto them like they were life vests. To me, the keys represented safety, a sanctuary in the Divine Library, and the *Timeless* book possibly held more messages from Zola. There was no way I was letting these items out of my sight.

As each second passed, I could feel the power growing, twisting, and changing inside me. It was indescribable and strong. I had to be prepared, and I knew that was why I gathered the electricity at my core. Behind me were the angels I had grown to love and care for. But more important than any of this was the fact that Abelie needed to be buried. It was time to lay her to rest, as Andrew said, and no matter how much it would kill me to place her six feet under, I knew I had to. She had lived a long life—a happy one with Aiden at her side. Jealousy flitted through me again at the thought.

Wind whipped through the small doorway and the silk dress-like robe I was wearing clung to my body. It was the only black robe Abelie had in her closet, and wearing it made me feel closer to her. My hair flew up in the air but I was too busy gazing down at the quiet scene below me to care about the frosty October air that beat against my skin.

"Come on, Gabriella," Andrew said, taking my hand in his. He led me down the stone steps. When we reached the section of stairs that I had destroyed, he let go of my hand, jumped, and looked up to where I was standing. It was probably only fifteen feet, but that seemed mighty high to me, the one who is absolutely terrified of falling. The rocks below were mocking me as I stared down. "Jump," he called.

I stared at him with a look of disbelief. "Andrew . . . I—"

"She's scared of falling from heights," Joseph chimed in from behind me. I nodded in absolute agreement.

Andrew flew back up to where I was and knocked me off my feet, literally, and into his arms. He smiled down at me. Shadows darkened his face, but I could still see the amusement there. He dropped gently back down to the ground and set me on my feet. "Better?" he asked.

"Much."

Andrew started to take off to help Joseph, but Joseph had already landed on his feet with a thud right next to me. I looked up at him in utter shock. He just shrugged and said, "I learned all kinds of cool tricks while training to be an FBI agent."

Lucia and Ehno soon joined our ranks. The only two who were left were my parents. Andrew flew back up to the last step again and held out his arms for Abelie. Aiden kissed her on the cheek and then held her out to him as a golden tear slid down his charcoal skin. Andrew landed gracefully on his feet with Abelie securely in his arms. Aiden followed and they awkwardly moved Abelie between the two. She looked like she was sleeping and I wished that were true.

"We have to move at least fifty feet from the Divine Library for my portal to work," Lucia told me as we walked out into the silky blackness of the night. The moon was still a big orb in the sky, bathing the land in a ghostly reflection of daylight, hidden by a mist of clouds.

Fifty feet wasn't far from the bottom of the stairs. Lucia had closed her eyes and put her arms out, palms up. The air rippled before us. It was just like before, a weird disturbance, nothing like what you would see in the movies. There was no tunnel-looking vortex or wild electrical colors—it was almost as if there was a heat wave in the middle of the cold, dark air.

"I think we should go first." Andrew pointed to himself and Ehno. "It's better to be safe than sorry."

"You should stay here with Gabriella," Ehno contradicted. "You know I can go through and inform you if there is any danger on the other side."

"I'll bring up the rear," Lucia added.

"Keep her safe," Ehno said to Andrew while he pointed at me.

"I'm standing right here," I replied and rolled my eyes. "You don't have to talk about me like I'm not two feet away from you."

He seemed embarrassed, but turned and disappeared into the portal.

"Where are we going?" I asked Lucia as the cold wind whipped through the air again.

"Abelie and Aiden's home."

I turned toward Aiden. "You had a house together?"

"It was a secret." He looked down at the angel in his arms. "It was our small slice of paradise." His eyes cast toward Lucia. "I'll go next."

"Is everything clear on the other side, Andrew?" Lucia asked.

"Yes."

Aiden pivoted with Abelie close to his chest and disappeared into the quiet night air.

"You three should go next," Lucia pointed out. "Joseph has only been through a portal once and Gabriella was injured before. She probably doesn't remember what it was like."

"Just the horrible ache in my side," I agreed.

Andrew nodded once and grabbed my hand to pull me in the direction of the portal. The current raced between us and I tried to send as much love and adoration as I could through the connection. He looked down at me with a small smile and squeezed my hand in acknowledgement. As the three of us entered into the portal, wind rushed at us like a tornado had landed right next to our heads. I looked around me and was surprised to see two suns bright in the sky, and before I had the opportunity to take in my surroundings any more than that, I was suddenly sucked away as if a vacuum had pulled me through a tiny tube. I took a step and almost fell flat on my face but Andrew caught me before I hit the ground. Joseph walked through, unfazed by this new method of travel. I turned to him, gawking in surprise. He just gave me a mocking smile and said, very nonchalantly, "What? I travel like this all the time. In fact, I have enough frequent flyer miles racked up to circle the world three times."

I just shook my head at him.

The grounds were just as dark as before. It was so dark, in fact, that I could barely see two feet in front of me. As I stood there in the dark I started to panic. Since I had met and been tricked by Karen I had become extremely suspicious of everything, even the jet-blackness surrounding me. Andrew's fingers brushed against my hand and I jerked, surprised.

He lowered his head to my ear and whispered, "I'm sorry." My eyes shot around the line of trees I could barely make out in the night, as if there were spies in the trees.

Suddenly, we were blinded by lights that flooded the area. I blinked, trying to remove the imprint from my irises. When I finally accessed my vision again, I saw a beautiful house with richly brown stone walls and large arched windows. It was more than amazing; it was spectacular. The front door opened and through the door, light flooded the yard, silhouetting Aiden in the opening.

"Come on in guys," he waved us forward.

Inside, I circled around trying to take in the scene. There was a staircase that dominated the center of the house and railed around the second floor. The colors on the wall were all rich, earthy tones and the floor was a striking white and tan marble. The walls were covered with beautiful paintings, some of them ancient.

"This is your house?" I asked Aiden in awe.

"No," he sighed. "This was *our* house, mine and Abelie's."

I stopped my spinning and looked at him. He was leaning against the door frame of a darkened room. In my awe, I forgot about how hard this must be for my father. I inched toward him and held my hand out. He took it without looking up.

"D—Dad, where did you put Abelie?"

He didn't say a word, just led me down a hallway behind the staircase. He opened the first door to our right. She was laid upon a bed, another silken cloth over her body.

"Do you want me to leave?" he wondered.

I squeezed his hand tighter in mine. "No," I whispered and pulled him to the floor next to my mother. "Do you know where we are going to bury her?"

His hand rubbed against her cheek through the sheet covering her. "Yes, in the cemetery down the road."

"When?"

He looked up at a large clock on the wall. "It's still relatively early. I'll probably call the funeral home tonight and see if we can set up burial arrangements."

"So quick," I mouthed. "Isn't that kind of weird, burying her in a regular cemetery?"

"It is rare for an immortal to die in the first place, and I know that Abelie would have wanted to be buried here, close to home."

As I sat on my knees between my mother and father, I realized this would be the last time we would be together as a family—just the three of us, sitting in the room in silence. After several heavily weighted seconds I said, "I wish I could have known you both long before now."

"You don't know hard it was to let you go," Aiden barely whispered. "We had to, to keep you safe. Gabriella, you probably don't know this yet, but angels cannot bear children. How Abelie became pregnant with you is still a complete mystery. Please know that we were elated when we found out about the pregnancy. We had been given a gift that no angel had ever been given. We had huge plans for our family and refused to take one second of our lives as a family for granted.

"To lose a child—no, worse—to give up a child that we loved more than our own lives was nearly unendurable. Abelie cried for months and sometimes in the middle of the night I would find her sitting in your bedroom, looking at pictures of you. It was difficult for both of us." He paused to take a deep breath. "You have to understand that we both loved you; I still love you, Gabriella. You are my daughter even though I wasn't there to do all the father/daughter things that I had planned on doing."

"I know," I said, placing my hand over his. "You were protecting me—I know that. You kept me safe. Please don't feel guilty about it anymore."

He sighed. "It's difficult not to. If we would have just found another way to hide you or to protect you, Abelie would still be alive and we would have been a family for all these years."

"This is not your fault," I told him firmly.

We were silent then.

Dinner was a quiet event. My stomach was finally

full of food, but there was an odd, sick, empty feeling that didn't seem to be sated by any amount of substance. Upstairs—sitting on a bed, *my* old bed, in *Abelie's* pajamas—I wondered if my childhood memories
would ever return. Now, more than ever, I wanted to
remember those five years that I had been constantly
trying to find a link to. Now here it was—here I was.
There was some magical *thing* blocking my memories,
and I was determined to find a way to fix that, to break
through that wall preventing me from remembering
my mother. Those memories would be more precious
to me than before her death.

There was a soft knock on the door. I looked up
from the pink bedspread I was sitting on. "Come in."

The door slowly opened and Andrew poked his
head in. His eyes seemed to be a mixture of the gold
I remembered and the saddest blue color. "There is
a room down the hall for you to sleep in, whenever
you're ready. Aiden brought up some of Abelie's
clothes, too." He opened the door all the way and I saw
for the first time that he was barefoot, wearing pajama
bottoms and a cotton t-shirt. It was almost funny, the
thought of a celestial being in pajamas.

"Okay." I stood and he gestured for me to go down.
"It's the door at the end of the hallway."

I could hear our footsteps echo down the hall

until suddenly all I heard were mine. I stopped and turned around to face Andrew who looked at me with a mixture of expressions on his face. He seemed upset and tortured, possibly struggling with some internal thought he was having. His eyes seized mine and I walked towards him.

"What's wrong?" I wondered.

He opened his mouth to say something then shut it. I raised my eyebrows. He sighed and then said, "Two times I've stayed with you in a bed. I've tried to be a complete gentleman, but of course I—"

I put my finger on his lips to silence him. "Andrew," I sighed, "I have only ever allowed one other man to stay the night with me, and it was awkward . . . I ended up spending most of the night in my living room surfing the internet." His expression twisted into something unreadable. "But being with you," I continued quickly, "it was different. It felt *right*." His eyes bore into mine, even more fiercely than before. "Come on, we need to talk," I said as I pulled him into the bedroom at the end of the hall.

My hand reached along the dark wall for a light switch and finally found it. Lamps all around the bedroom flickered to life. The room stunned me for a moment. It was beyond lavish. The ceiling was tall and everything looked old and expensive, everything except a big comfy couch under the windowsill of a large arched window. We were reflected back perfectly in the glass. I dragged Andrew over to the couch and we both sat. We held hands in silence for a moment before I broke it.

"Andrew," I began. "I really don't know that much about you, but there are a few things that I do know. You are a warrior, a protector of mankind. You take care of those you love and you are an honorable man. I've seen some of the past, and I've been around you for a couple of days now and you have been nothing but caring, sweet, and kind."

He opened his mouth to speak but I put a hand up to stop him.

"You have put my safety before yours. Everyone has been so great, and through all of my overwhelming feelings of being thrown into this world, you have made the adjustment much smoother than I ever thought possible. And honestly, I know we are meant to be together.

"When I was 'reading' the *Timeless* book, I saw Zola. She practically told me that you were my kindred soul, and I believe her. You know it and I know it. There is something that I can't explain, and neither can you—we have a connection."

I saw Andrew's lips twitch up. "I just don't want

you to think I am taking advantage of you."

I groaned. "Before I knew what was happening to me, my dreams were scaring the living hell out of me, and you helped to take away those feelings when I thought I was losing my mind. If it wasn't for you, I probably wouldn't have been able to survive the past couple of nights."

He shook his head. "You would have survived."

"That's not how I meant it," I conveyed. "I was an emotional wreck, and you kept me together, helped me hold the pieces in place. And though this is completely unconventional—*we* are unconventional—please don't leave me tonight. I need you, now more than ever."

"I won't," he promised.

"Good."

He held his hand out and towed me to the bed and pulled the covers down. I scooted across the soft cotton sheets. He followed behind and then I cuddled in his warm arms for only a few minutes before sleep pulled me under. The last thing I remembered was Andrew whispering, "Goodnight," in my ear.

It was a dreamless night—my first dreamless night in what felt like a year. The sun poured into the room through the large arched window and made everything in the room glitter and shine in return. Though it was beautiful, the thoughts of my mother only seemed to dull everything around me—everything except the angel fast asleep in the bed with me. His dark, almost black-blue hair was tousled and he had the most tranquil and serene expression on his face that I had ever seen. I didn't want to wake him up, so for several minutes I just lay there and stared at him.

Suddenly, he smiled. "Are you watching me?"

"No," I lied.

He opened his eyes. "You were very calm all night. Did you have any dreams?" He reached up and traced a finger along my jaw. The sound of tiny sparks could be heard.

I shook my head. "None." I sighed in relief. Maybe there was hope after all for getting rid of the dark circles under my eyes, but at the same time I didn't want to lose the connection with my mother. My two dreamless nights had my brain reeling. "Andrew, do angels dream?"

He chuckled and pulled me tighter to his body. "Of course we dream; we are similar to your average human in many ways—we were human at one point. Last night, for instance, I had a dream that you and I were at a baseball game, back in America. I read about baseball at the library; it sounded like something I would enjoy."

I laughed at the thought of Andrew, in all his celestial glory, wearing a baseball hat and eating a hot dog and garlic fries. I had to admit, the image in my head was adorable and surprisingly sexy, making the blood rush into my cheeks. I hid my face in the pillow to hide the blush and stifle the giggles.

"What?" Andrew asked, seeming completely confused by my reaction.

"It's nothing, really. Just the thought of you doing something so common—*so normal* seems strange to me."

"Well, angels do enjoy *normal* activities. We don't always run around saving lives." He grinned at me, his eyes almost back to their golden color. "That makes me wonder, though. What do you like to do when you're not disproving the existence of mythical creatures?" He was looking at me so intently that it made me feel self-conscious. Could this beautiful man really be interested in the trivial aspects of my daily life?

"Well," I began hesitantly, "I enjoy snow skiing. Skiing is a sport where you—"

"Gabriella," he sighed, slightly rolling his eyes in amusement, "I know what skiing is. I may have been *dead* for a few hundred years, but skiing was around before I *died*. Though I'm sure it has changed a lot since I last went."

"You've skied?" I asked. I didn't even bother to hide the amused expression on my face.

"Yes, well, I've lived in several places where snow was quite common. Skies were necessary for travel. I couldn't fly while trying to blend in with humans."

"No, I guess you couldn't. Well, I'd love to take you skiing sometime, show you what it's like now."

"Like a date?" Andrew asked, a phony surprised smile plastered on his face. "Are you asking me out on a date, Gabriella?"

There was no hiding the blush that I knew was covering my cheeks now.

"Well, um . . ." I fumbled for words. How could I be so forward? I had to recover this conversation—and fast! "Well . . . I guess a date is not the most practical idea right now, what with the Soul Stalker after me and all." This thought brought me back to reality. "Or the Shadows and the Ladies of Light . . ."

Andrew saw the change in my expression and tenderly took my face between his hands. "Gabriella," he whispered, "I will not let anyone hurt you. What you said last night, about us being kindred souls, well, I feel the same way. You have suddenly become my entire life and I will not allow anyone to take you away from me."

Reality came crashing back down on me. Aiden—

he must be paralyzed with grief. Abelie had obviously been his kindred soul. How could he possibly deal with her loss? He and I may not have a normal father/daughter relationship, but I knew that I wanted to be there for him, to support him as he grieved for his wife.

"We better get up. I'm sure we need to help Aiden with arrangements for Abelie. He can't do it on his own."

Andrew sat up, stretched, and put an arm around my shoulder. "Yes," he agreed. "It's time for her to be at peace."

#

29

Another dreamless night had passed and I wasn't quite sure what that meant. Did the Sight fade when the one who gave it to you passed? It worried me, and for a whole minute I thought I was going to panic at the thought of losing one of my last connections to my mother. Andrew had stayed with me again, and he was nothing but a complete gentleman. It was amazing how much my life had changed within the past few days. The fleeting thought of going back to work in the fishbowl was kind of surreal—*was I ever going to go back to that life that I once knew?*

Special arrangements had to be made for Abelie because of the circumstances surrounding her death. For a whole day, I wandered through her house—my parent's house—while I traced my fingers along their belongings and soaked up everything I could. This was where Abelie spent her time with Aiden and with me when I was a child. The feel of the floor beneath my feet and the smell in the air made me feel like this was my home. It smelled like Abelie—honey and vanilla. Each room was extravagant and different. Some items

456

were old and priceless and others were more modern. You could tell she had been collecting trinkets for centuries. They especially liked old paintings of angels, which almost made me laugh.

The sun flooded down like liquid light into the room from the window high on the wall, but then a cloud passed over and it turned dull and grey. When I looked up I couldn't see through the dew that hand built up on the glass. Little rainbows shimmered through the water droplets as clouds passed and the sun faded in and out.

My feet dangled from my perch at my mother's bed. It had a large canopy with wrought iron metal that twisted into beautiful designs that connected over my head. I had a family photo in one hand and the phone in the other. My life felt torn between who I was and who I was becoming. It literally hurt when I thought about my family back in the States, especially Jenna. At the same time, my heart was still trying to put all the pieces back together after losing the life I never had, the life I had almost returned to. In the photo, Aiden looked so human with Abelie and me in his lava-cracked arms. We looked happy, like a family should. I was young, of course—long golden curls cascaded down my back. There was so much love in their eyes, even in my father's, which were nothing more than flames.

The door squeaked when Joseph pushed it open and he took just a few long strides toward me. The bed sank when he sat beside me on the deep red comforter. "Who you gunna call?"

I snorted. "That line is never going to be usable again."

He cocked his head to the side and smiled at me. "Yeah, I guess not." He shrugged. "But really, who were you going to call?"

"I thought about calling my sister, Jenna. But I don't know what I would say to her."

"Probably not a wise idea," he suggested. "At least not yet. I made a phone call, earlier this morning, to the FBI."

"Oh," I said, looking up at him. I bit my lip, an automatic reaction when I was nervous. "And what did you say—what did *they* say?"

"Honestly, I had nothing. I just told them not to ask." He chuckled anxiously. "I mean, it isn't like I can tell them that I went through a portal and ended up in Italy—even if I do work in Paranormal Investigations. My boss would ask me how many hallucinogenic mushrooms had I eaten."

I burst out in laughter, the first real sound of joy I had made in several days. He smiled back, a look of confusion on his face.

"It's—" I tried to speak through the fit of giggles that had overtaken me. I would take in every happy moment I could get because I knew it wouldn't be this lighthearted for long. "When I first found out there were angels, like *real, live* angels, I thought that some-one had put some hallucinogenic mushrooms in my coffee. The whole day I was questioning whether I was losing my mind."

After reigning in my insane outburst, I asked, "And they just said"—I tried to imitate a man—"'Sure, Agent Carter, just come on back home'?"

His smile vanished. "Not exactly, though they did say to come back immediately. And not in a pleasant way."

Any humor I had left was swatted away by his words. "Are you not staying for the funeral?"

"Of course I am." He grabbed my hands in his. "I can't express to you how sorry I feel about everything. I didn't know your mother, but she was brave and she fought side-by-side with the other angels to keep us all safe. She was a hero."

I looked down at the golden rug beside the bed. "Aiden said that word spread quickly of her death after we made arrangements with the funeral home." I took in a deep breath. "It looks like I have to stay hidden during her funeral." Before I knew what I was doing,

I was on my feet, marching back and forth, wearing a hole in the rug. "She was my mother," I practically shouted. "I deserve to be there—to not have to hide from her."

Joseph ran a hand through his dark hair. "It's not fair, it really isn't—" His forehead creased.

"What?" I stopped pacing.

"How did the angels find out? Because, you know, we're in *hiding*."

"Apparently," I sighed and joined Joseph on the bed again, "Abelie had made many friends in the community around here. They were all human friends— one human happened to know an angel."

"Do the humans here know that they are angels?"

"Nope." I popped my lip on the "p." "Angels were—are encouraged to mingle with humans. Aiden and Abelie were apparently good at hiding their relationship from public view, so at least Aiden is safe. He said they rarely had people over. Abelie was loved in the community and word spread quickly of her death." My eyes shot down to the gold rug again. "Of course she was loved, she was wonderful and I—" I cut myself off, knowing that if I started to talk about it, I would choke on my sobs again.

"So how are you going to stay 'covert' during the funeral?" he wondered, as he ran his hand through his hair again. I was surprised it wasn't standing on end.

"I'm not sure"—I shrugged—"but Aiden told me not to worry about it, that he would cover that part."

Joseph shifted next to me and I looked up to see that Andrew had walked into the room. He was absolutely stunning in an all-black suit—from the deep black button-up shirt with jacket, all the way down to his polished black shoes.

"Wow, Andrew. *You look amazing.*"

He gave me a small smile. "I'm not interrupting anything, am I?" he asked. "Because I have something for you."

"No." I stood. "You have something for me?" I didn't know what he had up his sleeve. "It better not be a puppy. Hercules will be jealous," I tried to joke. It didn't sound right. Laughing, joking, being happy felt wrong. I gave Joseph a tiny wave good-bye which he returned.

Andrew smiled with a confused expression on his face when I turned back toward him. "Hercules?"

"My dog."

"You have a dog?"

"Yup."

Andrew's smile grew and then he gestured for me to exit. He pointed down the long hallway toward the room we had been staying in. "It's on the bed."

My feet were bare and didn't make any noise against the hard floor. The walls were a soft cream color and had beautiful red designs woven at the edge of the ceiling. I wondered if Abelie had painted them and then I instantly felt empty because I didn't know anything about my mother. I made a mental note to ask Aiden more about her. When I reached the end of the hallway, I thought I could hear Andrew say "Thank you for being so kind to Gabriella" to Joseph. I smiled. He really was a kind soul—a *kindred soul*.

Lying on the dark green bedspread was the most beautiful black dress I had ever seen. I skipped over to it and ran my fingers along the silk. The angels sure did seem to love their silk. Underneath was a knee-length, black pea coat.

Andrew peeked his head in. "Do you like it?"

"I love it," I whispered in awe.

"Put it on," he said. "The funeral is in about an hour."

So soon, I thought dazedly and then nodded. He frowned but turned and closed the door behind him with a small click.

Andrew held a large black umbrella over my head as we walked through a path in the woods that lead us to the burial grounds. Though the air was chilly, the grass was still a very vivid green, more pronounced in the misty rain that scattered across the cemetery. Aiden and Lucia had joined forces to form a sort of bubble around us. He said we would be invisible to everyone during the ceremony, but we had to be quiet because we could still be heard, and we could still disturb the area around us. As we approached the dark wooden casket that was being held over the deep hole that would eventually swallow Abelie—or as close as we could feasibly get—I could feel the grief starting to swell in my chest, as if I were drowning or wading through heavy waters, unable to stay afloat. I didn't know if I was ready to handle these emotions again, but I had no choice. They came rushing back more fiercely than before. Aiden's face reflected mine in his grief. I reached out and held his hand as we moved closer to the coffin.

We stopped farther away from the tent than I would have wished. I stared straight ahead, feeling hollow. This person that possessed me was different—*broken*. Before, I always felt like there was something missing, and there was. But now—now I felt like a train had severed me in half, like the two parts of myself would never be able to reattach. I was torn. The dark wooden casket taunted me, telling me it was entirely my fault. If it wasn't for my birth, or my ingenious idea to flee the underground lab, we wouldn't be here right now.

463

For a few seconds, I thought I would be sick all over Andrew's shiny black shoes. Bent over at the waist, my stomach heaving, I felt Andrew lean over and pull my hair away from my face.

"Are you okay?" he whispered so low I could barely hear him through my heavy breaths—the sound like putting my fingers in my ears and speaking.

I shook my head and let the tears roll down my face. I had thought I knew what pain was before, but I was wrong—so incredibly wrong. Something had ripped through me and shredded any strength I had left inside. Before, she was still there—covered on the table in the library or lying on a bed in her house—but now she would be devoured by the earth with dirt and rocks. There was just something final about that act—permanent. The thought of that barrier between us almost made me faint with sickness. I didn't know how Aiden was still standing. When I looked at him, tears littered his face.

All around me, those who had been blessed by this glorious being wept and held on to each other, coming together as one entity for the support they each needed. The mass of humans surprised me, and I realized how many lives she had touched, changed in some way. In the distance, I could see angels beneath the shadows of the encroaching forest. Their golden tears glittered in the small glint of the sun beaming down through a slit in the clouds. Maybe the heavens were shining upon them. No one else seemed to be able to see them, or maybe they weren't paying them any attention, but I could—in all their magnificent glory. They had always possessed a celestial glow, but today it had been taken away. There was a darkness that surrounded them as they mourned the one they had lost. The one I had lost.

"If I ever see Jeff again, I'll kill him. That is a promise," Aiden barely whispered.

The other angels shared a look of approval before nodding. "Agreed," they all said. For once, I agreed to this death.

There was a short, grey-haired man that walked toward the podium and pulled a book from beneath his black robes. He looked Catholic. He began speaking reverently in a deep, rich Italian. The rain pounded against the umbrella above my head and drowned out his speech. Instead of listening, I let the humming of the rain soothe my brain. Andrew held me against his side and began to sing into my ear. The words were loving and beautiful. It only made the tears come quicker, like a soundtrack to my sorrow.

I was silent as the tears descended my face, contributing to the heartache around me. As the service came to a close, the crowd dispersed and the angels seemed to vanish before my eyes, some just completely popping out of existence.

We moved closer to the coffin covered in white roses. We were still invisible, and I wondered how long Aiden and Lucia could keep up their strength. Once everyone was in their cars, making their way down the windy drive, workers converged upon the tent and began disassembling it.

The rain scattered across the ground, soaking the flowers that were lying upon the tomb of the forgotten angel. Someone had once told me that when it rained, it was God weeping for the beloved who were lost. Today I believed this more than on any other day, because this was a more grievous death than that of any mere mortal.

We stayed to watch when they began to lower the body into the ground. A perfectly smooth, warm hand found its way to mine. The thumb compassionately stroking my palm was soothing. I never looked to see whose hand was holding mine, and its owner remained slightly behind me, out of view. I knew it was Andrew—it was always Andrew. He didn't pressure me to leave, or try to tell me that it would be all right, because it wouldn't, and he knew that. That was just fine with me; I needed time to grasp the concept of this monumental death.

It was then that I looked down at the mound of dirt that would soon be covering this benevolent angel, my mother. In that moment, it felt like something was breaking away from my heart. It fluttered away, and the hole it left would forever be there. A reminder.

Andrew's warm hand never left mine, even when I collapsed to my knees, unsure if I would ever be able to leave this place, and leave this angel who had never left me. My mother, who had secretly watched me grow into an adult, even though she couldn't reveal herself, for fear of losing me. To imagine the kind of sacrifices she had to make only made me choke on my breath. I needed it—the tears, the release—so I could get past this, make a special place for her in my heart and seal it for eternity, because that is what I had now, eternity, forever . . . a timeless immortality.

When I struggled to rise, Andrew reached for my waist and pulled me to my feet. I just looked into the eyes of my angel through my own water-filled ones. They were deep pools, so blue you would think that someone had painted them that way. Perhaps someone had. Maybe there was an exalted artisan in the sky using water colors on the red-golden fall day, painting the angelic being before me. I'd never seen such a devastatingly beautiful day before in my entire life.

As we reached a path in the trees that would lead

us back to Abelie's hidden house, the invisible charm disintegrated from around us, a white mist falling to the leaf-strewn ground. Still, the support of Andrew's warm hand never left mine, as if we were melting together. Besides the sound of our feet shuffling beneath the canopy of trees and the small drips of rain making their way through, we were all silent. I had yet to really look at the other angels, to see their golden tears trailing down their faces. But I knew in a time like this, that we were here to comfort each other so I snaked my free arm around Aiden's. His head turned to the side as he gave me the most anguished smile I had ever seen on someone before, patted my fingers wrapped around his huge charcoal bicep, and continued our silent parade through the ever rain-drenched trees.

When the huge stone mansion came into view, the light of day had already begun to fade in the background. The sky was slowly thickening with the languid darkness of night. It was twilight again, just as it was when Abelie's soul was severed from her body. Ehno opened the door for us, but before I could find my way to the bedroom to weep in solitude, he called out to me, "Gabriella, wait." I turned around, curious. Everyone else, besides Joseph, went their separate ways. Ehno continued after seeing my expression,

"Joseph has a plane to catch. I thought you might want to say good-bye before he left."

I nodded. "Of course."

Ehno walked off to give us some privacy.

"Gabriella—"

"No, Joseph. Let me speak." I raised a hand in protest when he opened his mouth. "You've been far beyond amazing these last few days. It's my fault you got caught in this whirlwind with me. I'm so glad that you survived, because I don't think I could handle your death on my hands too." My voice had lowered so much that he leaned in to hear me better. "I'm glad you are finally going back to your normal life and—"

"You've got it all wrong," he protested. "You changed my life. Remember when I said you were a skeptic?" I nodded, raising my eyebrows. "Well, I was a bigger skeptic than you. I'd seen things that your lab never had the chance to investigate and I still didn't believe—but on that plane, falling from the sky . . . there are no descriptions in my head that can make you understand how that felt. My heart lifted, rejoiced, even though we were about to die. And if it weren't for me sitting next to you, I probably would have crashed with the rest of them. If anything, *you* saved *me*."

And with everything heavily weighing down on me, I collapsed in tears once again. I was really growing tired of the tears. It was actually a mixture of grief and a twisted sort-of-happiness. Joseph caught me and gave me a huge hug.

"We'll see each other again, won't we?" he mumbled into my hair.

I pulled away from him and wiped the golden tears away. "You know it. Once all of this craziness goes away, I'll definitely come visit. You can count on that."

"Good." He smiled. "Well, I better go. Ehno called me a cab before we went to the funeral and I just heard it pull up into the drive." His eyes darted to the door.

"Be careful," I ordered and reached up on my toes to give him a kiss on the cheek. He blushed and walked outside into the rainy abyss.

I watched as the brake lights of the cab disappeared through the trees and then I shut the door.

"Are you okay?" Andrew asked from the bottom of the staircase.

I shook my head. "Not really. Let's just go to bed." It was early, but I didn't care. I was exhausted. He reached out a consoling hand. I took it and we started to ascend the stairs. "Will you just . . . hold me tonight?"

"I wouldn't want to do anything different."

⚭

I jolted upright. I didn't know why my heart was pounding a million miles a minute, but it was racing.

Trying to take deep steadying breaths, I looked over Andrew's sleeping form to see the alarm clock that said it was almost five in the morning. The pattering of the rain could still be heard against the large arch window above the comfy couch. Trying not to jostle the bed too much, I uncurled myself from his arms and tiptoed across the room toward the fogged-up window, and looked into the misty darkness. Even in the cloudy night I could see the path where we exited earlier. In that moment, I wanted to see my mom more than anything and all I would have to do was follow that trail. Even if the only thing I could do was stand at her grave, it would be enough. I just needed that closeness.

Through the fog, I found my way easily down the path in the middle of the trees as the sky began to dilute into a grayish blue. I practically tore through the forest until it suddenly ended at the clearing of the cemetery. Not too far away was a stone bench. I wrapped my new coat around me securely and pulled up the hood up over my head from the hoodie I was wearing underneath. The wind lashed out with harsh rain.

As the sun began to rise, the bright yellow ball seemed to find larger and larger holes in the clouds until the day was almost full of sunshine. Abelie's grave was still open and I just couldn't will myself to look over the deep hole with her casket covered in rainwater and roses. I couldn't believe they left it like this.

Two cemetery workers materialized from the mist. They didn't pay me any attention as they continued their day's work like it was nothing unusual. One of them drove a Bobcat while the other directed his actions. It was then that I noticed what they had planned. They lifted the fake grass off the pile of dirt next to Abelie's grave and proceeded to push the dirt into the hole.

I flinched when I heard the first bit of mud fall on the wood. Something inside of me sank down with the coffin, as if I was being suffocated by the dirt that was now being thrown over the my mother. I stayed to watch as the ground swallowed the coffin whole. Each time they backed the Bobcat up, and it forcefully pushed more muddy dirt into the hole, I would jerk out of reflex.

Soon, there was nothing left but a smooth layer of earth above the angel . . . *my angel . . . my Guardian . . . my mother.*

There were soft footfalls behind me. I figured it was one of the workers coming back to do something else to Abelie's gravesite.

"Gabriella," a gentle male voice spoke softly in my ear. I hadn't noticed that he crouched beside me.

"Andrew?" I cried as I recognized his face.

"It's time to leave." His breath was so affection-ate, so *healing*, that some new strength grew inside me. He reached for my hand and I gladly gave it to him. He had a look of panic on his face and I wasn't quite sure why. Did something frighten him?

"What are you doing here?" I asked. It wasn't out of exasperation that I had cried out, it was pure intoxi-cating relief. I hadn't realized how much I needed him as I watched Abelie become one with the earth.

His hand tightened in mine before he released me. He wrapped his graceful arm around my waist to move me toward a black limo. I wondered where it had come from. Did he steal it?

"No time for questions. It's not safe here any-more," he whispered. I mouthed his words back ques-tioningly as he pushed me towards the car door.

Reflexively, my eyes darted around the area. There was nothing out of the ordinary, nothing strange in the least. No Shadows, no Ladies of Light. No angels to speak of except for the one holding me against his body. After one last sweeping gaze around the forest that seemed to be choking the boundaries of the ceme-tery, I noticed a form materializing under the shadows. I couldn't see a face, only the red-orange glow of fiery eyes.

Andrew reached for my hand and began a quick

sprint.

No, I thought stupidly, *it couldn't be*. Wasn't this death the end of it all? Could there possibly be anymore tragedies? The door flung open on its own accord, and suddenly we were inside and speeding away.

His hand still had not left mine, and he continually gave me the strength I so desperately needed. My heart pumped my new golden blood through my veins so quickly, I was surprised I wasn't exploding under the pressure.

"I don't think he'll follow—not while he's alone," Andrew whispered into my hair. My head rested upon his shoulders as tears continued to trickle down my face to land on his jacket, staining it with golden salt water.

"I'm sorry," I said softly as I tried to wipe away the tears on the fabric. He caught my hand to stop me, as if this action displeased him.

"Don't ever be sorry about weeping over an angel. This truly is a heartbreaking day." He cupped my chin to get a better look at my face. Again, just the warmth of his hand was enough to feel like he was healing me. And perhaps he was—Abelie had, why couldn't he?

He kissed the tears on my face and then wrapped his arms around me protectively. "Ehno and Lucia went looking for you in the opposite direction. You really had us frightened."

"I'm sorry, Andrew." I looked down, feeling embarrassed. "I didn't mean to make you worry about me."

The road curved some as we headed out of the cemetery.

"And what about Aiden?" My question was muffled against the lapel of his jacket as I tried to avoid his skin. "If he finds out a Shadow is here, he will come looking for him and try to kill whoever did this to Abelie." And once again, just like before in the library, I felt a thirst for retribution—*justice.*

"The dark one." He nodded, as if to some thought he had just had, still ignoring my first question. "He is not far." He pressed a button, and the window between the driver and us slithered away.

"Driver," he called out. "How much longer till—"

Sudden and violent metal twisting against metal echoed in my ears as the limo seemed to bend sideways. The sound hurt my ears, but my head hurt worse as it slammed into the side of the limo. It was as if my reality had just warped into something new. Then I was exposed to the elements. *Odd*, the sun had disappeared again as rain started beating down on the ground. I was way too dizzy. Rain splattered across my face and wind rushed through my hair as I felt my body being pressed tightly against Andrew's hard chest. My head felt faint, but with all my might I clung to him, absolutely confused at what was going on.

There was a blur in my vision, and I wasn't sure if we quit moving or if we were high in the sky at this point. But for some reason, we were not in the air. I was on the ground looking up at the beautiful maple tree above me, with its big yellow leaves.

"It's just you and me now," Andrew breathed into my ear. "I'm your Guardian now." He helped me sit up against the tree.

"And where will we go?" I asked, my lips against his collar bone as he leaned forward to hear me. What did he mean "I'm your Guardian now?" Were the others gone? Dead? Worse?

He shuddered slightly under my breath.

I ignored the meaning of that. Or I tried to, but I still wondered if something was wrong with the others. Or maybe he was quivering in anger.

Something hot and wet seeped from my head and down my neck. My hand automatically went up to a sore spot on my temple, and when my fingers came away they were covered in rich molten blood. When I looked into my protector's eyes, I saw they were full of regret and torture. He also had a splattering of blood on his clothes, but that could have just been from my head. All I could think about was soothing him, even though *he* was here to protect *me*.

There was no time for that now, though. We were in danger.

I finally saw a woman. She stalked toward Jeff, the Shadow who had caused our accident. It was the Soul Stalker—Karen.

"Is that why—"

"I can't fly?" Andrew finished. "Yes. She's preventing me from using my abilities." He sprang forward, shielding me from her.

But not my abilities, I thought dazedly. But there was no strength within me. I was tired and hurt, worse than I previously thought. The horrible ache in my side seemed to have come back. Abelie had said she wasn't able to fully heal me and now I could tell. I was in pain—a lot of pain. Each second the scene seemed to go in and out of focus around me. One moment Andrew was crouched to spring before me, and the next thing I saw was—

"It's him," I whimpered. "Aiden. Just like he promised." This was my fault. If Aiden was killed, I would die too. Surely there were no other guardians left for me. This would be the end. I didn't want this to be the end. I'd lost Abelie—I couldn't lose my father too. I refused.

He shot a murderous glare in Jeff's direction, right at his temple—like a sniper preparing to shoot.

I must have blanked out because the next thing I knew the ground was shaking beneath me, like one of those cheap beds in a trashy motel where you have to pay a quarter. Everything stilled.

The ground shook beneath us again as a dark shadow loomed overhead. Andrew tensed for action as the ground shook again. We were in complete darkness now, only the headlights of the limo illuminated the vicinity. It was my office all over again, like the dark mist was creeping up and around every inch of my skin. I wanted to swat it away but my arms felt heavy, like they were broken. Fire sprang up and ringed around us, and the rain seemed only to intensify the raging flames that licked at the air.

"Only one guardian?" a vicious voice said mirthfully. It was Jeff. I squinted to see an expression of gloating pleasure, or was it just vicious satisfaction on his face?

"It's so easy to pick you off one by one." That was the Soul Stalker.

Did that mean they killed Ehno and Lucia? *No*, it couldn't be. I wouldn't allow it. *No*! I blinked, transfixed in horror. Swallowing, I tried to muster up the strength to stare at him with every sign of great dislike—hate, even. Hate indeed.

As I went in and out of consciousness, I saw light flashing left and right as fire and magic twirled in the air like pretty fireworks. There was a swirl of colors, a rush of wind, as if something just flew overhead. There were no other words for it except complete and utter chaos. I had no idea how they were keeping up with each other. I was thankful all over again for everything Andrew had done for me, and I hoped that between my father and him, they could fight the two creatures who wanted to kill me more than anyone else on this planet or even in this universe . . . because I couldn't.

"You won't take her," Andrew shouted. I really thought daggers would roll off his tongue and pierce Jeff's heart if he even had a heart.

"Won't I?" Jeff laughed. "I will kill everyone who tries to protect her until she has no protectors left." Again, he laughed. "Did you hear that, Illuminator? Everyone you hold near and dear will die as long as they stand in my way."

Maybe it was my faint state, but I thought I was going to freeze from his words, so icy and—not threatening but *promising*.

The encompassing fire crackled and flickered into an ominous red as a shape appeared before us. It was so easy for Jeff to embrace the same fires that had snapped the neck of Abelie. I tried to fight against my heavy lids and continued to fail miserably. I felt heat wrap around my ribs and up my shoulders and creep around my neck and I was sure in that second that I was going to join Abelie. I could feel my ribs folding under the pressure.

There was shouting and a grunt as the sensation disappeared. I tried my best to shake off my faintness and the pain in my side so I could help, or at least see what was going on. And I did, though I was having trouble concentrating through the haze of pain. When I stood, my hand on my side, I could feel blood leaking from beneath my clothes. I lifted my shirt to see the wound that Abelie had tried to heal ripped open, and blood dripping down my side. My back hit the tree behind me and I sunk back to the ground, unable to stand any longer.

Fire shot from the palm of the dark creature. Andrew ducked, and the fire-ball hit a branch above us. Then he flung himself in front of me as another fireball came rocketing in my direction. It pierced into my chest and for a fraction of a second I could feel the anger boil up like a black wave right along with the pain. It did me no good. He had me. I was a goner, the Shadow and Soul Stalker had won. Andrew yelled something close to my head, but I couldn't make out the words. Suddenly, the branch above me came clattering down, hitting me against the head and then, as a new darkness began consuming me, I knew I was finished. The world as I knew it disappeared into a silent, black oblivion.

30

death is only the beginning

There was a moment when I knew that my life was over. And then it passed. Or maybe I passed on. There was no pain anymore, no horrible ache in my chest from the death of my mother or wounds on my head, or the searing pain of my opened wound; it was like my mother all over again—I was healed. I was . . . okay. More than okay. I was fantastic. Incredible. Whole.

It was silent. Ridiculously peaceful. Suddenly, I was standing in a hallway. I stared down at my clothes. *Where did this come from?* I wondered as I lifted the silk blue dress which draped over my body like extremely smooth satin. The hall I was standing in seemed infinite—the white walls, like silky curtains, expanded for miles or maybe even forever. My bare feet moved over the soft ground—like clouds. *Was I in heaven?* My heart wasn't beating the normal pounding against my rib cage. My heart was just as quiet as this place.

Realization hit. "I'm dead," I whispered to nobody.

"Not yet, beautiful angel."

I spun around excitedly, looking for the culprit to that earth-shattering, beautiful voice. "Mom?"

"Yes, sweetie. I'm here."

Again, I did a three-sixty trying to find her face. I'd lost her twice before and now I could hear her voice. This was heaven, it had to be!

"Where are you?"

"Right here." A warm hand touched my shoulder.

I whirled around to see Abelie staring at me with her same bright-green eyes. She barely had time to take a breath—if you even breathed in this *place*—before I seized her and hugged her to my body. She returned my embrace just as fiercely.

"Where are we?" I wondered aloud against her hair. "Are we in heaven? Because I am pretty sure this looks and feels like how heaven would."

She pushed away from me slightly, cradling my cheeks in her hands. She inspected my face, her eyes devouring every last inch. "This is the place between," she told me. "Our Timeless Oblivion."

Her face was full of motherly love—something I always saw with my adoptive mother, but this was different, more pure. My whole life I wondered what would happen when I saw my real mother, and then I had lost her. But there she was, right in front of me. She loved me; I could see it in the set of her eyes. It felt real, wonderful, to be loved so completely by a mother; *my mother*. Now I knew what it would be like. It was complete and fulfilling. There were no words to describe it.

It was a Herculean effort for me to tear my eyes away from her, but I had to look at this place one more time. It was almost blinding the amount of white there was. It was so bright. Once again, I glanced back down at the ground. It could be clouds. The white fluffy surface was solid, but soft and felt pleasant between my toes, like the softest grains of warm sand. I couldn't even describe it. The words wouldn't make sense, "it feels like a cloud."

I gazed back at her, waiting for an explanation. Though I was thrilled—*more* than thrilled—to see her, it was difficult for me to believe she was real. When I didn't receive any kind of response I asked, "And what do you mean by 'Timeless Oblivion'?"

"Between mortality and immortality—life and death." She laughed, the sound was whimsical. She twirled away from me and danced around like a little girl. For the first time I noticed she had on an identical dress—the color a vivid red. At each twist it turned a different color. She was magnificent with her long, curly brown hair and her tall, slim body.

"I don't understand," I said, confused. "Are you sure I'm not dead?" I mean, it made sense—my being dead and all—considering the last thing I felt was being hit with a spell and a large object hitting my cranium. Plus, the lack of my heart beating steadily in my chest might also be a sign.

"You are," she smiled back at me.

"But you just said—" I was . . . dead. What was the point of the word "immortality" if it wasn't as timeless as everyone perceived? I had things I needed to do, people who I wanted to save. How was I supposed to do that here, in the Timeless Oblivion? Maybe this is what it meant to be timeless after all.

The peaceful feeling vanished.

Aiden, I lamented. Hadn't he lost enough for an eternity? *And Andrew*—this would crush him. *And my family . . .*

"Immortality doesn't come without consequences," Abelie clarified. She didn't seem worried about my state of . . . *oblivion?*

But I was already an angel—an immortal. *Wasn't I?*

Abelie glanced at my bewildered expression. Her smile dissolved into a frown.

"So," I finally spoke, "if I'm 'dead,' how does that

translate into being in between mortality and immortality?" What was with the angels and their cryptic words? You didn't know if you should take things literally or look deeper for a metaphor.

An easy smile crawled across her face. "You're *becoming* an angel. Your abilities go beyond what any of us have *ever* seen." She moved closer to me, her dress back to the rich ruby color. "When we, the *Senza Tempo,* became immortal, we all had to prove ourselves worthy. The first step was death."

"What?" I gasped. They never told me that.

"It was different for us. When we went through the process we didn't know that death was the price we would pay. Not until we came here, and then it was too late. None of us remembered afterward. *I* didn't remember—I just woke up and I knew I was *different.*" She shrugged dispassionately. "But now that I am here, my memory's restored, I know. *I remember.* We each made sacrifices to prove our virtue." Her voice was calm.

"Sacrifices?"

"Each one of us endured our own personal test." She looked thoughtful. "When I was here last, I was given the option to return to life as an immortal and lose Aiden, or to truly die so he could live."

"And what happened?"

"I gave up my life for him." She smiled. "I loved him too deeply to be selfish. What I didn't realize was that that was the test. Actually, I didn't even know I was there to prove my worth."

"And . . . did everyone make it?"

"All but two." Her facial expression didn't even flinch.

How could she speak like this was all just a normal everyday conversation? She was . . . and I was . . . It just didn't make any sense. This wasn't Heaven, or Earth. For a second, I was going to ask her what I would have to sacrifice, or what my "test" might be, but I decided not to. I didn't want to know. I figured I would find out eventually. I shuddered at the thought of what else I might have to sacrifice.

But even as all my thoughts started piling on top of each other, for some reason I was able to thrust them all to the side, and be content that I was standing in the presence of my mother, Abelie. The one person I thought I had lost forever. Did this mean that she was going to come back? That she wasn't dead after all? If this *was* the Timeless Oblivion she knew before... and the other angels came back from here, couldn't she do it again? The peaceful feeling returned in full measure. Maybe I could have her back.

Abelie continued talking without noticing my

internal musings. "We were all here at one point—lost and confused. A young woman guided us through the Timeless Oblivion."

"Guided?"

She held my hand as she walked me across the soft cloud-ground. "Death is only the beginning, Gabriella. Sometimes we need someone to guide us through our difficult times." Her eyes filled with an indescribable sadness. "And you have been through too many difficult times already."

It was silent between us as we seemed to float over the bleach-white ground.

I broke the silence. "Will you come back to . . . life?" I asked.

"No," she barely whispered. "I'll go on to the Ethereal Eternity." Her eyes were staring at me, but at the same time she seemed as if she were stuck in the past. I put my hand on her arm—her very real, incredibly warm arm. I didn't want to leave. If she couldn't go back with me then I wanted to stay here with her. It was too much for her to be taken from me again—I just couldn't go through that loss for the third time. She looked down at my hand and put hers on top of mine and smiled dejectedly back up at me.

"What is the Ethereal Eternity?" I wondered. Was *that* heaven?

"Where your journey will end—" She paused, her eyebrows knitting together like she wasn't sure she should say anymore. She took in a deep breath and let it out. The words "everlasting death" were nothing more than a sigh on her lips, but I heard it clearly. "They thought it would be best if I was the one to be your first guide on your journey," she continued. "But it looks as though you won't need much guidance while you're here, seeing as how you are already divine."

Journey. I remembered Andrew telling me about the Illuminator's journey, but he didn't know any specifics. But now I knew that it was a journey to a true, *final* death. I gulped.

"Who's 'they'?" I spluttered.

"'They' are the Guardian Spirits," she replied simply.

This was all so confusing. "What now? And what kind of sacrifice will I have to make?" I asked reluctantly.

She smiled again. "Haven't you sacrificed enough?"

I nodded. "More than I care to remember." I caught sight of her emerald eyes, which were full of tears. Real, human tears. "They're not gold," I barely mouthed, reaching up to touch her tears. They were so real; *she* was so real.

"I'm not an immortal anymore. I have no body, only a soul. That is all that is left of me. What you see—what you feel—it is an illusion, but *I* am still here." She cupped my cheeks between her palms. "It's still me and I still love you. I'm here for you." The heartwarming look on her face was enough to prove she loved me more than her own life.

"No more sacrifices?" I double checked, even though *everlasting death* seemed pretty sacrificey to me.

She shook her head. "Not any more. You have given of yourself to protect those around you. You have sacrificed your life and placed others before yourself. You don't need to be tested. You are worthy. You always have been. Why do you think those three angels awoke in that plane?"

"Andrew said it was because I was worth saving," I admitted.

"Exactly. They were here, in this Timeless Oblivion, waiting for you. The Ladies of Light had bound them to the earth when they turned them human and murdered them, because the Guardian Spirits refused to let the three angels continue on. They had a destiny—a purpose.

"When Lucia was turned human by the Ladies of Light, and murdered before all the Halos and Guardians, the Ladies didn't realize the problem it would cause. First it was Ehno who lashed out, and then Andrew followed to protect his friend, his brother. The Ladies of Light were fed up, angry at their efforts being thwarted. So, they tried to eliminate their problems permanently. In their efforts to kill the entire Halo of the Sun, the Guardian Spirits fought back and refused the Halos and the Guardians entry to the Ethereal Eternity or to the Timeless Oblivion. The Guardian Spirits turned them to Shadows, creatures that would fight back against the Ladies of Light and never die.

"The Ladies of Light altered the other angels' minds to fight back against the Shadows—turning some of the Shadows into brutal beings after fighting many wars.

"When the prophecy came about, the Ladies of Light erased pages of Zola's words to prevent the others from knowing what they did—what they truly are. They didn't destroy it all because they needed the angels to have hope in them. Little did they know that the Illuminator would come in the form of a human, not a Lady of Light—an innocent, beautiful, *human* child. Aiden and I were clever. We beat them at their own game; we had seen pages of the prophecy that no one else knew about. We knew there was an assassin, the Soul Stalker, and we knew you were in trouble.

"Then the Shadows found out about you. They thought the prophecy was about them, since they are the dark ones. But they were wrong—it was about the Ladies of Light. The name 'Illuminator' was chosen because you will bring light to those who are in shadow—not to kill them. Of course, the Ladies of Light already knew this and all I could think about was saving you. And our only choice was to turn you into a mortal—which is why you are here now." She paused, watching my reaction. I urged her on with a flick of my wrist.

"There will be no tests, no sacrifices. You are the Darkness Illuminator and your journey has already begun," she concluded.

"Does that mean you will come back until it's . . . over?"

"No." she almost spat the word as if she were furious about giving me that answer. "I wish I could."

I hugged her to my chest, feeling every last inch of her. "Will I remember any of this?" I whispered in her ear, repeating her words in my head, *None of them remembered afterward. I didn't remember—I just woke up and I knew I was* different.

"I'm afraid not," she admitted.

I was jerked away. A jolt of electricity flooded through my body. Through my blue dress I could see an even brighter, electric blue haze cover my skin. I looked like a blueberry. Another shock shot through me. It hurt and I put my hand over my heart. It pumped once in my chest before giving up on me.

"What's happening?" I shouted. Again, my heart tried to start its jagged beating in my chest and failed.

"*Shh*. It's okay sweet Gabriella. It is not time for you to die. You must go back. The Illuminator will not be hindered by death—not even her own. Your journey awaits you."

Now it felt as though a live wire was touching every last inch of my skin. My heart exploded in my chest, pumping my rich, golden blood through my once still veins. Abelie began fading before me and I reached out to her, trying desperately to grab her, hoping to bring her back with me.

"I thought you said no more sacrifices?" Didn't she know that losing her for the third time was yet another sacrifice?

She blew me a kiss. Was that all I was going to get? I tried to cry out to her, but suddenly I was sucked out of the white place I'd like to call heaven. It felt like I was tumbling through the air. I knew where I was going—to a place of punishment, torment and misery. I was brought straight back to Earth, the embodiment of hell.

It was dark and I was on my back. I had a strange feeling I was in a refrigerator. It was cold. *Really* cold. *Where am I?* My fingers reached out and came in contact with something frigid and hard—like metal. Claustrophobia hit and I began reaching out on all sides of me. Each time I hit freezing metal. Underneath, on top, to the sides, where my feet were—I was trapped. I screamed. It didn't seem to help. Where was Andrew? He wouldn't leave me, would he?

"Andrew?" I cried out. There was an echo then . . .

Nothing.

Silence.

Suddenly, everything came flooding back to me; the funeral, the limo crashing, Andrew fighting against Jeff and the Soul Stalker. The last thing I remembered was something hard hitting my head and a branch piercing my skin. My hand automatically reached up to my temple and then down to my side. *Did the Shadows kidnap me? Is Andrew okay?* I started to panic and strings of electricity shot from my fingers, jumping from one conductive surface to the next until the wall beyond my feet burst open. Fresh air came rushing in and I took in a deep breath of freedom.

Hastily, I pushed myself free of the frosty, confined space. It wasn't any lighter outside the box-fridge. But it was warmer, much warmer. My body still shook from the cold. I stilled in hopes of hearing something to give me a clue as to what was going on. There was warmth on my hand, but I couldn't see anyone.

"Hello?" I called out.

"I don't have much time, Gabriella." The voice was angelic, one I never thought I would hear again. A ghost-like shape shimmered before me, but I recognized her all the same. She was insubstantial, but I could see her wearing a red silk dress and see her shiny brown hair over her shoulders. She was more like a goddess than an angel.

"Mom?" I breathed. I didn't question my sanity because I wanted it to be real and I refused to try to deny what was right before me.

"Yes, sweetheart." She moved closer to me, the outline of her shining like a seraph. "Listen to me, I only have seconds. They don't know I'm here." Her head jerked behind her like she heard something. I couldn't tear my eyes away from her face to see for myself. Who were "they" anyway? "The other key, it will open the door to Zola," she continued after a second. "The Ladies of Light have her locked up. She will have the answe—" There was a rush of wind and then she was gone.

"Mom?" I screamed. "Mom! Come back. Please.

Don't leave me!" It was still silent—she had gone. I couldn't believe it. "No! You can't leave me again. No!" I whimpered. The room was in absolute darkness again. I dropped to my knees, grief-stricken, alone, and terrified. My mother was a . . . ghost. What if she was trying to get back into her body and she couldn't because she was buried beneath the earth? The words that had haunted me flashed in my head; *Her soul was severed from her body*. I felt ripped to shreds all over again. But it was what I needed—the pain—to remind me of her sacrifices, and her love for me.

On hands and knees, I crawled on the hard floor and searched for a wall. Tears leaked from beneath my eyelids relentlessly. I put my hands out in front of me to determine my surroundings. My fingers came in contact with more metal before I flipped something over, my face landing hard against it. Several things dumped onto the ground. The noise was thunderous in the quiet space around me. It sounded like I just dropped a tray of silverware. Things clanged and bounced until it was silent again. Moving whatever I knocked over out of my way, I moved forward again.

Whatever I pushed over was all over the floor; little metal instruments of some kind. It wasn't silverware. One piece felt like scissors and the others were bent in an odd shape. I put my weight on one hand so I could scoot the stuff away from me. As I brushed the metal pieces away, something sliced deeply into my palm when I accidently knocked it against another hard object. It sliced through my skin with no effort. I quickly shifted my weight to my knees.

"Ouch," I whispered furiously, more tears welled in my eyes. I still couldn't see a thing. You would think immortality would give you night vision, which I thought it had after the fight outside the Divine Library, but now I didn't believe it for a second.

I sat up on my knees and gently felt with my other hand a piece of something sticking out of the top of my hand. Something had gone all the way through and it hurt like hell. But for some reason it was nothing in comparison to seeing my mom brutally killed. My fingers rubbed over the object again. Maybe it was a knife. What was I doing around knives? My fingers gently felt over the cool metal one more time. It wasn't a knife, it was a scalpel. I would know it even in the dark. I used one all the time in the fishbowl.

As I held my hurt hand to my chest, I dragged myself across the floor. There was a wall only a foot away from me. I stood and followed it until I came across shelves. I was careful where I placed my good hand, afraid I'd cut myself again. My heart was beating wildly in my chest. Here I was, in a dark room, a hand wound and only a fuzzy memory of what happened at the cemetery.

"Andrew?" I cried out again.

Zilch, nada.

Tears came quicker then. I was in pain, horrific pain. My body shivered under the coldness of my skin, and at the same time I broke out into a sweat. I was probably going into shock with this wound and the rest of my circumstances. I knew it would be better for me to wait until I could see what I was dealing with before I took the scalpel out. But no matter what my previous medical training was, I was dying to pull it out and throw all my commonsense out the window.

With my uninjured hand, I continued to sweep the side of the walls whenever possible. After stumbling over who knows what, I finally came across a light switch. I flipped it up and several lights hummed to life. Why did I feel better immediately?

Well, I did, until I got a good look at the room I was in. My back slammed against the wall as a scream begged to escape my lips. I was in a morgue, or some kind of medical facility—possibly in a lab for experiments.

"Oh, no," I barely whispered under my breath. Where was Andrew? Where was my angel when I needed him?

My eyes shot from one side of the room to the other. I could easily see where I had scooted across the ground and where I had previously walked from the trail of . . . silver blood? Not golden blood. My heart hammered in my chest. What was going on? Each second my eyes zoned in on the different supplies; autopsy tables, morgue gurneys, examination lights, stainless steel equipment everywhere, and an organ scale. Acid rose in my throat. A wash basin, X-ray boxes, morgue instruments, biohazard containers . . . my head began to swim and I felt faint. There were even organ jars sitting next to an autopsy table.

Why was I here? What was going to happen to me? The tears were relentless. Silver tears. Where did the gold go? Did it mean something? And as my eyes finally made their way across the room, they landed on the far wall where there were several stainless steel drawers. One of the doors was hanging off of its hinges; blackened from being electrocuted.

I cringed away from the whole sight, by putting my back as flat against the wall as possible. The pain in my hand brought me back to my predicament. I tried to shake the terror off. It wasn't working, but I knew I had to get my act together or I wasn't going to make it through this. My head was the first body part to move away from the wall, and the rest of my body followed.

I turned to see a door and went immediately to the knob. My good hand reached out to rotate it, but nothing happened. It was locked. I needed to fix my hand up before I decided to do some famous, prison-break style escape. But first, I wanted to see what was behind door number one.

I inched toward the stainless steel doors, my good hand out stretched. I thought my heart would explode with the adrenaline. My breathing was heavy. Why did I feel so weak, but only days ago I was so powerful?

Pull yourself together, Gabriella. Sheesh!

I yanked the first door open. Inside was a body, the toe tag showing. I'd seen many, many dead bodies before, but for some reason this one really bothered me. I slammed the door shut and closed my eyes, trying to shake the image from my head. This time it didn't help and I fell back down to the floor, useless. I rocked back and forth for a few minutes, trying to regain my composure. When I finally opened my eyes, they landed immediately upon a small piece of paper with a string tied around it lying only feet away on the ground. It looked eerily like a toe tag. With tears in my eyes, I scooted toward the paper. I held it in my grasp for several seconds before I looked down at the name on it.

Gabriella Noelle Moretti.

"No," I mouthed. "No!" I got to my feet, the paper still in my grasp. "No! No . . . this can't be!" I looked down at the paper again. Nothing had changed. It was me. I was dead. I was in a real morgue—not in some prison or being held captive. I had died.

This isn't happening. This couldn't be happening. No!

I dashed across the floor to where the charts were and started tearing through them until I found mine. There was an autopsy paper which I quickly tossed away because below was my death certificate, signed by the coroner. I read over it to find the cause of death. "Blow to the head," was listed. My hand automatically went to the back of my head where my hair was matted with blood. There was no wound, just the evidence of it. I slid to the ground, holding my own death certificate and cried over it.

My injured hand, with the silver blood, long forgotten, all I could think about was my family and Andrew, and how I was so close to being with my angel mother again in heaven.

I yanked the scalpel out of my hand and watched as my skin healed immediately, quicker than before. The power was back, the pain stronger than ever as I lifted my hand to blast the morgue door open, grabbed a lab coat and tore out of there.

epilogue

It was the hardest decision I've ever had to make. Ultimately, I decided to conceal myself from those who thought I was deceased—which was everyone. Jeff had made a promise, and if he thought I was dead . . . and the Ladies and the Soul Stalker thought I was dead, hopefully my angels would be safe. That was the only form of protection that I could safely offer them. My mission was to find Zola, restore the minds to those that had been altered, and return the light to the angels who had been turned to Shadows. I could save them all—I would save them all. Light, Shadow, or Soul Stalker wouldn't stop me now. With their precious Illuminator out of the way, and Gabriella in full force, I would solve this mystery. *It's what I do best.*

It had been one week since I died horribly in Italy. My body had been shipped to Oregon—shocking news to someone who died in Italy and rose from the dead on another continent—and now, through the cover of the morning darkness of shadows, I had arrived at my burial site.

Anyone would be curious, I told myself.

Oregon had never looked so beautiful. As the sun rose, the fall colors were bright on the line of trees hovering on the border of the cemetery. Everything looked on fire. I watched as my grave was dug and the tent was set up. And I watched as flower wreaths were placed around the hole that my casket would soon descend to; the same casket that would be empty of one, Gabriella. I wondered how the morgue explained my missing body, or if they explained it at all.

As the hours ticked on, I could see in the distance a small crowd of people moving toward the tent. It wasn't long before they were all gathered under it.

"*Invisible*," I whispered. The air around me shimmered and went still.

As each day passed I could feel power flourishing and multiplying within me. There was something different with the electricity zinging through me, like my death had changed part of me. Invisibility was one of the new tricks I had learned from watching Aiden and Lucia. I'd been told several times before that I was powerful—*special*—but never in my wildest dreams did I believe I would possess abilities of this magnitude. But even I had limits; I felt drained after holding myself in a covert, concealed charm. I didn't care—it wasn't every day that one had the opportunity to attend one's own funeral.

As I hovered dangerously close to my grave, I was surprised by the amount of people who had come to say their final good-byes. Before the angels, I had practically drawn into myself and had effectively become a recluse in the past year—no one else had been around to love me besides my family. There was Adam, but we saw how embarrassingly that ended.

My father and mother, dressed in all black, held on to each other. It broke my heart to see them this grief-stricken when I could easily reveal myself to them. But I couldn't; it would be too dangerous. Not just for them, but for all the angels. I knew too many secrets; my life was best spent "dead." I couldn't risk being protected by those who would die doing so. I had come to one conclusion while waiting for my funeral: it would not be the Shadows I would destroy; it would be the Ladies and the Soul Stalker. When I illuminate the Shadows, I will not deliver death—I will deliver life, light. The only problem was that every angel's mind had been altered, their perception changed. I knew I needed to get back to Abelie's. The *Timeless* book was still there and I knew it would lead me to the Prophetess. She had answers; now all I had to do was find her.

Jenna walked up to the podium to speak. Her face was tear-stained and her nose was red from wiping it. My heart gave a horrible, wrenching jolt. What made the whole scene even worse was little Jules, holding several white roses in her tiny palms. She was a doll in her black dress. She stood next to the silver casket, her tiny tears dripping from her tiny cheeks. Right then I broke down. I cried, not for my death, but for my family. I knew what it was like to lose someone you truly loved. It was only a week ago that I was placing my own mom—the most beautiful angel of all—into the solid ground below.

"Not many people knew Gabriella as I did," Jenna said through her tears. "And that is too bad. She was self-righteous at times, but she was humble when needed. She placed others before herself and loved deeper than anyone I have ever known. She was there for me when times were tough, and she was always there for Jules. She was not one to let someone into her heart, and she was fearful of relationships with people. Because of this, many of you don't know the care-free, fun-loving girl inside. So let me tell you a few things I do know about my sister that you might not know. She was intelligent beyond her years. Well, you all already knew that." There was light laughter. "She was beautiful, inside and out and had a fantastic sense of humor, not to mention her sarcastic side." Jenna smirked then, her eyes reminiscent.

"Since she is no longer here to share her smile with us today, I thought I would tell you a story about my sister."

505

Oh no, I thought, but was smiling all the same, the new silver tears still finding their way down my cheeks.

She continued. "When Gabriella first moved to Oretown, I had only been living in Portland for a few months. Nicole was with her to help her unpack. They both had decided to come up to the city so we could go out. So, I got a sitter for Jules and we went to a bar. She was so nervous because she had a fake ID."

I knew where this was going . . .

"At the time, Gabriella drove a Jeep Wrangler. Not exactly the best vehicle to own in a rainy costal town. It had been a beautiful day, so the top was off when she parked in my driveway . . ."

Jenna continued with the story as I searched the crowd under the tent. There were familiar faces—particularly my family members, but others I only knew professionally. As I scanned the crowd, I spotted my cousin Nicole standing next to my mother. Her stunning blue-green eyes were accentuated by her dark green wrap style dress, which hugged her pint sized figure perfectly. She was listening intently to Jenna's story when she suddenly broke down in sobs. My mom reached out to comfort her, stroking her silky blonde hair. It was too much, I had to look away.

When the angel I was looking for couldn't be

seen, I searched along the tree line. In the far distance, I found my four angels; Andrew, Ehno, Lucia and my father. My world, the one that I thought was about to spin off of its axis, seemed to realign itself at the sight of them standing there. It was such a huge relief to see them there. They survived—all of them. *They are alive!* Deep down, I knew that was another reason I had come here today—I had to know they were okay.

Standing close to the angels was Joseph. He looked distraught, but it was nothing compared to the tortured expression Andrew was wearing. It was like the life had been sucked out of him. His golden tears were numerous and his eyes were the brightest blue I had ever seen—even more brilliant than when Abelie was brutally murdered. I hated the fact that I couldn't comfort them, but I was a magnet for death, and I wouldn't let it follow them any longer.

Jenna had finished her story which ended in the three of us being drenched in mud and two revoked fake ID's. There was light laughter in the crowd, but it died out quickly. As the service came to a close, I knew that I couldn't stay invisible for much longer. My power was draining quickly. Vehicles began to start up and soon everyone was gone except my angels, Joseph, Jenna and Jules.

Jenna had her hand over the casket, her tears trickling down onto the silver. I hated seeing Jenna there, with Jules' all in black. They were mourning me. And as I saw the angels move closer, I even began to mourn for myself. This truly was the death of Gabriella, and the life of the Illuminator—*I was alone.*

Joseph was the first to come up behind Jenna. I saw them talking to each other, and I even saw Jenna smile a small, sad smile. Through my tears, I smiled too. She always loved a man in a suit. After several minutes, he walked her to her car. But what I was intent on watching was not them, but the angels who were now surrounding my coffin. Andrew put his hand upon the silver coated casket and several golden tears splashed onto it, which then slithered down the side. I hadn't noticed how close I had gotten and backed away quickly. Aiden had a hand on Andrew's shoulder, gripping it as if he were holding him up. Ehno and Lucia were holding hands. But what shocked me more than anything about the whole scene was that Ehno was looking directly at me.

I vanished, going back to my neighbor's beach house. For a moment I was stunned. That was the first time I had "popped" from one place to the next. I had been staying here for the last three days. I was lucky that my neighbors did not live up here—they only visited in the summer months. Taking in a deep breath, I leaned back against the wall. I wasn't sure if Ehno had actually seen me or not, but I wasn't staying to find out. It was amazing how easily I had taken to this new life, these new changes and this new power. But I knew deep within my soul that this was who I was meant to be. And if I had to hide in shadows for a while, I would.

It was only a matter of time before I would need my angels again. More than anything, I missed Andrew holding me at night during my dreams. But right now, the angelic world needed to think I was dead—that the Illuminator had failed. Though I was far from failing—I was only beginning my journey, a journey I knew nothing about.

It had been two long days since my own funeral. A plum brick colored house stood with sandy brown shutters in the darkness of the cloudy night. No light flooded through the windows.

He was asleep, but I knew he would be there.

I knocked on the front door. It was three in the morning, but that was why I had picked this time of night. It was the dead hour—perfect timing for me to show up on his doorstep considering I was "dead." The door flung open and Joseph was silhouetted in the dim light coming from the kitchen. He was wearing only flannel pajama pants, his bare abs exposed, his hair tousled and his eyes heavy. He didn't say anything, just looked at me in sheer disbelief. I could understand; I was *dead,* or so he thought.

"Gabriella?"

"Joseph, I need your help."

acknowledgements

There are so many people I want to thank for their help with making this book possible.

First, and foremost, Lisa Langdale; she stuck with me through every sentence, each comma, and every crazy quote that she could convince me to trash . . . *or to add*. There has never been a better Beta reader! She might have even taken a Lamaze class so she could coax me down when I was having a "freak-out." She was the first Team Joseph supporter, and hopefully not the last. Love you like crazy, woman!

"The beta-ing never ends, even on the acknowledgments." –Lisa, self proclaimed Captain of Team Joseph

Second, I want to thank my family; they cheered me on, helped me when I desperately needed advice, and have been nothing but supportive in whatever I wanted to do in life, even when it was to become a writer. (That was out of left-field, eh Mom?) Most important to acknowledge of this bunch is JD, for understanding me when I was being an anti-social, crazy lunatic for months. (And for letting me have TWO men in my life besides him; Andrew and Joseph.) Michael, my brother, for calling me almost every night for three months begging for new material, and when I was finally done, he read the whole thing again in one day. Of course, my parents, who dedicated their lives to me. Don't worry, I didn't forget about how amazing you are, Grandma, and all the wonderful notes you gave me to help improve my writing. You'll always be an English teacher at heart.

Third, I'd like to thank DJ Urquart, who is an excellent English teacher and friend who gave it to me straight! Sorry, his name is still Jeff, not Geoffre or Frautz. Are those even names? Haha.

Fourth, there were a few who edited only parts of my book that gave me great, new insight on my characters. Big thanks to Brianne Villano, from Mindful Media Management, who was able to make me laugh at my own stupidity without actually making *me* feel stupid. Thank you to Marissa at First Editing. She transformed some of my badly formed sentences into something readable!

511

Gabriella is back.

soul stalker

Being the Illuminator is not all happiness and light,
especially when everyone thinks you are dead. When
Gabriella decides to finally let her angels know that she
is alive, Joseph and an unexpected friend help her. The
Darkness Illuminator is not as in control of her power
as she believes, which makes for a very comedic and
endearing relationship that blooms between the three.
A fender-bender debacle, a run in with the cops, and
a hiccup at the airport seem to all be worth it until
Gabriella finds out her plan has backfired.

The three angels are missing, more mysteries pile
up, and a new evil is brewing—so terrifying, in fact,
that even the Soul Stalker herself is cowering in fear.
Our heroine begins a jarring, romance-filled, heartbreaking journey that will lead her back to Italy, and
ultimately to the answers she is desperately searching
for. What will she do when they aren't the answers she
expected? What happens when she unveils a truth, so
deeply hidden, that it causes an angelic war?

Coming soon.

http://timelessseries.blogspot.com